# THE CHILD AT FORTY

A Novel

*Written by*

MICHAEL WURTH

Scriptwise Partners LLC Publishing is a wholly owned subsidiary of Aubreywerks LLC, who is solely responsible for its content. For more information, contact www.aubreywerks.com

# Acknowledgements

It's always legally messy to critique a cultural icon.  In this case, great care was taken not to unduly quote or take advantage of characters I did not create, despite how ubiquitous their influence has been for anyone born after 1965.  All characters and references belonging to Sesame Street™, The Electric Company™, the Muppet Show™, and other Jim Henson/ CTW products remain the exclusive and sole property of their respective copyright holders.  As cultural icons they are evoked as fair use for cultural critique.

No Muppets were harmed in the making of this novel.

"The Rainbow Connection" is by Ascher Kenneth Lee and Paul H Williams, all rights reserved to them.  Buy the recording via legal means, even those not recorded by Kermit the Frog.  The Brothers Cazimero do a great job with it as a Hawaiian tune.

There are buried quotations from Dr. Spock's 1968 edition of "Baby and Child Care" that I am grateful to remember and sprinkled through-out the mansucript.  Interested people might revisit older editions of the book, which were social manifestos rather than childrearing manuals.  Our characters here also live lives of unintended consequences from those ideas.

Many thanks to Erin Brown, Sue Wyshinksi and Scotty Lisetor, Jon Brekke, Shawn Hiatt, Jason Suapaia, Dick Hershberger, Brett Wagner, Chris Vogler, Cheryl Bartlett, Taedra Kogan, Judith Karfiol, Gary Pearl, Audra Arr, E. Rahn (Road) Keucher, Steven Wyman, Eric Gilliom, Greg Harman, Larry McMurtry, Sally Apgar, Keith Berry, M-Henn, TVKL, Richard Stovall, Cruz, Big D, Non-Sequitur Girl, Mericia Palma Elmore Esq., Captain Danger, the venerable Col. Dann Seki, the not yet so venerable but always stimulating Cary Henson, Liedeke Plate, the late Cliff

Flanagan, and everyone else who encouraged me when I was unsure of my thesis.

Special thanks to Eugene Eoyang, who hates this book, and Michael Wisser, who loves it. And Jack Past and Chuck and Linda Smith, and Lawrence Wade Wurth, who promised they wouldn't read themselves into it, but did anyway.

Thank you Shelagh Vale, for rescuing me. And thank you to our children Matthew, Kathryn, and Aubrey, for helping me remember why we tell stories. And why they can't always be true.

Generation X was the laboratory for the free-thinking childhood experiment. We don't have all the data in yet; but it's not optimistic. It is my best hope this is an exhibit in the final hearing.


For Barbara and for Jasminka, forever.

# Introduction

Every novel is a suicide note. Since storytellers tend to be cowards, stories rarely fulfill their promise. Sure, you get the occasional ritual death, like Mishima finishing his last novel shortly before committing hari-kari. But if you've read his last books, you might not be so hard on him.

Still, suicides are frowned upon. By the survivors, at least, or by people who've never been truly tempted to commit such an act themselves. As well it should be. There's nothing that quite says "fuck you" to one's friends and family than by offing oneself. It's the height of narcissism: it's unilaterally declaring that your own problems are larger than anyone else's and that this is the only solution you find workable.

Steven didn't mean to kill himself. I'm convinced of that. Nor was he crying out for attention. Sometimes, people just get things wrong. Sometimes we fuck up. And sometimes, if you do it enough, you earn the title of perpetual fuckup, which is an honor bestowed utterly without ceremony. You just wake up one morning, look in the mirror, and know on a deeply intuitive level that you've been put on the list. Then you shower and go to work, or to the sofa to watch *Sesame Street* reruns all day.

I don't think Steven deserved that appellation, but I have to admit it's going to take a little persuasion for you to believe me. What I do know, and what you need to know to follow me, is that Steven was guided with a deep-seated desire to do the right thing. No matter how many times he found himself in tough situations, state-ordered confinements, or strangers' bedrooms, this core value continued to lead him further and further away from anything resembling redemption.

It wasn't absolution he was seeking. The bigger the hole he found himself in, the harder he'd dig to try to tunnel out: he wasn't worried about whether a God approved of his actions. Redemption to him meant having at least one outcome in his life that validated his desire to do the right thing. Just one thing that would allow him to look at himself in the mirror and say, "Yes, I followed my heart, and life was better for it."

Maybe he found that one grand instance and didn't need any more. After receiving that great and utter validation, there's nowhere to go but down. So why hang around? After all, we should all have the right to decide when the canvas of our life has been adequately rendered. If you have achieved your masterpiece, whether at forty or eighty, sign it and move on. Before you're forty, you really have no idea what a masterpiece is. After you're eighty, you don't really care. So this is the window for meaningful exits. Which is perhaps what Steven chose.

Or maybe he didn't. You decide.

# CHAPTER ONE

Near the outskirts of Woodward, Oklahoma, Steven Watkins, five, sat unbuckled in the back seat of a brand new 1972 Mercury Montego wagon as his mother Barbara sped towards an unguarded railroad crossing. She glanced quickly over at the approaching freight train, then shot a quick smile in the rear view mirror to Steven as he sat next to his sister Judy, who was three years old and completely occupied with the taste of her own thumb. Barbara chirped optimistically, "Hey kids, I think we can beat that train!"

She was wrong. So Steven never really got to know his mother, and his sister never became more than a gauzy memory – in his late thirties, he could recall that Judy bumped into things often while she was learning to walk. And when Barbara divorced their dad in 1971, Judy seemed to have no clue what was going on. Maybe once she bit him, but his memory of the bite was as though she did it in a "hey, I want to know what other people taste like" fashion, rather than a punitive sort of way. Nothing was certain for Steven in the spring of 1972, other than his mother and sister were gone.

The police couldn't find his father, who had long ago absconded to someplace Steven only knew as Nebraska. It sounded exotic and lonely.

Steven's dim memories of his father were pleasant. He kept returning to the somewhat fuzzy image of his dad sitting next to him on the back porch, a beer in his hand and several empties beside him, waiting for charcoal to get hot in a beer keg that had been converted to a grill. It was going to take a while.

In the meantime, it took a few months of rehab for him to regain the strength in his broken left arm after the train accident– in Oklahoma at the time, physical therapy for a such an injury consisted of lifting an eighteen-ounce weight over and over again in different positions, something that even at the age of five Steven believed to be medically unproductive. He articulated his displeasure at the inefficiency of the process with the most powerful tools in his vocabulary: "This is stupid."

Words are much older than we are.

Yet the therapist kept putting him through it for nearly six months, even though a doctor with yellow-gray hair parted ruthlessly down the left side of his scalp told Steven that his left arm was going to be weaker than his right, probably for the rest of his life. Steven sat at the end of a shiny metal gurney when he got the news, and wasn't all that bothered by it. The doctor had bad breath, which was a far more immediate consideration. Steven wanted to run outside and breathe fresh air.

The rest of his life. These phrases have no meaning when you're five years old. But Steven was self-aware enough to ask himself, "If my arm will never be strong, why do I have to do the damn exercises?" He quietly giggled when curse words appeared in his head. Sometimes he would just sit still, remember a grownup conversation he'd heard, and not be able to contain his joy at knowing the words he wasn't allowed to say. It used to drive his mother crazy. "What are you thinking?" she'd ask. "Nothing," he'd usually answer, and giggle some more. Sometimes, to try to get his thoughts out of him, she'd tickle his tummy and make him almost cry with laughter. He still never told her what he was really thinking, and there was some kind of respectful bond they formed as a result. She would keep smil-ing at him, but at some point during the process, her eyes could become suddenly somber, as if she were watching something beautiful unfold right before her, something so beautiful that even to say it out loud would make her cry.

He would only realize this years later, as he combed every fiber of his memory to remember her. It got harder as he grew older. By twenty-five, he'd forgotten how she dressed. By thirty-five, he had a hard time even describing her hairstyle. But the look of those eyes never left him – not the serious look at the end of their tickle-sessions, not the stern eye contact she'd make when it was time for him to get out of bed when he didn't want to; above all, he never forgot the playful wink she gave him in the rear view mirror just seconds before she and his sister died in an avalanche of noise he'd only hear once more in his life, which was sometimes too strong of a contrast to the cheerful tone of her voice just before.

Her voice, in fact, would come to him at odd times, with such uncomfortable force that he had to train himself to ignore it. He would sometimes think she was talking to him, only it was as though her voice were in italics, never being directly engaged, but never completely separated either.

This was to come. At five, he did the exercises, because grownups told him to, and grownups knew best, even grownups with bad breath.

His aunt and uncle took him in to their home in West Texas, being childless themselves despite multiple visits to fertility doctors, where Barbara's brother, Lawrence, was given the astonishingly sophisticated advice to wear boxers instead of briefs, and his wife, Maria, was told to keep her legs pointed straight up at the ceiling after coitus to give Lawrence's sperm a better chance of reaching their target. She did so regularly, making herself laugh at the thought of his seed actually being millions of tiny salmon that she was helping to swim upstream.

Surprisingly, none of this advice had resulted in a child. So they were aware of the great responsibility they were taking on by raising Barbara's surviving son, and they went to a used bookstore in San Antonio and bought Dr. Spock's book *Baby and Child Care*, never really understanding that it was meant for infants and toddlers, not kids who were old enough to start school, although they liked the motto that they should trust themselves because they knew more than they thought they knew.

Even if they knew more than they thought they knew, and liked the idea, they refused to be arrogant. They asked for advice, they spoke to other parents of adopted children, and more than anything else, they grew to trust one organization to help them raise their newly acquired responsibility: Public Television in general and the Children's Television Workshop in particular.

Over the next ten years, *Sesame Street*, *The Electric Company*, *Zoom*, and *The Muppet Show* became their best allies in making sure that Steven was keeping up in his reading and math skills, learning how to play well with others, and being exposed to enough Spanish to keep his mind open to other cultures. Each show had its own format, but shared the same basic premise: everybody's cool no matter how different they are from you, and you can be whatever you want to be in this life if you only work hard at it – and our television show is going to give you the tools to make that easier. Lawrence and Maria liked that message, and encouraged Steven to pursue his dreams at every opportunity. This was a challenge in Fort Stockton, Texas.

Steven never called out for me until 1986, when he was a freshman in college. There's a lot about him I'll never understand. But I will say that I hold the Children's Television Workshop responsible for his death more than any other single factor.

This is the story about how Jim Henson, the CTW, and PBS may have single-handedly ruined an entire generation. Or it might not be: I may be a bit older, but I was intimately involved with the same shows and I'm doing just fine. Perhaps it's too much to blame Steven's death on a single muppeteer or corporation when so many other people were involved in screwing up his life. But this is my story and I get to determine how it's told. Steven is dead. He shouldn't be.

I want you to be as pissed about it as I am.


# Jeremy

Jeremy Schultz, five, didn't actually make an audible plop when he was sat down in front of the television, but plop is the appropriate verb. His mother Naomi very quickly plopped her son down in the living room of their East Allis home, turned on the TV, and switched to the UHF dial to find public television. The reception wasn't perfect, so she tweaked the rabbit ear antennae on top of the set, unaware that rabbit ears were meant to enhance VHF signals and had literally no impact on reception of UHF signals. That never stopped her from trying. Jeremy always silently watched her, waiting for the reception to improve, but ultimately had to settle for the same slight haze over the picture. Naomi had even tried aluminum foil once, but took it down after her husband, Donald, found it inelegant.

I personally believe they set the bar for inelegance fairly high in the greater Milwaukee area, so I can only imagine what kind of contraption he objected to. But Donald was working hard to mature from a cash register repairman to a computer engineer (there were very few of them in 1970, especially ones without college degrees), and his brother had just been appointed to a judgeship at the young age of thirty-six, and they should be prepared to have important people over on a regular basis.

So Jeremy couldn't see all the detail in Big Bird's feathers as he talked with Bob about how to be friends with Oscar the Grouch. He didn't need to. *Sesame Street* was cool. He couldn't tell you why. It just was.

The folks at the Children's Television Workshop knew why. They had begun *Sesame Street* with two distinct formats: the Muppets, performing their own skits by themselves, and the human actors, who would clarify the message and make sure kids understood they were learning.

Fortunately, the CTW had found out early on in a test market in Philadelphia that kids responded enthusiastically to the Muppet segments, but lost all interest when the adults appeared to preach about how to share, be nice to your friends, listen to your elders, all that crap. So they tweaked the show before going national and made sure the Muppets appeared with humans in the segments, thus closing the embarrassing American chapter of Muppet segregation forever, and now real educators were conversing on a regular basis with Muppets, and ratings, because of people like Naomi and Jeremy, were skyrocketing.

It turns out Big Bird just needed to accept Oscar the Grouch for who he was. Sometimes that takes patience. *Do you know what patience is?*

Naomi heated up a Swanson frozen dinner while Jeremy learned what patience was. Just accept people for who they are. That was key. In fact, that seemed to be the lesson a lot of the time. Even at five, Jeremy could tell the difference between an educational segment and an "accept people for who they are" segment.

But of all of the segments he watched during 1970, he laughed loudest when Bert and Ernie had an argument over a birthday song. Ernie was singing to the letter U, and Bert thought that the "Happy Birthday to U" was being directed at him, though it wasn't his birthday. There was an actual foam letter U on the set, and still, Bert didn't get it. Bert, Jeremy thought, was a moron. But he didn't know the word "moron" yet, so he expressed himself at the height of his current vocabulary: "Bert is stupid."

Jeremy was a pretty sharp kid. Normally children start to grasp paronomasia around seven, but he was ahead of the curve. He liked to prove it at dinner, when he and Naomi would eat together as Donald stayed out late (often traveling all over Wisconsin repairing computerized cash registers, sometimes for other reasons altogether), and the mashed potatoes in the aluminum foil tray were undercooked and the apple cobbler in the center portion would scald the roof of his mouth (Naomi never learned to cook or wanted to) as he tried to distract himself by coming up with or repeating he had learned.

"Where does the king keep his armies? In his sleevies!"

He'd lost Naomi on this one, and it took her a few seconds to figure it out. Naomi wasn't stupid by any means, but she was very literal and could be taken by surprise by any sort of figurative language. She started to suspect that there was something special about Jeremy, and had even checked out if there might be a program for him at school because his reading and writing skills were so advanced for his age. Sadly, there were no "Gifted and Talented" programs in his district until he reached middle school, so Naomi just made sure he got his dose of *Sesame Street*, every weekday. This show seemed to have more of an effect than anything else.

So when Jeremy, over an aluminum tray of Salisbury steak with mushroom sauce, asked "what am I going to be when I grow up?" Naomi had overheard enough of the broadcasts to know exactly what to say: "Whatever you want to be, sweetheart. All you have to do is work hard."

Jeremy shrugged, stirring the scalding sauce into his cold mashed potatoes. Naomi would never study physics enough to learn what "specific heat" was, and why it made those old frozen dinners so dreadful; it took Jeremy himself years to understand why he had to mix them to keep both courses palatable. By then it was too late: he had already been burned, and it was his own fault.

Specific heat refers to the fact that it's harder to raise the unit temperature of some elements than it is for others. Some things (like mashed potatoes) take a lot of energy to warm up, so spending thirty-five minutes in a 1970 oven in Milwaukee wasn't quite going to do it. Whereas a high-fat concoction like apple cobbler takes less energy to heat up, and after that point it begins to radiate heat instead of storing it, which is why it was so damn hot and the boxes carried a warning to not eat it first. Before placing the dinner in the oven to cook, the consumer was directed to peel back the aluminum foil on the cobbler; not so it would be exposed to more direct heat, but because it reached edible temperature so quickly that it needed to radiate away excess heat well before the other sections of the tray were warmed enough to serve.

In other words, you can take different foods from the same oven after the same cooking time and temperature, and some will scald your mouth and some won't. Ever burn your mouth with a pancake right off the grill? Doesn't happen. Tomato sauce? You bet you will, as we've all discovered at least once in our lives with a fresh slice of pizza. Specific heat.

Jeremy only needed a scalded roof of his mouth once to learn this lesson, so he was patient as his TV dinner cooked. It helped that Bob, Gordon, Big Bird, and Oscar told him to be patient, on a regular basis. He should accept people as they are and not bite into boiling cobbler. These two rules cover most of the questions we have about life.

What he didn't yet know was that there were mothers all over his neighborhood – and even a few fathers – who didn't buy all their groceries in the frozen foods section. He might have felt less content with his diet at the time had he been aware of his neighbors' habits, but this was all he knew. Come home from school, let mommy turn on PBS and spend five minutes trying to improve the signal, then have dinner together a couple of hours later. Sometimes after going to bed he'd hear his dad come home; sometimes he was already asleep.

This was before his dad and mom got divorced when Jeremy was eleven. That would change everything.

# Tiffany

Tiffany was the first born to Leonardas and Melissa Morales, and was supposed to be a boy. That is to say, her life would have been a lot easier all the way around if she'd just changed chromosomes in the womb and popped out of Melissa sporting a penis. But womb-bound fetuses rarely get to exercise decision-making skills, even if Sartre once made an elaborate argument to support the idea that we do in fact choose to be born. So if babies choose to be born, why can't we blame them for choosing their sex? Mostly because Sartre was wrong. But Tiffany never got through a complete book of Sartre's, even as an adult, and so denied herself the chance to get annoyed at how white-knuckledly desperate a philosopher can become when he's defending a pet idea.

She did, as a freshman at the University of Texas, manage to make it through half of *Being and Nothingness* before getting some crib notes from a big sister in the sorority she was pledging at, which allowed her to pass the class and stop reading the actual texts. Just knowing the essence of Sartre was enough, she'd decided, and she said it out loud, without a trace of irony, at Kingsolving Dormitory's cafeteria in 1986. The space shuttle Challenger had blown up a few weeks before, so people were still fairly quiet and unwilling to joke much in public.

Tiffany defended her use of Cliffs Notes by arguing about the essence of Sartre, which is practically quoting him, albeit inadvertently. Steven laughed. As Sartre would have. Tiffany wouldn't get it, and in fact, her entire table full of freshman girls nodded in solemn agreement that really, the amount of reading they'd been assigned was too great and they were justified in using Cliffs Notes.

For instance, when Tiffany was born in Austin, Texas, in May of 1968, hell was breaking loose all over the world. The peace talks between the U.S. and the North Vietnamese had started in Paris, riots were springing up at the Sorbonne, and at Columbia, and Berkeley's disobedience was just getting started. The more left-leaning students at the University of Texas felt they were missing out on all the fun, so they threw their own demonstrations as well, but they were nowhere near as destructive as their East or West Coast counterparts. That wasn't the point.

They just wanted to be in on the outrage, it was very trendy; but their anger was genuine. They just didn't have the stomach for real violence; mostly because the majority of the students were from working class and rural families who knew how hard it is to rebuild things when nature tears them down (like a tornado or a strong Texas wind along a two-mile wooden fence line), and were reluctant to cause that kind of trouble. This is just my theory.

Hesitant or not, the Texas students were still a pain in the ass for Tiffany's father Leonardas, who was already an Austin Police Commissioner. The Commission had learned very valuable lessons from Columbia University's response to their riots. The sooner the police rolled in, the faster the film crews from television stations would arrive. So it was Leonardas's job to inform the UT administrators that the City of Austin considered it an internal matter for the school to handle itself. University cops had no power whatsoever, all thirty of them in a campus of over 20,000 students. And the Sheriff's department was more than ready to run in and kick the snot out of the little shits, so Leo had to warn the University to keep them in check, as they were a bigger potential headache than the students, and had to be contained. Then Melissa went into labor, and Leo lost the sex lottery. There would be no Leonardas Miguel Morales the Third. At least not yet. The fact that Melissa had made a hard stand on Tiffany being the baby's name ("if it happens to be a girl," she'd say almost apologetically) only aggravated him further.

If she was to be a girl, the woman could name her. Melissa was the latest in a long stream of lily-white ranching daughters (her family had been in Texas since before it won its independence from Mexico and was its own sovereign nation, which meant she had no idea what her ethnicity was except for, "white, probably from England."). They also were not without influence, and had Leo (her parents resisted the uncommon fullness of his name) not possessed such obvious career promise (college degree at twenty, law degree from UT at twenty-three, assistant city attorney at twenty-four), Melissa might not have been given permission to marry *"an* Hispanic."

Tiffany represented a fragile piece of glass, Leo had decided, and he wanted his firstborn to be tougher than that. So rather than just accept that she was a girl, he more or less decided to treat her as he'd treat any first-born son. More discipline. More regimen. She was half-Latino, which means she was *all* Latino in the eyes of polite society, so she would have to work twice as hard than anyone else for half the respect. There would be no speaking of Spanish in the house. Being bilingual would make her English skills suffer, and she had enough disadvantages to look forward to. Leonardas Miguel Morales the Second didn't spend a lot of time studying the development of children, and how growing up with a second language might make her more linguistically supple later on. But most of the research in that field was in its own infancy at the time (*I used to like linguistics, but now I'm not Saussure, etc.*), and Leo went from his gut, or from Father Diego's down the street, whichever happened to reinforce this belief more articulately.

This wasn't easy on Tiffany, especially as the seventies began and she began gaining not just an awareness of who she was but what was expected of her. She was not to play with dolls. Her room contained nothing that could be considered girly or frilly. She was absolutely forbidden to watch Saturday morning cartoons on television, because serious people don't watch cartoons. *Sesame Street* was permitted, however. Melissa would use the time to play bridge with friends in her rotating social, and Tiffany would sit with whatever other kids came over and learn letters and manners while their mothers got louder and louder as the gin and tonics flowed. Tiffany liked it best when they went to Mrs. Madla's house, because she could stare outside at the horses in the pasture adjoining the home and wonder what it might be like to ride one.

Little girls were permitted to like horses, but not like little boys were. If any boy said he wanted to be a cowboy, everybody thought it was a noble avocation. When she declared that she wanted to be a cowgirl, the room went silent, and looks were shot to Melissa from all over the kitchen, looks Tiffany didn't understand, words she couldn't understand ("barrel rider" and "slut" were uttered often and in close proximity) but she could tell they disturbed her mother. So she kept quiet about the horses, stealing glances whenever she could.

She rarely got positive reinforcement for conforming; the fear of not conforming was generally enough to keep her from inviting a scolding. Still, every once in a while she would sit in the living room while her father read the paper in silence, and he'd fold down half the paper and stare at her. She often felt the stare was expressing a disappointment she could never overcome. But occasionally, Leo would seem to realize she was staring right back, and he'd react by winking at her playfully and returning to his paper. He rarely saw the huge smile it left on Tiffany's face.

It was an uneasy peace, but a peace. It would be shattered three years later when Melissa had a second baby, another girl, and this one Leo seemed to welcome with open arms. She got the traditional name: Maria Louisa Wells Morales. Tiffany was confused that Melissa's family name got snuck in there too. She was just Tiffany Morales. Not even a middle name. Maria got two.

Along with the new baby's crib, Tiffany received a new color. When Tiffany was an only child, her room was always a soft powdery blue, which she didn't know enough to think anything about at the time. But the moment Maria was home from the hospital, overnight it was painted bright pink, with frilly window treatments which clashed horribly with the plush chocolate deep-pile carpeting.

This upset her greatly. Not only had Tiffany been unable to anticipate that she'd be sharing the room with the new baby, she had been given no warning that her space would be completely transformed.

Tiffany would continue to be astonished many times during Maria's first years: at how often she was allowed to wear dresses, at how Melissa would get to have pink bows tied in her hair (by Maria's third birthday, the "pink-ribbon count" was Maria: forty-three, Tiffany: two, and both of Tiffany's pink-ribbons were worn for parties at the Wells side of the family, where the denial of Tiffany's gender wasn't generally known.) Tiffany herself didn't know the exact breadth of the imbalance, but she felt in a strong sense that it was lopsided.

What was perhaps the worst of all of it was that Maria was allowed to flirt and giggle with grownups, something Tiffany had been slapped across the hands more than once for doing. Maria was a world-champion peek-a-boo player with Leo's important friends, while Tiffany's social contribution to the gatherings consisted largely of reciting the state capitols on demand. She even knew Montpelier, which was the most predictable tough question she would get as the lawyers interrogated her playfully.

All of this remained a growing but general displeasure, a disappointment without words, until at the age of six she summoned all of her linguistic talent to declare, upon seeing Maria being brought out for a party in a pink dress with a matching ribbon: "This is stupid."

She spent the rest of the afternoon in their shared room, sulking. Melissa had made it clear that if she couldn't be polite, she needed to be by herself. This would be called "time out" later on in the nomenclature of parenting, but in 1974 in Texas, it was just called "get the grumpy kid the hell out of the room before she ruins everything."

Like many grumpy six year olds, she couldn't stay mad long, or even let her anger keep her awake. She drifted to sleep looking up at the ceiling, hearing her mother and her friends as their laughter devolved into gin-blazed cackles, and closed her eyes just as the end theme from *The Electric Company* was blaring on the TV set in the living room.

Tiffany hated Maria, she decided. Let her be the girl. Tiffany could work harder. She could get her own room and not have to look at this stupid pink.

Tiffany and Maria would not get along for nearly thirty years, and that only came about because Tiffany had just told the biggest lie of her entire life. She was desperate for Maria to support her; and even though Tiffany had tried to convince her that her life was at stake, Maria knew for a fact it wasn't true and that she was being lied to, and that pretending to believe Tiffany was going to cause an immense amount of damage to someone else. But she backed her big sister up anyway.

They'd be much better friends after that.


# Katherine

I don't think Sartre ever went so far as to say we choose our parents. We appear, and unless we have some immediate or temporarily concealed medical condition, we are ostensibly created equal. But it should probably be noted that if your father isn't in the hospital because he's sitting in a smoke-filled bar drinking Coors at the rate of six an hour, it may take more than average effort on your part later in life to make you feel like the Declaration of Independence applies to you.

Katherine appeared after thirty hours of labor, was a breach baby, and the procedure cost Millicent, her mother, so much blood loss that for a short time Katherine's health became secondary to ensuring that Millie would survive the procedure.

It didn't seem like Wally was going to make a bad father up to that point. During Katherine's gestation he bought *Dr. Spock's Baby and Child Care* for Millie to read ("the raising-kids Bible," he called it), and he'd put in overtime at the machine shop to try to store up a little more money so they could possibly get out of the trailer park by the time the baby was born. He didn't see why it was necessary – a lot of people he and Millie went to high school with were living in trailer parks, and their double-wide was easily the biggest in the Ballerina Court, as Katherine would hear her father repeat to Millie four years later when she first tried to leave him.

But that night, or rather, earlier the previous night, Wally had taken the pre-packed luggage they'd kept by the door and driven Millie to the hospital. He sat with Millie's parents, Marion and Linda, in the waiting room (nobody was admitted to the delivery room) for roughly forty-five minutes, until, unable to handle the tension any longer, he announced that he needed to go to work and squeeze in some extra hours, and that Marion was to call him there if anything new developed.

When the phone at the machine shop rang a few hours later, indicating there seemed to be a problem, nobody picked it up. This was before there was anything so fancy as retail answering machines, and small towns in Colorado didn't have personal answering services. Wally always figured he'd hear the phone if he placed it right outside the doorway, but it was Buck Owens and the Buckaroos night on the jukebox at Mikey's Bar across the street, and Wally never heard a thing.

It didn't help matters at all that Wally's father himself had died of a heart attack the month before. Twenty days before, actually, at the age of fifty-four. He'd died at the table directly behind where Wally was sitting as his daughter was being delivered.

It was 1966, but Fred, Wally's father, had been drunk since he returned from the war in 1945. He had fought at Guadalcanal and had seen things that knocked him forever from the orbit he was supposed to be in; he'd divorced his young wife and left their three children only a few years after the war ended.

That he'd lived to 54 surprised several of his friends. There had been several drunken shootings at Mikey's over the years, especially since Mikey rented out the second floor of his bar to vagrants whom he knew were having problems with their lives. Sweep out the place, stay out of trouble, try to get regular jobs, and they could get drunk every night in a controlled environment and have a bed to fall into upstairs. Most couldn't keep regular work; but Fred wired new houses as they were being built, and something resembling a suburb was being built north of Denver. Ranch-style houses were springing up by the dozen in North Glenn.

Fred enjoyed it mostly because a workday meant he could stay away from Mikey's until five or six – although sometimes he'd work with more haste than usual, his left hand trembling from just a few hours of alcohol withdrawal, so he could get back to Mikey's sooner. Once he volunteered for a double-shift purely to see if that would stop him from getting drunk at all that day, and was both delighted and disappointed when the second-shift workers pulled out a green steel Coleman cooler filled with Coors during their lunch break. Fred passed out before the end of his shift drunk, but not before managing to leave the new dimmer switches grounded to a hot power line: so six months later, when the house caught fire from the dining room rheostat, he kept a low profile at Mikey's until the insurance company settled the matter. Nobody died, everybody got made whole. "That wasn't a bad deal," he'd tell Mikey, a little more often than was necessary or desired.

When Wally decided he wanted to know his father, he knew it would have to be at Mikey's. So that's where he'd spent three or four nights a week over the past seven years, beginning when he was eighteen and old enough for Mikey to serve him. Mikey was more enthusiastic about his presence when Wally got a part time job at the machine shop across the street and could pay, or at least reduce Fred's bar bill.

Wally hadn't been there when Fred died. Instead, he'd been sitting with Millie watching *The Smothers Brothers' Comedy Hour*, arguing baby names. Wally had no real preference, but Millie was fretting endlessly about it, and couldn't be contained. Occasionally he'd try nodding and grunting his way through the conversation while not taking his eyes from the television, but Millie required eye contact from time to time. And the eye contact she received, one night when she interrupted a particularly interesting skit on the TV, was enough for her to leave the room. When the phone rang at midnight that might have informed them of Fred's heart attack, neither one was in the mood to answer it, and Mikey had to walk across the street to the machine shop to deliver the news the next morning.

Wally stopped sitting at that table. He even stayed away from the bar.

But it was different now that Millie was in labor. He sat with his back to his father's old chair and contemplated what he'd have to do to take care of his family.

He was surprised when Marion stormed into Mikey's at around 1:00 a.m. "Your wife is in trouble," he grunted with more disgust than Wally thought was respectable, then threw a twenty dollar bill at Mikey behind the bar, who was more than willing to apply it to the running balance. Marion grabbed Wally's arm and literally pulled him out of the bar. Wally wasn't unwilling, but Marion's daughter had just survived a near-death delivery, and goddamn it, Wally was going to be there.

Wally was drunk as he stuck his face up against the glass looking into the nursery. The baby was fine, wrapped in pink. Wally was so excited that he kept breathing too hard against the glass, so he and the nurse had to shuffle down the length of the window every few seconds to avoid the opaque fog he kept creating with his banquet-beer exhalations.

Marion and Linda were with Millie. When Wally joined them he entered the recovery room with as confident a stride as he could muster, (believing that walking firmly didn't give off any sign of intoxication), he was, to Millie's eyes and everyone else's, quite firmly drunk.

He approached her and caressed her hair. "You alright?"

Millie could only nod, too exhausted even to say yes.

"They say she's out of the woods. We're staying till the morning to make sure." Marion's contempt was audible.

Wally nodded and turned back to Millicent. Typical Marion, the old cowboy, he thought, not letting his daughter answer questions herself. He was an overbearing son of a bitch.

"I love you." Wally said. "I'm very proud of you."

Millie managed a smile. This is when they both knew he should kiss her on the forehead.

Wally knew if he leaned in, his breath would overwhelm her, and he wasn't yet ready to admit he'd been unable to handle the whole thing. So he stayed put.

"Kiss her, you idiot. She just went through hell for you." Wally felt the unspoken command coming from the strong eye contact Marion and Linda were making with the back of his head. It had only been a few seconds, but it was enough.

"You're in great hands. Get some rest. I'll be back in a few hours to check on you."

Millie concealed her disappointment, nodded, and smiled.

Wally stood upright, and with barely a nod (unreturned) to Marion, started out of the room. As he was nearly to the door, Marion grunted, "Her name is Katherine."

Katherine was Marion's younger sister, who had died of smallpox in 1934 when Marion was one of nine kids who lived in a dugout near Cheyenne Wells.

Wally stiffened somewhat. He'd wanted a bit more say in the matter, and didn't remember that he'd abdicated that responsibility to Tommy Smothers.

None of them knew this, but on that very day, a small band of scrappy television producers had just received enough grant money from private corporations and federal agencies to start their own production company. Their goal, and it was a passionate one, was borne out of the increasing social disturbances in large urban areas, so they were to create an educational show that would take place in a single street in the kind of urban environment that their target viewers, kids around three to five, would find recognizable and perhaps unthreatening enough to learn in. There would be skits with wildly colored creatures that were a mixture of marionettes and puppets – and a whole generation would learn tolerance, respect, and spelling in a whole new way.

As Wally headed back to Mikey's, he could have no idea that the single most destructive part of Katherine's upbringing was not her drunken father behind the wheel leaving St. Joseph's hospital in a '62 Impala with only one headlight working, but rather the television show that was going to be revealed eighteen months later from several of the most brilliant minds in education who, one has to assume, were secretly praying that they might change the world.

# CHAPTER TWO

The very first *Sesame Street* episode premiered on November 10, 1969. Why it premiered on a Friday is somewhat confusing. It began with Gordon, a black man with an impressive-but-not-frightening-to-whites afro and muttonchops, leading a little white girl named Sally into Sesame Street, telling her all kinds of things happened there.

There were a few skits, the Muppets appeared – Ernie was naked in the tub and Bert walked in on him, demanding tub time himself. Ernie wasn't yet sporting his soon-to-be-famous horizontally striped shirts, which as a heavy-set character only emphasized his roundness. Muppet fashion is not to be emulated.

The part of that show that catches my attention happens about just about twenty-eight minutes in. A Muppet that resembles a hand sock walks up to Gordon and says hello. The Muppet has no eyes, no nose, and no hair, but her hello is a soft, female greeting. Gordon is not fazed by this in the least; apparently he has seen more gruesome things than Muppets without features. But to make sure the viewer is at ease, he turns and tells us that, "This is one of our anything people. She can be whatever she wants to be."

Over the next couple of minutes, Gordon provides the hair the Muppet wants, the eyes she prefers, the nose, and then proceeds to do the same thing for the rest of her family of four. Dad even gets a moustache. It's a pretty cool thing, asking for your features and getting them.

Milan Kundera wrote that we don't get the faces we deserve until we're at least thirty. Since the features we were born with are so genetically random in terms of how they may or may not shape our personalities, it takes roughly three decades for our smiles, frustrations, and the general muscle movements and dietary choices we make to manifest themselves to the point that our face can actually explain to some degree who we are.

I believe Kundera because he articulated the notion while he was still a dissident writing in Czech. Dissidents are always so much more truthful, I find, especially if they aren't so angry that their passion befuddles their arguments. I'm not a dissident. It is not a solid career path in the United States, certainly nothing like it was when *Sesame Street* and our players first appeared. I'm just angry, which means I have to be careful not to piss you off. I also don't speak with an Eastern European accent, which means I probably don't appear as soulful as someone who does. We're so much more willing to accept anger from soulful people than others.

I wonder what Kundera would think of the Anything People. Philosophically, it's colossally offensive to reason, and if you're an academic in the humanities, you're likely a Marxist, which means you believe we cater to the few people with the resources to be whatever they want to be, at the expense of poor workers like Gordon, whose job was to on their faces in a shameless reminder of the oppression of lesser-known thespians worldwide.

But few philosophers or Marxists watch *Sesame Street* unless it's to publish a paper about its educational shortcomings. But in 1969, just a year after the Soviet invasion of Prague, what would Kundera have thought of this kind of notion? He would almost certainly have decried the lack of sensuality in the program, which is one of the reasons that producers of children's shows rarely come to authors like Kundera for advice.

What does it tell children? Gordon seems to imply that there are certain people who could be whatever they wanted to be just by asking. Are they supposed to represent the all the kids who are watching? Can they too become whatever they want? Or is it just a special kind of person who is afforded that privilege?

There are too many long-winded assessments of what television programs are actually communicating to children, so I'll just tell you what

Barbara thought when she was alive and watching the show with Steven, who wasn't really paying attention. Gordon doesn't seem to have an accent. She couldn't place where he was from. Everything about Sesame Street seemed to suggest it was in New York City, a place that frightened her just because it was so big and the people there were said to be so rude and rough and everything people were *not* in Oklahoma.

He was a nice, polite, colored man. This was a show she could allow her boy to watch, because he needed to know he could be whatever he wanted.

Steven, during that airing, rolled around in a half-crawl-half-walk that he would use for locomotion for the next few months. Occasionally he would turn to the TV, usually when the Muppets were on. He never had any one thought in particular in his head, but he'd just stare until they were gone, and then go back to his business of using the coffee table as a support as he 'walked' across the room. Barbara was the one who was captivated by the program. This, she thought, was a good thing.

It was seven years later that Steven sat in a doctor's office, his thin limbs dangling from the side of a very cold metal table, while his pediatrician calmly explained to Uncle Lawrence that Steven had rheumatic fever; it had already damaged his heart, and he would be lucky to live through his teens. The best thing for him, the doctor advised, was to avoid all rigorous activity and stay indoors as much as possible. He might just make it to young adulthood if there were not too many strains on his heart.

Steven listened while his uncle nodded. Steven was the captain of the third grade flag football team, despite his slightly weaker left arm – he was even the quarterback, and they'd won the "Toy Bowl" between Ft. Stockton and Midland just the year before. They would have gone undefeated for the season, but Steven, on a quarterback end-around, lost his orientation on the field and ran full speed out of bounds at the thirty-yard line on the last play of the game. If he'd just been able to keep his head straight, he would have known where the end zone was and would easily have scored. This, by the way, would be a felony in Texas if some legislators had any say about it. But as of this writing it remains a misdemeanor whose punishment is strictly enforced by the player's peers. Steven was beaten up after the game by two fat kids who played offensive line. It was the first bloody nose he'd ever had that wasn't inflicted by the invasive curiosity of his own index finger.

He wouldn't be playing again. His uncle was taking it all in stride, so he should too. He nodded as wisely as he knew how to as the doctor explained that he'd need penicillin shots every month to avoid infections that might stress the heart and would likely be fatal; that he'd have to have blood drawn every week so they could keep track of whatever was or wasn't growing in his bloodstream.

On the way home, Steven looked out the passenger side of the 1971 F-150 pickup truck his uncle drove everywhere. It had cool lights on the top of the cab that made it look like a big-rig at night. And while he never consciously thought of *Sesame Street*, a part of him was slowly beginning to digest that, as a matter of fact, his dreams were done. The doctor had just told him he couldn't be what he wanted to be: a professional football quarterback. That was over. Just like that. No matter how hard he would work or how nice he would be. He couldn't just be whatever he wanted. He'd have to find something else to be.

The world smelled vaguely of motor oil. Steven watched the Texas clouds whipping themselves taller above Fort Stockton; a storm was coming, he could tell by how dark the bottoms of the really big clouds were getting.

Maybe the doctor was wrong. Maybe this wasn't that big of a deal. He could still play football, he just wouldn't try as hard. He was still faster than almost everyone – he didn't have to run at full speed. He didn't have to be *rigorous* about it. He'd run at half speed to protect his heart. That's what he'd do.

"Want to go to McDonald's?" Uncle Lawrence's voice was cracking, like a radio station you can't quite receive.

"Sure." Steven looked at his uncle and felt a sudden drop in his internal organs, like everything from his throat to his stomach had just landed in his lap. McDonald's was a big deal. You don't just go to McDonald's. He'd even stopped begging to, despite the fact that he could recite the recipe for a Big Mac, and the commercials said that if you could sing the recipe for a Big Mac, you'd get one for free. Aunt Maria would say no without even letting him finish the song.

This must be serious.

Ten minutes later, Steven stood in front of the counter at McDonalds, and sang, his own voice wavering, "Two all beef patties special sauce lettuce cheese pickles onions on a sesame seed bun."

He got the Big Mac; and after his uncle whispered something to the attendant at the cash register, they came out and gave him a white tee shirt with green neck and armbands with an artist's rendering of the Big Mac as an image comprised of the words of the ingredients.

Steven sat in his chair across from his uncle and just waggled his feet back and forth. He counted the number of sesame seeds that came off the bun. Thirty-six. His uncle didn't notice how little of the sandwich he ate.

Leonardas noticed everything Tiffany ate, to the point of grabbing uneaten food from her during meals.. "That's enough," he'd say with always a gentler voice than she expected. "You have to mind your figure for the competition."

The Austin Mid-Town What-The-Hell competition. Raise a baton. Talk about world peace. Why didn't anyone want to talk about how powerful static electricity was, and harnessing it could provide electricity for half the world? Mr. Hardy himself said that in class, and-

"Enough about that. There's plenty of time to go to school when you're older."

She had said that same thing yesterday, like they'd had a conference and decided Tiffany wasn't girl crazy enough. It made Tiffany fume. She knew she was smarter than all of them and was uninterested in throwing a baton anywhere but at Maria's head.

"Wait a minute?" Leonardas stared at Tiffany clinically. Then, to Louise. "What is that?"

Tiffany's mom saw nothing.

"The way she sits, no?" He leaned back and watched her. "Go ahead, eat."

Tiffany did as instructed, four sets of eyes watching her. "What." She said as blandly as possible as she turned over a page of her science book.

A week later Leonardas decided she had spent too much time leaning over tables and desks and books; it had damaged her back somehow.

He would check into it soon.

As normal as it is for children to blame themselves for their parents' divorce, this wasn't Jeremy's problem. He was thirteen, and had spent the first month of his eighth grade year avoiding gym class. He'd feigned illness, he'd volunteered for administrative work in the school offices, and even tried to launch a mimeographed school newspaper during gym hour, one that he might sell advertising for and help the school. Everyone loved the idea until they discovered it wasn't a legal means of fundraising for Wisconsin public schools.

Jeremy's attempts to delay his admission to gym class hadn't worked. Now, after climbing rope as well as anyone, he was expected to strip naked and enter the group shower bay without a single pubic hair, and a penis that resembled the baby corn that his mother put in their salads.

Every other boy was swinging. Some were larger than others, but all of them had hair. All of them were on their way to becoming men. Jeremy wasn't, and had no idea when he would be. Maybe his father would know.

One day a month before, he'd awakened after a sensual dream, and as he took off his shorts to take his morning shower his heart leapt at the curly fibers above his penis. That excitement lasted only a few seconds, when he realized his mother hadn't cleaned the filter on the clothes dryer, and that lint adorned every inch of his body his pajamas had covered. He skipped school that day and told his mother that the automatic garage door opener broke with the door wide open, and he had to stay there to guard the place.

This was the height of absurdity. But so was being nearly fourteen and not having a single pubic or underarm hair to show for it. He looked at himself in the mirror and saw a ten year old. He hated that boy.

In part, because that boy had run out of maneuvers. It was time to take a shower among the hairy genitals of his friends.

He walked in wrapped in a towel, a towel that wouldn't attract attention. Lots of guys did that. He reached up and turned on one of the shower heads. It was common to let the water flow for a few seconds to ensure it wasn't too hot or too cold before walking in.

Jeremy looked around. Everybody was about to see him. Everybody was about to see what an underdeveloped boy he was. Somebody would probably beat him up, but he was more concerned about the laughter. It would come from everywhere.

His hand trembled as he removed his towel and stepped into the stream from the showerhead.

The water splashed shame onto his head, most of it flowing around in his hair, but enough ran down his face to give him a good excuse not to open his eyes. He groped for the shampoo dispenser and made sure suds covered his entire face. Nothing existed but the soapy foam, he hoped.

"Hey, Jeremy . . . " Danny D'Aguilar, a linebacker on the varsity football team, was about to call him out.

Jeremy opened his eyes and felt the sting of the shampoo while staring at the wall. "Yeah?"

"Good job on the rope, man. Made me look bad, you gotta slow down."

That was it. Jeremy rinsed himself off, got dressed, and nobody said anything about his Vienna Sausage penis or his utter lack of development. All they cared about was how quickly he climbed rope. He would climb faster. He would make the other guys work harder. That way he'd never have to defend himself for something that he couldn't do anything about.

He bounded into the house when school was out, excited to tell his mother that he'd been the hero of the gym class – and was astonished to find her sitting at the kitchen table, her mascara running down her face, a paper napkin in her hand, stained black with attempts to halt the meltdown of her makeup. Despite that, her yellow leisure suit sat perfectly on her slight frame.

"Mom?"

"Jeremy."

"I have to tell you something cool!"

"Let's hold onto that for a minute," she said. "There's something I have to tell you."

"But I climbed rope faster than anyone else in gym today! Even the football players! They noticed and everything!"

Naomi pulled her dirty blonde hair back, and managed a smile. "That's great, honey."

Jeremy rushed off to his room to do his homework before she could tell him the news. It would take her a full month to explain that Jeremy's father had left them for "a new life." She didn't explain that "a new life" was a euphemism for "some twenty-four year old bitch in Oshkosh."

The night she did explain it to Jeremy, he nodded as she explained life would be different. They'd spend less money. They'd spend more time at home. Daddy was confused and trying to make sense of his life and would eventually come home, because you only have one home.

Jeremy sat at the dining room table, staring at his place setting.

"Do you want to talk to Uncle Ted?"

"That's Daddy's brother."

"He's still your uncle."

Jeremy shook his head no. Naomi began breathing harder, as though holding something back.

"What should I do?" Jeremy asked, dispirited.

"Jeremy, you don't have to do anything. You're just a boy. You just need to know it's not your fault."

"I want to help."

"I know you do. But you can't right now." Naomi left, her shoulders convulsing in grief, quietly giving away her sobbing.

That night, Jeremy pulled his pajama bottoms down and felt around his crotch. Still no hair, just tiny testicles and a child's penis. He needed to be a man, and he needed to be a man right now. His mother needed him to be a man right now, and he was still a child. What good is a child when a man is needed?

For reasons he couldn't understand, he grabbed his penis in pure anger and pulled at it. It hurt. Grow already, dammit. I need you.

He promised himself that when he did develop, he'd never disappoint anyone by not being mature enough.

Steven was in the seventh grade, and had a thing for Natalie Kowalski. He also had a serious gas-monster in his immature lower intestine that had convinced him it would end his existence if he didn't do something about it.

Natalie Kowalski sat next to Steven in fifth period math, right after lunch. He never really talked with her. His body kept screaming at him to stare at her, but he didn't entirely know why. He just complied.

He enjoyed sitting directly beside her. She wore cotton blouses with very short sleeves, flawless bangs and honey-rich hair flowing down past her shoulders, wearing a blue headband that gave away her regal bearing - and her arms were so thin that Steven could occasionally peer through and see her training bra. Or sometimes, on special days, she'd wear something sleeveless. Good times.

Natalie had a very slender body type, and had probably developed as much as she was going to – so even back then, her bra was already something she used to lend gravity to her curves. She certainly had body issues of her own, but she wasn't about to make those known to Steven. For instance, he would never know that she'd asked her mother, who was also athletically built (translation for those of you who have never placed a personal ad: it means, "small breasted"), if she'd ever grow larger. Her mother, remembering the pointed bras she'd worn in the early sixties to conceal her own "athletic" build (the adjective only becomes painful when used by non-athletic women), had said simply "I don't know – your grandmother was always bigger than I was."

This didn't matter. Steven was turned on by Natalie to the point of distraction during class. It wasn't just her chest. He liked her smile. He liked her laugh. And he liked the idea of her somehow looking at him someday with the idea of kissing him, and had imagined it more than once in the evening while a Hall and Oates tape played in his new cassette player and he tried to figure out what to do with his peach-fuzz covered erection.

There are shockingly few books on the market that instruct boys on how to masturbate. It's one of the few skills that you have to learn completely without guidance. It's dirty, it'll ruin you for women, it'll make you go blind ("what if I just do it until I need glasses?") – there continues to exist such a huge chasm between what we are and what we are expected to be as teenagers that no institutional resources exist to help boys (or girls) learn to masturbate. This is highly offensive in an advanced society.

Steven didn't take offense, he just didn't know what to do with his erections and was struggling to figure it out. He knew from experience that his uncle was never going to take him aside and say "boy, this is the way to relieve your sexual tension." Although Steven could swear somewhere in his memory that he'd heard Aunt Maria talk of Uncle Lawrence being taken to a prostitute in LaGrange when he'd turned fifteen, and she apparently was still mad about it. But that was back in the 1950s. It just wasn't going to happen in 1980.

So he lived for the days when he could see Natalie's bra. He didn't know why.

That wasn't the issue on this particular day. The State of Texas was very specific about what is to be served in its school cafeterias. Every child enjoyed a certain amount of protein, a certain amount of carbohydrates, a serving of fruit, and a vegetable (a requirement that could be satisfied by a package of ketchup).

What nobody told any of the parents or students was that no research was done whatsoever that might predict the effect of this state-dictated diet would have on the digestive system of boys in emerging pubescence. The law resulted in an explosive concoction of elements uncontemplated by the legislators who passed it.

Steven was shifting in his chair, the gas building up in his digestive tract having become so unbearable that he honestly believed that without some relief he might actually lose consciousness.

This was a chemical problem. Added to that was the fact that only a few weeks before, he'd committed the cardinal sin of actually trying to grant himself that relief in the relative anonymity of the back row of the same math class, and with disastrous results.

He'd decided, like many people in his position, to just let everything out slowly. He'd sat very still and relaxed his clenched sphincter just the slightest bit.

It was by any measure a phenomenal blunder. His attempt to "sneak one out" made a logic-defying high-pitched noise, like air escaping from a tightly-held balloon – and it went *on and On and on.* The trumpeter Chuck Mangione had just made a worldwide hit out of his song "Feels so Good," and it suddenly sounded like Steven's anus was warming up Mangione's embouchure.

He couldn't stop it – and he was mortified. It lasted so long that everyone in class had time to not only notice the sound, but to look around until they located its source. He could read their faces as they thought: "what's that? Oh wait – it can't be – seriously, someone is farting in class? Who is it? Wait, it's Steve!"

That is an eternity for a thirteen year old.

He was been purple with embarrassment by the time it was over. Everyone turned back to their work; a few sniggers at best. The teacher, Ms. Liszt (or as she was known by many, "Miss Slit,") chose to ignore the situation, therefore almost everyone had to ignore it. She was in her late twenties, wore a home-permanent that made her head resemble that of a poodle's, but the hormonally-charged boys in her class only noticed her hourglass figure, and she had a complete hold on each one of them. Steven knew this. What he didn't know was that every girl in the class hated her, if for no other reason than she commanded so much attention from the boys in a seemingly effortless fashion.

As the squeal from his buttocks faded, Steven couldn't even look at Natalie. He returned to the task at hand. Complex equations were a greater relief at that point. And he had to admit he felt better.

But now it was a couple of weeks later, Steven had another monster gasball in his abdomen (*thank you, state-mandated broccoli*) — and he was determined not to let there be a repeat of the long, slow flatulent death of his social standing.

Steven decided to use logic to address the situation, in exactly the way he'd learned on TV.

Problem: in previous gassy instances, the "clinch and creep" had resulted in squeezing himself together, so when he did let some gas escape, it had to go through a narrow type of opening, so it made that awful squeal. He thought of air from a balloon, and realized that if instead of pinching it nearly shut, you hold the nozzle of a balloon wide open, the air doesn't squeak, but escapes with barely a sound.

Solution: open the gate wide and expel all the gas at once.

Problem number two: the little plastic student desks they all sat in. A hard steel frame holding a molded plastic seat, with a laminate desktop bolted to the right arm (there were never any lefty chairs, which made Steven feel at a disadvantage during tests.)

Obviously, his earlier disaster had been exacerbated by the echo that was formed by the imperfectly shaped chair. There had to have been some little chamber he couldn't perceive while seated that nonetheless amplified any noise originating from his butt. So if he were to gain any relief at all and not be a spectacle, he obviously needed to kind of roll up to one side so he was only half-seated on the plastic, thereby eliminating the chance of the chair making noise.

Solution: pull up one cheek.

Why on Earth didn't everyone know this? And why hadn't anyone ever told him?

So Steven, quite proud of his skills in logic, leaned over to one side, fully expecting that if he forced everything all out at once, and did so only half-seated, the sound, if any, would be something akin to a *whoosh* that would be over in just a portion of a second; some people might hear it, but nobody would know what it was, and certainly nobody would know that it emanated from him – especially since he was doing Natalie the courtesy of situating himself so the business side of the transaction was facing away from her. Instead, he aimed at some exchange student, a kid from Germany named Gunther who spoke English better than any of them did. Gunther could handle breathing foul air for a few seconds. In fact, he wasn't at all sure that the Kraut hadn't done the same thing to Steven before.

Wonderful. A solution reached through calm and passionless logic, even in the midst of serious discomfort. Steven was proud of himself.

He reared up, literally, swallowed hard for luck, and began the short journey to relief.

*Oh my God. Oh my God. Oh no. Oh God No.*

This was perhaps the loudest fart ever released by a human being.

Steven was more stunned than anyone. He imagined parents yanking their kids off the street as bricks fell from the stress of an earthquake. He imagined seismograph needles leaping into action in some faraway lab. He pictured sonar operators in submarines deep underwater, tearing their headsets off, yelling, "what the hell was that?" He could easily have been convinced that somewhere in Switzerland at that very moment, an avalanche was released onto some unsuspecting climbers, who had only enough time to say to each other "dude, did that come out of *you?*" before a wall of snow swept them from the mountain.

All these images flashed in Steven's mind in a fraction of a second, before he realized, in the most lonely conclusion he'd ever made in his short life, that it was not a worldwide event: it was simply a tremendous fart in Ms. Liszt's class – a social nightmare, unadulterated, unhindered, unleashed.

Total mayhem in the classroom. Fifteen of the twenty-five seventh graders lost their cool completely. As the papers flew and the howling began, he was still frozen in his starting position, completely stymied that every piece of logic he'd assembled to make no noise at all had in fact achieved the opposite: a mighty, tremendously voluminous, incredibly loud surge of intestinal wind that probably parted Gunther's hair.

The reactions were not universal, he saw after the initial cheers from some of the other boys. There was a sense of shock, to be sure. Nobody does that. Nobody *does* that. Some of the girls managed a look of disgust, but the overarching sense was one of utter disbelief – and most of the guys just looked at him, slack-jawed, their expressions containing an odd type of respect – as if to say, "whoa, you really went for it, dude." Actually, because he was truly mortified, Steven would never put together the fact that despite his slim seventh-grade build, he was never picked on by the larger boys from that day forward. The kid had balls. This would be the general consensus.

But in the moment, Natalie Kowalski was dumbstruck. Steven looked at her and wondered if deep down she was also in awe of his accomplishment—if only her awe was just obscured by the total horror in her eyes, like when you find out your next door neighbor, who kept to himself and didn't talk much, actually killed half a trailer park and had your name on a piece of paper taped to his refrigerator.

Ms. Liszt, who had to do something to restore order, because there was no ignoring this kind of interruption (when someone blasts a trumpet in your ear during a sermon, you have to react somehow) cleared her throat, and said with a voice that was practically quivering with fear of what Steven had just unleashed:

"Steven, would you like a bathroom pass?"

Without even thinking about it, he answered, with utter sincerity: "no, I think I'm fine now."

The laughter began again.

Five minutes later he was standing in the bathroom, Ms. Liszt having scribbled his pass so quickly that none of it was legible. He walked from stall to stall, taking that internal measurement we take as to whether or not we're in need of relief.

He wasn't.

He leaned up against one of the sinks and felt like cursing, only the dirty words no longer made him giggle. If he hadn't been in middle school, he might have contemplated the limits of logic when determining our behavior. Instead, he grew angry at Ms. Liszt for refusing to even let him finish his explanation about how he'd tried to avoid trouble. What was the point of explaining your logic when nobody wants to listen.

He said out loud, "this is stupid." He kept checking his digital Casio watch until eight minutes had gone by, which he figured was the middle-school minimum time for Ms. Liszt to assume he'd had a bowel movement to eliminate the chances of further embarrassment.

He curled the pass into a ball and tossed it from hand to hand. "Next time," he thought, "I'm not going to explain anything. To anyone."

Tiffany sat in her usual seat on the back seat of the bus. It was the last week of school, the last week before she was scheduled to have her back brace removed, and today's ride was particularly excruciating. She was a little concerned. The pain didn't bother her so much, she'd long ago decided. But why so much so suddenly, just before she was to be free of the metal contraption? Just her luck, she thought, another complication. She'd gotten some grasp of the medical lingo required to talk to the doctors for the last three years, but overall, her fifteen-year-old mind only knew that it was the last week of the ninth grade, and scoliosis was a bitch.

If anything about the situation didn't completely suck, it was that she almost never had to explain to anyone what scoliosis was. When Tiffany showed up to her seventh grade homeroom in a metal brace extending from below her hips up to the middle of her head, keeping her back and neck almost completely immobile, very little was directly asked.

Not that the other kids weren't curious, and she heard the whispers. But that lasted only a week or so, and after the first month, all curiosity regarding her condition had disappeared. Next week would be the end of three years wearing the brace, the end of three years of being invisible.

Shortly after seeing Tiffany tumble down the stairs in the first month of her affliction, her father had decided that since her body had already been rendered unattractive by the brace, it was the opportune time to undergo every embarrassing procedure a teenaged girl could endure. Or, as she once heard him say to a friend "so long as her body's in the shop anyway . . ."

Braces with headgear to ensure her teeth would be as perfect as her little sister's. A tiny operation to remove what seemed like an embarrassingly Asian epicanthic fold that developed over both of her eyes when she hit puberty. Actually, it was derived from the Mestizo side of Leonardas's Mexican family, but that mattered not at all.

"My daughter isn't going to look like some half-breed Chinese," Leonardas said when Tiffany's mother initially objected.

"But it's too much all at once - it will make her so hideous!" Tiffany stood stock still in the hallway around the corner. *Hideous.* Melissa was vaguely insulted, and struck back. "And when she tans, she gets that yellow hue. I think that's from your side of the family, frankly."

This fight wasn't going to be resolved in the hallway. So Tiffany went into the shop.

The eye surgery necessitated thick glasses for the last year, as puberty had also ruined her vision, and contacts would potentially impede the plastic surgeon's work. She would, much later, be told this was a false notion.

There was no way to exercise, and eating was always painful. Tiffany would take showers carefully, and sometimes stare in the mirror before drying off. She hated the glasses – red-rimmed, bottle-thick, the wrong shape for her face. They magnified her eyes so much she felt she looked like a caricature of an owl. She didn't know how her body looked compared to anyone else's, because she was never in gym class, and nobody ever invited her for sleepover parties.

For her part, Tiffany, either from lack of exercise or a plethora of genetic material, had a curvaceous figure, but nobody could see it beneath the brace. In fact, nobody seemed to see her at all. Both the boys and girls at her school were ruthless to each other – about what they wore, how their hair looked, what kind of music they liked: nothing was off limits. If you deviated from the cool you got yanked back into the cool, or you became nobody.

But the keepers of the cool never teased or taunted Tiffany. Ever. There seemed to be an unspoken agreement that the girl in the back brace got a pass, which Tiffany had come to hate more than the idea of being teased. Even the cruelest girl in the school, Heather, wouldn't criticize her directly. Tiffany knew that some things had to have been said behind her back – and she wanted to know what they were, just so she could respond. But she wasn't even good enough to be teased.

Another unforeseen result of the scoliosis was that since she was invisible, people around her began to act like she wasn't there. They'd tell their friends secrets to each other right in front of her, as though she were a piece of furniture.

As Tiffany had struggled with her locker combination one day (it was painful to raise her hands above her chest) Heather came up to Ellen and hissed "Joe is cheating on Laura!"

"No way!" Ellen slammed her locker door closed, which made Tiffany jump, then wince in pain.

"With Shawna, can you believe that?"

Ellen turned around to see if anyone was listening. Tiffany was standing right there, so Ellen turned back around, secure in their secretive space.

"How do you know?"

All secrets were safe with Tiffany, because nobody cared what she thought. This felt mildly amusing at first, like a perk, even – but the sheer enormity of what horrible things people would say right in front of her began to overwhelm her after a while.

Leslie and Camille were best friends until Mark Lasko decided he had a crush on Leslie instead of Camille, who had been angling for him for months. Then Camille held a girl-council in the cafeteria when Leslie wasn't there, and told ten other girls (and Tiffany, playing the role of the Scoliosis Credenza) that Leslie had had sex with a guy from UT and had contracted "one of *those* diseases." Within days, Leslie went from head junior varsity cheerleader to slut. Tiffany never thought that it was a very long trip to begin with, but she also knew Camille was making it all up. She'd heard Camille say so to Angelica during history class the day before.

So this is how people are. It doesn't matter if you're nice, or if you work hard. If you took one step wrong, if your body didn't measure up, you were toast. Nobody ever tells you that when you're a little kid.

Or maybe she'd been too cynical. She decided one way for her to get attention was to start applying herself more assiduously to her homework, especially math and science, which were fields that most girls seemed to avoid, so she could be spared a little bit of the cattiness; not to mention that some of the cutest boys in school, who wanted to be engineers or work in the sciences, suddenly saw her as a resource.

Another jolt in the school bus reminded her that she was about to lose that access. She looked at the pattern of fingerprints on the dust on the half-down window beside her. They resembled the constellation Leo.

The luxury of being asexual would go away soon, and so naturally it would follow that the cute boys wouldn't talk to her anymore. Maybe her days as a credenza were over, but transforming into a mildly fat girl who was part of the scene was never going to get her any popularity. The cute boys would stop talking to her because she wasn't medically off limits anymore: she was just ugly. That would leave her with the nerds.

She looked up ahead at David and Earl. Both of them would be scientists, but for now they were wearing similar plaid shirts with pocket protectors, essentially begging the football players in the front seats of the bus to beat them up. She knew all about the nerds. One of them looked up at her and nudged the other. A woodsy glare from her glasses made them turn away. Nerds weren't nice, they were just cowards. You can be smart and cool. They were just afraid to try, having bought into the crap from the keepers of the cool. She wouldn't make that mistake.

Maybe. She'd worked damn hard to make sure her grasp of calculus and physics were the best in the school. She'd even helped Elian Sanchez nail his final exam in AP Physics. And he was a senior. It was an open book test, so they agreed it wasn't cheating when he came to her house and she walked him through calculating the mass of two stars in orbit with each other. Leonardas, now *State Representative* Morales, had even walked in to grab ice for his bourbon and nodded approvingly to Tiffany when he thought Elian wasn't looking. *You've brought home a fine young man*, his look said. She tried to make her facial expression reply, *he doesn't even know I'm a girl,* but few people could read any of her expressions behind her glasses. Elian had passed with flying colors, was now at UT, and had even asked if he could come talk to her about his homework if it got "too gruesome." *Of course, you idiot*, Tiffany thought as she'd nodded politely. *You look exactly like Tom Cruise. Don't you know anything?*

Removing the brace was going to change everything, but she didn't know exactly how. Would she have more girlfriends than Karen, "the Stork," who sprouted a foot taller than every boy in the fourth grade? Did Karen just like her because she was an outcast too (Karen was probably the only girl in school less coordinated than Tiffany, something that flummoxed the volleyball coach)? Would Karen still come over and listen to records on her stomach while they talked about boys they would never date? What would happen if Tiffany suddenly became dateable?

All this boiled down to few central questions. Could Tiffany be cool? Did she even dare to dream of being cool? Did she even want to be cool after seeing how cruel the cool kids truly were?

And her sister. This would be tough. Maria was already being groomed for local beauty pageants, because that's what the daughters of powerful men in Texas did. Maria had been given music lessons on just about every instrument (the back brace kept Tiffany from everything but the piano, and even that worried Leonardas so much that he'd stopped her after just a few lessons). Maria had been taught how to walk the way dancers walk so she could look elegant. Tiffany's walk was more of a continuous series of pivots. And her parents gave Maria the prettiest dresses, dresses that augmented her figure in what Tiffany doubted was an age-appropriate way (she was not armed with the vocabulary to express this thought precisely, so she merely replied "this is stupid" when she was forced to go shopping with Maria and their mother). Maria was only twelve, but once she'd gotten made up in the right dress, she looked twenty. Tiffany got the frumpy clothes, because nobody wanted to admit that underneath the steel getup and headgear there was a developing woman.

Tiffany took it like a man, which is how she was raised to take such disappointments. That is to say, she said nothing about it and let her resentment quietly grow. It wasn't as though she were actively mad about it – if anyone asked what was wrong, she wasn't lying when she said "nothing."

The only exception to this had been one night after one of Maria's dance recitals. Maria had literally pranced onstage, her barely pubescent body springing forth with signs of fertility, and danced to Stevie Wonder's song "Ribbon in the Sky," while trailing a limp ribbon attached to a long stick in her hand. It had been an unimpressive routine. At the end of it, she'd released two handfuls of glitter into the air (not nearly as subtly as she had hoped to), and spun in the glitter as it rained down upon her. On the way home, Leonardas had said, his voice nearly breaking, that the dance was so beautiful he could swear he saw magic in the air.

Tiffany just thought her dad needed to see an optometrist.

Everyone else just took the comment for what it was, but when Tiffany looked over at Maria next to her in the back seat and saw her self-satisfied grin, Tiffany couldn't help herself. "It was glitter, daddy."

"What?"

"She threw glitter in the air to make it look like that."

"I did not!"

"Then show us your hands. I bet there's still glitter on them. Come on, show me your hands!"

Maria refused. "You can't make me do that! You can't make me!"

"Enough," Leonardas said, shooting a harsh look at Tiffany in the rear view mirror. "It was beautiful. You should be proud of your sister. It's not her fault you can't dance yet."

The memory of that statement coincided with a harsh right turn, rocking all the students in the bus over to the left. She felt a harsh pain in her neck — the very kind of pain the brace was supposed to prevent. She had an epiphany.

She wanted the brace to stay on. This is why the jolts in the bus were so difficult for her on this particular day. The brace was asking to stay on her body; and in that moment, she wanted to agree. The orthodontics with headgear, which she was to lose next month, and her glasses, which could be replaced by contacts by the end of the summer — she didn't want any of them to go. It was her armor. It was her -

"Hey, Tiff." Michael Smith nudged her. She hadn't even realized he'd moved to sit beside her.

Michael fidgeted a bit as she stared at him. She liked that her stare could make people a little nervous. He was mildly cute, but was wearing Duran Duran parachute pants, which she knew earned him a lot of laughter in Heather's circle.

"What's up." Tiffany was good at not expressing curiosity when asking questions.

"Math homework was a killer. I worked on it *for hours*. Did you get it done?"

"Yeah. It wasn't that hard." In fact, she had done it the night before while watching *The Cosby Show* and was surprised at how elementary the questions were.

"I just need help on number twelve, here." He presented his unfinished homework. She examined it. How on Earth did he not see how obvious the solution was?

"Yeah. You want me to do it for you, or talk you through it?"

"Whatever you want, babe. This is the last big one of the year, man. I just want a good grade."

*Babe*. Right. Like that was going to work. She knew he really wasn't that interested in learning calculus. He wasn't going to be a mathematician — she'd learned from all the unfiltered gossip that he was going to join the Army right after high school anyway, so why waste the time explaining anything.

"Give me your pencil."

"Won't Mrs. Hershaw know you did it?"

"I'll make it look like your handwriting."

Michael was overjoyed. "You're so cool, Tiff. Awesome!"

Yeah, she thought, and you have no clue.

He took his notebook back with him to the part of the bus where the jocks sat, and soon several of the boys were copying the answer down in their own notebooks, looking back at her, nodding their mulletted appreciation.

*Armor, my ass.* There would be no going back. Tomorrow, the brace would come off, and she would no longer be anyone's credenza. She would decide how people reacted to her, and if that meant pissing off the boys, she had no problem doing that. She had dirt on them they wouldn't believe.

Tiffany felt an anger within her growing, and was familiar with it enough to not let it overtake her. She'd been ignoring it for nearly three years; she wasn't about to let it control her now. Small steps. She'd become a woman to reckon with, in small steps. Beginning tomorrow, nobody would treat her like furniture.

It would look suspicious when half the boys in the class got number twelve wrong by making the same error, Tiffany knew. She'd have to answer for that socially at some point. But she was about to become a different person, and that person needed to take the offensive. Even be offensive, if that's what it took.

# The Rainbow Connection

There were two outs, three balls, two strikes, runners on second and third, and Katherine in left field nervously drumming her ungloved hand against her thigh. Amy would get this last out, Katherine knew. Amy always came up big.

Amy looked at the base runners, then looked back at the catcher, Melissa. Katherine couldn't see Amy's face but knew she was scowling, that scowl that scared everyone, even the older boys from the high school. Katherine had even noticed Eddie and Sam in the stands—high school boys—and knew they were there to watch Amy, which Katherine thought was just a little weird. They didn't even cheer. They just watched Amy as she tucked her long red hair into her cap on the pitcher's mound and went to work.

She threw a windmill fastball, the one she saved for situations like this ("you always save the windmill for situations like this," she remembered) and Katherine was completely surprised to see that the batter not only got her bat on the ball, but by the time the metallic clink of the aluminum reached left field, Katherine saw Amy fall in a heap. It was a comebacker that had caught her square in the right thigh.

Katherine ran to her without waiting for the umpire to call time. The whole team gathered, indifferent to the fact that two runners scored before the shortstop picked up the ball and threw it right at the runner from third as she sauntered to the plate to score. It smacked her square in the back and she collapsed momentarily before crawling the last few feet to tag home plate. You didn't run on Amy, period. And the girl who tried to steal a run after a cheap comeback would wake up for a week remembering that lesson.

"Get off the field!" the Umpire yelled at the offending shortstop, who complied. But if anyone thought that shooting for Amy was okay, they didn't anymore.

Amy was twisting in pain, her eyes squinted shut as her tears tried to leak out. She kept rocking back and forth, holding her leg, until she opened her eyes and saw Katherine leaning over her. Her face changed instantly and she said, forcing a smile, "Don't worry. I've got another leg."

"Yeah," Katherine said, "but this is the one that hurts, right?"

Nobody could keep from laughing, and Katherine was happy about that, if a little confused. People laughed a lot when she talked. When she was a little girl, she assumed it was because she was cute. Now, with her father Wally already gone for three years, Katherine was beginning to figure out that she didn't always know why. I mean, how cute can a 13 year old be? Cute is for kids. Older kids needed other words. Like pretty. Pretty the way Amy was.

Amy had such smooth white skin, and she easily freckled. She was going to have an awful bruise. Other girls were going to make fun of her in gym. Katherine began worrying for her.

Amy got up, nodded off the umpire, and finished the inning with three straight windmill strikes. As they reached the dugout, Amy slapped Katherine on the butt with her glove and said, "Thanks for cheering me up." She sat down beside her gingerly on the bench. "What's for dinner tonight?" Amy took off her cap and shook her hair free.

"Mom's working late, so Daddy's going to cook spaghetti." Katherine had been periodically calling her stepfather "Daddy" for nearly a year.

"Is that all Mark knows how to make?"

Katherine shrugged. Mark had three dishes: chili, spaghetti, and macaroni and cheese. She didn't have a problem with that.

"Maybe I should call my mom and see what she's making." Amy winked at Katherine.

Katherine knew she was kidding. Amy spent maybe one or two nights a month at her own house – almost a year ago, when Amy had first asked to stay overnight during a school night, Katherine's mother Millie called Amy's mother to ask permission. Katherine didn't know what was said, but Millie never called Amy's family again. It had been settled: Amy was welcome any night she wanted to stay, even school nights. So she did. A lot.

"You girls shacking up again tonight?" Melissa asked with a smirk. Katherine was about to simply say "yes" without a touch of irony, when Amy repeated their usual lie, but this time she said it with a snarl. "She's my sister, you dumb bitch."

Melissa looked around the dugout to see who had heard the exchange, and seemed relieved that it was private. Amy always knew what to say, and using the b-word was pretty tough. Melissa was scared, and Katherine felt a slight surge of adrenaline knowing that. Amy showed no sign of feeling anything. She almost never did.

One night almost a year before, as they were going to sleep together in her full-sized bed, Katherine asked the back of Amy's head why she stayed over so often. It was a soft question, and Katherine had been afraid for months to ask it. "Are your parents mean?"

There was a long pause. A silver beam of moonlight seemed to give Amy's hair an amber penumbral glow. The low murmur of the box fan in the window softened the silence and shielded most of the sounds of the crickets and night insects outside. Amy finally sighed. "I'm tired."

Katherine accepted this. "Amy doesn't want to talk, Amy doesn't have to talk," she said to herself. She'd remembered when her mother gave her a stern exhortation when Katherine wondered why her real father Wally had just abandoned them. The answer was simple. "Your father's life is in

Wisconsin now, and he'll tell you more when he's ready. You have to let people tell you what they think when they're ready to tell you."

She had still been surprised to hear what she was certain was the sound of Amy crying.

She wasn't crying today, even as she limped out to the mound for the last inning. Katherine headed out to left field, and just smiled when Amy looked over and nodded to her before throwing the first pitch.

The first batter went down swinging. The second drove a shot directly to first and was out in a flash. The third hit a long fly ball into left field. Katherine ran backwards, her eyes never leaving the ball, caught it right at the wall, and threw the ball straight to home plate, where the catcher snagged the ball in perfect position to tag an imaginary runner. Katherine didn't have to do that. She knew it was the third out. She just liked the practice, and she knew she was the only 7$^{th}$ grader who could make that throw. She deliberately didn't look at the high school boys as she jogged to the dugout. But she knew they were looking at her.

Once they'd started gathering their equipment after their victory, Amy leaned up to Katherine and whispered, "show off."

Katherine just smiled.

Rolph the dog was playing a veterinarian on that week's episode of *The Muppet Show*, which Katherine loved more than anything else in the world, except purple flowers. The Muppet nurse walked in and told him his next patient was going to be some kind of large dog – and Rolph hung his head in disappointment.

"I really wish it were going to be a dachshund," Rolph said.

"Why, doctor?" The Muppet nurse was concerned.

Rolph suddenly sprang to life, "because I always wanted to get a long, little dogie!"

Amy laughed, so it had to be funny. Katherine took the cue and laughed uncertainly as she heard Mark snicker behind her.

Mark was cool. The spaghetti had been seasoned with a jar of Prego with some extra fennel thrown in, which he liked to declare his "doctored-up sauce."

And he liked *The Muppet Show*. Sometimes he'd do Statdler and Waldorf imitations at the breakfast table just to crack up Katherine and Millie, or Amy if she was staying over. Amy liked him, Katherine liked him, and her mom had never seemed happier. She didn't know much about Wally anymore other than that he lived in Wisconsin now, fixed old cars, and liked to hang out with "the boys" (a term Millie almost spat out when she used it) in the garage after hours way too often. Mark was different. Mark paid attention to Katherine and Millie, and had even agreed that they would host Amy anytime without being mad about it.

This episode was a particular hit; she and Amy and Mark were having a great time, and she was laughing so hard during the last musical number that she didn't hear the phone ringing, and she barely noticed as Mark stood up to go answer the phone in the kitchen. All she knew was that a few minutes later, he came back into the room and sat back down. He pulled out a cigarette (Mark usually went to the back patio to smoke) and burned half the cigarette with a single drag.

Amy seemed to know something wasn't right, and Katherine followed her lead as she turned around to look at Mark just as the half-spent cigarette stopped glowing. Mark just stared at the TV, his eyes watery, and motioned with his hand for them to keep watching the show.

When it ended, he stood up and said "Amy, can Kathy stay with you tonight at your house?"

Katherine hated being called Kathy. But she never corrected him.

Amy's face darkened, and Katherine wanted to explain that Mark didn't know how mean Amy's family was. But Amy and Mark made strong eye contact, and Amy nodded.

"Thank you. Kathy, grab some stuff for overnight. I'll drop you off."

"What's wrong?"

"Let me talk to Amy a moment, will you? Go on now."

That night, just before Amy and Katherine were to go to sleep, Amy's mother Dorothy stuck her head in Amy's bedroom, a pencil-thin cigar dangling from her mouth and a glass of foul smelling liquor in her hand, and said to Amy in a harsh and unsteady tone of voice, "Just one night. They have to start making funeral arrangements, and I'm not turning this place into a damn hotel."

Amy turned to Katherine as soon as the door closed, her face a look of alarm. Katherine could only look back calmly and say, "what?"

Amy took her hand and sat her down on the bed. "Katherine. It's your mom."

Katherine cried all night, and Amy held her. Katherine tried to get up to walk home twice, but Amy kept her from going. Katherine only fell asleep after Amy rocked her in her arms in the corner of the bed. She kept whispering "It's okay, it's okay. It'll be all right."

Katherine wanted to argue. Of course it wasn't all right. What a silly thing to say. But finally, as she grew exhausted, she allowed herself to think that if Amy said it would be all right, it had to be. She fell asleep with her head resting softly against Amy's soft tiny chest, feeling certain that there wasn't a single ounce of water left in her for another tear.

The funeral arrangements took three weeks, and Katherine understood why. When you die in a car they have to do an investigation. Mark had finally explained it all. Mom had been driving home when she died. She crashed into a tree, but the doctors had to examine why the accident would kill her when she was driving so slowly. It took them a while, but they discovered Millie had suffered a heart attack just before she drove off the road.

"She was probably gone when she hit the tree, sweetie."

"Oh." Katherine didn't know what to say.

"That means she probably didn't feel much pain, so that's good."

Katherine nodded. But she was a bit worried when Mark got down on one knee in front of her. Grownups only did that in the movies. She frowned at him.

"There's going to be some changes, though."

"I know." *Duh.* She didn't like it when people talked down to her. She might only be twelve, but she knew that everything would be different now that it was just her and Mark and Amy.

"Katherine, your father is coming down next week."

This was a surprise. "Wally?"

"He wants to take you back to Wisconsin with him."

Mark seemed to see Katherine's eyes get unnaturally large, and tried to pre-empt her response, "I don't like it either, and we've talked to lawyers about it, but since we never got around to me formally adopting you, I don't have a say in the matter. He's your father. It's his right to take you to his home."

"But that's not fair!"

"I know it doesn't feel fair, but that's what your parents agreed to when they got divorced. We wanted to change that, but it was very difficult to do."

"I don't know anybody in Wisconsin!"

This response seemed to shock Mark somewhat. "Well, you'll make friends there."

"When do I have to go?"

"A few days after the funeral."

Mom had always said to take good news and bad news the same way. Katherine tried to live up to that. She had to live up to it. Mark was starting to cry again, and Katherine felt a part of herself harden. "Okay." She stood up and walked away, proceeding into her room, closing her door, and lying on the bed. She couldn't make Mark cry anymore. She'd been watching him cry for three weeks and couldn't add to his worries. She had to be the level head. Mark loved her more than anything. It wasn't fair to ask him to take care of her right now.

She'd only been in her room a few moments when Mark knocked. "Katherine?"

He got her name right. "Yes?"

He opened the door. "I'm sorry, sweetheart. I can talk about it more with you if you want."

"Do I have to talk about it if I don't want to?"

"Of course not."

"Then I don't want to talk about it." When Mark closed the door, Katherine grabbed her pillow and curled into the fetal position. She rocked back and forth until all alertness faded from her.

On the way to the funeral, Mark tapped the steering wheel of their Toyota Corolla while Amy and Katherine sat in the back seats. Katherine stared at the back of Mark's head. He was dressed better than she'd ever seen him. He worked for the phone company; phone company guys didn't have suits, she'd thought. But he looked nice.

Amy reached over and touched her leg. When Katherine looked over, Amy seemed to be asking a question with her eyes. Katherine shrugged, unaware of what was being asked. She saw Amy look out the window at

Denver sliding by, then was surprised to see her grin when she looked back. Amy was up to something.

Katherine's forehead scrunched up. "What?"

Amy began singing:

Why are there so many

Songs about rainbows

And what's on the other side . . .

It was the opening song from *The Muppet Movie*, which they'd seen with Mark and Millie a few months before. Katherine began singing with her.

Rainbows are visions

But only illusions

And rainbows have nothing to hide . . .

Both were surprised to hear Mark singing along in the front seat, but Katherine could tell he wasn't up to it.

So we've been told and some choose to believe it

I know they're wrong, wait and see —

Someday we'll find it

The rainbow connection

The lovers, the dreamers, and me.

Together they sang the entire piece. They stopped when the song was over, paused, then Amy began again — and Katherine heard Mark give out a little laugh when she did. Soon Amy was singing with more power, and finally Katherine sang at the top of her lungs as well, all three off-key, (or rather, in different keys entirely), crying, laughing, and inexorably headed toward the funeral home.

After the third rendition they stopped, dried their eyes, and got out of the car. Katherine smiled because she knew their faces were red for reasons different than anyone else's. You weren't supposed to laugh so hard on the way to a funeral. Mark held both of their hands, and as they entered the building, Katherine realized in a slight panic that it would hurt her mom's feelings if she didn't act sad. So, effortlessly, she let a wave of sadness flow over her, like it had been contained in a room whose door only needed to be touched to fly open. She began crying uncontrollably but subtly, just a stream of tears that she didn't even try to stop. She felt Mark squeezing her hand, and looked up to see him crying as well. It helped. They were a team.

Three weeks later, the counselor at her new school in Madison, Wisconsin, asked her what she liked to do when she wasn't in class, if there were any activities she'd like to be a part of. Her reading and writing skills were prodigious, she'd said, and she was such a well-rounded girl. Was there anything special, any clubs, she'd like to join? Katherine looked away for a second, then turned to the nice old lady and said with unexpected firmness: "I don't like sports."

I can handle this, Steven thought. It's no big deal.

Steven and his best friend Scott (not really his best friend, but they sat next to each other in every class) had been busted going off campus during lunch. The students at Rayburn High School were supposed to stay on campus. Steven and Scott ignored this rule with impunity, especially as the end of their senior year was almost upon them. But this happened to be the one day that Deputy Dawg (nobody knew his real name, or cared to) caught them high-tailing it across the parking lot to make it to Calculus II on time, and had slammed on his golf cart's brakes in front of them in a fairly hilarious attempt at masculinity.

They had been in the vice principal's office for about ten minutes. His name was McDonald, a thick eyeglass-wearing, pencil-moustache sporting limpdick. There were other insulting adjectives used for him; in fact, the record for McDonald insults in one sentence was upwards of twenty by some sophomore, but Steven couldn't remember all of them. He did remember that one of the latest versions had contemplated how deeply a hamster could be forced up Old McDonald's ass, but the precise wording eluded him.

The facts were not in dispute. Steven began to daydream as he pointed his eyes towards the vice principal: if he let his eyes blur just a bit, McDonald looked like Beeker from *The Muppet Show*. His voice was high pitched and nothing he said made any more sense than his doppelganger's. So Steven smiled as discipline was doled out – until he noticed he was alone in the office with the VP. Scott had disappeared.

"I'm sorry, I got distracted. What?"

"I said," McDonald pulled down on his shirt authoritatively, "you can have detention after school for a week, or get five whacks on the ass right now."

Steven raised his eyebrows. He'd have to tell his uncle and aunt about detention. That, he couldn't hide. "Anyone need to know about this—if I get the smacks?"

McDonald's eyes widened when he heard "the smacks," as though he'd just gotten a streetwise primer on what spankings were known as among the cool kids. "Nobody needs to know."

Steven nodded. "Whatever. Let's get it over with." Steven wasn't trying to be stoic; his cowboy uncle had just always hammered home the importance of fessing up and taking your medicine. After all, a good-hearted person is going to mess up from time to time; it was a worse crime to cover it up or blame it on someone else than it was to just own up to it and take what was coming to you.

The eminent pubic-hairless, mushroomed-boogered platter-eyed pie-freckled lambfucker, Old McDonald, (no, that wasn't the right sequence, Steven thought,) got up and retrieved the paddle – something that looked like it used to be an old crewing oar, but now had several holes drilled through it. Steven had heard about this paddle, how the holes were supposed to eliminate wind resistance and thus make each swat more powerful. It also decreased the overall mass of the paddle, however, and Steven wasn't intimidated as he was supposed to be.

As the clove-footed dick-licking swamp-assed Vaseline-rimmed-mouth pigfucker, Old McDonald, waved the paddle in the air, Steven did his calculations. The problem was one of momentum as the paddle struck: momentum is expressed as $P=mv$, where m is mass and v is velocity.

An undrilled paddle would weigh about 30 ounces. Let's call the velocity 30mph. So whatever the final value would be (he knew it should be metric, but he never bothered with exact unit terms,) it came to 900. About ten percent of the mass was gone because of the holes. So, 27 ounces multiplied by a ten percent increase in swing speed would be 891. The holes made the paddle less powerful, if you were willing to do the math. If you don't do the math, you'll fall for the myth. Did I learn that from Oscar the Grouch, he wondered. No, probably the Cookie Monster. He dealt in quantities.

What if the holes increased the velocity by twenty percent? That would result in a swing speed of 36mph, which would be an overall unit-without-term value of 972, which was considerably more momentum, and might hurt more, but Steven's appraisal of the arm strength of that miserable abandoned-in-an-overflowing-outhouse unibrow Boxer-the-horse faced (Steven remembered *Animal Farm* from AP English) ankle-grabbing cock-smoking dickhead Old McDonald indicated that three or four swats at full strength were all he could do.

Fifteen seconds and this would be over. What's the big deal?

"Stand up. Put your elbows on the desk."

Steven complied. Obviously this was going to hurt and the venerable ass-sucking, donkey-felching, toejam-football-helmet-wearing Vice Principal was going to get a rush out of it. Whatever. And why wasn't Scott there?

The first spank came before Steven was ready for it, and he exhaled involuntarily.

"Not so tough now, are you?"

"Whatever." Steven had regained control of himself.

Which was possibly the worst thing he could have done. In the course of the next twenty seconds, Steven was spanked harder than he ever had been in his life – and some of the strokes didn't land on his buttocks. His upper thighs took two stinging hits, his lower back took a jab that made Steven actually cry out in pain.

The feel of hot breath on his neck. "Are you sorry? Are you sorry you broke the rules?"

Steven wiped a tear away from his left eye and stared at the motivational poster that McDonald had on the wall behind his desk: a crewing canoe filled with high school boys in tight athletic wear with the word "TEAMWORK" spelled out in bold below it, with some other crap sentence in a smaller type that Steven couldn't see through the mist of his eyes clearly enough to read. "I'm just fucking sorry you're a limp-dicked asshole in charge of children." He didn't know he was going to say this. It just came out.

The paddle's next destination was on the back of Steven's head. He fell over and clutched the chair behind him to keep from hitting the floor. "Hey –" was all he was able to get out before the paddle smacked him on his knuckles. A second later and he was on the ground and the paddle came at him sideways, like a cleaver, and glanced off of his scalp.

"Oh yeah??? Got anything else smart to say?" McDonald's comb-over flopped down like a curtain in a theater relieving the audience from an awful play. Steven snorted involuntarily, trying the best he could not to laugh. He breathed heavily a few times to make sure both of them knew no more comments were forthcoming.

Steven watched his assailant straighten himself up a little, then bend over to examine him again. At first, he thought he was checking to see if there was evidence that he'd wailed on his head, back and legs. But that wasn't it. For the first time, Steven began to feel scared.

He felt McDonald's hand reach down and caress his buttocks through his jeans. "You'll be fine," he said, his hand sliding under his crotch and then down the inside of his left thigh. You're a spirited young man. Very strong will. I admire that." He put out his hand to help Steven up. Steven took it, vacantly.

He was helped up to his full height. "Is that all?"

McDonald backed away a step, but kept looking at him with faraway eyes. He stroked Steven's cheek tenderly with the back of his hand. "You're excused from detention. Let me write you a note for class. Nobody has to know what you did." He returned to his side of the desk, sat down, and filled out a form with quiet precision. "You know, you're lucky I was the one on duty today. Mrs. Gardner would have given you detention for the rest of the school year without even asking your side of the story."

"I appreciate it, sir." He turned and walked away.

Before he could clear the principal's suite, he heard Mr. McDonald call out behind him, "if you need anything, I hope you know you can come to me."

Steven walked back to class with a slight limp.

What the fuck was that. He didn't know what to think. This was not the kind of thing he could talk about with anyone. There were getting to be so many things he couldn't talk about. He felt like a liar all the time just for keeping his mouth shut. He didn't need to be in this fucking high school anyway. He already passed AP exams for all his major courses, and would start at UT as a junior when he got out. Who cares if his grades sucked. He didn't like doing work for people who couldn't appreciate it. And like the TV always said, if you were good at what you did, nothing else should matter.

You even thanked him, you weak son of a bitch.

He limped back into Calculus. Scott was sitting in the back row, and began chuckling as Steven entered. Several other kids joined him; obviously Scott had told the story. Scott had accepted a week's detention, because Scott's mom didn't give a damn about what he did at school. He'd spread the word that Steven skipped detention because he was afraid of how his uncle and aunt would react, which was considerably lower on the man-scale.

Steven considered this. He didn't care how his uncle and aunt would react. In fact, he decided in that moment that he was going to tell them everything that happened. That is, everything but the fondling, which he still hadn't wrapped his head around. He'd just rather get his punishment over with right away.

As he reached his chair, next to Scott's against the far wall, he winced and said, far more loudly than Scott expected, "McDonald says you're a fucking pussy."

Scott stopped laughing. The other kids started an entirely new kind of laugh, this time directed at Scott, who visibly shrank in his chair. Despite his sore ass, Steven realized he'd done the right thing and was the hero of the moment. Right then he made a mental note to go off campus again the next day. This time, if Deputy Dawg stopped them, Steven would kick him in the nuts. McDonald had done something undeniably creepy. Enduring that, Steven concluded, won himself some kind of immunity from high school crap, which had bored him for far too long already.

That out of the way, he began to reconsider. Uncle Lawrence and Aunt Maria didn't need to know about this. Steven felt the top of his head. It was moist, and he pulled down his hand to see blood on his fingertips.

Ms. Bichsel noticed his distraction and had apparently shot him a question. "What is the solution, Steven?"

"Could you repeat the question?"

"Were you listening?"

"How could she expect me to be listening," he thought, " I just got my balls cupped by a man who beat me with a cricket paddle."

He ignored her. "Could you repeat the question?"

"No, Steven. You need to pay attention."

Steven's felt a surge in his pulse, and, barely aware of his actions, picked up his textbooks and began exiting the class.

"Steven!" Ms. Bichsel was harsher than usual. "You have not been dismissed!"

"How about that." Steven said as he left the room, loudly enough for her to hear, softly enough so that he wasn't broadcasting the insult. He wiped away a tear as he exited the classroom and headed off campus.

Just before driving out of the parking lot, Deputy Dawg cut him off in his golf cart. He stepped to the Steven's door and peered into his car with a smirk that only people with little to no power can form.

"Where you think you're going? You got a pass?"

"None of your goddamn business."

Dawg puffed out his chest and affected the deepest Texas drawl he could muster. "Wher' you 'posed to be raht now?"

"Someplace safe, where I don't get fondled by perverts."

"What do you mean?" Dawg looked genuinely concerned for a flash of a second, then seemed to realize that kids will say anything to skip school. "Go on back to class."

"Fuck you, sir."

Deputy Dawg took a step backward and turned on his radio, which emboldened Steven. The only person he could be radioing was McDonald. That's fine, Steven thought, let him repeat what he'd just said.

He did.

Steven slammed the car back into drive, floored the gas pedal, and plowed through the front of the golf cart, spinning it into Chuck White's Camero (his daddy would just buy him a newer one, he realized), and drove off while Dawg tried to catch him on foot. Steven slowed down enough for Dawg to get close, then peeled out farther away. Deputy Dawg stopped the pursuit and got on the radio again. Steven could tell he was listening to something on the handset, then turn around and walk back towards his cart.

Seconds later Steven was on the freeway, feeling his pulse pounding in his ears. Screw him. McDonald wouldn't do a damn thing.

That night, Steven went over the syllabus from Calculus, and then the syllabi from the other courses he was taking. It was late in the year. His application to UT had already been accepted, and he'd even won a ¾ tuition scholarship for essay writing. According to the math on the syllabus, he didn't have to turn in another daily assignment anywhere: all he had to do was pass the final exams, which he could do in his sleep anyway. He had three weeks of school left, and since he'd had a perfect attendance so far that year, he could miss nine days without it being considered an official disciplinary problem. The last five days were exams. He'd go in for exams, that's all. Let his teachers complain to McDonald. Let McDonald say one word to him and see what happens.

"This is stupid," he said to himself, wiping away a tear. It shouldn't be this easy to mail in your senior year.

But there it was.

By the time he settled into bed and turned out the light, he noticed he was crying. Not a bawling, attention-grabbing explosion of emotion: just every few minutes, a tear that he couldn't predict would suddenly roll down his cheek.

He couldn't tell himself why, he realized as he heard the phone ring in the living room. He heard Uncle Lawrence's deep voice answer, and while he couldn't make out the words, he could feel it growing deeper, more intense, faster than Uncle Lawrence's velvety smooth cowboy drawl. This would be serious.

Steven sat up and tried to overhear through the thin wall:

"I'm been strugglin' with him 'bout that. . . . what? Oh, don't ya reckon I should hear his side of things first? Alright then, I'll call you back. God Bless now."

Steven scurried to look as innocent as possible. He slammed himself into bed, then realized he always kept PBS on the black and white TV he'd built from a Heathkit with Uncle Lawrence. He quickly turned it on and lay as still under the covers as he could when his bedroom door opened.

"Steven?" Lawrence's voice was soft.

The night had turned the plains of Fort Stockton into twenty shades of gray, inconvenienced only by the constant 18-wheeler traffic passing through. Even though there were signs everywhere that said "No Jake Braking," haulers did it all the time, and the noise dotted every conversation with a pause for the machine gun effect to pass by.

"Here's somethin' ya need to know."

Steven waited to get hit by the .22 rifle in his Uncle's hand.

"Shoot me the edge off that prickly pear."

Steven tried; the dust that puffed up behind the plant told him his score.

"Y'always done that. You know why, don't ya?" Uncle Lawrence got on his knees. Steven was just starting to relax. "It's because you cain't show the difference between pull and squeeze. Any old jerk at a school can push a kid around, pull him back into line. It takes a special kind of marksman to know what the only way you get the results ya want is to squeeze the trigger."

"It's that simple?"

Wordlessly, Uncle Lawrence took the rifle and picked off a pear. "Truth is," he continued after giving the rifle back, "it ain't. But it's enough to let you know I understand your point of view in all this. What do you plan to do about it?"

"Nothing." Steven put his hands in his pockets to offset the size of his taller uncle and the even taller challenge.

Uncle Lawrence just nodded. "I understand that. I do. Can you live with that outcome?"

"Sure."

Uncle Lawrence looked away at the last strain of the night and started walking towards their tiny house. Steven didn't recall very many talks in the aftermath of that.

# CHAPTER THREE

As opposed to Steven, who had to take the GED to qualify for college, Tiffany, Jeremy, and Katherine all graduated as members of the National Honors Society. Katherine went to the University of Wisconsin eagerly, that being the only university she'd applied to. It was close to home but far enough away for her to feel independent. She didn't understand why so many of her friends were intent on getting as far away from Milwaukee as possible.

Jeremy wanted to attend Alfred University in upstate New York, which had accepted him but not offered money. Uncle Ted was willing to pay for college anywhere, but ultimately Jeremy chose to stay in state so he could see his mother, Naomi, on a regular basis. She needed him, and New York was too far away. And who knows what nonsense Donald (Jeremy hadn't called him "Dad" for years) would pull if Jeremy weren't around to protect her. She might even go back to him and get hurt again. It had happened twice so far. The second time Jeremy had called Uncle Ted for advice, forgetting he'd just been promoted to Chief Circuit Judge, and Ted called Donald, and Naomi scowled at Jeremy for weeks. That was a good time for a few weeks of summer school in Mexico.

Tiffany, however, was told in no uncertain terms that she was to attend UT as an undergraduate, where she would study liberal arts (a term Leonardas almost spat out) and would get her graduate training in the serious sciences at A&M. This would ensure she could work with anyone in the state, Leonardas said encouragingly. Texas society revolved almost entirely around those two campuses, and she would behave like someone who belonged to Texas society.

It was a great battle for Tiffany to win the dispensation from her father to take a dorm room. She argued that no sorority would take her seriously if she was a "homer," and Melissa agreed.

Steven was expelled the day after hitting Deputy Dawg's golf cart, and McDonald had revised his notes to say that during the swatting session Steven had threatened him and his wife and children, and Steven's fate was decided so quickly that he'd decided that speaking up would only complicate matters, especially upon seeing the muted disappointment on Uncle Lawrence's face. Best not to make this a bigger deal than it was.

He passed the GED and showed up at UT on time for his first semester, which, owing to his test scores, was technically the beginning of his junior year academically. His scholarship had gone away because of the drama, but he qualified for student loans, and took them.

Many of their contemporaries had similar adventures. One of Steven's smartest friends, Eric, surprised everyone by dropping his college plans to become an Army Ranger. Tiffany's only friend, Karen, went to nursing school in San Antonio, and they never managed to keep in touch. Jeremy watched as many of his friends left school entirely and went to Chicago, hoping to make it in theatre or art. As the time went by in college, all of them at one point or another wondered, if only for a moment, if they were on the right path, because there seemed to be so many paths they could follow.

Except Katherine. She was going to be an elementary school teacher, and that was that, until she took a business class late in her junior year. After doing well in the course, she found herself daydreaming about working in human resources, which most people wouldn't consider an impossibly ambitious dream. Aside from this occasional distraction, she was at peace with who she was and in what direction her life was heading.

Until her father, Wally, died of complications of cirrhosis. Katherine was surprised at how little she felt when it happened; more pressing was the fact that his death left her with her stepmother Mary as her only legal family, and though she still called Mark from time to time, he'd become a distant voice that reminded her of a time she didn't like thinking about.

When Katherine knew what rules to follow, she followed them precisely (which is why she'd make such a great underwriter and a lousy primary school teacher). She showed up at the funeral and cried (these were not false tears, she just wished she could have had them as a first reaction to his death rather than before remembering from Amy how she was supposed to behave.)

So she stopped thinking about it, and felt much better in general. Senior year would involve her teaching practicum, and she was looking forward to it. She felt a strange kinship with second graders. She liked pretending to be the Easy Reader from *The Electric Company*. She could help a lot of kids, she thought, as long as her life didn't get too complicated.

As she walked into her very first solo classroom, she took a deep breath, and heard some kid say "bitch!" while sliding his chair to make sure he wasn't entirely concealing the noise. She was interrupted five times in five minutes before walking out of the classroom.

"Everyone goes through this," her counselor, Miss Kreth, said soothingly. "You'll get it – you just have to remind them that you're smarter and stronger than they are."

"But I've never been smarter and stronger than anyone. I've always had someone to, you know, handle things when they got rough."

"Do you want another in-class advisor?" Miss Kreth always lost a few elementary teachers like this, but few on the first day.

"Business. I should major in business. They're nicer to you in business, I hear."

Miss Kreth seemed to stifle a laugh. She grabbed for the transfer paperwork.

"Good luck," Miss Kreth said with a half-smile that Katherine counted each tooth of in a flash.

So a much happier Katherine began her senior year of college inauspiciously, spending the first two weekends in her apartment alone without a date. The first weekend had been uneventful: everyone was just getting settled back into Madison, and a few girlfriends had agreed to go out for drinks (they were finally all twenty-one), but arranging the nests for the last year whittled the number of confirmed attendants to less than three, and Katherine didn't like going out with just two girlfriends. Going with just two girlfriends to a club was practically an invitation to be hit on. If she had to hear she was beautiful one more time, she'd scream. Not that the words themselves were bothersome: it was where the eyes of the speaker lingered that made the words irrelevant to her. What we look at changes what we mean.

Being a senior, it was time for her to stop being hit on in bars. She'd been single all summer and had enjoyed dating a few guys, but nobody who she thought might be a good candidate for the next step. She was, after all, about to finish college, and after graduation she would get married. This is just how things worked. She despised even the idea of casual sex.

She never really had liked it. By the time she was fourteen, she'd experimented a little. He was a senior, she was a freshman. She'd been in Wisconsin long enough to know the nice boys from the not nice boys, and it was as good a time as any to try the whole sex thing out. She saw her first erect penis ever in the flash of a second before it burrowed its way inside her; the act itself was painful and very quickly over with, leaving her sore and still not entirely sure what the penis experience was supposed to be. Did all boys make those noises? It was the lack of an opportunity to examine the flesh that made the event unfulfilling for her at first. It was only after he left that she realized, even though Barry had been as polite as he could be about it, she was sure her inexperience annoyed him. So she decided to try it again. The second time with Barry, after asking some girlfriends' advice, she made sure to take his penis into her hands and look closely. A purple hat on a pink sheath of skin. A pulse that seemed to connect directly to her heart through her fingers. A pliability in movement that grew less limber as she pulled it in any one direction, slapping firmly back into its original position as she released it.

The manipulation was too much for Barry, and he finished all over himself before he could even begin the task he'd set out to achieve. Katherine was mesmerized, but he folded himself quickly back into his underwear, which had yet to have fallen below his knees.

"Let's go," he grunted, waddling across the room for his keys with his Levis still wrapped around his ankles. Katherine didn't know what to make of the situation, and as she was prone to do in embarrassing situations, she let slip a nervous laugh.

Barry wheeled on her. "Shut up and get dressed."

She hadn't undressed, which made Katherine laugh even more. Barry's face turned red and he said nothing as he grabbed her elbow and escorted her out to his Ford Pinto.

She didn't like that kind of rudeness. As he dropped her off, she turned to him and said calmly, "I think we're not going to go out anymore."

"What? Why? Shit!"

"I hope we can be friends. Good night." She shut the door and walked towards her father's house, happy that she was home thirty minutes before he expected her. He always waited up for her. Before she got to the door, she heard Barry turn up "Working Man" by Rush at the loudest his car stereo could oblige. She turned to see him speeding past her house again (he must have turned around, which was silly, because if he turned left a block down he'd be right next to the highway), flipping her the bird as she opened the door.

That was high school; the first time she'd experienced what a boy could do if he didn't get what he wanted. It was the very next night. He arrived unannounced, and she had to divert him so her drunken father and step-mother wouldn't know who he was) and sat with her on her porch swing, and he made a compelling case as to why they should stay together. There was a lot of pleading involved. In fact, Katherine briefly thought that Barry would fall completely apart if she stayed broken up with him. So she consented to stay together that night. He probably wasn't home yet (again with the loud music when he left) when she realized he'd just talked her into something she didn't want to do, and it made her angry. He talked real smooth, but it was all about what he wanted; the whole evening had been a deliberate exercise in disregarding her thoughts on the matter. So she broke up again the next day, less politely. She walked up to him just before he left for tennis practice and said "Barry, I'm not going out with you anymore." She turned and left, hearing some murmurings from the other guys on the team. She had done the right thing, and that was that.

At least, it was supposed to be. Over the next days, Barry followed her through the hallways at school, stuffed messages into her locker ("don't you know I can't live without you," "you don't believe me but I really do love you," "I've never felt this way about anyone before," etc.). She didn't dare mention it at home: her stepmother, Mary gave dirty looks to her routinely and could not be trusted. But Debbie Carter, a junior, had told her these were harmless notes and for her not to take them seriously. Boys will say anything to have sex.

Katherine believed her, and broke off contact with Barry. At first it was tough, because he seemed to be so wounded and she didn't like the idea of hurting anyone, but just as Debbie promised, it got easier with time. The guilt gave way a little when he was overly persistent, and she had transitioned all the way from having a guilty conscience to being mildly annoyed in just a couple of weeks. It got to where she could pass him in the hallway without making eye contact, but without appearing obviously to be looking away either. That was fine with her.

Until she came home from an evening of putting brightly colored golf balls through miniature plastic windmills and artificial livestock with some girlfriends to see Barry sitting in the living room. Mary was trimming the stems of some roses.

"Katherine," her stepmother said, "your friend Barry is here."

This, Katherine thought, was a pretty stupid thing to say. Of course he was here. He was sitting right across from her in the den. Why do people say things like that?

"Hi Katherine," Barry said, "I just saw these and thought of you, so I dropped them by."

"Thanks." Katherine walked past them into her bedroom, shut her door firmly (one mustn't slam doors), sat down on the edge of her bed, and reached to her night stand to put the Bay City Rollers album on. A few minutes later, she heard the front door close, and soon afterwards, Mary was at her door.

"What was that about?"

"Nothing." It would take too long to explain. Katherine didn't like to explain things.

"He's too old for you."

"I know."

"But he says he's taken you out."

*S-A, T-U-R, D-A-Y, Night.* This was her favorite song on the album, and the only one she listened to. It was crackly and hissy and skipped ahead a few seconds in the last chorus.

"Don't you know about older boys? Does your father know about him?"

Katherine snapped her head up with an anger that surprised even herself. "I don't have to answer your questions!"

The next ten minutes had been dedicated to a soliloquy by Mary about the dangers of boys in general and older boys in particular. She finished quite proud of herself, and this would stay between them. After all, her father's health wasn't great and there was no need to stress him out.

"Just between us gals." As Mary left, Katherine felt an odd sensation that seemed to be a mixture of having her trust violated, while at the same time being vaguely understood, and something of value had been imparted to her regardless. She would not feel this again until about a decade later when she bought her first used car.

But at that moment, not having ever knowingly met a used car salesmen, Katherine simply lay down and listened to her music. She thought about Barry's relentless notes (were they called mash notes because he mashed them into her locker?) and how Debbie said the whole problem was caused by the fact that she was a freshman who put out, and it was best she didn't do so again. Once was okay, but agreeing to have sex twice gave him the idea that she would do it anytime, which is what made Barry so dumb to get Mary involved, who would do anything to be her buddy.

Katherine was confused by how complicated it seemed. To her it was simple: everyone should just shut up and stop talking about it, especially Mary.

She hated Mary in a quiet way that would never quite reach her consciousness, much less her voice, and being asked too many questions was threatening those sequestered thoughts. She rolled over on her side and thought of her mother. Her mother would know how to handle Barry. She'd tell her to just stay away from him until he calmed down and got over it. But Katherine wasn't sure that was all she wanted, to be left alone. She wanted something else. The details of that desire eluded her, so she let a tear drop down to her pillow and whispered "this is stupid."

"This is stupid," she said again, this time alone in her apartment, her senior year at Wisconsin just underway. The shrink-wrap that encased her new CD was nearly impossible to rupture, and she couldn't for the life of herself get access to Edie Brickell and New Bohemians. They were too cool to be "the" New Bohemians, which she never quite understood, but she knew the record company sucked for packaging the damn CD so solidly. She'd already torn a nail; five minutes later a paring knife had only allowed her to stab herself, and the CD remained on the kitchen counter, tinged with a little blood on the wrapping, and defiantly staring at her as if to ask why on Earth she was spending her Saturday night at home instead of going out like the rest of her friends.

The CD had a point. Almost all of her friends had serious boyfriends by now. Some were engaged. Katherine was about to get a degree, and she should have a serious boyfriend by now. That's just how it works. You get out of school, you get married, you have kids. Even Mary had started making a habit of asking her about the men in her life: after all, hadn't most of her older friends paired up by now? But Mary didn't know Louisa, who was two years older and had been her roommate for six months in sophomore year. Louisa finished her degree in economics, shaved her head, got multiple piercings and moved to Seattle, where real music was happening that nobody else knew about. Katherine liked the local bands in Madison just fine, but took Louisa at her word because she was so smart. She didn't always like her, though. She'd always smirked at Katherine in an annoying way, as though she knew something Katherine didn't about almost any given situation. They hadn't stayed in touch, largely because of Katherine's lingering resentment at feeling talked down to so much.

But she was sure Louisa hadn't gotten married. No reason to argue about that with Mary. She enjoyed being right and being quiet about it at the same time. She knew people like Louisa thought she was stupid, and it contributed to her own quiet happiness to know those people were wrong.

Katherine went into her living room and sat cross-legged in the recliner she'd inherited from her father. Mary still had almost everything else, and that was fine. She just liked the Laz-Y-Boy recliner he read newspaper in. When she sat in it, things were less complicated; Mary was mean. Katherine would stay in on weekends and get ahead on her reading for her business class. She still liked the idea of working in human resources, where she could help people (she had yet to learn that the active verb of the HR charter was not "help" but "herd," but it would be too late by then). As she began to read about how a boss could fire an employee and convince the employee it was for his own good, she felt a little better about staying where she was.

The doorbell rang. Katherine froze. She was in a Wisconsin sweatshirt and pink pajama bottoms, and her roommate (Janet? Jane? Katherine kept forgetting) was at some activist meeting where she would find out strategies on how to end racism everywhere. Maybe she forgot her key. It was easy to forget your keys when you were working on something so important.

She opened the door and was a little shocked to see a guy about her age, wearing a t-shirt with Miles Davis on it and a pair of shorts, even though it was only sixty degrees or so. His hair was scruffy and dark, and he had a round face. He looked up at her and his eyes widened.

"Whoa, sorry." He said, backing away a little.

"What do you mean?" Katherine asked, leaning forward to see if anyone else was outside on the elevated walkway that connected all the front doors of the apartment building's second floor. Mark always told her to never stay on the first floor of an apartment complex or hotel room, without ever explaining why.

"I'm sorry, you just look really pissed off and I was just . . . never mind." He began to walk away.

"Wait!" Katherine stepped outside her apartment, leaving the door open. "I'm not pissed. I mean, I am, but that has nothing to do with anything. You knocked on my door."

"I'm your neighbor. I did one of those mondo shopping runs that, you know, we all do at the beginning of the semester . . . yeah, and I forgot to buy salt, and I'm cooking some pasta and thought I'd borrow some. I'll leave you be, though. Sorry."

"I have salt."

When Katherine led her neighbor into the kitchen, she reached up into the cabinet to grab the big barrel of Morton's and could feel him scrutinizing her body from behind. She hated leers and had just walked into one.

"Edie Brickell. Cool."

She turned and was surprised to see that he hadn't been looking at her at all. Instead, he had taken a paper towel and was wiping the small specks of blood from the shrink-wrap, as though it was the most natural thing he could have done.

"I can't get it open. That's why I'm in a bad mood. They make these things so hard to get to."

"I know, right?" the young man said, "first there's the impossible shrink-wrap, then the stickers sealing each side. Makes me miss albums. I was an idiot and got rid of all my vinyl right when CDs came out. But you want to learn a trick?"

Katherine just looked at him, which he seemed to take for an answer. He picked up the CD, found the edge of the kitchen counter, and scraped the CD across it at a perpendicular angle.

"What are you doing?" He was going to scratch up the place.

"Here you go." The motion had ripped the shrink-wrap and sticker completely down one side. He removed the wrapping with a flick of the wrist, and dragged his thumb through the other two stickers as he pulled on the CD case. They sliced open instantly, and suddenly Edie Brickell was free. "You can just peel the stickers away once you've opened them like this. If you try to peel them using the tiny little 'pull' tab, you'll never get it open."

The counter didn't have a scratch.

"Oh cool, glad you like that." He seemed to be reacting to her eyes, though she was certain she hadn't changed her expression. She stood staring at him for a moment before being jolted by the realization that she was holding a canister of salt.

"Here."

"Thanks. I didn't want to spend all week eating unsalted lasagna. I'll bring it back tomorrow morning if that's cool."

Katherine nodded.

As he walked down the passage to his apartment, she shut her door and listened to his footsteps. He knew from just a glance at her that she was in a bad mood, and he knew he had cheered her up, and he then just gone about his business.

She sat in her father's chair and wondered. She'd never seen a guy do that.

Ten minutes later, Katherine stood in front of his apartment wearing the same baggy Wisconsin sweatshirt and some jeans she knew that boys liked on her. The young man opened the door.

"Hey."

"I gave you the salt."

He smiled. "I know."

She stood in front of him for a moment, until the silence began registering as awkward.

"I mean, if I give someone salt I want to know their name." She felt stupid all of a sudden.

"That's a wise policy," he said, standing aside in the doorway. "You hungry? Want to help me make my lasagna?"

In the next two hours, Katherine learned he was a philosophy major, even though his divorced parents wanted him to be an engineer; that he didn't like clubs much; that he liked cooking; and that she couldn't keep a thing from him. Katherine talked and talked, only stopping herself periodically when she felt a touch of nervous energy infused in her speech.

He liked to make two giant pans of lasagna every weekend, usually while watching football on TV. Then, during the week, he would have something to nosh on. It saved a lot of money and it was a great way to de-stress; it was always especially handy during midterms or finals, but it was a weekly tradition he'd started observing even the second week of the semester. He was studying business contracts for his minor, and while it wasn't hard, it was a foreign language to him. "Philosophers," he said with a laugh, "don't do contract law very well." She laughed in response, hoping he didn't notice that she had no idea what that joke meant.

It had taken her thirty minutes before she remembered he'd never answered her question. "You never told me your name."

"Did you ask?"

"Yes."

"Oh. I'm Jeremy."

"I'm Katherine."

"Nice to meet you."

She walked back to her apartment later on with a Tupperware container of steaming lasagna and a commitment to cook together the next Saturday night. She put it away in the fridge, and went back into the living room and sat in the chair. She turned on the TV and enjoyed the butterflies she felt deep below her stomach as she realized he hadn't asked her a single thing about her, but acted as though he knew everything she'd ever felt. Besides, she'd practically told him her entire life story, unprovoked. It felt a little embarrassing now, but he wanted to see her again, and she didn't have to go to a Greenpeace meeting or a dance club to meet him. And once, just once, she'd caught him scoping her out, which her outfit made nearly impossible. He didn't seem to mind doing it so plainly, without even try-ing to conceal it from her. She was used to nearly eight years of watching boys play "catch up," where their eyes would dart back up from her breasts whenever she made eye contact after having looked away.

He made good lasagna. It reminded her of her mom's cooking. Katherine decided she would make a salad and bring it next weekend. She'd add hom-iny. Guys never chose it when they got salads at restaurant salad bars, but they always loved it when they didn't have a choice.

Her excitement might have been a little tempered had she seen him at that very moment, on the other side of the wall from her television.

Jeremy was pacing back and forth, in near disbelief at what had just oc-curred. The most beautiful woman in the apartment complex followed him home. *Can I keep her?* Jeremy laughed out loud at the thought, like he was asking about a kitten — who was it who told him all that anyone needed in order to be happy was a kitten, a sunset, and the smell of bacon? He didn't know — maybe nobody told him that; certainly nobody who was allergic to cats, or Jewish. He was just was so beside himself he couldn't sit still. He had reason to be so excited. For once, he didn't stammer when a beautiful woman looked him dead in the eye.

In fact, for the first time ever, Jeremy had the feeling he'd done every-thing right. He was cool without being distant, interested without being fawning, everything his Uncle Ted told him would work when meeting women. It wasn't all perfect; he'd still had to bite his tongue four or five times to keep from just running on about his life, and he was still fairly certain he'd been too much of a show-off. Who cares that he was on full scholarship because he worked for a judge when he was only sixteen? His problem was, he always tried to squeeze camouflaged boasting about his entire life when he met new women. He was happy to have avoided that tendency this time.

But he'd used too much basil. She hadn't noticed it tonight, but tomor-row, after the flavors had a chance to meld in the freezer (the condensation always intensified the spices), she'd notice and realize how nervous he was.

Or she wouldn't. That long dark hair, the figure that her clothes only suggested but never confirmed, the eyes that were not only beautiful, they seemed to him to be utterly honest, incapable of concealing any feeling at all. Here was someone whose eyes literally told him what she was thinking, even what she wanted to hear, at any given moment. All he did was follow their lead, and she was coming back. She was coming back.

If he didn't blow it before next weekend. He decided he'd use the library more than usual this week, just to reduce the possibility of the accidental encounter. Her parking space was two cars away from his; he'd seen her drive up in her Corolla a few times and wondered who she was. He decided that instead of his emasculatory LeCar, he'd ride his motorcycle to class all week. If they saw each other, he'd just wave or say hi. But by no means have an extended conversation with her before next week. Don't you dare.

He slowed himself down enough to hear the slight noise of her television on the other side of his apartment wall. It was a quiet complex; the small sounds never bothered anyone. But this wasn't just a noise; it was an opportunity to know her better. He walked over and put his ear to the wall. Nothing but people on TV talking. He rushed to the kitchen to fetch a drinking glass and placed it against the wall, because he'd heard somewhere it could serve as an amplifier. It did. The white noise was louder, almost like a seashell, and the voices on the TV were even less comprehensible. What was she watching?

He grabbed the bowl with the left over spiced ricotta mixture and sat down, wondering about who this Katherine person was as he scraped up enough for three large spoonfuls. The taste gave him pause. Maybe the oregano will calm the basil down.

That night Jeremy's concerns were amplified as he put his head over his open toilet, having forgotten that his ricotta mixture had raw eggs in it, which always made him sick. He was grateful that his bathroom was on the farthest side of the apartment from her wall. He knew he hadn't undercooked the lasagna, but still couldn't help but doubt himself as he took breaks to rest his forehead on the cool, unconditional acceptance of the commode rim. If she got sick, she was not coming back. He'd better skip class tomorrow and stay inside just in case she saw him not feeling well.

It was important not to be seen when you didn't feel well.

Tiffany only had a few minutes between code courses. It infuriated her. One was up at the Robert Lee Moore hall, where she wrote Fortran code in five minutes and waited for the rest of the class to catch up – and her next immediate course was in the Smith building, half a mile away, and she had fifteen minutes each day to run across the verdant University of Texas campus to show up late and out of breath. Fortunately, that class was extremely elementary also, so after the first few weeks she'd stopped the habit of running with her backpack across campus, and confined herself to a brisk walk.

She only slightly enjoyed being noticed during those first weeks, running late, she had to admit, was being noticed for what you did more than what you looked like. There were a lot of pretty girls, and she didn't feel like she was a particularly outstanding physical specimen, especially compared with most other sophomores. But she couldn't ignore what boys always said to her. Of course, boys who met her at parties would talk about her hazel eyes and how lost they were getting in them. She wasn't falling for it. No, they wanted more. This had long become boring for her, so she'd only go to parties when she wanted sex, which was rare, she thought, for a girl her age (maybe once every couple of months) and would hang around long enough to find someone who didn't seem like he got laid very often (a plethora of this demographic were freshmen, but the older the virgin, the more grateful), and then make his year in one night, so long as he wore protection. Smooth talkers likely had some kind of venereal disease (or AIDS, even; nobody knew anything about AIDS except that it was spread sexually and was killing everyone who got it).

She knew she wasn't quite sure what she was getting from the experience. Validation? Too simple, but she couldn't entirely dismiss the notion. An orgasm? Sure, a good orgasm took the pressure off before hard assignments, but what kind of shallow person did that make her? It was best not to think about her power, just to feel it and use it wisely.

And in the back of her head, she knew this wasn't supposed to be about power at all. In fact, she was willing to learn as much as she could about someone, and give more than a night on her back to them. But these bozos? She imagined taking any of them home to Leonardas. No, no, Tiffany decided, the boy she'd take to Leonardas would impress him.

"The transformation" had been remarkable. In one summer, she'd lost her back brace contraption, her teeth braces with headgear, her bottle-thick glasses, and was finally able to exercise. She lost twenty pounds and discovered she had a Playboy bunny's measurements (a fact confirmed by a perusal of Leonardas's bathroom reading basket), and had gone from a scoliosis credenza to Miss Austin in her senior year, and the third runner-up for Miss Texas in the statewide pageant. The winner, who went on to become Miss America, was a ringer brought in from Chicago who got sponsors for her dress and her hairstyles. The bitch had spent less than a year in Texas, and more on her dress than her father had spent on Tiffany her entire life. It disappointed Tiffany to lose, but she was comforted by the fact that she lost to a cheater. Anyone whose mother had to make her dress and whose father had primed her on world events would have lost to Tiffany. She lost to someone who couldn't even make the finals and quietly relocated back to Chicago during her junior year of college.

The boys had certainly treated Tiffany differently. Suddenly she'd become all they could talk about, as though she were a new kid in school. She had dates every weekend, and every boy was clumsy, and what's worse, they all wanted the same thing. And as much as she thought she knew about the boys when they were sharing their secrets with her when she was back-brace credenza girl, she was still surprised at how numbingly similar they were when expressing their newly-discovered ardor for her alone.

"I've never felt this way before."

"You make me feel so special."

"I want to just wrap you up and keep the world from ever hurting you."

To be honest, the last one was the most original, and perhaps the most frightening. Austin grew like a longhaired landfill in the 1980s, and there were wide, accommodating roads out in the suburbs where houses had yet to be built ("the sticks" they called it) the perfect place for high schoolers to go to make out or have other adventures. Even as a junior, she'd accepted a date from the valedictorian of the senior class, Edward, who was on his way to Yale. His father was even higher up in Texas politics than Leonardas, and Leo liked the match. They'd gone to prom together, and he drove her in his 1982 Impala out to the sticks. Tiffany knew full well that a few boys had probably said that she enjoyed parking.

But that night, when Edward unveiled that line, all it did was piss her off. She'd worn a dress that took her mother a week to make, and the best this guy could do was drive her to a remote suburb? Even some of the nerds had gotten rooms at the prom's host hotel. He thought he'd get in her pants without even buying room service? No, no, no. *Protect me?* Fuck you. You've never spent three years in a back brace being ignored.

"What's wrong?" Edward was genuinely confused after kissing her and receiving no passion in return.

"Why aren't we in a hotel?"

Edward looked down at his lap, as though trying to console his shrinking erection. "I never thought of that."

Tiffany stared a hole through his brain.

"Do you want to go home?" Edward asked. This was the height of arrogance. Of course they were supposed to fuck after the prom. Everyone knew this. He was prom king, and even Heather, the prom queen, knew that he would have a hell of a night. Tiffany liked sitting among the seniors, seeing them alternately hate her and like her. Heather just couldn't deal with her. Tiffany was too smart, too sexy, and too cool. That, combined with the accumulated knowledge of a family credenza, made her untouchable.

Especially in the front seat of an Impala out in the sticks. What did he expect? That she'd just open her legs for him in the car? Other girls might, and Eddie might be used to it, but he needed to be taught that Tiffany was not one of the other girls.

"Yeah, I'll go home. Your idea of a prom night really sucks."

Edward looked legitimately confused.

"Why didn't you get us a room?"

"I didn't think about it."

"Fine. Take me home. I'm tired of dating high school boys anyway."

She knew the barb would sting him, but let it fly anyway. It didn't matter all that much if she screwed the prom king, but it would have been nice because Heather really wanted to. Going home was a good solution. Maybe he'd call Heather afterwards, if he could reach her. And no matter what lie he told about why he had to drop Tiffany off early, Heather would know the truth: Tiffany wouldn't put out for him. The word would spread like a virus and Tiffany would start her senior year as an even more powerful figure.

Eddie angrily slammed a tape into his car's cassette player. Like everyone else she knew, he had an aftermarket stereo system, probably installed by Lance, the pepperoni-faced nerd who made no bones about his attraction to Tiffany. Once, when she'd been talking to Lance about a calculus problem, she interrupted him to say "stop talking to my breasts." Lance's response was as instantaneous as it was innocent: "but they're so nice to look at." They had been good friends since: he never asked her out and therefore, she never had to refuse him. All it took was a little cleavage and he'd helped her master diffy-q before her junior year was over. She drew the line at letting him take photographs of her ("fully clothed, tasteful of course."). It was just too creepy.

The Psychedelic Furs sang "The Ghost in You" as they left the parking area. Edward shot sideways glances as if he was wondering whether or not the music was getting to her.

*Inside you the time moves and she don't fade, the Ghost in you she don't fade.*

She had no idea what the song was talking about, and thought it was rather stupid. She kissed him on the cheek when he dropped her off, and enjoyed how he turned up the stereo and floored the gas pedal so much his tires squealed as he left her driveway. She knew Leonardas would hear "the call of the unlaid high school boy" and would be proud. Even so, when she walked into the house, when Leonardas asked how her evening went, she only answered, "it was interesting." She walked into her bedroom and closed the door while he held a half-eaten apple in his hand, trying to reconcile what he'd heard outside with what she'd just said.

What Tiffany couldn't say but was beginning to sharply see: a lot of these boys didn't just want sex. That was a horrible cliché that she'd believed in for far too long. They wanted just an ounce of tenderness. They wanted someone who would help them take shelter from the world they lived in. This was her theory, and it restored kindness to her for some while. She even began writing about it once, in a thing she called her "breakfast pages." She began her first entry with her common refrain. "This is stupid." In fact, she considered it a simple matter.

So she was not the first young woman to bring this firm knowledge of man to UT and have it blow up in her face. Everyone was as pretty as she was, everyone was as smart as she was. At least that's how her freshman year seemed to make her feel. She'd chosen Kingsolving dormitory, an all-girl bastion of chastity, and had grown tired of it quickly. Kingsolving girls weren't sluts (well, many of them were, but they only served to reinforce the image, much like the image of the librarian with her hair in a bun and thick glasses: boys just couldn't wait to see what happened when the hair came down.), so whenever she said yes to a boy, it seemed to mean more. To them, anyway; Tiffany was more interested in collecting data on their behavior and the psychodynamics of sexual power. Screw the idea of attracting tenderness. She decided having power was good. And power meant not giving a snowflake's care if someone needed you for anything.

Now that young man was sitting next to the live oak tree outside of the Smith Building, where all the diffy-q she'd already mastered in high school was being taught. He held a broad build and an almost Caesarian flop of black hair, and was writing something in a notebook. He always was. And he conspicuously never seemed to notice her. It made her suspicious. He clearly wasn't gay (too uninterested in his appearance), but he seemed to view her as nothing, no matter how quickly she answered questions from the teaching assistant in class, no matter how obvious it was that she would have tested out of the course if UT had allowed it. As it was, to get an information technology degree, the course was necessary, and since precisely one percent of Texas students even knew what diffy-q stood for when they entered college, no test had been prepared.

He just never seemed to notice her. She had beautiful black hair, a figure that exceeded Misses September through January, and boys slobbered over her. He treated her like she was still a credenza. He made her feel like her back brace and thick glasses were still on.

She arrived in class five minutes late, and got an acknowledging nod from the TA as she took her seat. Some fifteen minutes after she pulled out her pad to pretend to take notes, the young man came in, utterly unbothered by the dirty look the TA gave him. Apparently he hadn't explained that he had to cross the entire campus to make the course. In fact, Tiffany realized, he never made any excuses. He never apologized for anything.

He also never sat in the same place. Sometimes he'd sit in the back of the class, sometimes right up front; sometimes he sit to the far left next to a window and doodle during the entire session. The TA couldn't stand him, in part because whenever he was called on, he'd ask the TA to repeat the question (because he hadn't bothered to pay attention to it the first time), and he would always, always answer correctly–not with an "I told you so" tone of voice, but more of a "is that the best you got?" attitude.

Today he sat next to Tiffany. Half the lecture was over. He glanced at her notepad as though trying to get a bead on what had been said so far. She pulled it away. He smiled at her.

About ten minutes later the TA asked him a question. "Steven, given these variables, is a solution possible?"

Steven looked at the chalkboard for a second, then turned to Tiffany. "Don't you hate idiots?" He asked. Half the class heard him and started snickering.

He cut off the snickering by stating loudly to the TA, "No."

"Are you sure, Steven?" The TA seemed pretty proud of himself.

"I just mean I don't think *you* can solve it. If you want me to, I'll come down and do it myself."

The TA flushed red as he solved the problem on the board himself, and Steven just continued his scribbling, which seemed to have nothing to do with mathematics. When the TA finished, he turned to Steven and said with quite a bit of anger, "there. You happy?"

"To be honest, I wish I gave a fuck."

The class erupted in laughter, which was clearly humiliating to the TA, who wiped the chalkboard clean as though he were sanitizing a kitchen table after a bitch had whelped on it.

Steven leaned towards Tiffany. "They pay him to do this, you know."

Tiffany decided she liked this Steven character. She leaned towards him and said, "you know, I live in Kinsolving."

Steven was unimpressed. "Sorry to hear that."

"I just need to cut loose a little."

"Good luck with that."

Tiffany suddenly felt pissed. She'd just thrown himself at this guy with the "Kingsolving Come On," which was virtually a fool-proof way to get laid, and he showed no reciprocal interest at all. Screw him. Actually, don't screw him. Let him make his doodles and stories and waltz in late to class.

Steven leaned towards her suddenly. "Let's to go Captain Quack's – a hell of a lot more interesting than this is."

She gathered her books and Steven got up, and they walked out of class together. It didn't matter that the TA dropped his chalk when he saw them leaving. Tiffany was going to go to Captain Quackenbush's Intergalactic Café (i.e., a coffee house next to a University campus with a bizarre name – something *de rigueur* at colleges in the 1980s) with this guy. She was going to have a talk over a latte with someone smarter than she was, who had no interest in her sexually; and she wasn't used to that. This was, she was sure, a better use of her time.

She felt a deep sense of excitement in her belly, and below. Stop it, you idiot, she thought. It's just a talk. The dumbest thing she could do is to start liking this guy.

# CHAPTER FOUR

oys, even the smart ones, are dangerous. Boys can be controlled. Just watch your step around them. Tiffany had been ingrained with "statement one" since her father first saw that she was going through puberty; boys are dangerous.

Boys who told her she was beautiful were a load of crap, which is why Steven had turned out so special to her. He didn't shovel crap. In fact, for the first few months they hung out, she started wondering if he was just impotent and embarrassed about it. He only cared about what she thought. And as the weeks went by, she discovered, almost like a personal betrayal, that she trusted him.

But this does not make for good wedding vows. So she smiled as she was primped and looked out the window at Steven with his uncle and aunt. Funny, Steven never really looked like one of those bumpkin engineers when he was standing in the office. But put him next to some cowboys and he fit right in.

Maria hurried into the room. "Mama." "Mama" was code for "mother, something is wrong."

Melissa took the phone. Tiffany expected the next word out of her mouth to be "when?" As in, "when did he die?" It was just the face she was making: eyes closed, a tissue instantly grabbed, free hand to her forehead.

"Look, you bastard, this is your daughter's wedding. I don't care what you say you have to do, you come to your daughter's wedding. Oh, it's the foot now, I get it. Can't leave the house with that foot on fire. Then why don't we all go over there? We can all be there in your house, in your kitchen, in your library, all 150 of your friends. Let me get a carpool going. What? Okay, then."

Melissa handed the phone to Tiffany. "Daddy?"

"Sweet Tiffany, I cannot make it. I am so sorry. I just have had these problems – "

"Is it Steven, Daddy?"

"I wish I knew him better." A long pause. "No."

"What do I do, Daddy?" Tiffany was becoming embarrassed at how all the women in the room were just staring at her.

"You just go have a happy day." He hung up.

Melissa hung over her shoulder for the verdict.

"He, uh, doesn't feel well. Wishes he could be here. Say's it'd be a kick if you walked me down the aisle. Will, you Mom? Mommy?"

Maria covered her eyes as Melissa patted Tiffany's shoulder in confirmation. And as they continued to work (or re-work, for the first ten minutes) on making Tiffany the Tech a beautiful woman for a moment, all Louisa could think of was Leonardas's real words:

"If you think for a second I'm going to sanction that bitch of a daughter of yours, you've got another think coming. How long has she lived with him? And we've met him twice? And him with that smirk, like he always knows something we don't? And he won't introduce us to his family? I refuse."

As though Tiffany couldn't hear them, he was yelling so loud over the receiver. She finally leaned forward long enough to appraise the crafts-womanship of the makeup and said "yes. This is perfect. Thank you mom. Thank you, everybody."

Everybody agreed that while it was too bad Leonardas's gout had flared, it was a beautiful service. And that night, Steven learned what Tiffany called the difference between living-in-sin sex and married sex. He was so scratched up and pulled at he resembled a rodeo dummy.

"Why?" Mary was incredulous.

Katherine listened to the clinking of tableware on white porcelain coming from tables all around her. You were supposed to have salads for lunch, but she didn't have an appetite. The clinking was all she could hear. "I love him and he's wonderful and I can make him happy." Katherine wouldn't let Mary derail her.

"But does he make you happy? You're so young."

"Making him happy makes me happy, Mom. Don't you like him?" Katherine only called Mary "Mom" when she wanted approval: both women knew this, and neither thought of it as a manipulative device. It's just who Katherine was.

"Jeremy's fine, but it's not about me. The boy doesn't know what he wants, and he's scared to go into the world all alone. He'll stay with you until he figures out what he needs, then go off and find it."

"But he already has a job lined up! His Uncle got him that marketing thing for the City."

"That wasn't his choice. My point is . . ." Mary suddenly seemed to gather herself, and breathed evenly like a sniper about to take a long shot in a Kentucky wind. "What would your mother say?"

Katherine was surprised by this. Nobody mentioned mom, not ever. "I think she'd be happy for me."

Mary nodded, knowing it was useless to argue. "Your father set something aside for this. Let me know your plans, and I'll send you what you need." She sipped her coffee.

"Thank you! Will you help with the plans? I've got so much–"

"Absolutely not," Mary said, firmly but without raising her voice.

Katherine sat, stunned, watching the tiny bubbles at the circumference of her coffee line come together and break off again, changing allegiances constantly. What on Earth was that about?

Mary must not be over Dad's death yet, Katherine thought. She'll calm down when she sees how happy we are.

"She's not thrilled." Katherine said as Jeremy made dinner. He liked cooking for her. And he was better at it. "She doesn't want any part of it other than writing the check."

"Are you surprised?"

"No, I guess." Katherine flopped down on the sofa and turned on cable. All kinds of reruns. Nothing she liked until she settled on an old *Sesame Street*. "But I was at least supposed to ask her to be, I don't know, happy."

"Who told you that?" Jeremy was beating two steaks with a claw hammer. He covered them in wax paper. He knew where was a tool out there somewhere that was supposed to make this easier, but a hammer was, after all, a hammer.

Tiffany muted the program. She'd seen this one about Big Bird missing his friend Snufalufagus. He'd find him. Everybody finds everybody on Sesame Street eventually. "You know, it's just the way things are. Even stepdaughters are supposed to let this kind of news out with their families, and even if the families don't like it, their role is to say 'why, that's wonderful' and say yes. They can say whatever they want when they go home, but that's where she failed."

That was enough to pull Jeremy out of the kitchen, the claw hammer hanging utterly unthreateningly in his left hand. "What if she just doesn't like me?"

Katherine thought. "Then the answer should have been yes, but her lips would have been pursed closer together, like this:" She made the face. Jeremy made it too. They kissed extendedly like two people who hated everything but had to admit it was in their lives for good.

Jeremy laughed as he returned to the kitchen. Katherine went back to the Muppets. "That makes me think," Jeremy announced as he pounded two innocent flank steaks into commission, "I mean, come on, have we ever in our entire lives just known somebody who accepted all of our decisions? The world would be pretty boring in that case, I imagine. Or every flight leaving Milwaukee would be one-way. Hmm." This is what Katherine brought to him, he thought. No matter how up in his head he got, she knew the rules. He'd trust her to guide him. "Kath?"

He didn't know that the TV had gone off in the other room, and Katherine was sitting in darkness, her chin resting against her knees, almost unperceptively rocking.

"Yeah."

Steven got a new job he hated, calculating concrete pour designs for state contractors. It made him a little cranky, certainly, but nothing Tiffany couldn't handle. She could always handle boys.

Which is why the plus reading stared her in the face as she shook the plastic stick in front of her again. A small speck of urine flew off to the side somewhere. Tiffany had no intention of tracking it down and cleaning it up.

The line was clear. She was pregnant.

It was starting to sink in now. She hadn't had a period in two months, but the test was what it took to convince her. It was an EPT brand test, which her friends had always referred to as "InEPT" because of its history of false positives, but she knew it was accurate in this case. Her body had been telling her so for a month.

She'd noticed about then that her breasts had swollen outside of her bra, and nothing annoyed her more than when she gained weight – she knew she was going to be a big old woman, but was raging against the dying of the spotlight. Her outfit still looked great, but it was clear that her breasts were larger than the bra she was wearing was designed to house.

Steven didn't care, of course. He had blurted out once when she was fretting over an outfit (probably because Tiffany rarely fretted over outfits) that she should stop worrying about what she looks like.

"What, because I'm too old or something?"

"Don't be an idiot," Steven said completely without anger. He said such things to her precisely because she was not and idiot, so he didn't like her speaking as though she were. "You're the most beautiful woman I've ever seen. You should be on TV."

So did she have to go all out and get pregnant now? Being on TV wouldn't be so bad.

But here she was in Austin, always thirsty. She had never read that as a symptom of pregnancy, but it was something new in her life that coincided with the last great lovemaking she and Steven had had.

It had been a special night. He'd just gotten the new job and title bump, and was the equivalent of a professional engineer at his firm. He might be a partner in the company in fifteen years: ten if he went back to school, finished his degree, and lived up to his promise.

Steven so rarely lived up to his promise. He simply didn't care, and he'd only gotten an engineering position a year after joining the firm, instead of having had that title from the start. He wasn't credentialed enough to be paid as an engineer, but was too talented to let go to waste, so the company exploited his impatience with UT and gave him an engineer's work without an engineer's pay. That didn't seem to bother him nearly as much as it bothered her. He made enough money so that Tiffany could stay home and decide what to do with her life. That arrangement had been going on for five years now, since Steven dropped out of UT to take the job halfway through his junior year.

And now she was sitting in a cheap apartment with milk-crate bookshelves, pregnant by a college dropout. Maybe he was one of the few in the country to have a PE designation without a degree, but ultimately, he was a dropout. Which was why Leonardas never came to their fucking wedding..

That evening at dinner, Tiffany spoke up over Jeopardy, which was blaring from the living room. "I don't know what I want to do yet." Tiffany was trying to express herself at dinner.

"Do what makes you happy." Steven had had this conversation enough times to know that engaging her at such times was a mistake, so he kept his eyes trained on the newspaper.

"What if I'm one of those people who can't be happy?"

"What is: we're both in serious trouble."

This aggravated Tiffany. She wanted a real dialogue, and Steven was answering her in the form of a question, game-show style.

"What if I'm crazy? What if nothing I ever do will satisfy me?" Tiffany stood up, found the remote control, and turned off the TV.

"Get a kitten, I don't know. What's bothering you?"

"What if I'm crazy? That's all I'm asking." Tiffany sensed that there was no right answer to this, and she was being horribly unfair to Steven, but as her heart pounded she couldn't be bothered by fairness.

"Then I guess I'll have you committed," Steven said, without a trace of irony.

"I'm serious."

"So am I." Steven took another bite of mashed potatoes.

"You're not listening to me!"

"You're not saying anything. You're asking me silly questions."

"You just *don't get it*!" Tiffany yelled and stormed out of the room. Steven stayed where he was as the bedroom door slammed.

As she lay on her bed, waiting for Steven to come up and apologize, even though she knew he hadn't done anything wrong, Tiffany realized she was crying. Not bawling. She'd been raised better than that. But she felt tears trickle down from her eyes to her ears, and wiped them away. It's okay, she told herself. Pregnancy does this. You're not really feeling this way; it's only chemical, it will pass.

He'll leave.

He'd only married her in the first place because she could prove with an Excel spreadsheet that it would save them over three thousand dollars a year. He was thoughtful on occasion – he even bought her roses on the day he thought was her birthday. He was a week late, but she never told him. She just reveled in the fact that he remembered that she liked purple roses and he'd made sure that three dozen were delivered. Even her parents routinely forgot her birthday (everybody remembered Maria's, whether they wanted to or not, Maria always ensured that). Steven might have remembered late, but he'd done the most gentlemanly thing he could once he realized it.

That was the problem. If you had all of Steven's attention, he was the most thoughtful, soulful, vulnerable, brilliant man on the planet. He once noticed that she liked a particular sport coat once; it was sitting on their chair the next night. Not a word. And at those times, she'd get him to open further as well: knowing that he hated massages or any hands on his body, she'd sneak up behind him, begin rubbing his neck, and not be pissed off at how hard he'd jump with shock. "I live here too," She'd whisper, and massage his neck until all she heard from Steven was a series of increasingly somnolent groans. If she could put him to sleep, she'd bring down a pillow so he'd awakened feeling loved. After awakening he'd never say a thing – it was as though their relationships were a series of love notes left in the room to each other, never too effusive, the authors never visible. They'd just take turns reading them and looking around to see if they were noticed.

That had to be enough; it was more than most people got. He was a foot smarter than her, handled his life with a causal ease that pissed her off (like doing absolutely every, every assignment he ever did at work or in school without being seen doing so), but she could never hold that against him. Well, sometimes yes, when she deliberately made him cornbread (the cowboy/cornbread thing disgusted her almost as much as the idea of cooking) with little chips of plastic in it from a broken mixing spoon. Oops. She couldn't figure out why she was even doing it – it wouldn't kill him, it would just get his attention, and weren't there nicer ways to do that?

He just took one bite, set it aside, and went without.

Even his desire for Tiffany had come across almost too casually for her to notice. They'd been friends at UT for over a year, taking the same classes, making fun of the same TAs, joking about the nerds who devoted all their time to mathematics, when it was so easy for both of them.

It began one night when they were in his dorm room at Simpkins Hall. Steven's roommate, Doug, was gone for the night, and since Doug still wore pocket protectors and black-rimmed glasses, she was pretty sure he wasn't on a date. Steven had to have sent him to the movies or something.

He had said, very simply, after they'd finished a particularly challenging question regarding how much differing specific heat values impact rebar-reinforced concrete in fire resistance: "Hey, Tiff."

She'd looked up at him. "What?"

"I sure would like to make love to you right now."

She'd stared him down for a second. He didn't break eye contact. She had to. "I need a shower." She stood up and left his room. She didn't know what Steven did during that time, and pretended not to care as she let the hot water run from the showerhead over her.

Simpkins Hall was an all-male dorm and had no private bathrooms. She closed the curtain on her shower stall, but her presence was very quickly noted by a few guys, and word traveled fast: a woman was taking a shower in their communal area! They didn't overtly congregate to peek at her, but some boys standing at the urinals within sight of the shower stalls had been holding their penises until they were entirely too engorged to perform the services a urinal demanded.

She'd walked back into his room wearing only a towel. "We doing this, or what?" She asked as she let the towel drop from her body.

Even this didn't seem to overly excite Steven. "I think I should brush my teeth," he said as he got up. She grabbed him by the neck and kissed him, hard.

"You taste fine to me."

They had sex: awkward, we-don't-know-each-others'-bodies first time sex. She was a bit embarrassed that her genitals were so dry at first, so she had to slow him down, but she got there.

When he was inside her, she was amazed at the look in his eyes. It wasn't geeky gratitude, it wasn't some jock's self-fulfillment, or some A-student's self-affirmation. She'd seen all of that. This was something different, something that was actually gentle. This was a man who understood her. She had actually begged him to come inside her, to feel that contentment of receiving him, not just because she was on the pill and she knew nothing would happen as a result, but because she wanted that part of him resting inside her. She'd never felt that way before. He was the first boy she didn't require to wear a condom. She wanted all of that experience.

He pulled out just before orgasm, and ejaculated on her stomach. He excused himself and came back with a warm wet towel and wiped her clean, then held her for what seemed like hours. He'd decided on *coitus interruptus* because they'd never talked about birth control, he explained. My stupid fucking fault, she thought, while she played with his hair. She still wanted that part of him inside of her.

As the night went by, he just listened as she talked – about her childhood, about her father, about the expectations she was trying to meet. He didn't judge. He just held her, until she noticed he was caressing her left breast and it was responding.

She responded by opening his robe. He would give her what she wanted that night, with or without his consent. She consumed him with her mouth, and she enjoyed scarring his buttocks with her fingernails as he tensed up, trying to withhold his ejaculation. She loved how he worked to keep it from her and how easy it was to win it from him; and what's more, he'd think of her every time he sat down for the next few days.

That was how they started. Specific heat.

Nothing about their experience prepared her for the fact that Steven, without consulting her, dropped out of UT the next week and took the job at an architecture firm..

"You don't have an engineering degree!"

"So why'd they hire me?"

"You don't belong there yet!"

"Like I belong here?"

"I like being with you, dammit!" Tiffany hadn't used these words for anyone before.

"Then marry me, dammit."

Tiffany spent the night throwing up. The next morning she looked at all half-eaten boxes of Chinese food strewn about the floor in celebration, and woke Steven up.

"Hmmph?" Steven seemed inconvenienced.

"You get your act together with this job and finish your degree, and we'll get married."

"Okay." Steven rolled back over.

Tiffany wanted to ask if she were the reason he was leaving school to begin with, but that broke some kind of rule she'd sensed about their communication. Steven was committed to non-commitment. She'd settled on the idea that they shouldn't marry because he seemed to understand that marriage was an old fashioned institution designed to oppress women. But she still wanted to be his wife. Her mom never failed to mention that Maria's husband was going to be a politician, and when was Steven going to make something of himself? Leonardas's feelings were obvious, but at least he kept quiet about one thing in his life. He was more concerned about Maria marrying up; Tiffany wasn't expected to.

Which was probably why she went off the pill last year, although she wasn't ready to admit that.

Now, with a real live baby growing in her stomach, she had no idea how anyone would react. Who was she kidding, she knew exactly how her parents would react, and was already preparing for the silent treatment. She figured Daddy wouldn't talk to her until late in second trimester, at worst until a healthy boy is born.

So it had better be a boy.

Steven, she honestly couldn't predict. She could easily see him borrowing money from his Uncle, buying and remodeling some beat-up house out of baby panic (my God, that house would be in *Fort Stockton*); she could also, just as easily, imagine him picking up his newspaper and walking out the door, without speaking a word to her ever again.

She picked up the plastic stick that was going to change her life, and watched it as it sat in her hand. There had to be a logical way to talk to him about it without scaring him off. It just wouldn't be tonight. She'd have to bake on this a while.

She heard Steven coming up the stairs to bed. He entered the bedroom just after she'd tucked the EPT under the mattress.

"Everything ok?" Steven acted like they'd never had the fight. He did this more than she liked, which is why she'd sometimes go nuclear on him, just to get a response. But tonight was the wrong time to become radioactive.

"Yeah, honey," Tiffany knew she was being too self-conscious, "you coming to bed?"

"I read an article in *Popular Mechanics* about solar cars. Turned me on."

"You want me to do something about that?"

Steven seemed surprised, as though his choice of words had nothing to do with sex.

"I guess."

Tiffany unzipped his trousers and glanced at the clock. "It's 10:25. I'll have you home by 10:30."

Steven laughed. "No way."

"You wanna bet?"

"Sure." Steven's eyes glistened, which didn't happen often, and the clue told Tiffany she had a good chance.

Steven lost, and had to do the dishes all week. This was a good thing (she could never stand wearing dishwashing gloves; indeed, any new apparati attached to her body were unwelcome), and Steven didn't seem to mind. But as she watched him keep his end of the bargain on Friday night after they'd had his boss and his wife over for dinner, she realized that she loved Steven.

She still wasn't sure, but that was a secondary thought. She thought of her logic classes: she didn't need to be sure, because her doubt was a secondary thought, and secondary thoughts, by definition, involved primary thoughts. Could either of them love anyone? What was love, and how did it feel? She'd have to settle those primary questions before addressing a subset question.

And honestly, the time to have asked those questions was before marrying him.

She had enough to talk to him about. Like it or not, they had a primary problem to deal with, one that would require primary solutions.

For the next four weeks, Tiffany resumed her morning pages habit: she kept a pad of paper at her side at all times, just in case she had the courage to talk to him, and just in case she needed it to explain how it wouldn't end the comfort of their life so far. Steven needed reason, even if it was symbolic logic or a spreadsheet. She could provide it.

During an Astros game on TV he glanced over at her. "You trying to work something out?"

"No."

"Because the only time you carry that pad around is when you're trying to work something out."

As impressed as she was that he deduced something was amiss by her notepad, this observation pissed her off somewhat. Dude, I've gained ten pounds. I'm moody as hell, and I throw up every other fucking morning.

Men were stupid. It was driving her crazy.

"I'm cool. Want a beer?"

"Sure."

She got up and grabbed him a craft beer from the fridge. Steven would drink anything, but she liked giving him more of a variety. There had to be some way to tell him.

# CHAPTER FIVE

## This moment brought to you by the letter M.

t was Saturday morning, and the sunlight filtered through the gauzy yellow sheers of the kitchen window, creating in front of the dining table a small company of dancing particles of dust, and, Jeremy noticed, changing the whites of his over-easy eggs into an unappealing chartreuse. He suddenly wanted toast. He shifted his chair to cast his own shadow over the plate, and his appetite resumed, his eggs now properly white-balanced.

Katherine walked in with her robe half open, her bed-hair still managing to flow down in front of her neck as though directing his eyes deliberately down her figure. She kissed him on the forehead and he could still smell their sex from hours before. Some Friday nights meant two times. This had been only once, but with some insanely powerful oral sex, which he had successfully initiated. So breakfast was waiting for her.

She plopped herself down, mashed her two sunny-side up eggs with a strip of not-quite-too-crisp bacon until the yolks spread around the plate, and began sopping everything up with an untoasted English muffin. She had told him three years before that of all breakfast breads, English muffins had the best yolk-absorbing properties because there were so many nooks and crannies to absorb it with. So he kept packages of them in the cupboard for weekend breakfasts. Weekday breakfasts Katherine was dressed for, and was compelled by the decorum of her bookkeeping wardrobe to use utensils (she had lasted one year as an elementary school teacher: the children frightened her, they seemed to know her too well). On weekends, everything was finger food. This morning it took just a few seconds and a forgetful self-tousling for Katherine to have a streak of egg in her hair.

"You were a good boy last night." Katherine was playful.

Jeremy didn't feel like it. She'd had an orgasm, he was sure of that, but his jaw was still sore and it had taken longer than usual. That wasn't the problem, though.

"I'm having lunch with Lisa at three," Katherine continued casually.

"Three?" Jeremy had developed the habit of listening to only the last few words of Katherine's sentences. He found it relieved the Milgram-box anxiety that had preoccupied, but not unduly disrupted, the first few years of their marriage. He'd resisted the urge to run away and hide, one that came to him with unexpected ferocity on his first day of work after college. But he said nothing about it, knowing that Katherine needed him, and finally making peace with the idea that parsing the money spent by the City of Milwaukee on their campaigns to attract business downtown was good enough.

"I know, it's all she has. It's her afternoon off from the kids, so we're going for a hike. Hey! You know what would be great? We should do the Appalachian Trail! You always liked to hike when we were in college, remember?"

Jeremy stared at the egg in Katherine's hair. "You've got a little Bride of Frankenstein thing going on," he indicated.

She laughed and ran her fingers through her hair, making it worse, and was not distracted. "Remember?"

Jeremy wanted to sleep with Katherine in college. Everyone wanted to sleep with Katherine in college. Katherine loved hiking. Not all the other guys loved hiking. So he had made a deliberate decision to love hiking. It created a smaller pool. Socratic syllogisms had landed him her virginity, he believed.

"Yeah, still do, you know that." He found hiking to be ninety-five percent boring (the hike to wherever) and five percent breathtaking (the view from the destination); Jeremy liked bigger returns on his physical investments. It was an inconsequential lie.

"Then we'll do it!" Katherine bolted out of her chair and into the den to hop on the computer. As she left the room her robe billowed from the unexpected movement and struggled to catch up with her naked body before she turned the corner. Within seconds he heard the modem dialing America Online. AOL knows everything, Katherine had once pronounced. Certainly they know all about the Appalachian Trail.

Katherine wasn't being herself lately. Or perhaps the sore jaw was making him grumpy, though the inconvenience of that was mitigated by the scent of her that he could still trace on his upper lip. No, if anything, Katherine had been more herself lately than usual, and that was making him feel a bit like a mouse waiting for the floor to shock him. If you're a mouse, walls define your world. Until the electric shock comes. Then it's a "holy shit" worth of energy, you no longer trust anything, and you find yourself voting for libertarians. He smiled at his own analogies.

She had been coming up with wild ideas for vacations lately. Not just vacations, but a whole host of different ways for them to "do new things" and "broaden our horizons." She'd attack each new idea with the same frenzied energy, research it thoroughly, and completely drop the idea in about a week (it took two weeks for bungee jumping, then the carnival with the bungee crane left town, leaving Jeremy relieved and unbounced). He had never discouraged this behavior, nor was remotely surprised even the first time it appeared. This was a woman who took six years to finish college because of her habit of taking courses that were wildly divergent from her education major (usually in sociology, anthropology, or in one disastrous instance, scuba diving. Lake water is cold, murky, and generally unentertaining in Wisconsin), then dropping them just before the deadline. Katherine ran towards things. It was best not to get in the way. She comes back.

There had been a look in her eyes last night, just for a second, less than that perhaps. She adjusted the moment she realized he was looking up at her, his eyes struggling to hold focus through her pubic hair to her face, hoping to make eye contact. When she caught him, she smiled and placed both hands on the back of his head and pulled, making sure his nose rubbed against her clitoris, and he'd gone back to the task at hand with renewed vigor.

But there had been a distinct look. It wasn't like she was bored, or was waiting for him to finish (he was on the second spelling of the alphabet with his tongue, right at the halfway point, and he'd decided that this round would be in upper case for fuller coverage); in fact, there was no dissatisfaction at all about her glance. If anything, she was enjoying his efforts, but in the five years of their marriage he'd never seen that look.

It struck him suddenly. He replayed the moment in his head as he heard the AOL voice say "Welcome!"

He knew exactly what she had been thinking.

He stood up and slowly walked into the den. Weekend mornings were often naked (Katherine had read in a magazine that proclaiming the occasional "naked day" would keep a relationship fresh. It was, Jeremy now believed, an article written by a very young person who had a lot of time to spare at the gym), but he'd been the one who made breakfast, and nudity combined with the act of frying bacon was an experiment you only try once. Katherine considered keeping an open gown to be naked enough, probably because the kitchen chairs had been caned with a natural fiber that was rattan-like in its capacity to pinch the one hair that could cause the most pain.

He was directly behind her. Katherine was disappointed already, he could tell. Maybe her shoulders had slouched a bit; he didn't know. But he could always sense disappointment from her, even without looking. And last night wasn't disappointment. It was–

"Shoot! I didn't know it takes months to walk the Appalachian Trail! We could never take that kind of time off. That sucks. This is for old people or rich kids right out of college."

Jeremy let this pass, as they'd spent their first three months out of college on trains all over Europe, courtesy of Uncle Ted, or as they liked to call him now, "Judge Poo-Bah." "You're making the responsible choice," Ted had confirmed in his office, just after Jeremy informed him that he wanted to start a career now instead of more schooling or a military obligation in a job he wasn't prepared for, "so go be irresponsible for a while with your pretty new wife. Start in Venice, you'll love it."

They did. Donald, already incensed that Naomi had the temerity to move on fifteen years after their divorce, became incensed with Ted's meddling as well. Surprisingly, a rift formed, and Jeremy had avoided his father ever since. As far as Jeremy were concerned, Donald lived in a fantasy world, where he wasn't a baby boom failure and he could start over again at any time. Life didn't work that way. Well, actually, it did an astonishing amount of the time, but Jeremy didn't put it that way to Katherine when she asked on the airplane to Italy. Katherine preferred "life didn't work that way" kind of endings.

Five years later and Katherine was just playing on the computer. Jeremy didn't necessarily demand attention; it just always seemed to be flowing his way. As his was towards her. But something in this other realm bothered him a bit. So he walked up behind her, firmly committed to grabbing her shoulders, turning her around, throwing her robe to the ground and seeing if that engineer's chair really could hold its weight rating. Then he got to her, and-

"Do you have any fantasies I don't know about?" Jeremy blurted to the back of Katherine's head with unexpected hesitation.

Katherine turned around innocently. "What do you mean?"

"I mean, you know, last night."

Katherine smiled. "What about last night?"

"It seemed like you were somewhere else for a minute."

"Um – yeah! I told you, you were a good boy!" She turned around to face the AOL connection screen. She didn't have any new email. She never had email. It annoyed her.

Had Jeremy seen her face at that very moment he might have shut up. He didn't. "I mean, do you ever have - you know – fantasies? Things you want to do that we don't do? Some couples start having fantasies and they don't tell each other, and before you know it –" Jeremy realized, almost with a start, that he was starting to sound insecure. Uncle Ted preached that insecurity kills relationships. Stop right there. Correct yourself.

Katherine hadn't turned around. She faced the computer screen, completely still. Dammit, Jeremy thought, you blew it.

"I just mean," Jeremy said with as commanding a voice as he could muster without seeming to overcompensate, "if there's ever anything you want to explore, just say so. I'm totally cool with it."

Katherine typed in another search term. "Look, there's a two-week hike some people make. It's not the whole trail, but you get a sense of it."

Jeremy nodded to no one in particular, his lips pursed, and turned around to leave. Katherine kept typing until just at the moment he was at the kitchen threshold.

"—Jeremy."

He turned around. Katherine looked at him for a moment and cocked her head. Her brow was a little furrowed, which told him something serious was coming, so he was surprised at the impish tone of her voice when she said -

"What if there is?"

"This isn't exactly what I had in mind." Jeremy stood nervously in front of Katherine while she sat back in the chair. The whole place smelled almost like a dentist's office, and the chair was no different. There had to be some central place where that kind of upholstery was made: that medical-grade vinyl that smelled of antiseptic. Was there a regulatory body that ensured uniformity in tattoo chairs?

If there was, this was the only place to conform. They'd gone to five different parlors in a month, and none of them seemed a place even remotely suitable to having their skin stabbed thousands of times per minute and injected with ink.

The choice of the first parlor had been by design. Jeremy led Katherine to a spot he knew had been busted for hygiene a few times, a fact made even more grave by dark entrance off an alley in Metcalfe Park. Katherine had been excited by the thrill of being in a dangerous neighborhood at first, but the experience was short lived. Adrian, the tattoo artist, wore dark shades at midnight and was applying the chiaroscuro to a unicorn's head on a drunken young man's forearm while giving Jeremy a quote.

"One hundred bucks an hour." He looked up and saw Katherine, who was just coming down off of her gentrified high. "Sorry. One-fifty."

That was supposed to be it. Adrian, the veiled obese tatter who was willing to put the most feminine tattoo possible on a wasted guy – he was supposed to be enough for Katherine to realize this was a bad idea. She'd get grossed out, and that was enough, so long as Jeremy let the matter drop.

They were on the way home from Adrian's parlor (cleverly titled "Adrian's Tattoo Parlor"), when Jeremy said it. "How do you think that guy is going to feel tomorrow morning?"

Katherine looked out the window. "I know, right? That's just not cool. I mean, a tattoo is forever – not just a prank you play on someone."

Jeremy smiled to himself and relaxed.

"We've got to make sure whoever does ours is a real professional."

Her continued focus was a bit of a surprise, but it didn't faze Jeremy. It would take a few more places over the space of a week or two. There would be something wrong with each of them: too dirty, too dark, not the design she wanted . . . Not to mention the pain. Katherine could be immobilized by a paper cut. Jeremy wasn't worried. In fact, he was looking forward to having a Friday night, even though it was Wednesday, because he knew Katherine would be happy they tried.

So when she rolled over and went to sleep right away, Jeremy realized he might have to rethink his plan. He'd have to be more patient and let her pickiness gradually overcome the romantic notion of dual tattoos on her own schedule.

Steven watched the tiny ball wander across his screen saver for the seventh time in the same minute. Sometimes it sank slightly as it crossed, sometimes it suddenly changed direction. The ball was entertaining, and it helped him pass the time, but it wasn't designing the new prison walls for him, and Steven was beginning to feel the pressure more acutely.

It was his job to determine the size of the walls of the new prison outside of Tucson, Arizona, which was being built right that very minute. Each day he configured the dimensions according to the concrete mix, how much weight the wall must bear, and what lateral pressures its location in the building would exert on it. It was revolving math work, it required no extraordinary feats of cognition. Steven had long since turned the more active synapses of his brain to other, more important affairs, such as the bouncing ball screensaver, its origins, uses, applications in other fields, ability to distract kittens, etc.

His body carried out the autonomic functions: find the wall in the plans. Calculate the drawn dimensions. Compare that to the type of concrete used, the tension of the rebar, and find the theoretical breaking point.

Compare that point to the known stresses of the design, whether the wall curves, where the corners are. If the known stresses are less than twenty-five percent of the breaking point, pass the drawing along. Otherwise, refine the wall design until it meets the standard.

The fact that this wall would be poured within forty-eight hours of his approval of the design was a little bothersome as well. If the construction workers knew he spent most of his time watching a screen saver or playing Unreal Tournament on company bandwidth, they'd pour the concrete with considerably less confidence. As it was, he'd put off walls two or three days at a time in the service of other minutiae, then show up to Paul's desk with six walls already scoped and RTP (ready to pour). Paul always looked at him with a mixture of admiration and disgust when he did that (as he was about to do) and Steven decided he lived for the look. It gave him something to look forward to. Paul was known as "the owl" because of his round head and rounder, thick glasses. It looked like it would take him entire seconds for his eyelids, were they ever to blink, to get through the motion.

He sat up, accidentally nudging the mouse, and the computer screen came back to life, the diverting ball bouncing no more. It was time. Steven grabbed a sheath of design paper and sauntered to Paul's office.

The room was completely enclosed in glass, only the door was opaque, something laminated in wood-colored plastic. Because Paul still wanted some privacy in the room, he'd taken to putting up posters, (mostly third-party vendor ads, but some sports pictures also) on both sides of the glass, filling up the area from about knee to neck high. Consequently, many of the engineers called Paul's office "the strike zone," and if you emerged from the office looking like you'd just been chewed out, someone would yell "strike one!" from the back of the cubicle farm.

Steven had a full count. All week he'd been sandbagging the walls, doing Internet searches, reading the news or finding as many joke websites as he could, and he knew Paul was getting nervous. He'd done this last month, and could hardly keep from smiling when Paul scoured five different exterior wall refits and couldn't find a single error. "This is good work," Paul conceded, visibly disappointed.

He'd go in the office now with nine walls. They were interior walls, granted, not terribly load-bearing, and mostly his analysis had demonstrated that the original designs were adequate. He'd made a few changes here and there just in case, just to prove he didn't merely rubber-stamp the design.

"Close the door." Paul didn't look up as Steven walked in.

Steven closed the door and sat down. Paul was going over some figures on graph paper. Steven looked around, playing with the drawings in his hand, casually rolling them up and unrolling them. Close to a minute went by.

"Need me to come back?" Steven offered, playfully.

The Owl would not be distracted. "I need you to sit there and shut up. I'll get to you when I get to you."

"Oooh." Steven tried to walk the line between being an upstart and being disrespectful, but nobody talked to subordinates like that anymore. This wasn't the military.

Paul looked up suddenly. "You have something for me?"

Steven smiled broadly and handed over the designs. Paul placed them in his outbox.

"They're all there."

"I know."

"Want to check them out?"

"I'm sure they're fine."

Steven got up. "Okay, then . . ." he searched Paul's face for any sign of bewilderment or of being impressed.

"Sit down." Paul could have been playing poker.

Steven sat back down and began actively worrying about the situation.

"I'm transferring you."

Steven more upright and began questioning in his most clinical voice. For the first time in over a year, Paul had his complete attention. "Where?"

"Iowa."

"What's in Iowa?"

"A couple of pretty good colleges, beautiful farm girls who gain five pounds a year after they're married, and your new office. We're moving the architectural support group."

"We're all going?"

"No."

"I don't understand."

"The task is going to Iowa. You're staying with the task. We're retasking here to International support."

Steven quickly tried to appraise whether this was a lateral move or a promotion. "Why send me to Iowa?"

"Because they can deal with the kind of engineer who screws around for four days and works for one. I can't. The International group needs engineers who I know are working every day."

So this wasn't a promotion. "Iowa?"

"It's not bad. In fact, the office there is newer. Faster computers. You're still on the same network, though, so you can play whatever games you like."

"I do good work, Paul."

"That's true. And if you did great work, we'd keep you with the International group, and you could spend two months a year in Europe."

That was unnecessary, Steven thought. "So your decision is made?"

"It is. I'm tired of trying to manage you. You don't listen and you make a plain show of being bored with every task you do, and I've had enough of trying to keep you busy."

"Is that going to change in Iowa?"

"You know, Steve, I don't care. It won't be my problem, and that's what matters to me."

Steven sat back and looked around. Rickey Henderson's record-setting stolen base photo took up half the wall behind Paul. Nolan Ryan pitched his 7th career no-hitter that day as well, Steven remembered.

"When does all this happen?"

"The retasking will be phased in over three months, and you'll be needed out in Iowa in about two weeks. They need someone over there who can help with the adjustments, and since you do seem to have a lot of free time on this project, I volunteered you."

"I don't have any say in this, do I?"

Paul looked directly at Steven. "Not much." He smiled.

It was the smile that put it over the top. That was the Mr. McDonald smile. "Actually, I disagree. I'm outta here."

Paul leaned back in his chair, his face dispassionate. "Really."

"I'm not just going to pick up and move to the Midwest just because you want to shove off a management problem. If you can't motivate me to work harder, that's your failing, not mine."

"You actually believe that bullshit, don't you?"

"I'm not going to Iowa."

"You're not staying here."

"Then fire me?"

"Are you kidding? It costs corporate $20,000 to fire someone and re-hire a replacement. You're already a disciplinary problem, I'm not going to let you be a budgetary one."

"We'll see about that." Steven threw the door open and walked outside.

"Strike one!" Was called from somewhere around Adam's desk.

"Fuck you." Steven said plainly to nobody in particular as he went to his cubicle. He started to walk out of the pit. Paul was standing by his doorway, leaning up against the jamb, his arms crossed as Steven walked towards him.

"Are you sure you want to do this?" Paul looked almost amused.

"Go to hell. I quit." Steven brushed past, letting his briefcase gently chock Paul in the leg. He could feel his left hand trembling, and shoved it in his jeans pocket. This was the right thing to do. He could find a better job someplace else local anyway. This job was boring him to tears all by itself, and Iowa wasn't known for moving the meter much in that regard. Tiffany would never leave Texas, period. They'd have to have "the talk," and she'd insist that he take some flunky state job that Leo would arrange . . .

No, Steven thought as he sat in his Volkswagen in the parking lot. This would just be a blip. Paul was doing him a favor. He really wasn't a prick, just one of those guys who gets hurt while he's young and never gets better. Steven needed to get on with life anyway, he was wasting time here. There was real engineering to be done, real science to apply to the real world, and he'd find a job that would let him do it. Someplace in Austin there was a manager just dying for an engineer like Steven. He'd just have to find him, that's all.

And Tiffany would just have to deal.

Steven walked in the door to find Tiffany, hands in her lap, wearing the plainest grey-plaid housedress she owned. In fact, Steven was pretty sure it was Melissa's. Why on Earth it was here and on her was a mystery.

"Hey," Steven said, and proceeded towards the bedroom. He grabbed a couple of beers and brought them back to the living room. It was only then he'd noticed she hadn't said anything.

"Oh good," Steven thought, "drama."

"You're going to hate me." Tiffany said, unable to look up.

"What's his name?"

"No, nothing like that. Steven, I'm – "

"Here in this country illegally. I always suspected that about you."

"No, I-"

"Secretly, you've always wanted to buy a foreign car."

"Dammit Steven, I'm pregnant." Tiffany burst into tears.

Steven took a large sip of his beer. "Yeah?"

"Well?" Tiffany's question was a plea as much as anything. As she sat there, tearfully waiting for something from Steven, Steven knew very well something was called for. This is the moment, cowboy. Say the right thing. Make it up if you have to because you sure as hell don't know what it is.

"Is it mine?" He laughed.

It was a miscalculated joke. Tiffany stood up to storm out of the room when Steven stopped her with just a clearing of the voice. "Tiff, what's wrong with being parents?"

Tiffany paced as she tried to answer. "You don't know. You don't know my family. Hell, you don't know yours. All I've got is mine to go on. And if it's a girl, it's likely to be a little Maria. And if it's a boy, I'm afraid it will be my father."

"Tiff, you're being too hard on yourself. What if it isn't either?"

Tiffany's face turned beet red and she tried to conceal it in her hands as she screamed, "then I'm scared to death it will be *me!*"

She turned abound and ran into the bedroom, where she slammed the door.

Steven turned on the TV. This was one thing too many. He could find a job anywhere, no need to bother her about that tonight. As for being pregnant. Well. That would be Tiffany's call, wouldn't it? If she said no he couldn't do anything, wouldn't want to do anything.

And he didn't want her to say no to this.

"This is stupid," he said, and slammed his beer. He went into the kitchen and saw a bottle of expensive sour mash whiskey on the top, unopened.

She knew she'd run into the bedroom and he'd run into the kitchen. Love works that way sometimes.

Nah, they'd be fine. This was Austin. They didn't trust tech gurus *with* degrees. How long can it be before he's back on his feet?

"You're being so picky!"

Katherine was right. In their fifth parlor in two weeks, Jeremy kept thumbing through the pages of "flash"—pre-drawn tattoos that artists make for royalties—and finding problems with every design. One was too big. She wanted a Celtic design, but they weren't even remotely Celts, which seemed silly. Tribal armbands seemed to be an idea from Mars. Marketing consultants don't wear Polynesian tattoos—even Polynesian marketing consultants probably didn't, Jeremy had said jokingly just a moment before.

"Then what do you want?" Katherine used the distant, clinical voice she only employed to try to hide her impatience. Jeremy was certain she was calling him on his cowardice.

"There!" Katherine's face lit up. "That's what I want!" It was a green Celtic knot, about the size of a silver dollar, with black outlines. "That's what I want! Say you like it Jeremy, please say you like it!"

Jeremy had nodded, and now she was in the dentist chair with the requisite green vinyl cover, her skin below her left ankle sterilized, and the tattoo taking shape before his eyes. There was less blood than Jeremy expected; he was certain that if someone ran a miniature sewing machine into *his* flesh a hundred times a second, he'd be bleeding all over the place.

Katherine could only get a limited view of the goings-on. If she sat up to get a full glimpse, she'd move her legs for balance and yank them out of their supports in the chair. Doug the artist (with unbespectacled eyes) had been very clear: she could be strapped in, or she could not be strapped in, but she couldn't pull away without letting him know. She'd yanked her foot away twice already out of sheer excitement. Doug just sighed and stared at his unfinished work until she replaced it against the pad.

"Can you believe it? It doesn't even hurt!" Katherine was joyful. "It's like an Indian burn – kind of annoying, but not really painful. Is it painful if you like it? 'Cause I kind of like it – wait, is this the endorphin rush they were talking about? Maybe I'm reacting to that, oh god is that it? Is this the high I'm supposed to want to chase later on and get my arms covered or something? Watch, I'm going to get like the whole story of Alice in Wonderland on my left arm. 'Oh no, she's addicted!' That's what they'll say, anyway. Oh, we can't tell Mary about this right away, you remember that, right? When should we? Maybe I'll just wait until we're up in Door County this summer – do I have enough socks? Make sure I *always* wear socks around her for a few months . . ."

Katherine appeared to realize she'd been conducting a monologue, and an irrational one at that. She hadn't seen Mary in three years; just exchanged holiday cards and the occasional phone call.

She decided to ignore this incongruity and to giggle instead, "What are you going to get?"

Jeremy couldn't decide on what to do. He wanted to make Katherine happy, but if there had been one thing in the world that he knew now that he didn't know for certain at the beginning of the day, it was the fact that he couldn't get a tattoo. It just wasn't something you did. It was something thugs and sluts and sailors did. He'd been telling himself for the last three hours that times were different, nobody really thought like that anymore, but he couldn't dismiss the thought entirely. Nor could he express it, because he knew it was likely fear-based and more than willing to seize upon stereotype, and Jeremy thought seizing anything was uncivilized.

"I can't find anything here that I like."

Doug, dabbing small drops of blood away from the new green shading on Katherine's skin, made it known he'd heard it all before: "Dude, like I told you, I can design something that's totally you; but sometimes getting what you want means just walking away. No shame in that. Not the first guy to have a change of heart."

Jeremy went back to the pages of flash in the lobby while he heard the inconstant buzzing of Katherine's evolving skin. Her name in Fraktur script along his bicep. That would be stupid, like some heavy metal band from the 80s that put random umlauts over vowels in their name or album titles. Some of the bands had been pretty good once he looked past that, though; he wondered how many people would take longer to warm up to him if they saw that font on his upper arm.

He turned pages until he heard the buzzing stop. He walked back into the vinyl room in time to see Doug applying a bandage. Katherine beamed up at him.

"You missed the end! You'll see it, though. You have to rinse it and clean it in an hour."

Jeremy smiled and nodded. He looked over at Doug, who seemed to have forgiven Katherine's exuberance.

That night, she reread the small card of aftercare instructions fourteen times: twice in the car on the way home, once out loud when Jeremy removed the bandage and cleaned the tattoo (which turned out to be an unexpectedly beautiful array of green and black curves and angles that did in fact suggest infinity in a tightly enclosed space) once more as she got ready for bed, and at least ten times as Jeremy lay beside her, stroking her hair and waiting for her to notice him. It wasn't going to be a Friday night. But he knew that when she came to bed wearing a t-shirt. Coming to bed topless meant the gig was on; wearing a tank top meant it could go either way; a t-shirt was definitely a sign that persuasion was needed. Unless it was one of his t-shirts, which carried with it a probability between topless and tank top.

She fell asleep with the instructions in her left hand, draped lightly over her chest. When Jeremy attempted to remove the card to the nightstand, her fingers tightened. He let them be, and lay back down beside her.

He stared at the ceiling. *Next time, idiot, walk the damn Appalachian Trail.*

# CHAPTER SIX

Tiffany parked her compact next to Tim's SUV and thought about her journal entry from that morning's journal. He was there already. He was always there. He was always there for her, she thought, a little embarrassed about how she could turn almost any observation into something that related to her and Tim. It was the sign of sickeningly sweet infatuation, and she felt it in full force.

This was Steven's fault as much as anyone's. If he'd just get off the couch and work, she wouldn't have had to take this job. If he'd only been responsible, she could have stayed home with Tony and nothing would have changed. She could have gotten one of those new online MBAs and taken a real job as soon as Tony went to kindergarten, which would be next year.

"You're here." The stunningly obvious became romantic; Tim was sitting at his desk, his hands clasped behind his head. She hated his smirk, but her infatuation made it maddeningly charming to her.

"I hear somebody's got a bad network card." Tiffany practically sang the sentence.

She closed his office door behind her, and sat down across his desk from him.

"That must be the problem. I feel disconnected from everyone else in the world but you."

Tiffany smiled and glanced down at her fingernails. Steven would never say something like that, something so obviously stupid, clichéd, and, well, wonderful.

They were too close to it. She had to moderate herself. She leaned back in her chair.

"What's wrong?" Tim, a burly, rumpled man, much taller than Steven, reacted quickly to even the slightest sign of her removing intimacy from him. His size made his pretense of delicacy somewhat comic.

"What are we doing, Tim?"

Tim sat up and rested his head on his elbows on the desk. It occurred to Tiffany that he always had his hands someplace near his head: behind, underneath, holding it up – he also tended to stand with one arm across his slightly extended stomach, and the other resting vertically on top of it, propping up his chin. And every time they walked out into the parking lot together, he'd grab his head with both hands and turn it sharply to pop bubbles from the synovial fluid in his upper vertebrae. Crack. Tiffany suddenly wondered if his neck was capable of holding his head up at all.

"We're getting to know each other," Tim said, "and there's nothing wrong with that."

No, there probably wasn't, Tiffany told herself. She'd only been there six weeks, but there was an undeniable spark of attraction between them. She'd noticed it from the first time he met her. There wasn't anything wrong with him being her boss, because he wasn't. Well, not really. As a Vice President of the H-E-B grocery chain, he was everybody's boss at the site, but he didn't directly supervise her work, so it wasn't really a conflict.

Neither was his being married. *They've been unhappy for years, they don't even have sex,* Tiffany tried to quiet her internal disgust for that excuse. She didn't care if Tim still screwed his wife. Why do all men tell the same stupid lies to convince themselves into believing that having an affair was okay? If you're going to do something evil, then call it what it is and take responsibility. Say it: I'm married and fucking around. Why on Earth is that so impossible? It's not like she was asking him to act like a saint: in fact, she wanted him to screw his wife. That more than anything would prove to Tiffany that she was turning him on, and she liked the idea of

Tim screwing Lisa when he was thinking of her. That's power, she thought. That's what Tim gives me.

Tiffany felt herself engaged in a long, soulful look into Tim's eyes. So desperate. So clueless. So what if she was violating her father's conception of her morality. Not like he wouldn't do the same if she had the chance. Actually, he probably did have the chance. Mom always looked so ashen in public with him. He probably screwed around more than anyone she knew.

"I have to make the choice between a smart man and a rich man," she'd written that morning in her journal, "And I honestly don't know what to do. We're so close and we both know it, and we're dancing around the subject, and if I let this happen there's no going back."

Tiffany never liked being summoned to Capitol Hill. Even though everyone there knew her, and asked in their polished and phony ways about Steven and Tony, for the Great One to call his daughter into his office meant she had done something wrong.

"Sit down, he'll be with you in a second." Leonardas wore a short-sleeved dress shirt, his portly frame resembling an egg for just a moment as he shifted in his chair. His reading glasses were perched far down on his flat nose, pinching his nostrils enough that he emitted a slight wheeze as he breathed.

Tiffany did as she was told and examined the books displayed in his antechamber. At first glance, it looked like he had read every single book ever written about Texas. The whole place was an "I dare you" to question his Texan bona fides.

Tiffany knew that the UT Press simply supplied every member of the Legislature with a complete library upon request, and Mrs. Villareal would take the new catalogue every year and order what she would ever read if she could only get around to it.

The buzzer sounded. Tiffany wordlessly entered. Leonardas was finishing up a phone call. "Tell him it's a matter of doing the right thing. He'll know what that means. Yes, Frank, that's a code. Yes, Frank I know you're never playing dominoes with us again. Thank you." He hung up, clasped his hands on his desk, and sighed as Tiffany sat down.

"So," he said belaboredly, "what's wrong with my little girl?"

"Maria's you're little girl, Daddy, remember?" She raised her chin in a somewhat defiant pout.

"Yes, yes, I know. Can we not go through that again?"

"Why did you require me to come here?"

"Nobody's requiring anybo-goodness, Tiffany, you'd think you came here sporting for a fight."

"Well?"

"You're not happy."

This was enough to break Tiffany's eye contact. "What makes you say that?"

"A father knows."

Tiffany glared at him.

"Even one you don't see as often as you should."

"So, what did one of your Tejano spies tell you about me?" Tiffany heard her voice raising, and realized instantly that this was one of Leonardas's biggest, fattest, reddest emotional buttons. Having real power meant never mentioning it. Mentioning it made him human; making him human meant he could be wrong about something.

"Enough!!" He slapped his hand on his desk, then scurried up and shut the door, unaware that Mrs. Villareal had never turned off the intercom. Mrs. Villareal had decided to save money on subscription magazines that year.

Leonardas reared back. "I hear about you taking a job. I've made ten job openings to that man."

"His name is Steven."

"I heard he's the babysitter."

"Great intel, Dad. All you'd have to do is show up once in a while. Hell, you visit Maria all the time."

"There is no comparison. I love my daughters both the same."

Tiffany rolled her eyes.

Leonardas rumbled on. "Here is what I will do. You keep that job for appearances sake. You let me put some money away for you. As soon as you have enough to stand on your own, you leave."

"What?" Tiffany's jaw dropped.

"That way we can keep appearances, and you will not have to demean yourself much longer, and Antonio will spend time with his mother."

"Steven does fine, Daddy."

"Steven refuses to care for himself. If there's one thing in nature I cannot abide, it is a creature that will not fend for itself. If you do not leave him – "

"What, your goons will do something?"

"I am not that kind of man. But if you do not leave him, you will wish you had."

"Steven's a good man."

"Steven is a child."

Tiffany stood up. "I don't have to take this." Leonardas stood up also.

"It is the only way for Antonio."

"Why is everything a goddamn morality play with you, Daddy? Why is that? Someone beat you up when you were young? Uncle Chico, he take a few hits at you? That drunk from the grocery store in Saltillo bend you over a barrel when you were twelve??"

Leonardas slapped her, hard.

They both backed away, looking anywhere but each other. When Tiffany restored her demeanor, she kept quiet. Steven always told her: in a showdown, whoever speaks first, loses. She kept quiet. So did Leonardas.

The only thing audible was Mrs. Villarreal's quick breaths on the other side of the monitor, which Leonardas finally shut off. He looked at her with a deep pain, as though something in him had done something profoundly wrong to Tiffany. And more than just a slap. In his eyes Tiffany saw reflected a waste of skin.

"I'll send you an account number," Tiffany said, straightening herself. "Goodbye."

She slammed the door and walked out through the antechamber, eyes following her. She did not see Leonardas's reaction, which in later years she would imagine in twenty different ways.

Four years later, she had $75,000 in her private bank account, a boy enter-
ing second grade, and was still in the middle of a flirt-fest with someone
whom Leonardas might actually approve of.

Tiffany looked down at her nails again as Tim cradled his bowling ball
head in his hands, watching her. It was hard to keep nails growing and polished when you're yanking PCI cards all the time. For a small peripheral
warehouse, this facility had an astonishing number of network problems.
They'd bought their hardware from a bargain-basement vendor, and one of
the executives' sons, who knew something about Windows, had configured
their servers in an arcane if not outright Byzantine way, and it had taken
her nearly a month just to get everyone's user accounts set up properly.
Now it was the hardware itself that was rebelling, and she'd had to replace
several components in about thirty of the desktop machines. Putting on
the static strap, opening up computer cases, yanking the little green plastic
cards, installing new drivers . . . this isn't what she wanted, and if Steven
could just get back on his feet, everything would be fine and she could go
back to school.

But Steven wasn't about to do that, so long as there were *The Muppet
Show* reruns all day on cable. Every day she'd come home and hear about
how clever Jim Henson was.

Sure, he was looking for work, but you don't often find it in the
television.

Partially inspired by her frustration, he decided to be a home engineer
and start fiddling with electricity. He'd built automated lights all over the
house, which was stupid because you don't spend money to improve a place
you're renting. He'd set up the oven timer so it would automatically dim
the lights of the living room when dinner was ready. He bought cookbooks
and Teflon pans and insisted on a royal culinary production each day when
she got home from work.

Tiffany didn't want to come home from work anymore. All that care
didn't impress her in the least. He's stalling.

"Steven is fixing Chinese tonight." She broke off her deliberately callow
stare.

"He has time on his hands," Tim said, "I wish I had time to cook. I'd
make you a feast."

Everything, everything, everything with this guy came back to a com-
pliment or a chance to show his affection. "I get it, okay?" She thought

to herself, "Jesus, this is hard enough without dealing with all the sappy bullshit."

As though he could read her expression, Tim sat back, his left hand under his chin. "Seriously, you've done a great job fixing the mess you inherited. I went ahead and accelerated your benefits."

"What's that?"

"You're insured, as of last Friday. You and Tony and . . . Steve. I took care of it. I also adjusted your contract to reflect Union rates now. Most contractors don't qualify, but I've been legitimately blown away by what you've done here."

"Tim, that's so sweet of you."

"No, it's good business. I've been blown away," he repeated, a bit too ardently. "I want you here, we all want you here, and I know when Steve gets his life back together you'll be tempted to leave, and we would suffer for it."

Tiffany nodded and noticed the clock behind Tim's desk. 8:35 a.m.: the Noggin channel just started their daily CTW marathon. Kermit the Frog is babysitting her baby and husband.

"And I would suffer for it." Tim continued, leaning over his desk, his hands cradling his head. It pushed his cheeks forward and made him look like an infant. Did Tim's son look like that? She'd only seen six-year-old Patrick a few times, and didn't really like him. Too mouthy, and he did in fact have those cheeks. At least he came by them honestly. Tim's wife, Lisa, was as thin as a rail. Effortlessly so, it seemed, which pissed Tiffany off.

"I think I'd suffer too."

Tim smiled in triumph. "So: where for lunch today?"

"I don't know yet, is that okay?"

"Sure, sure. We've got some stuff to do before then anyway, if you think of something, let me know. Just remember, anything you want." Tim smiled.

Anything she wanted. Steven used to say that, but it never happened. She didn't want to go back to work. She didn't want to work in computers. He never listens. She certainly didn't want to flirt with some guy who's ten years older than she was and hasn't run the length of a city block in that time. But there it is.

She looked at Tim more closely, and worried briefly that she'd unintentionally cocked her head to one side like a spaniel. He was kind, everybody saw that. He'd yell at you for not getting things done, but that's what you needed from a manager, or at least that's what some people needed. Once that door was closed, he was a different person – genuinely caring, interested in your dreams, your desires, your passions. . .

It was stupid staying this close, playing with fire like this. It was more dangerous doing this than it would be just to try it. Steven was still technically looking for work, and was smart enough to find something soon. She was still a little shocked that years had gone by without a single offer, but that was the state of the market right now. Things would change, and she'd rather have a boss who respected her than one who was just lusting after her all the time.

Okay, he wasn't really her boss, but all the same. Maybe it was better just to get it out of the way. Things always were better if everyone knows the score, not if there's this lingering tension of "what if" hanging around. She'd been in too many misunderstandings – people start reading things into innocent glances, or small flirtations become big deals, and soon that's all they could talk about.

She needed to cross a line. She looked up at the clock. The first commercials were probably playing on the TV in the living room. They'd be selling feminine care products or baby stuff. Steven was alone with Anthony and their credit card. She'd almost killed him the day she got home from work and found a fully assembled as-seen-on-TV Abmaster 2000. Steven had stood proudly behind it, not realizing that buying your wife an Abmaster 2000 was an implicit criticism.

"Seriously, is your network card out?"

"I think it must be. I can, what do you call it, 'ping' the loopback address? But the lights aren't on."

"It's under your desk, right?"

Tim wheeled back his chair, and Tiffany got on her knees before him to inspect the computer. She looked back behind the machine and saw that the link lights were off – there was probably a problem with the card, and Tim was right. She'd have to repair it without moving it; Tim needed his computer to be on all day. "Yeah, it's out. I can grab a new one and install it by the end of the day."

She turned her head and realized she couldn't see all of Tim. He had rolled back in his chair, but from her position under his desk all she could see was from his belly down, and she noticed the slight bulge in his slacks.

She looked down at her fingernails and noticed a chip in the color. It was one of those specialty colors whose name had nothing to do with the shade. This one was called 'I'm not really a waitress' and she found it was her favorite. This job made her have to redo her nails almost every night, and by the end of the year, she'd have those little stubby fingers that women engineers or scoliosis credenzas have.

And Steven was just like Daddy said. Daddy saw it all along.

*I hate this job.*

"Come here." She said, reaching out and grabbing behind Tim's knees, pulling his chair towards his desk again. He rolled forward with a small noise of surprise, and her hands were instantly at his belt, sliding it out of the buckle.

"What are you doing?"

"Is your door locked?"

"You know it isn't!" Tim's voice had legitimate alarm in it.

"Then I'd better make this quick," she said, unzipping him completely. He sprang out like a purple Jack in the Box, and Tiffany winced at the unexpected excitement it displayed.

A barrier was about to be breached, and she didn't even have to kiss him to achieve it. There wasn't any doubt about where they were now. This should take care of it. It needs to be right out there.

She rose up, closed her eyes, and crossed the line.

A single banker's lamp competed with the computer monitor for space and illumination on Jeremy's home office desktop in the living room. The lamp was losing. Katherine had recently purchased a bigger monitor for her AOL surfing, and the twenty-one-inch screen required a cathode ray tube that weighed about thirty pounds and took up almost all usable space for the desk. The lamp was relegated to a small corner behind the screen, where the monitor tapered off to a more reasonable size.

Jeremy still liked how the glow of the lamp's single bulb was altered by the green frosted glass, so whenever he had work to do, he'd reach around the monitor and turn on the lamp anyway, and pay bills from his lap as he sat in front of the desk. He liked the sense of being closeted away when he did financial or other important things. It just made him feel better. You bring things out in the open, people can tell you you're wrong, and then you have these self-esteem issues, and etc. When he got something wrong at work, his assistant would whisper it to him. When he got it wrong at home, Katherine was too much in Kathyland to say anything – which is not to say not to notice. She could read a column of numbers in their check register like a race driver. "That's not right." "Oh, I'll look into it." "Ok, sweetie!" A quick kiss and it was over.

The computer monitor stayed on. Katherine had read that computers use the most power, and run the most risk of operating problems, if they are turned off after each use. Just like florescent light bulbs. Cheaper to keep them on all day. Even the government does this, she'd said authoritatively when Jeremy asked why, from their upstairs bedroom, he could still hear the slight but steady hum of the giant monitor. He didn't sleep well with it on; and the computer itself had a fan that escaped notice if there were any other noises in the house, but once it was time for bed, the sound climbed up the stairs and perched in his ears. But he stopped complaining after a couple of days. Even the government does this.

This was the big night, though. Worthy of turning off the television and focusing all their efforts on AOL. Katherine had taken to Internet chatting with a few friends – AOL had private 'rooms' that one could create and invite other people to when they were online. She'd sit as she and Jeremy watched prime time and chat with people she'd never met in different parts of the country.

Jeremy thought it was a good thing for Katherine, but it didn't appeal to him much. Why you'd want to talk so much with perfect strangers was beyond him. And he was certain that half of the people weren't who they claimed to be – the person who kept logging on as Tom Clancy certainly couldn't be – and there had been rumors about a woman online who had claimed to have been an eighteen-year-old leukemia patient, but was actually a forty-year-old housewife and mother of two. These were just two among the many "friends" that Katherine had.

She'd eventually understood that, so when she presented the case for her new horizon it was explicitly understood that it would not involve any of her AOL friends. They'd do it anonymously like everybody else.

After the tattoo there had been more than a year of quiet in the house – not the awful, sullen quiet of disappointment between couples, but not the peaceful, contented quiet Jeremy was certain they'd enjoyed before. It had become a quiet much like after something awful had happened – even though nothing awful had. The quiet of people cleaning up and doing dishes after a wake. "Nice that Mrs. Elmore brought the strudel, wasn't it. Oh yes, very nice. And the Taggerts were very kind to come over, you know he works for the Brewers and is hardly ever home this time of year. . . "

Actually, Jeremy realized he'd never really been to a wake. Had he even known anyone who died? His grandparents had passed before he was born – his grandfather on his father's side, who apparently was not the best liked man in Milwaukee, dropped dead of a heart attack two weeks before Jeremy was born. Uncle Ted had to step in because Jeremy's father was such a wreck that month.

But Jeremy didn't know what it was like to be that kind of wreck. And Katherine's infertility made it fairly certain he'd never know what kind of wreck being a new father made men into. He'd seen it happen, several of his friends whose wives were late in their terms would just do crazy things: pick fights with strangers at bars, choose the worst time in the world to demand a raise; one friend of his, Richard, even disappeared for almost a week during his wife's last trimester. No phone call, nothing. Nancy had gone out of her mind and was just in the process of moving back in with her mother when Richard reappeared. They apparently proceeded on in life like the event had never happened, but obviously it had taken some negotiation to get to that point.

Jeremy had been wondering for a couple of years now what kind of negotiation he and Katherine would have long-term, ever since the news that they couldn't have children of their own really sank in. He was certain the news had been easier for him to bear: it was a fact, they couldn't have kids – their first attempt at a pregnancy was ectopic and the doctor who performed the procedure to terminate had damaged her uterus. He hadn't screwed up; if anything, he'd been very frank about the risk of that happening. "There is almost no chance of a positive outcome regarding future pregnancies," he'd said, sitting on the corner of his desk and peering over his glasses as they fidgeted on the sofa in his office. Why did old guy doctors do that?

But Uncle Ted made sure he was investigated for malpractice anyway, and the doctor had been litigated out of town; the last Jeremy knew, he was practicing out of a strip mall in some clinic in Henderson, Nevada, next to one of those dry cleaning joints that posted their sign upside-down.

Jeremy had accepted the infertility news quickly enough to help Katherine adjust, he thought. He'd stayed with her constantly after the procedure, even though she was home the next day. Jeremy was even so close he barely stopped himself from asking point blank, "honey, what's it like to have a uterus?" Thankfully he backed away from that one. There are questions and there are childish questions, and the latter usually appear most attractive during stress.

But in fact, she appeared to grow weary of his hovering over her. One night, about a week later, it had come to a head:

"You can tell me," Jeremy said. "You really can."

"And I would, I promise." Katherine was sitting up in bed, her beautiful breasts still somewhat fuller from the pregnancy. Or maybe Jeremy just thought so. He could never stop watching her body. "But there's just nothing to talk about. The way you fuss over me makes me feel like I have to go through some kind of mourning that I just don't feel. We tried. We can't do it. Let's move on."

Moving on did not mean adoption at that point, they had decided. After all, who said that life had to work on some set schedule: too many of their friends got married right out of college and started the kid thing, and while they universally praised the experience, they sure seemed a lot more tired and less interested in doing things than they did before their babies took over their lives.

Which is why so many of the guys had freaked out anyway. When your wife is pregnant, your life is going to change pretty damn quickly and you'd better man up for it. That meant for most of his friends that they had to do about a decade's worth of maturing in just a few weeks, and that kind of pressure made freaking out pretty likely as the pregnancies neared full term.

Adoption would be easier. When they were more financially stable, when they felt like they'd enjoyed life together as a couple the way a young couple should, they'd find a child to adopt. Don't go to the car dealership unless you are ready to buy. This was an easy enough principle. They looked at each other one night and made the decision. They'd do it when they were ready.

Now Katherine was ready for something else entirely. "Married woman, thirties, seeks woman for NSA play. Not interested in threesomes." Katherine read the text aloud again, then looked at Jeremy with anticipation.

"Shouldn't you say something about how you want her to look?" Jeremy didn't exactly know what the protocol was for advertisements on "the back page" of *The Onion.*

"Oh, you can't really say that," Katherine confirmed, "but you can say this–" She continued to type, then read aloud again: "Married woman, height-weight appropriate, seeks same for NSA play."

"You're restricting yourself to married women."

Katherine frowned. They'd have to keep at it.

This was the idea that had broken the uneasy, "maybe-this-is-how-it-felt-after-a-wake, post-tattoo, post we're-going-to-be-childless for a while" silence. Katherine had rolled over into Jeremy's arms after a lovemaking session and played with the few light brown hairs on his chest (Jeremy was growing a distinct fear that they would soon outnumber the ones on his head) as her chin dug into his shoulder. "Remember that time you asked me about my fantasies?"

Jeremy felt another tattoo coming, and braced himself. "Sure."

"Are you still comfortable with that?"

Jeremy answered the only way a man could, he figured. "Of course. I want you to have whatever you want." It had the added benefit of being true. He did want her to be happy, and a big part of his job was to make sure she was – if their infertility had made any direct impact on Jeremy's life, it might be in the fact that more pressure was on Jeremy now to make Katherine happy, because she wouldn't have kids to distract her. Not that kids were a distraction – he'd just seen a lot of women who weren't living the lives they had wanted to lead because they had children. And the children were their own reward, this was something everybody who had children agreed upon (the only other topic of unanimity was that people like Jeremy, who did not have children of his own, would never understand the love, the love, the incredible love that would make any sacrifice in the world worthwhile). Whatever. He was innately suspicious of anyone telling anyone else they had to have a certain experience to understand something. Bullshit. That's what language was for, to describe experiences so others might have them. You don't have to be in a situation to understand it. Every philosopher knows that.

The clinical experience meant that Katherine's innate happiness, then, would fall upon Jeremy. Or at least, he'd become more acutely aware that he'd better not be an obstacle to it, because they wouldn't have kids to mitigate an unhappy marriage or the slow toxins of unrealized ambitions. Jeremy hadn't used those particular words to come to his decision in the matter – it was more like a gut feeling when Katherine asked him things like this. No matter what the question was, if it was important to Katherine, he should say yes.

"What if I picked up a woman at a lesbian bar or something?"

Jeremy's post-coital drowsiness was instantly shattered. "Are you serious?"

"Before you say no – "

"I didn't say no – "

"I mean, before you do – just realize, this is something I've always dreamed of."

"Being with another woman? You've always dreamt of this?" The only way Jeremy would ever correct someone's grammar was to reply to them with the improved usage: this annoyed far more people than Jeremy was aware of, including Katherine, who frowned.

"Not always, but you know what I mean. I think the name for someone like me is bi-curious. I'm just interested in what it would be like, that's all."

Jeremy went along. "Since you were – "

"About ten."

"Ten?" Jeremy was more jealous than accusatory – he'd had his first erection at age seven and had had no earthly idea what to do with it except press hard down against it in his jeans, which only made it feel worse – and better – and it had been until he was twelve before he figured out he could masturbate – and only when he was about fourteen did he put together the fact that thinking of girls he knew was directly connected to a more efficient ejaculation. But for Katherine to have those feelings at ten –

"Wow. Did you ever think of guys that way?"

"Not until later. And it's not like I didn't like guys – it's just that I've always wanted a girl to kiss me, that's all."

"Well," Jeremy still didn't know where this was going to go – he could no longer say with certainty that any impulse of Katherine's was going to be short-lived, "I can report from experience that it's a good feeling."

Katherine's face burst into a smile, and her eyes flashed. "You mean, like this?" She began to kiss his chest.

"Ummm, something like that."

Katherine pulled up and settled her tongue along Jeremy's right nipple. "Or this?"

"Yeah, I remember something like this – "

"And when a girl makes a tent out of her hair for you?" Katherine adjusted, and her hair did just that – a flowing brunette canopy over his chest, her concealed face slowly working down his abdomen. Only as she began using her hair to stroke his inner thighs and drag over his penis, did the rest of her hair slowly follow down his chest, until finally, just as she engulfed him, he felt her hair caressing everything around the middle of his body – his hips, his stomach, his thighs – the longest strands even played with the sides of his knees; and when her activity seemed to bunch her hair around her face she would flip it out again and the process would begin all over. Jeremy closed his eyes, began swimming in the experience, and giggled slightly: she wasn't just giving him head, she was giving him hair.

This was wonderful. If she wants to feel this way, what kind of a husband would he be to say no?

"What do you think?"

Jeremy was jarred from his memory back into his chair before the giant computer screen.

"Married woman, thirties, seeks discrete NSA play with lesbian or bisexual woman. HWP please."

Jeremy smiled. "Go ahead and send."

"Really?"

"Yes. I meant it when I said yes."

Katherine beamed and hit the send key. Jeremy got up and went to the kitchen. Some bourbon would be nice.

"Dammit – Jeremy!"

"What?" He turned.

"They need my credit card. Do you think it's safe?"

"It's how we pay for most things online now, isn't it?"

Katherine smiled. "I guess so."

As Jeremy poured his Jim Beam over two ice cubes, he laughed to himself. Of all the things about this to bother Katherine, it was using her credit card online. He took a drink, and as he felt the welcome sting on the back of his throat, he realized that she'd probably get some hardcore lesbian responses, real bull-dykes that wouldn't interest Katherine in the least. She'd mentioned a red-headed girl in pigtails a few times, and Jeremy assumed that's who she was looking for. You can't use a new attraction to heal the wounds of the old ones. It never works for long.

But these were things none of us could be told, Jeremy thought, feeling suddenly quite wise and generous, almost philanthropic: these were things we all have to learn for ourselves. People who aren't brave enough to live their fantasies could never understand that.

Inexplicably, he felt his stomach churn, and leaned over the sink just in time to regurgitate the bourbon he'd just swallowed. That was odd, he thought. He must be coming down with something.

Sally had responded to the personal ad almost immediately. Katherine got an email saying there was a voice mail in her 'personals' mailbox. She'd listened to the message a few times, and was still excited when she handed the phone to Jeremy. As Sally spoke, Katherine felt warm and proud and hunter-gathery: like she'd just handed him a present she hoped he would love. So this is what it felt like to be a man, she thought.

"Hi, I'm, um, Sally. I'm calling about the ad in *The Onion*. I've never done this, so I'm a little nervous. I'm married, and my husband doesn't know — so if we meet or anything it has to be discrete. I guess I should tell you what I look like. I'm kind of tall, I used to run track and I'm still in pretty good shape I guess. Red hair. Anyway, my mailbox is 433. Hope you'll call. Bye."

Katherine's face lit up when she heard "red hair." Jeremy smiled, and that smile made Katherine put her arms around him. She knew how he loved it when she held him like that.

She'd called back that evening and left a message, after consulting with Jeremy about the language. She always consulted Jeremy about language.

"Dear Sally: Thank you for your response. I had a bunch to say but – um – I guess it must have been too rehearsed. I've never done this either. Or does everyone say that? Is that what you're supposed to say? And I'm married, my husband knows but he honors boundaries. I'm just over 5'5" but everyone thinks I'm taller than that because I have long black hair. My husband loves my body so much I think it's a sharing thing. Now I've said too much. Call back if you want. If not, thanks for listening and have a great life."

She hung up the phone and her heart was in her throat as she looked over at Jeremy with two tentative thumbs-ups. He returned them, and she exploded into his arms, pulling herself at him as though she wanted to be one part of his body. Jeremy absolutely knew what to do. Every time.

Which is to say, it had gone well. By the end of the week, they had their first phone conversation. Jeremy had decided not to listen, so he mowed the lawn until Katherine came running out, saying they were going to meet at a coffee house a few miles away. She then took Jeremy inside and made love to him in his favorite position, with her on top of him so he could lay back and relax and just watch her face and her breasts and her hair. He was always happiest just looking at her when she was in that state. She'd told him that it wasn't an easily orgasmic position for her, but that didn't have to matter every time. She had just as much fun watching him watch her.

They made love like it was Friday night, deep into the morning hours while a summer rain tapped like thousands of tiny nervous fingers on the roof. Katherine had fallen asleep against his chest, and as he'd drifted off himself, Jeremy listened to the rain and let his fingertips trace ever so gently down along the back of her head. She'd murmured approvingly without waking up.

Katherine made little cooing noises in her sleep; if you'd ask her why, even if she didn't remember, she'd report that she could only sleep that way because she Jeremy loved her more than anything in the world. And that she loved him more.

Katherine kept playing with a piece of red duct tape on her pants leg as Jeremy drove them to the café. She liked making little pieces of art on her clothes, especially when she was nervous. Usually she'd grab a pen and just doodle flowers – but today the tape was there, left from when Jeremy had inexpertly patched up a small tear in the upholstery. She tore it into five pieces, about an inch long each, and arranged them in to what she thought was some kind of southwestern pattern, like a petroglyph from those caves in New Mexico or Arizona or something. She had seen pictures.

Jeremy was trying to stay at the speed limit. He'd find himself going too fast, and was certain it was because of the excitement of the day. Then, minutes later, he caught himself driving fully ten miles per hour below the speed limit, and was suddenly convinced he was probably too scared to go through with this.

When they got out of the car in front of the café, Jeremy noticed that Katherine hadn't removed the tiny pattern of red duct tape on her right leg of her jeans. Maybe that was a sign she and Sally had agreed upon, but he hadn't planned to leave the tape in the car.

She hugged him. "Okay, I'll be back in about ten minutes. You stay here, okay? I don't think anything's going to go wrong, but you promise you'll stay?"

"I said I would."

"And you promise you're okay with this, right? You're not just saying that?"

The tent of hair was something everyone should experience "No, I'm okay with everything. This is for you."

She bounded to the door of the café like a kid running home from a school bus; then, as though realizing that unbridled enthusiasm might not be her sexiest look (she was wrong about that, however. Jeremy lived for it), she collected herself, turned at the door, waved to Jeremy, and went inside.

Jeremy walked through the parking lot and peered into a few stores that shared the mini-mall with the café. He thought about a presentation he was supposed to finish the next weekend; he liked doing the numbers thing, but he had the most fun when they were put to bed and he could focus on the language. How can these numbers tell a story? How can he get the client to see that spending more on their plant right now would not only be a good idea, but the only idea. It was obvious, given their P&L; but too many people were afraid of numbers for that to happen alone.

He suddenly wondered how long he'd let his mind wander and turned towards the café. Katherine was standing next to a tall redheaded woman with an athletic frame who was wearing a tank top and tight shorts that made it appear like she could sprint in any direction on a moment's notice.

Katherine was waving for him to join them. His pulse quickened as he tried to talk in a controlled pace. As he got closer and closer, it became more obvious that it had gone very well. Katherine was wearing that smile.

"This is Sally. Sally, this is my husband Jeremy."

They shook hands. She had a firm grip, but pulled away after just a quick touch; just enough to be brave. "So," her voice had a nervous edge to it. "I guess we're doing this. Awkward, huh?"

Katherine's eyes flashed. "Let's go back to the house." She turned to Sally. "You want us to drive you?"

"I think she'd feel more comfortable if she had her own car." Jeremy added with as helpful a voice he could muster. There were all kinds of perverts out there, something Katherine just refused to understand, and Sally probably needed the assurance that she could take off if things got weird.

"No, I live about a mile from here. I walked. You can drive me if that's okay."

Jeremy coughed to conceal his surprise.

As they drove back home, he couldn't help but look back at Sally in the rear passenger seat. She and Katherine talked – about music, about what she did (she was a lawyer who specialized in intellectual property). Jeremy figured it was his place to keep quiet and be the cool husband. But as he looked at her, the casual lilt in her voice as her anxiety abated, and watched how she'd mindlessly keep pulling a few strands of her long red hair behind her left ear, and would sometimes repeat the motion even when her hair was in place, one thought kept coming back to him over and over again:

The world cannot be this generous. It just can't. This is exactly what Katherine wanted. And they find her on the first try? And she wants to come home with them now? Sure, she was probably thinking something like "if I don't do this right now, I'll never do it." He understood that. Katherine might be thinking the same thing, he'd have to talk with her later.

They pulled up to the house, and as Jeremy held the door for them both Sally whispered a tremulous "thank you."

The three of them stood in the living room. Jeremy thought he could actually hear Katherine's heart pounding. Sally looked around and saw the museum posters Katherine and Jeremy had hanging on the walls. Manet,

Monet, Renoir. The canonical decorations of middle class Milwaukee, Jeremy had once thought.

"I like your posters," Sally said. "I've got the Manet too."

Katherine was somewhat jolted by the statement into realizing some basic hospitality was in order. She asked if Sally wanted anything to drink – water, beer, they had some liquor.

Sally smiled shyly and said "yeah, that might be best. Got any Jim Beam?"

Now Jeremy was in love. The world is not this kind. He walked with Katherine into the kitchen and poured two drinks. He gave them to Katherine and told her he'd go out and finish mowing the lawn.

"But it rained all night. It's going to be a pain in the ass."

"Yeah, but I want you guys to have privacy. I'm right outside if anything happens."

"What could happen?"

"Go find out." Jeremy smiled. Katherine gave him a quick kiss, turned, and went back into the living room alone. Jeremy went out the back door.

When he got to the lawn mower, which Jeremy had left in its place with the backyard half finished, had accumulated a pool of rainwater in the small indented ring below where the motor was attached to the housing the protected the blade. It would start rusting soon after.

Dammit, I just cleaned up and oiled this thing, Jeremy thought as he pulled back had on the motor cable. The engine puttered to life and Jeremy prepared for a wet, sticky, grassy afternoon.

Steven's birthday fell on a Thursday that year, and because Tiffany had to work late, they decided to push the celebration off until Friday. Steven spent Thursday night watching college basketball, and for the first time since anyone could remember, North Carolina wasn't a national threat. Despite being a Texan, Steven took it personally, and it threatened to ruin his evening. Too much of this server maintenance had to be done on weeknights. Steven knew a little about computers. Tiffany could schedule the maintenance cycles for weekends; a lot of LAN administrators did that.

And North Carolina had no chance against Duke that year. Dammit.

Friday was easier. Tiffany had to go in early to have a 'geek breakfast' as she called each ENS meeting. Steven could wake up leisurely (or as leisurely as Tony would allow), take a long shower, make sure his hands were perfectly clean and dry, and catch up on what Tiffany was doing during the week.

Her journal was in the bathroom, under the sink, beneath a box of electric curlers her mother had given her years ago and which she never used, but couldn't stomach to throw away. Steven always felt very guilty about reading it – so much so in fact it made him paranoid, it made him feel as though his crime was obvious and that everyone knew he was the kind of guy who couldn't trust his wife – and so he restricted himself to reading it once a week, on Fridays, so he could know going into the weekend, when he had to spend the most time with Tiffany, just what it was he was up against.

The first time he read the journal, it had been a romantic accident. He was cleaning out one of their dressers so he could give her more room for clothes now that she was working, and in moving her underwear he found it, a small steno pad in a fluffy calico cover. No lock, no prohibition on the front page (why do people do that, anyway?), just a notebook with Tiffany's writing in all of its neat, angled beauty. Steven instantly felt lucky, like he'd found a way to crawl into the secrets of her heart – and as he opened it for the first time, he truly believed that he'd find out things that she really wanted, and he'd be able to give them to her. A peek into her dreams would help them become reality.

He was completely unprepared for what he would find. In the early pages of this journal, which began just a few days after Steven quit his job (which was approximately six months after he in fact did lose it. Tiffany was too worried for him to bring it up. Or, if he were more honest with himself, he knew what her reaction would be), there were comments about how he'd find work again soon, how she wasn't worried because Steven was smart and resourceful, and he'd shake out of the depression he was in, and Tony (she always called him A. in her journal) was beautiful, and how he looked like both of them.

But the pages darkened after that. Suddenly Steven found himself described as the Loser, which shortly afterwards became Loser Husband, then L.H. for short. He was 'lazy' and 'unambitious' and 'lied to me.' Steven tried to figure out what the lie was, but couldn't imagine. After all, one lies to women routinely to keep the peace, but he wasn't sure of any specific lie that would give rise to such heated anger.

Steven set the journal down that first day, his hands trembling, and vowed never to look at it again. Some people did that, some people vented on paper and let loose their most disturbing, violent thoughts. It allowed them to act normally in front of the people they love, and it keeps their frustrations from bottling up. Steven knew he himself had a problem with those frustrations, and would often go weeks at a time without letting anything bother him before blowing up over a minor annoyance. Maybe this was healthier, especially since Tony was the most statistically likely target if she let loose in public, being a toddler who pushes boundaries for a living.

Still, to have no idea that she had such angry, violent thoughts, or that she could smile at him and still think those things – this was difficult to stomach.

The first week or so after that, Steven managed to keep his word to himself and not read the journal. But then, Tiffany wouldn't want to sleep with him one night, or she backed away from him suddenly as he came to kiss her, or even that one day when she 'left her cell phone off' for most of the afternoon (IT specialists never leave their cell phones off) suddenly everything became imbued with suspicion and he had to know what was going on.

When he found the entries about Tim, he didn't know what to do. He couldn't demand she quit her job – it was all they had right then, and besides, it would reveal that he knew all about the relationship, and he could only know that by reading her journals. He couldn't tell her that she had betrayed his trust without admitting he'd betrayed hers as well – and he was still wise enough to figure out that people didn't compare betrayals very well – the betrayals you commit never seem as painful as the ones committed against you.

This morning, though, it was different. The journal wasn't really in code, but Steven had a hard time figuring it out. Her latest entry read:

> TK too much on my mind. I think he's psycho sometimes. Generous to a fault, then he lashes out. Why can't he take it out on the page? Why does he have to take it out on me? Boy, Tiff, you can pick 'em. LH ruining your life, TK too scared to get out of his marriage, then he blames you for it. Why do I attract weak men? What do I do that

makes them find me? This must be my fault somehow, because I don't think I've ever really loved anyone. They have to sense it.

So maybe Steven should keep his mouth shut, and Tim wouldn't leave his wife, and when he got another job it would all blow over. He just had to keep his mouth shut long enough to survive it.

But occasionally, usually after lunch, (Steven wondered if it had to do with his blood sugar after eating) he'd become seized with a furious jealousy. All he could think of was Tiffany's body in Tim's hands, of the looks she would be giving him, looks that used to be reserved for Steven – of the slight way she used to moan when he kissed her. All of these gifts she'd be giving to another man, an older, overweight, slightly-smelling-of-cabbage guy who made about four times what Steven made when he was working.

Invariably, he'd call Tiffany's cell phone in the middle of that mood, and it would instantly ring over to voice mail, meaning the phone wasn't even turned on. And in the evening, while fixing whatever meal he designed for her that night, he'd casually ask about her day, and see her eyes quickly shift before finding some way to explain her phone being off.

"I was in the warehouse all day, where I don't get a signal. Did you try to call?" Before Steven could answer, she would regularly pick up Tony, almost as a prop, and continue, "I can't believe I forgot to recharge my batteries again. The battery doesn't hold a charge anymore. I think we should get a new one."

Steven would believe any one of these excuses if he'd asked for them, but he never did ask – it was too plain that she was trying to prevent him from becoming suspicious.

On his birthday, even. Tiffany had stayed with Tim after work, he was certain of that. He'd swung by the office and saw her car missing – and for the first time, thought about buying some newfangled GPS device so he could put it in her car and discover where she was.

But that was full-blown paranoia. Especially the very thought that Tiffany would use Tony as a prop. She ran to him the minute she entered the door; and horned her way in to the four good books they'd read together every night. She'd stroke his hair – and occasionally stroke Steven's, but that was a completely different motion.

When you're becoming paranoid, your powers of scrutiny seem to expand logarithmically. He'd find himself drinking too much. He'd see Tony give him that "you're there, Daddy, but you're not really there," look. And most of all he just stopped trusting himself about everything. Did he bail from UT because he was scared? Can he not find a job because he was scared? Was he hiding here with Tony because the world was too big to take on?

Fear is what you feel the first day of school. This was different. But he finally started to shut his emotions down after reading the home page of a private detective, someone who specialized in tracking spouses, he already knew the lesson he found there: if you feel you must take these steps, then trust is completely gone already, and you need to consider if the relationship is even worth saving.

It wasn't. Nobody who loved him would treat him this way. Nobody so deeply in love would read his wife's journal. But they had a little boy, and Anthony needed both parents.

Maybe being a better father was the trick. So over the space of a few months, he began using his free time with Tony to visit the zoo, museums, parks, and take walks together whenever possible. He became one of those dads who seem to exist to elicit questions from their children "Daddy, why are cars so fast?" "So you'll know what to drive when you're running late.")

All this seemed to be working, and though he hadn't found a job, Tiffany seemed finally resigned to the fact that Steven was at least being a good home-schooler. They couldn't afford that kind of care even if he worked at his last salary, so it was a wash.

Until his 33rd birthday. Steven found a sitter, and when Tiffany came home that afternoon, Steven was already dressed up, wearing a sports jacket and white shirt.

"Whoa, you're Mr. Fancy-Dancy."

"I thought we were celebrating tonight." Steven smiled.

"Okay, give me a second." Tiffany walked past Steven, pulling slightly away when he tried to kiss her cheek. Steven thought he smelled a hint of cologne, but couldn't be sure. As she walked back into the bedroom he scrutinized the back of her blouse. There were slight wrinkles – maybe from it having been removed then reworn, or maybe from crawling around behind computers on the warehouse floor. That was the problem. There was always a plausible explanation for all of these hints.

If it weren't for the journals, he'd have never known. Part of him wished he'd never found them.

At the restaurant, Steven searched Tiffany's eyes for some clue to how she was feeling. It was one of those dimly-lit Pacific Rim-themed restaurants where the menu had to be printed on double-wide paper because every dish had five adjectives in front of it: Cajun-inspired blackened deep sea Bass with Visayan adobo remoulade; Phuket Thai green chili curry with potatoes and rosemary bourbon chicken. Steven normally didn't go in for that kind of thing, but he'd noticed Tiffany was developing a taste for nicer restaurants, and since he had a good guess where that taste was coming from, he figured on a special occasion, he had to play along.

"What's wrong?" Tiffany asked, and Steven thought he saw genuine concern in her eyes.

"Nothing. I've just been thinking about us."

"Oh." Tiffany looked down. "I see."

"I know it's been a little tough with me out of work."

"It hasn't been so bad. I don't mind supporting us."

"Right. But it's kind of gotten in the way of some things."

"You're talking about sex, right? You want to make sure we have sex for your birthday?" Tiffany was suddenly very cold, as though they were negotiating fishing rights off the coast of Galveston.

"That's not where I was going."

"Well, I'm glad, because I just haven't been in the mood at all lately. It's not you, it's me, and I just don't have that in me right now."

"Okay, fine." Steven looked down at the list of adjectives while Tiffany continued to stare at him. He looked up and noticed, and without even realizing it, blurted out: "if I get a job, will you love me again?"

Tiffany leaned back and sighed heavily. Steven was instantly overcome with embarrassment – he wanted this evening to be romantic, to sweep her off her feet again, and now he'd just virtually begged her to stay with him; he'd reduced himself to nothing in just one sentence. Five years ago he'd have just stood up and walked away, knowing he didn't have to put up with anything like this. He even half-expected to get up now. But he didn't, and couldn't figure out why.

"That's so sad, Steven, that you could even think that way." Tiffany's eyes teared up.

"Never mind. I'm sorry. Let's have a nice dinner." There was no chance of mentioning her leaving her job now. He'd redouble his efforts to find his own, and he'd find one, one that would make Tiffany proud and want to get him out of Austin and her father and whatever the hell mistake she was making at work. Then Anthony would be taken care of, Tiffany could go home and stop working if she wanted, and maybe they could find a good private school for Anthony...

Tiffany suddenly grabbed Steven's hand across the table. "You have to know I am asking for everything from you." Her eyes were welling up with tears, and her lips seemed to have the slightest shake about them. "Everything. I'm depending totally on you."

Steven nodded, not knowing where this was coming from at all.

"Really. Everything. That's a lot to ask." Tiffany looked at Steven with even more passionate intensity. There was something else she seemed to be trying to say.

"I understand. Do you want some wine?"

Tiffany nodded, but somehow it seemed like Steven had just missed the point of the conversation, like there was something he was supposed to hear that he didn't hear. She leaned back in her chair and looked dully over the menu. "I don't need to feel drunk. I'll just have a salad."

Back home, Steven went straight to bed. Tiffany went into the bathroom, and he thought he could hear pages turning. He'd have to hold on until next Friday to find out what happened that night.

He was nearly asleep when she came out, naked, and moved towards her side of the bed. He leaned up on one elbow, and watched as her breasts swayed slightly as she situated herself under the covers. She caught him looking at her and pulled the sheets up.

"What?" She asked, as though he'd said something.

"Nothing. It's just that you're beautiful."

Tiffany sighed. "You want to have sex, don't you?"

"It occurred to me."

Tiffany sighed again, dramatically. "Okay."

"No, really, I'm fine. Sorry I mentioned it." Steven began to roll over.

"No, if you want it, you're just going to keep at me, if not today, then tomorrow or the next day, so you might as well get it now. Come on."

"No, really, I'm fine."

Tiffany threw the sheets aside, revealing her entire naked body. "No, come on. Let's go."

Steven rolled back over and looked at her. She looked so unfamiliar to him, like he didn't know her at all. He couldn't believe someone who loved him would speak to him like this – and he couldn't believe that she didn't love him, because, well, they'd loved each other too long.

He didn't understand what the look in her eyes meant – but she didn't give him a chance. She pulled the covers down from over him and moved down over his crotch, taking him into her mouth, and clinically stroking him with her tongue, awakening his desire in spite of himself.

Steven leaned back and felt himself growing, and tears welled up in his eyes. This isn't how birthdays are supposed to go. This isn't how wives are supposed to behave. This isn't right, none of it is right.

He looked down when she'd gotten him fully aroused, and she pulled him over on top of her. "Go ahead, dammit. Fuck me. That's what you want, so just go ahead and fuck me."

Steven was suddenly angry. He didn't know what he was supposed to do – be the strong silent guy and roll over and go to bed, let her talk to him like that? Or be the guy who meekly has sex with his wife because she wants to get it over with?

No. There was another option.

He entered her, discovering instantly that she'd put some artificial lubricant in herself, and he began pushing hard, harder than normal, harder than he thought she would like. He would do exactly what she wanted, and he'd enjoy it, and he resolved to ask her again tomorrow, and the next day, and the next day. If this is going to be her attitude, then let her do it, and he'd do it right back. Maybe it wasn't making love anymore, maybe it was a completely empty and hollow experience, but dammit, he was going to have sex with his wife if she asked him to, and that, each night, was a luxury that her boss didn't have.

He looked down at Tiffany, feeling himself nearing his climax, and saw a new look in her eyes. She wasn't even there. She wasn't angry, she wasn't sad, her eyes just didn't register anything. It frightened him.

"Are you okay?" He asked with a bit of alarm in his voice. What the hell was happening?

"Are you finished?" She asked, coldly.

"Not really."

"Then how about this?" She wrapped her legs around behind his lower back and began writhing against him, moving almost hysterically, her lips glued to his chest, her tongue flicking rapidly along his nipple between tiny bites – all the things that she knew would set Steven off.

Before Steven could pull out – even as he tried to – he felt himself literally yanked into an orgasm of surprising power. It seemed to resonate from his center all the way back into his eyeballs, down even to his feet, and despite how angry and humiliated he was, all he could do for several seconds was bob his head in time with the pulses of his center, moaning uncontrollably.

"There, that's better, isn't it?" With a tenderness so surprising that Steven felt it had to be sarcastic. He rolled away from her, breathing heavily, and she jumped out of bed and hurried into the bathroom.

Moments later, he heard the shower, and could make out the sounds of Tiffany crying under the running water.

Happy Birthday, dammit. He turned over, buried his head under a pillow, and was asleep within seconds.

# CHAPTER SEVEN

"Sally, you've never seen a street like Sesame Street. Everything happens here!"
— The first line from *Sesame Street*, 1969

Katherine and Sally were a hit, it turns out. Katherine received her first 'hair tent' with an amazing sense of gratitude, and Sally, who told her that very first time that she was nervous because she knew what she liked but had no idea how to give it to another woman, was a trouper.

As the months went by she trained her the way she'd slowly trained Jeremy, and she was just as enthusiastic of a student as he had been.

Katherine couldn't believe how cool Jeremy was about everything, from the first day on. He'd always stay near the house – for some reason, it was reassuring to both women that Jeremy was home. It was like he was their guard dog while they did something illicit—he made them feel like they could relax and enjoy each other, and the marriage police wouldn't be able to kick the door in all of a sudden.

Or something like that. He was just the best. Sometimes if she and Sally were making too much noise, he'd just turn on the stereo downstairs so they'd know it was okay and he was respecting their privacy. Every once in a while he'd even put on a song very loudly that he knew would mean something to them. He'd been collecting a series of CDs that had all the songs they grew up with in the 70s, and enjoyed teasing them with it. She didn't know where he found the old recording "Behind the Green Door," but when it drifted up into the master bedroom, Katherine and Sally laughed so hard that Katherine had to go to the door and yell down "very funny, Mr. DJ!"

Sally was so cool too. She was always in some high stress case, and her husband seemed like he was a good guy — she never said anything bad about him — but just like Katherine, this had been something she always wanted to try. And so far, so good. Sally was now willing to drive herself over for their meetings, usually on a Sunday afternoon. She'd bring some wine, or some bourbon for Jeremy. That was really sweet of her, and Jeremy appreciated it.

But mostly Katherine wanted to find ways to make Jeremy happy. She worked extra hard to keep the house clean and to do all those things that she figured wives were supposed to do, things that Mary did. Friday nights were still special, but now Sundays were fun too — after the first time with Sally, she laid by his side when they went to bed and told him every detail of their encounter. How Sally's lips trembled the first time they kissed, how Katherine herself realized it was harder than she'd thought to treat the clitoris with the right kind of pressure with her tongue. "You're really good, Mister," she'd added. "That's hard to do." That night he'd masturbated as she whispered directly into his ear, and she loved how it seemed to turn him on just as much as her.

As the weeks went on, it became more ritualized, and she and Jeremy would make love as she told him about her adventures with Sally. She described how Sally's tiny white breasts had nipples that seemed more like pink rosebuds than any other woman she'd ever seen. She talked about how delicate Sally's skin was, but how athletic and toned, and what a weird sensation that was for her. Sally's body was soft and hard at once, which she didn't think was possible. All while making strong eye contact with Jeremy as much as she could — sometimes he closed his eyes when she whispered, like he was trying to imagine everything about that afternoon himself.

His orgasms seemed more powerful when that happened, and even though she knew it was making him happy, she also knew not a lot of husbands would be cool with this. She was talking about it with Sally one

Sunday afternoon as they lie naked over the sheets, trying to think of a gift or something to show her appreciation for Jeremy. Maybe a power tool? Most guys liked power tools even if they used them only once. He could say he was going to build things around the house, then he'd put it off and put it off until it never got done, and she wouldn't say a word about it. The silence would be the real gift. Just as she was about to ask Sally about it, she was interrupted -

"I told Zachary." Sally ran her hand along the curve of Katherine's naked hip, but she didn't look her straight in the eye.

"Really? Wow! What did he say?"

Sally looked down, then back over at the window, then at the door – everywhere but at Katherine, who was leaning in closer and closer for the response. Finally, she just shot a glance at Katherine's eyes with just the slightest hint at a playful smile. She looked away coquettishly, then back again, smiling even more.

"Yeah?" Katherine was ecstatic.

"Yeah." They kissed. "He was really pretty cool. He didn't really like the fact that I'd gone behind his back, but he understood. You can't really know how a guy is going to react. I've seen so many computer nerds blow their stacks if the slightest part of their patent isn't right – he understood everything."

"I cannot tell you how happy I am for you!"

Sally smiled again, mysteriously, and Katherine's brow furrowed. "Well, after we talked and I described you, he brought up something. I'm not sure it's what you want."

"What, does he want us to stop or something –" Katherine stopped herself. She suddenly knew exactly what was coming.

"He wants to be a part of it."

Katherine leaned back. Yeah, of course he would. Typical guy. Come to think of it, why hadn't Jeremy ever asked?

"What did you tell him?"

"I told him that you were pretty clear when we started that this wasn't about threesomes or anything, and that Jeremy had never even asked or come on to me in the least little bit. But you know, we've known each other a little while now, and I told him I'd run it by you."

Katherine's sense of fair play immediately kicked in. "Only if he lets us do it with Jeremy too."

Sally took a moment to kiss Katherine's breast; Katherine felt herself warming and closed her eyes.

"I kind of anticipated that, and explained to Zach that we'd need full consent and a set of boundaries that everyone would be comfortable with, and we'd have to report back to each other's husbands exactly what transpired."

Katherine smiled. Every once in a while she forgot that Sally was a lawyer. Hearing her talk like one always made Katherine so proud of her – just like when she could get Jeremy to talk about his work. It was just so nice to be let in like that. Of course Sally would have thought of all the contingencies, because that's what lawyers do. She actually felt herself getting turned on at the thought of Sally driving her BMW through Wauwatosa thinking of all the contingencies of a threesome. She wondered what position Sally would like best. She'd have to go online to look some up; maybe there was a position she hadn't even thought of.

"So," Katherine said, already in a kind of dreamy sensual place that made logical discussion harder and harder, "what's the next step."

"We talk to Jeremy. If he says yes, we're a go."

Katherine snapped back into a more energetic mode. "Oh my god, he'll have a heart attack. I mean, he will be so grateful! Let's do it!

"Right now?" Sally laughed.

"Yeah, let's not even put any clothes on. Let's just go down naked and announce the new plan."

"But we haven't talked about boundaries – "

"It's easier to get a man to agree to a lot when there's two naked women in front of him." Katherine tossed out the comment so matter-of-factly that Sally rolled her eyes.

"I didn't think of that."

She kissed Katherine, a long slow, "we are going to the next level" kiss and they got up from the bed. They opened the door, and with Katherine leading the way, they headed downstairs, two nudes descending a staircase.

Jeremy was thumbing through a compendium of CDs he's just purchased called *Have A Nice Day* – all songs that weren't necessarily classics, but each one made him say or think "oh yeah, I remember that song." It came with a shag-carpeted cover and a voluminous booklet that more or less acted as liner notes for the whole ten-cd set.

Jeremy missed liner notes. They were the one cool thing about albums that most CDs didn't have anymore. They'd include lyrics now in little booklets, that was rare when he was a kid, but there was something cool about having just the back of the album cover to fit in all the text. He was about ten when he first read the liner notes to Boston's first album, and the writer kept interrupting himself to interject "Listen to the Record!"

As he was listening to The Ozark Mountain Daredevils singing "Jackie Blue," he was reading the lyrics, which he'd never contemplated before. It was kind of a silly song, and he was wondering why it had been so popular, when he heard the door open upstairs. He smiled, waiting for a smart-alecky comment from Katherine. Maybe she was so vain she thought the song was about her, he smiled to himself. But no comment followed from upstairs, so he figured maybe they just finished quickly this week. Nice to know it happens to women sometimes too.

"Ahem, Mr. DJ." Jeremy was reading the lyrics "you'll take an inch but you'd love a mile," and surprised so much by the proximity of her voice that he didn't look at Katherine or even notice Sally right away. Instead, he swiveled his chair around to the stereo and turned down the music, casually asking, loudly enough to be heard upstairs, "You guys want a bottle of wine or something?"

Which is about the time he turned around and physically jumped from shock. There was his beautiful wife, slightly tanned, her black hair flowing down over the top of her breasts, and Sally, in all her athletic fairness. Both naked, and certainly not finished for the day. Katherine stood confidently. Sally seemed to be trying to hide a little behind her.

Quick, Jeremy, the thought. Think of something witty to say.

"Um, I would have been happy to bring you a bottle." Dammit, Jeremy. Not witty.

"We want to bounce something off of you."

"It's getting hard enough right now that anything would bounce off me." Awful. Just shut up.

Katherine explained the proposition as Sally nodded in agreement, and even said it was just an experiment, and that the only way to keep Sally is if both guys get the same treatment. She was so calm, it was like she was talking about a house listing, the color of the kitchen, the size of the bedrooms.

Jeremy sat, dumbfounded as the details of the proposition were laid out. Katherine would talk, and Sally would amend the comment, and Katherine would talk again. Part of Jeremy couldn't believe this was happening. The world is not this good to people. He took his time before responding. "So I can't – you know – insert myself in Sally. And Zach won't – insert himself – in you."

"Right. At least, not there. Anything else I guess is okay." Katherine turned to Sally, who gave a surprisingly shy nod of approval, then stopped herself: "Oh, but I never liked that. Tried it once in college and it just felt too weird, like a giant suppository."

Jeremy laughed, but Katherine was all business.

"No, I didn't mean that. I meant blowjobs. Blowjobs are okay."

"Oh, yeah. Sure." Sally answered like she had just been offered black olives on her pizza and had merely forgotten that it was one of her favorite ingredients.

This was the boundary. They looked at Jeremy.

He looked at both women and couldn't quite decide what to do. They'd both obviously wanted this, or they wouldn't be there naked and so hard to say no to. And it was odd, the idea of being intimate with a new woman for the first time in seven years. And she was beautiful in such a completely different way than Katherine – and – and – and. . . .

And Katherine was already loosening his belt buckle, and gently placed her hand on his erection. "It feels to me like you like this idea."

"I do." Jeremy breathed out heavily and said one of the truest things in his life. "I'm just not sure I'm ready for it."

"Let me make you ready, then." She pulled out his penis and took it as deeply into her mouth as she could. He had been so shocked that he hadn't grown to his full length yet, and Katherine knew that one of his favorite sensations was feeling himself grow in her mouth.

"Yes. Yes, dammit. You don't play fair." Jeremy smiled. Sally walked up and tentatively kneeled down next to Katherine, who pulled away just a few inches and gently tugged his penis towards her, like she was offering to share an ice cream cone. Sally leaned forward and stuck out her tongue, but was still a few inches away. Jeremy felt his heart pounding as she slowly moved closer. Oh, this can't be happening. Life isn't that good to people.

When she finally did make contact, he sensation was so electric that Jeremy literally had to bite his lip to keep from exploding into her mouth. Even that didn't feel like it was going to work, until he came across the thought that doing so would be simply rude, and he didn't want to be rude to such a nice person in such a vulnerable moment. That thought made him giggle internally enough to resume control as Katherine undressed him while Sally began a more confident rhythm in his lap.

A few moments later there was the awkwardness of Jeremy standing up so he could remove his jeans and shoes, and the slightly comic look of his member waving back and forth near Sally's face as he shimmied the jeans down his legs. He'd been silly enough to think he could get them off without removing his shoes, and had to lay down on the sofa while both women finished disrobing him.

The next minutes were the best in his life so far, he thought at the time. Both women shared his erection as they gave him fellatio, occasionally stopping to kiss while dragging him across the cheek of one or the other. They laid out on the floor and continued, with Jeremy's head on a sofa cushion, so he could see both naked bodies stretched out at opposite angles from his center. He'd always loved looking at Katherine's body when she'd lie like this: it was as though you could follow a line from her feet all the way to her task at hand, like she was meant to do this. And to see it from both women was astonishing.

Sally was good at this, really good, Jeremy thought. He'd never spent much time imagining what it would be like to receive this from another woman – his sexual life with Katherine never had been unfulfilling at all. But she was different – she had a completely different rhythm, and when Katherine backed away and said "give him the hair tent. He LOVES that," just the feeling of Sally spreading her hair out over his body almost made him lose control.

Katherine sensed quickly that this was about to end, so she guided Sally away and mounted Jeremy directly. Sally looked at her questioningly, and Katherine nodded, before Sally bent down herself and settled her sex directly into Jeremy's mouth. He couldn't see anything, but he could feel the two women kissing and caressing each other as they maintained their balance. Jeremy knew that Sally had always been the louder of the two when they were together, so it suddenly became his goal to get her to moan the way he'd heard her from upstairs.

It didn't take long, and the sound was so passionate, and his wife's knowledge of his preferred rhythm in his favorite position was so expert, that the moment he felt Sally pulsating he simply lost control – a powerful, intense orgasm that had not matched Katherine's, but rather Sally's.

The women rolled off of him and each lied down. "I'm sorry, hon," he said to Katherine, knowing she hadn't climaxed. "But that was just mind-blowing."

She kissed him, a gentle peck on the cheek. "It's alright. That was the most beautiful thing I've ever done."

Sally seemed to be in a completely different zone, satisfied but shocked at what she'd just gone through. As both women settled their heads against a different side of his chest, Katherine caressed him. Sally just looked up into his eyes, saying nothing, but with an expression of bewilderment.

That's what Jeremy hoped it meant, anyway – and within a few minutes, he fell asleep. When he woke up, He was alone on the floor, Sally had left the house, and Katherine was in thick pajamas, heating up some lasagna. As he put his clothes back on, a part of him was certain that none of what he'd remembered of the day had even happened.

Tiffany opened her car door and felt the warm Austin sun on her hair as she climbed out. She liked to wear it up in the summertime, but it made her look too much like a little girl, and some guys were just a bit too much into that look for her comfort. She leaned back into the car and grabbed the brisket she'd cooked for her father's birthday. She had surprised Steven by insisting that she make it herself.

"You know I'm the better cook," Steven offered as charmingly as he could.

"I know you think you are." Tiffany flirted back.

"Besides, he likes me now, right? I could make some chili –"

"Steven," Tiffany cut him off. "He's my father. Giving him something from you would mean all he'd do was tell his friends what a great son in law he has."

"I thought we wanted that."

"Not when it's part of the 'why my daughter neglects me' speech he gives everyone. It has to come from me."

"Fair enough. Let me know if I can help." Steven went back to watching golf. There wasn't a sport that boy wouldn't watch.

What she didn't tell him was that she had a deeper objection: it was somehow crude to ask him to prepare a brisket when she knew she was going to leave him. She wanted to limit his exposure to her family. They were never that crazy about him anyway, and the feelings were mutual. Steven seemed to hate Leonardas just for being himself, and had once muttered something about how amazed he was that her father could do such emotional damage to people without even knowing it. She'd cut him off hard that night; it was one thing for her to criticize or complain about her family. He was not allowed to follow suit.

She also thought it was cruel to use Steven's time and energy on false pretenses. So she was doing him a favor, a favor she regretted as she pulled out the roasting pan from the back seat. The juices had spilled over and now the damn car would smell like brisket for a month. Steven would have drained the pan before transport. Why didn't he insist she do it? Loser.

She was now incapable of using any other term to describe Steven. She said it once in front of a mirror and it made her fair skin seem so remarkably old, in just a second, like a dash of poison had just washed over her. It was shocking at first. But as Steven reminded her back in their UT days, you can get used to anything. Now she didn't even feel like it was hostile. It was what it was.

As she approached the front door with her arms full, her mother rushed out of the house and met her on the stoop. "Tiffany, you need to go."

"Hey mom, I made this – what?"

Louisa was beside herself. "You need to go, honey. Daddy's really upset."

"What's wrong? Is he okay?"

"Tiffany – daddy has a friend at the warehouse." Louisa let the words linger in the air until Tiffany caught them.

Her world was over, right then. "Let me talk to him."

"Honey, you don't want to see him right now. You know how he gets."

"I can explain everything. Did Steven call?"

"No. He doesn't seem to know much."

"What do you know, mom?"

"I don't know anything. But Daddy's upset right now. Tiffany, *you have to go!*"

Tiffany relaxed a little. They knew nothing. "Oh come on, mom. I'll straighten this out. A lot of people don't understand what's going on."

Louisa positioned herself squarely in front of Tiffany. "Tiffany. No."

This was too strange, Tiffany thought, then said as casually as she could. "Ok, it's probably a blood sugar thing, right? Here, take the brisket, tell him happy birthday from me and Steven. I'll call later if you want." She handed the pan over to Louisa, who took it reluctantly.

"Let me call you," she said, looking harshly into Tiffany's eyes.

Tiffany went back into the car and started the engine, amazed at how heated up the air had gotten so quickly. She turned the air conditioning vents directly towards her face and felt it drying sweat all over, sweat she hadn't been aware of. Texas is just too hot in the summer. Maybe California would be better.

"Whore!"

Tiffany jumped and looked back at the front door to see Leonardas thundering out, the tray of brisket in his hands.

"Daddy?"

"Get the hell out of here! And take your damn meat with you!" He threw the pan at the car, where it bounced off of her front fender, the beef falling to the concrete with a hard angry splat.

She threw the car into reverse and pulled out of the driveway. Leonardas didn't look like himself at all; his skin was red and puffy, his eyes were wet and angry. What in the hell happened? She put down the window, "Daddy, what's wrong?"

"You're a goddamned whore, and everyone knows it! Everyone! I knew you'd do this to me, I knew it!" To make his point again, he reached for the limp brisket, which slid out of his hands as he stood to throw it again. As he turned to pick it up, it slithered out again, like some slippery Texas catfish of the prairie. The pause gave Tiffany enough time to put the car back into gear and drive down the street.

She'd been telling her mother for years that Leonardas needed to be tested for diabetes or high blood pressure. The mood swings were awful, he was out of control. And what did he think he knew? Tim wouldn't tell anyone, she hadn't said anything, and office gossip was always going to be office gossip. To get Daddy's attention, news like that would have had to come from someone who knew him and knew her, someone who –

She abruptly pulled over and wiped the tears from her eyes. She picked up her cell phone and dialed.

"Hey, sweetie. Did you sneak out to the garbage cans to give me a call?" Tim was clearly ready for some phone sex.

"My dad knows everything."

"What?"

"My dad called me a whore, Tim. He called me a whore!"

"Calm down, calm down. Where are you?"

"Meet me at Kerby Lane Café."

"Tiffany – how'd he find out?"

"Aaagh!" Tiffany screamed, a cry coming from deep within a tightly confined torso. She would never be free of it. She could never do anything without a man she cared about, knocking her down. She hung up the phone and pulled over harshly, nearly hitting a mailbox.

She turned the radio up and floored the engine. The car roared, still parked at the side of the road. Tiffany seized the steering wheel with all of her power, clutching it, slamming her forehead into the backs of her hands, crying, nearly howling, feeling her body begin to convulse against an absent brace - -

When the drama of the scene suddenly offended her.

She sat up abruptly and felt the tears dry on her cheeks almost instantly. Within two breaths she had eased up on the gas pedal; within ten seconds the radio was back at normal volume.

As she pulled back onto the road (after initially forgetting she'd instinctively put the car into park), she realized she'd hung up on Tim, which she knew would send Tim into a panic. Good. She wanted him to feel some urgency. He needed to feel as bad as she did.

She saw her eyes in the rear view mirror. More red than they should be.

Like her entire world had just shattered.

It was just after seven when the phone rang. Steven answered. There was no voice on the line, just a choking sound that lasted a few seconds before the line went dead.

"We have to go to the hospital." Steven hung up.

"Why?" Tiffany looked up from the newest edition of *Wired*, Tony asleep on her lap.

"We have to go to the hospital." Steven had nothing else to say. He rubbed his wedding ring with his thumb.

"Okay."

"Wait a minute," she said, "They don't let you take little kids into the hospital. Call mom and see if she'll babysit – "

She looked at Steven and her eyes widened. "Daddy."

Steven nodded.

"When?"

"If we hurry you can see him, before."

Tiffany nodded and stood up and walked to the master bedroom, where Steven heard the shower activate. He wished he'd revisited the water heater – but when Anthony was born, he turned down the core temperature so he'd never inadvertently burn himself. But what Tiffany needed the most right now was a hot hot shower; and she wouldn't get one.

That was his fault. Steven sat down in the living room and negotiated the channel guide until he found a rerun of *Sesame Street*. Big Bird had never met another Big Bird. It all seemed like some exploration of homosexuality; but nothing he could put his finger on. It didn't matter. Everything Big Bird did was okay.

Tiffany emerged from the bedroom in black. "Let's go."

"What are you going to say to him?" They were stuck in traffic. Stuck in traffic in Austin at 8:30 p.m. on a Saturday.

"How should I know." Tiffany fumbled with her hands.

"I've heard, a lot of times, that people who are dying just want to know that you're okay. It allows them to rest."

"He never rested."

"Then he might need it now. I don't know, I'm just guessing here."

"You've done enough guessing for a while."

Steven nodded. He knew Tiffany would eventually need someone else to be angry at. She just didn't know it was so soon.

"Steven, did you tell my dad about Timothy?"

Steven stared straight forward. Her father had two, three hours to live. "This isn't the time."

"Steven, did you by any chance think maybe, just maybe, my father couldn't handle that particular revelation?"

"Let's think about your father right now."

"My father died this afternoon, throwing a slab of brisket at me and calling me a whore. Why would he do that, Steven? Hmm? What do you think gave him that massive stroke?"

"You're mad at him, not at me. I'm not in a place for self-righteous anger right now."

"Turn the car around."

"What? No – honey, there's the hospital!"

"I said to turn around the car or I go crazy."

"You are crazy in this moment. My god, you can't be serious."

"STEVEN! PULL OVER!"

Steven pulled over to the side of the highway.

"Get out of the car. NOW!" Steven obliged, but came back to the window and said, "Look, you're pissed, you want to be angry, I get it. Be angry at me. I can get a ride home. But if you don't go up there and see him on his deathbed you will hate yourself for the rest of your life."

"I don't think so," Tiffany seemed to thoughtfully consider her words. "I think I'll just hate you."

She pulled away with such a dramatic swerve that it actually helped Steven somewhat. He saw the next upcoming exit and walked slowly towards it. He'd call his uncle in the morning; Uncle Lawrence would know what to do.

As he looked in the distance, it appeared at least she was headed for the hospital. Then, at the next street, she squealed hard left. She wasn't going.

# CHAPTER EIGHT

## It's Not Easy Being Green

They sat together in the café where they had first met, and Sally couldn't stop crying. She was clearly trying not to make a scene, but Katherine knew other people were noticing, and just seeing them give Sally such sympathetic looks was embarrassing her.

"Do you want to go someplace else?"

"No. I just have to deal with it. Give me a second." Sally took a sip of her coffee and held the cup in front of her face with both hands. Katherine saw how she was shaking.

"What did Zach do?"

"It's not really Zach. Honestly, it isn't."

Katherine had been expecting this for a couple of weeks. When they tried the experiment with Zach, it started off well. She'd met Zach with Sally at this coffee house, and felt comfortable enough with him to try what they'd done with Jeremy. He almost immediately ejaculated. It was over so quickly that he'd asked for a "do over" because he felt "a great opportunity just slipped away."

But Zach was a lot edgier than Jeremy. There was a possessiveness about his lust that just didn't turn her on very much. He looked at her like she was something to devour, a gift Sally had brought home for him so she could fulfill an obligation. She hadn't liked guys like that since high school, when none of them knew any better. They were all in their thirties now; men should learn to pick up pretty quickly by then if a woman is turned on by that kind of guy. Katherine wasn't.

But that hadn't been the biggest problem, at least not the second time that day. One of the positions they discussed after the first time with Jeremy involved Sally and Katherine pleasuring each other at the same time while Zach or Jeremy made love to his wife. Then the other one would tease the man with her tongue and augment his and her experience – or sometimes remove him entirely and take him into her mouth. Katherine loved it when she tried it the first time, not because she liked Zach particularly well, but because it gave her a chance to taste Sally upon his skin.

Sally reported the same with Jeremy in that position, and it was one that had the greatest chance of all three of them climaxing at the same time. When they discussed it with Jeremy during the second 'experiment' afternoon, his answer was a quick shrug and "let's go with the percentages." Katherine was proud of him for that.

Zach never got a second visit. During their "do over," Zach proved to have an almost annoying staying power. Nothing Sally could do would bring him to a conclusion, and it had gotten to the point where both women, without saying so in direct words, were breathing with sighs that reflected fatigue rather than passion.

But Zach broke the rules. He pulled himself out of Sally, and given their position, Katherine couldn't see what was going on. Her world was filled with Sally's sex, and Sally's world was filled with hers. Until suddenly, Katherine felt Zach's penis at the opening of her vagina, and she was still so excited from where the experience had been taking her, that he was able to slip completely into her in one quick motion before she could even react.

Sally was so upset about it later on that she considered calling it rape, but there was nothing to be done about that. Katherine viewed it as the failure of the experiment with Zach – and in the moment, after the initial shock, she had felt a twinge of a feeling that surprised her and she had yet to figure out. Sally eventually got to the point where she could say, "Zach was just hurt as a child and has never really gotten better." That was the best excuse she could give.

Katherine could obviously never go back, Sally insisted. They made excuses about her schedule, about needing to go slow – nobody had brought up the fact that he broke the agreement. They'd dragged him along for six weeks now, and he had to have said something by now. He had to know he'd screwed up the deal.

They were continuing to play with Jeremy, though, to the point that he looked forward to the visits as much as she did, Katherine thought. But the week before Sally had asked it to just be the girls. Jeremy had seemed fine with it. And this Sunday, when they'd invited Jeremy back into the bed with them, Sally had burst into tears right in the middle of things, then wouldn't say a word except for that she wanted to talk with Katherine at the coffee house. Jeremy had seemed frustrated that he couldn't be more supportive, but he didn't resist.

Now they'd been in the café for ten minutes and Sally hadn't been able to say a word.

"Zach's finally figured out that we're still playing with Jeremy, hasn't he?" Katherine knew that Sally had to feel bad about that; she hated lying to anyone and they hadn't been truthful to Zach. She probably told him in a fit of guilt and he was now punishing her by making her end it. Guys can be such idiots.

"Believe it or not, that's not the problem. He has no clue. Once he did that to you I think he decided you weren't a threat anymore. He's a caveman that way."

"Did Jeremy do something to upset you?"

"No, baby, no. No, baby."

Something about the way she said that stuck with Katherine. It wasn't the first time she'd used terms of endearment, but it was happening more often. First it was 'babe,' which was fine with her, but the 'baby' and 'honey' remarks hadn't really bothered her, but she'd noticed them. They seemed to really stand out now. Amy used to call her that, which is why they had such fights with all the other girls.

"I wish you'd tell me."

"I hated it when Zach did that to you."

"I know. But it's done, and he just got carried away. And all we can do about it is not see him anymore together. Do you want us to stop playing with Jeremy? He loves it, but he'd understand." That was true. Jeremy understood everything.

"You still don't get it, do you?"

Katherine didn't, and her face made that clear.

"I can't stand it now even when Jeremy makes love with you."

"Then we'll stop."

"Katherine, dammit, I can't stand the idea of anyone making love with you but me! I'm in love with you."

Katherine leaned back, unsure of what to say. This is what she'd been noticing about Sally's behavior lately, she just hadn't put it together.

"But I'm not a lesbian." Katherine said this without a trace of irony. Katherine, as a rule, didn't do irony.

"Don't you think I know that? You're just playing at being one because it's fun and you get to be different and it's exciting for you."

"You say that like I'm using you or something."

"No, that's the thing. I know you haven't been. You're so pure you've just had no idea. But you just can't love me back the way I love you. You're incapable of it."

Katherine took one of Sally's hands into hers. Sally tried to pull away, but just for a second, then squeezed Katherine's so hard it hurt.

"And," she said, gulping hard, "And I can't be around you anymore. I can't continue to do this with someone I love so much who doesn't love me the same way."

Katherine tried to speak up about how important this time had been for her, but Sally wouldn't let her. "Don't, don't do that. You don't have to. I know who you are, and I know why I can't have you. It hurts too much and it's not going to change. You and Jeremy are special together, that's so obvious to me. Even if you wanted something like I did, I'd hate breaking that up so much we'd never get over it. You need him. You'll never need me."

They sat in silence for a moment. Katherine looked down at the table.

"I guess the friend thing is out of the question."

"Katherine, we were never friends. I don't see how we can start being friends now. It's just too damn hard on me."

Katherine picked up her coffee cup and was surprised at how cold it had become. It made her think this was taking a long time, and Sally had made up her mind, and she should help.

"Well, then," she said, putting her mug back down – "I guess the best thing I can do is go away." She rubbed Sally's hand again, and watched as she tried to keep her shoulders from throbbing.

"Please." Sally whispered.

"Will you stay with Zach?"

"Please." She whispered again, almost desperately. Katherine got it. Going away meant Zach was no longer any of her business. That was how it worked. All those people who want to be friends after are always just fooling themselves into not admitting they've heard a no. Katherine wouldn't be one of those people.

Katherine stood up with some effort and looked down on Sally, who just stared at the table. She couldn't just leave it like that, it was so sudden, so final.

Or maybe it wasn't. She had to say something just in case.

She placed her hand on Sally's shoulder, bent down and kissed her on the top of the head, and said, softly, "thank you, Sally."

She turned and walked out without waiting for a response, and did not look back, even though she was dying to know if Sally was watching her leave. It seemed like she could feel her eyes upon her.

In the car on the way home, Katherine thought about how certain Sally was about everything. Of course she loved Sally, in a way – but by the time you use the phrase "in a way," you're usually breaking up with someone. That's how she'd always done it back when she was in college, before Jeremy.

She couldn't build a life with a woman. One, that's just silly, especially with Sally being a lawyer. Not in Milwaukee, not at Jeremy's expense. She loved Jeremy, loved everything about him. How he smelled, how his light blonde hair shone in the sunlight, how he lit up when she came into the room – she even loved coming downstairs half-dressed just because she could still turn him on.

What would Jeremy think of losing Sally? She hadn't thought of that. She remembered this was their seventh year being married – that's always when people stray and decide to want more, have affairs, all that. Maybe Sally was what was keeping things fresh for him. Would he have an affair if she didn't keep things adventurous? Could he go back to just having one sexual partner? He sure seemed to love the treatment they gave him together.

It might be time to adopt, she thought. Then she threw that thought away as easily as she let it in. Children are not things, they're people, and the work that needed to be done was by grown up people. This was not the place for children.

She thought briefly of that twinge Zach gave her, that undefined feeling that momentarily swept over her when she knew another man's member was inside of her. She still didn't know what that meant. Sally had told her it was the shock of being violated, but as the weeks went by she started to realize Sally wasn't right.

Something deep inside of her believed it was somehow connected to keeping Jeremy happy, and keeping him close to her. She might have just ruined everything. She needed to make sure that didn't happen.

When she got home, as she exited the car she discovered that she hadn't set the parking brake and had kept the car out of gear, and it began rolling backwards down the driveway. She dropped her purse, scrambled back into the car, and set the brake just before she would have drifted into the cross traffic of their busy street.

Once she knew she was safe, she started to get out of the car again, and realized it couldn't be an automatic move anymore. Someone could have been killed if they'd been behind the car. She couldn't trust her impulses. She had never felt like that before.

She burst into tears.

Tiffany rolled over and brushed Steven's hair away from his eyes, causing him to stir. She watched as his eyelids fluttered, his lips moved involuntarily like her aunt's, who'd been on Thorazine for two years—and he eased back to sleep.

She liked watching him nearly wake up, much more than watching him sleep. It was like she could see him coming from a place far away, and she could actually observe his subconscious mind make the decision to keep the world from him for a little while longer.

It was like that part of him knew she was leaving, and wanted to protect him. After a month or so of making up – and of insisting that he not go to the funeral, where Tim met her after the wake – she figured it was time.

She'd left enough hints, she thought, as she tried to hypnotize herself into this course of action. She complained when he wanted sex, and was surprised when it didn't seem to bother him at first–and mortified when she recognized that something in him seemed to enjoy making love to her even when she was clearly not in the mood. It wound up being some kind of sick power struggle—but ultimately, it became an issue all its own, and he'd missed the hint. He thought that her sexuality was just depleted by Anthony's birth. "Nobody wants to have sex the first years after having a baby, do they?" he'd said once while undressing her, with a confident tone of voice that was meant to assure her that he was about to change all that.

But no matter how committed his lovemaking was, or how old Anthony was getting, it didn't change the fact that he still didn't have a job that could support them, and still couldn't bring himself to be an engineer. It was all he was really qualified to do, unless you counted beer drinking, watching *Sesame Street*, and playing computer games; these were not growth industries. Tony was nearly six. There's no way they could afford to put him in a private school if Steven wasn't working at his potential.

She'd loved him for more than his potential, she thought. He understood her. But she'd gotten to the point where she looked at it as his weakness. Because beyond that, ultimately, potential had to translate into results sometime. Nearly ten years was more than enough. He'd had chances to make it work, and managed to screw them up with astonishing effectiveness: having a martini to relax just before a big job interview, then stumbling on the way into the office; forgetting to file on time the student loan paperwork to finish his degree, causing him to drop out and be the first on any company's layoff list because he didn't have the piece of paper, no matter how much smarter he was than the idiots who had degrees; and he always stopped his job search whenever one company seemed interested in him—and when that company didn't pan out, he had no prospects and had to start over. She'd grown tired of telling him to always be on the search for a job, and was tired of him not listening.

And he told Daddy about Tim. Probably just asked advice. But you don't do that. Because if Leonardas knew it, then in fact it was all over town: it had even taken a victim. She wasn't going to be the daughter whose infidelity killed her father. She had to have been driven to it by a lazy, crazy man.

Tiffany tugged slightly on his ear. His head moved to the right, his hand lifting just a bit as though ready to shoo away a fly. He wasn't waking up.

The car was loaded. Anthony was at her sister's. She'd already gotten the paperwork for a restraining order, and would file it that afternoon. Steven was a threat to her, and they'd believe it. He hadn't actually threatened her, or touched her with anything even approaching violence—but there wasn't a judge in Travis County who would hesitate to sign an order that a teary-eyed woman submitted, especially in that old grey house frock. The liability was just too great. The fact that he'd been drinking heavily for a year was enough. She'd been saving the receipts since Leonardas started trying to buy her away from him. So what if he never even had a DUI. If she said he was prone to domestic violence, he was. If she said he was a danger to her son, grandson of Representative Morales, it was a fact.

This would be a shock. And you never know, he could react violently. But it was his own fault. He'd told her that they'd land on their feet. That if they took risks, they'd be rewarded. "You jump, I'll catch" he said on the night he'd talked her into going full term with Anthony, "and everything else will take care of itself."

It hadn't, and now she was taking care of him. He'd lied to her. Not deliberately, not with some kind of willful deceit—he simply didn't know how hard the world was to live in, and had convinced her for a short time that it was much easier than it was. She needed someone else in her life, someone who could protect her and let her be wonderful, someone like Tim. Steven couldn't even fend for himself, and she couldn't let Tony be corrupted by that attitude. She had to protect him. If Tony were left under Steven's guidance, he'd wind up being the brightest mechanic in San Marcos, and spend his weekends playing pool and watching wrestling and going on about how the jet contrails in the sky overhead are really just mind-control drugs to make us all gay to control the population. She needed more for him. She needed him to be exposed to the life you can lead when you're truly ambitious.

It was nearly 7am now. Tim was waiting for her downtown. They'd go to a little apartment he rented for her, something temporary until his divorce was final. And they'd make love, and he'd wrap his arms around her, and tell her about the yellow kitchen they'd have, and how he'd make sure she never wanted for anything ever again. He was going to run dozens of stores soon. He could pay for private school. And he didn't self-destruct whenever the pressure was on.

She suddenly realized Steven's eyes were open, and looking at her questioningly.

"You okay?" He asked.

"How did you sleep?" She couldn't look him in the eyes. How stupid, she thought at first—and then realized, it had to be because he was so threatening. He had no right to try to intimidate her.

"Okay, I guess. But I'm still tired."

"Go back to sleep."

"You want to make love?"

She exhaled heavily. "Sure."

"No, that's okay," he said, "maybe later, though, huh?" He closed his eyes and breathed deeply, slipping back into sleep.

She kissed his forehead, letting her lips rest for just a moment on his skin, and took his left hand in hers. She squeezed it with more force than she expected to. "Yeah. Maybe later today."

Tiffany felt surprised by her own words, and the warmth it spread through her body. She was about to do something hideous. And at the same time, she felt herself compelled to make love with him. It was a strong compulsion, so strong she jerked up from the bed to control it.

The contradiction seemed to shatter a part of her, and she stumbled like a drunk down their hallway to the living room. She picked up the kitchen phone and called her sister.

"Maria." She always knew she'd have to be dramatic during this phone call, but she hadn't anticipated not having to act to achieve the affect.

"What's wrong?" It was still early enough that Maria would be in her bathrobe, preparing for a lunch with a fellow Junior League member or a trip to Nieman's. Anthony would be sitting in the living room watching *Elmo's World*.

"It's about Steven. I need your help."

"What happened?"

"I can't talk about it—it's—I just can't. Meet me at Quack's in 30 minutes?"

"Absolutely."

"And Maria—"

"Yeah, Tiff?"

"I'm going to need a lawyer. A good one. One who knew Daddy."

She hung up, knowing she'd thrown her sister into a panic. Without warning, she felt her digestive system twist-—and tried made it to the hall bathroom in time to vomit, but wound up leaving a trail of her stomach fluids on the carpet leading into the room.

As she wiped her mouth, she looked at herself in the bathroom mirror.

So this is what betrayal looks like. I'll have to look worse than this in court.

It had been two years, and the Sally Experiment, as it was earlier known, had become merely 'The Experiment,' and even then it had been almost half a year since it came up.

The first few months had been difficult for Katherine, but as always, Jeremy simply helped her along. She didn't want to have sex of any kind for several weeks, and would occasionally cry when certain songs came up. "Jackie Blue" somehow made a resurgence of radio airplay on the classic rock station Jeremy liked to listen to in the car, and he never objected when Katherine would spring forward and turn off the radio within a second of hearing even one note of it. Jeremy retired the entire *Have a Nice Day* collection to the garage so as not to needlessly upset her.

She'd not been as graceful in the breakup as she had hoped to be. She'd called Sally a few times at work (there was no way she'd risk talking to Zachary), and the first time Sally even took the call. Katherine had asked if there was anything she could do, Sally had quietly said no. Katherine was struck from how confident Sally's voice was when she answered, and how quickly it seemed to shrink once Katherine asked.

"I know you want me to leave you alone. But I need to know if you're in any danger." Katherine practically pleaded for more information.

Almost every child at forty knows that this question, when directed at you after a breakup, does not mean that the person is actually worried about your safety or emotional well being, even if they genuinely believe they are when they ask about you. The question is an attempt to re-establish intimacy where it has been denied. "I'm worried about you" literally means "let me back in, let me feel what it's like to be a part of your inner life again."

The parties who break things off know this, although they occasionally fall for it anyway. Most people who have been shut out usually feel the lie of it on some level. That doesn't keep them from trying, especially when their shock or loneliness is at its most acute.

Sally didn't say anything.

"I worry Zach is hurting you."

"Zach never hurts me. Please leave me alone."

Katherine sat on the phone, trying to fight tears back.

Sally's voice wavered. "If you ever cared about me, leave me alone. Please."

Katherine hung up without answering—then called back and got Sally's voice mail, and apologized for being so rude by hanging up. Then, sensing that wasn't enough, she called again, this time Sally's secretary picked up and immediately asked to take a message, and Katherine was forced to confine her final remarks to, "no, not really. Just tell her I understand."

She wasn't proud about this, but that happens sometimes. Sally wouldn't be angry.

Jeremy had been extra attentive—cooking for her again, everything she liked. She'd even put on some weight and he didn't say a thing, which surprised her because he knew her body so well, and although he'd never said so in so many words, he liked her to be fit.

When she'd come home after the breakup, Jeremy asked what was upsetting her, and when she answered, he nodded knowingly, which only made her more confused.

She slowly stopped thinking of Sally, and life began to run its normal path again. Friday nights resumed after a few months, and Katherine was pleased to know how almost nine years had passed since their wedding and she could still turn him on with a loosely tied robe.

But she continued to wonder if she was going to keep his interest. He'd loved The Experiment; so had she. When she fantasized, which wasn't as often as she used to, Sally was still a part of the daydream more often than she was comfortable with.

On a December morning, after taking a shower and distinctly imagining Sally soaping up her breasts from behind (this is how they would almost finish their afternoons, with a long, tender shower together. The motion was sensual, not erotic, and always gave Katherine a sense of peace and well being after what she on some level couldn't help thinking was the debauchery of the day), Katherine came down and saw Jeremy drinking a cup of coffee and reading the paper. He looked genuinely bored. This might be her fault. There was something she might be holding from him.

"Do you think I'm a lesbian and I just don't know it?"

Jeremy was shocked enough to fold his newspaper down with more than the usual snap. "I thought you'd settled that. Has she been in touch?"

"No, honestly, no. I just have this nagging thing. Do you think I am?"

"I'd find that a little hard to believe. Maybe you've just got a bisexual streak. Do you know any other lesbians?"

"No."

"Are you sure? I always just thought every woman has a little lesbian in her."

"Really?" Katherine was too upset to deal with any kind of humor.

"Well, not literally. It's just something guys say to each other when we're joking around. Probably because we find women so damn beautiful that we don't understand how anyone else couldn't." Jeremy assumed that smile he got when he felt very clever. She didn't always like that smile; it made her feel stupid too often.

Jeremy seemed to sense her response. "Look, if you're really worried, see a counselor. Or hell, find a lesbian and talk to her."

That night Katherine began her lesbian quest on AOL. She posted her question and gave a few details, but mostly what she got back were more requests for details—the sexual details, mind you, not anything about how Katherine and Sally felt about each other. They overwhelmed her mailbox. One did stand out, a short email by a self-described lesbian, who wrote very simply that these are the kinds of questions that you can only answer for yourself, which makes it harder, but most gay and lesbian people she's ever met have always known on some level that's who they were, even as small children. If she didn't have that intuitive feeling, it probably was just a curiosity.

Not to be deterred (because she hadn't found the answer she wanted—that one was too tough to process), she searched for "lesbians and Milwaukee" on a new thing called a 'search engine' (the web site was northernlights. com, which seemed really good, but it charged you for almost every result that had a document available. "That sucks," she thought. "What if I don't like the document I buy?" A thought which millions shared.) One of the prominent search results was for a lesbian choir; it was at a church nearby. She paid the website 99 cents to get a copy of the church's newsletter and found out the location and time. She was going to go talk to them.

Jeremy was curious. "A lesbian choir at a church in Milwaukee? What kind of church?"

"Unitarian Universalist Fellowship, it says."

Jeremy got that clever smirk again and didn't say why.

She arrived on a Friday afternoon, just before the choir practice began. A lot of the women there just couldn't be lesbians, they looked like every other woman she knew. She saw a short, overweight woman with buzz-cut hair and three earrings on one ear (this must be code, she thought), wearing a stained t-shirt. This was what real lesbians looked like.

"Excuse me." Katherine was polite.

"Hey." The woman responded with a nod.

"I know you guys are about to practice—"

"Rehearse."

"Yeah, well, I had a real important question about, you know, sexuality. Can I have a moment of your time?"

Katherine had felt like one of those telemarketers who called at dinner every night, so she was relieved when the woman looked her over (almost like Zach had, but Katherine didn't quite make the connection) and said, "shoot."

She explained The Experiment, and how things fell apart when they got their husbands involved, and that she thought she wasn't really a lesbian, but the breakup was bothering her more than she thought it should if she weren't one. She loved her husband more than anything, even loved sex with him, and wanted to make him happy above all.

She'd said it all so quickly she was nearly breathless. "So, am I really a lesbian and I just don't know it?"

The woman laughed. "No, honey, you ain't no lesbian. You were just curious, and you found out the most you might be is a suburban bisexual. Try to find another one."

Katherine explained about how Sally resembled so much the girl she'd had a crush on as a child, Amy, and she didn't want another lesbian. It was too complicated and she didn't really love Sally the way she loved her husband.

"Well, honey," the woman paused the way you do when you're about to say something harsh, "then what you are is a dilettante lesbian. And that's not one of us." She seemed to know instantly that her attempt to be blunt was too much for Katherine, then added, more softly. "That's okay, sweetie. There's a whole lot of you running around. Causes most of us a hell of a lot of grief because you walk and talk like a lipstick lesbian, but at the end of the day, you'll never leave your husband, and that shit gets old after a while. Now if you'll excuse me, I gotta join the others—we're singing Christmas carols next week and the Fellowship ain't all that happy about it. They don't much like us using the J-word. Believe that? Unitarians, they love the freaks, but don't you go talkin' about Jesus."

Katherine had no idea what that meant. But as the woman was leaving, she called out "thank you. Thank you very much."

The woman turned around, looked at Katherine again in that devouring way that Zach did just before Katherine had taken off her clothes that Sunday afternoon, and shook her head in mock sadness. With a chuckle, she just whispered "god damm," and walked away.

Katherine felt better and better on the way home, and when Jeremy arrived, she'd prepared a quiche and used as much bacon as would fit in the pan—his favorite. Actually, anything with bacon would do, but she wanted this to be special. He came into the kitchen, where she gleefully announced, like she'd just gotten the results of a pregnancy test: "Guess what? I'm not really a lesbian!"

Jeremy laughed out loud and gave her a big hug, unthreatened as though he knew that only Katherine could turn her sexuality into some kind of factual pronouncement, like "I got into Harvard!" But she'd always been that way, as long as she could remember. Things were settled or they were not. Why not get excited when they're settled?

"I suppose that's good news for me."

They had dinner together, Katherine talking a mile a minute about a vacation they should take, someplace far away and interesting, like the Caribbean. She was going to search online right after she cleaned up the kitchen.

She spent hours looking up destinations, and found that Puerto Rico might be fun, if they could learn enough Spanish. Jeremy seemed open to it.

When they got to bed that night, Katherine was so tired from the emotional roller coaster of the day that she fell asleep before Jeremy could even get undressed, even though she had fully intended to give him a long hair tent, one of the kind where she would sense his climax and ease off, making him last as long as possible. But she was simply too tired, and drifted away the moment she pulled the covers up. Her last waking thought was that she was so glad she'd put this to bed. It wasn't fair to Sally, her not knowing. She didn't want to be a pain in the ass to anyone.

In the middle of the night, she woke up with a start. She'd just had a dream about Zachary, a graphic, unsettling dream. She felt the blood rushing to her center and realized her genitals were moist. She turned to look at Jeremy, as though he might have caught her doing something wrong. He was asleep, his mouth slightly open, with the faint snore emerging every few seconds.

She didn't go back to sleep that night. She kept hearing the coo of a baby somewhere.

But two months later, as they were on their flight to Aruba (Puerto Rico seemed too foreign, she'd told Jeremy, eliciting that smirk again), she finally figured it out. She looked over at Jeremy, who was thumbing through the airline's shopping catalogue, looking at all the cool products that you should be able to buy anywhere but can't (that always frustrated her, because she'd get all excited about something she wanted to buy, then forget to take the catalogue with her, and suddenly have no clue what it was she'd been excited about). He was looking at solar-powered lawn torches, noticed she was watching him, and he pointed them out to her. "Could be useful," he said.

She decided they'd have a talk after getting settled in the hotel in Aruba. Someplace quiet, on the beach, and they'd have drinks with little umbrellas in them.

# CHAPTER NINE

## Formative and Summative Research

*esame Street* is the most researched television program in history. In fact, one of the off-putting elements of the show for the television producers involved, even before it was launched, was the fact that researchers would be telling them what to do. TV producers knew what worked for kids: they didn't need a bunch of Dexters in lab coats telling them how to be creative. Many suspected it was a power grab, in part because most TV producers are incapable of imagining that there actually exist people who have no desire to be TV producers.

But Joan Ganz Cooney was persistent, and, well, she had a boatload of money from the government and from the Ford Foundation, and TV producers can overcome their distaste for research if the research comes with enough cash. This keeps many marriages together as well, which Cooney perhaps knew when she described the creative and research partnerships of *Sesame Street* as being a marriage of sorts.

The formative research was innovative—in fact, the term was coined only a couple of years before. Test the hell out of the segments that comprise each show; design them to achieve concrete goals. Phrase those goals in such language as, "the child will learn—." Learn what distracts children from the television and heighten the segments' attractiveness. Repeat the hell out of segments, just as advertisers do, so that the lesson is learned. In the first seasons, it was not uncommon to see the exact same animated lesson run four times in one hour.

This was formative research. It's more commonplace now, but in 1969, when our foursome was about to be among the first to receive its benefits, it was groundbreaking.

"Summative research" is a 1960s lab coat word for "feedback." What's working? What isn't? How do children's tastes change over the years? Kids of *Sesame Street* age today wouldn't sit still for even fifteen minutes of a *season one* episode. The early ones don't move fast enough. Kind of bugs me. We worked hard on those.

It's this kind of awareness, being mindful of how effective your entertainment is, that continues to make *Sesame Street* such a strong program: it's also why *The Electric Company*, which was so trendy at the time that it had become unintentional comedy of the highest order by the time production stopped in 1977. It was popular, but it didn't have anything like the Muppets to make them money outside of the show. It wasn't a brand you could buy in stores. They used reruns until 1985 until words like "groovy" made kids smirk instead of smile.

What about that brand you could buy in stores? The Muppets themselves never saw any money, but their operators did. And summative research provided Jim Henson and Frank Oz and their Muppeteers with a competitive advantage no single troupe of performers have ever had: almost a decade of research-based feedback.

To this day, after producers finish a film or a TV show, they call in a focus group audience to give feedback. Sometimes the questions are basic: did you like the film, did you like the ending, what about character B, etc. Rarely are they more insightful queries, because producers still feel that their gut instincts give them a better read on what audiences want than any "research" could provide (add snarled emphasis, theirs).

Jim Henson didn't make that mistake. He listened, he offered new ideas, he abandoned the ones that didn't work, and grew. We all did.

This is part of our problem, a problem that isn't likely to be repeated. Henson was one kind of artist when Steven watched *Sesame Street* in the early 70s, but quite a different, more seasoned artist by the time *The Muppet Show* debuted. And our friends were exactly at the right age to experience both: they were the core demographic at each stage of Henson's development as an artist.

So when Jim died on May 16, 1990, there was no one left to take these four on to the next steps. The steward of their imagination fell silent. They were on their own. New researchers, new performers, new ideas were all around, and very competent ones, I might add; but they weren't Jim. Nobody misses him more than I do. He raised our imaginations and brought them to fruition.

To die of severe pneumonia was simply a waste on so many levels. At least, that's what everyone thought killed him. In fact, the bacteria that devoured him was the *Streptococcus pyogenes*, the bacterial species that causes strep throat and rheumatic fever.

The same kind Steven was slowly accumulating in his own body without even knowing it. And, like those around Jim Henson, nobody could see anything but a lack of energy and an occasional annoying cough. Unlike Jim Henson, Steven was systematically losing anyone who would care to notice.

Steven shuffled out of the hallway of his apartment, half-awake, scratching his pubococcygeus muscle when he entered the living room. He stepped back, the breath momentarily taken from him by what he saw. Complete disarray. Couch cushions thrown against the wall. Glasses shattered on the floor. Wide open pantry doors in the adjoining kitchen, their contents in pieces adorning the fake ceramic tile. A lamp shade askew on the ground, its base broken, its light bulb flickering along to the faint sound of electrical arcing in the receptacle.

His wallet was on the counter, untouched.

He tried to cross the living room when he stepped on a shard of glass. He hopped back towards the bedroom, bleeding profusely, and didn't even wipe off his hands as he called Tiffany.

She didn't answer. He left a message. "Tiff, you okay? Something happened, I don't know—was there an earthquake? I don't remember anything,

I must have been really knocked out. I can't believe – I can't believe this happened. Call me, let me know you're okay. What happened? I'm so sorry I didn't hear anything. Please be okay."

He was still dressing his foot when banging started on the door. He limped to answer it in his white tank-top and boxer shorts, and when he opened it just a crack, was shocked at the sight of the three police officers with requisite moustaches.

The lead officer's gun was drawn. Steven was instructed to lie face down on the ground as he was handcuffed.

"What happened?" Steven wanted to know why they were there.

"Shut up!"

Steven shut up as his rights were read to him; he kept quiet until he could ask for his lawyer, Francisco, a computer gaming friend of his, who showed up to tell Steven that Tiffany reported that he'd beaten her in a jealous, drunken frenzy before trashing the apartment.

This was nonsense.

"But this is Tiffany Morales, man."

He knew who she was.

Three days later, the recording was seamless. Steven sat beside Francisco as his voice played, heavily redacted. "Tiff, you okay? I don't remember anything. I was just out of it. I can't believe – I can't believe this happened. I'm so sorry. Call me, let me know you're okay. Please be okay."

The prosecutor explained this kind of call was common after a man beats his wife; the immediate remorse, the attempt to deflect guilt with a convenient memory loss. The evidence remained: recordings of frantic phone calls from the victim to 911, a completely trashed living room and kitchen, blood everywhere. Pictures of the victim's bruised face, testimony of the officer who photographed her and took her initial statement, the tearful deposition from Maria Louisa Wells Morales, Miss Austin 1991, who had known Steven was violent but was too afraid to speak up about her observations until it was too late and would consequently be haunted for the rest of her life for not standing up for her big sister earlier.

After a short recess, Steven pleaded *nolo contendere* on his lawyer's advice, and received a restraining order and a six-month probated sentence for assault, during which he could only see Anthony in a supervised setting.

On his way out of the courtroom, he was served with a petition for sole custody and a civil suit seeking to prevent Steven from visiting Anthony for no less than two years.

That was a civil matter, Francisco said, and shook his hand before leaving.

"I want to see my son." Steven demanded, in such a way that made Francisco begin to doubt Steven's temper. After three or four hallroom negotiations, it was agreed that Steven could speak with Tony right then and there, with both lawyers present. Tiffany would be shaking perversely as though in a petite mal seizure the entire time.

The lawyers approached with Tony. Francisco made a point of saying "off the record, right?"

"Right." The other lawyer had already won.

Steven got down on his knees in front of Tony, both of them trying not to cry, Tony succeeding better than Steven. "Listen, Tony. I'm not going to be around as much in the house as I used to be?"

"Why?" Steven sensed an interminable "why" debate and cut it short.

"Daddy made a mistake, and Mommy needs a little space. Do you understand?"

Tony shrugged.

"But I need you to do one thing for Daddy, okay? Promise me you will do this one little thing."

Both lawyers stiffened. Francisco put his hand on Steven's shoulder.

"No matter what Mommy says about Daddy; no matter what you think sounds wrong or right or mad or happy, I want you to believe her. Mommy will always tell you the truth and you are to do what she says. Do you understand me?"

Tony stepped back, then reached forward and hugged Steven.

"Whatever she says, Tony. She loves you more than anything," Steven lied. Tony would remember this conversation and Steven didn't want to be hated in twenty years. "Mommy is always right."

Tony cried in full voice, concerning Tiffany down the hall; her lawyer gently guided Tony back to the floor and walked away with him, Tony walking only halfway so he could keep staring at his father.

When they'd left the corridor, Francisco leaned over and said, "That was either the bravest thing I've ever seen, or you've set a time bomb in that boy that's going to go off in about ten years when he realizes what she's done to you."

"I'm the time bomb, Frank. Whether it's a giant bird or a gorilla eating cookies believing in something generally is better than fighting at that age."

Francisco looked confused.

"Quit trying to think and buy me a damn beer."

"You're on probation."

"Then buy it at your house."

Two days later he broke into the house while Tiffany was at work, packed a bag and his laptop, and left the state. He emptied his individual bank account of $8,500, and traded his 1998 Volvo ("Out of work, no commute, low miles.") for a 1966 Studebaker Cruiser and another $1100 cash.

Tiffany would come home, see what happened, and file a police report, violating his probation. It was time to start over. As Steven started his new car with Iowa plates, he wondered why he always had to be pushed to do something right. It fired up, and the hum of an old Studebaker made questions like that largely irrelevant.

Jeremy watched as the other men flirted with Katherine. Six men in their twenties, all of them strangers, but to look at them, there were no strangers in this bar. They were united by a common goal. Katherine laughed at all of their jokes, she flashed her eyes when they said something suggestive, and her hand fell on their shoulders regularly as she continued to drink.

Jeremy was prepared for this. They'd agreed upon it in Aruba. At the time he didn't know how he felt about it, and it had taken him months to come around to the idea. But Katherine had been patient, and her point of view was so innocent, and yet so ruthless, that he figured it had to be worth trusting. He'd trusted her with Sally and look how wonderfully that turned out for him.

The sun had been directly overhead, the perpetually bent palm trees offering little natural shade – all the palm trees on Aruba lean in one direction only, the wind is so consistent--he'd spent the morning gambling in one of the casinos, had won a little money playing craps, and then celebrated with Katherine by indulging her in what she liked to do most at the beach: sit still, drink blended concoctions with umbrellas in them, and read magazines about famous people. He couldn't stand just sitting still all day in one place, even though he could easily be accused of doing so at home in front of the television on weekends. But the tables had been good, Katherine wanted this, and he wanted to make her happy.

For his part, he drew the line at piña coladas in fancy glasses, and drank Balashi straight from the fire-plug looking can. And he was in mid-sip when Katherine blurted out the question:

"What if I started flirting with other guys?"

Jeremy spit half of his mouthful back into the can and said, with every ounce of his weighty vocabulary, "Huh?"

"I've been thinking about it. I don't want you to stop wanting me."

"Who said anything about not wanting you anymore? I'm crazy about you."

"I know," said Katherine with an aire that told Jeremy he'd told her that once too often, maybe a thousand times too often. A part of her couldn't believe it anymore, he feared. "It's just that I've read about the seven year itch and all that, and I know we kind of put it off with The Experiment," (Katherine would still never mention Sally by name if she could help it), "but that was a fantasy for me. What about a fantasy for you?"

"Trust me. That fantasy was doing just fine for me."

"That's what I mean! That was then – this is different. You let me have mine and we kind of, well, rewarded you for it. And it meant so much to me. What kind of fantasy have you wanted that I've never given you?"

Jeremy stopped to think, his backwashed beer halfway to his lips. He knew the honest answer. He didn't even have to think about it. It was what he'd always wanted from a woman, but could never ask for. And he could never ask Katherine.

"I don't know. Never really thought about it."

"Oh come on. Guys have fantasies all the time. Who is on your exempt list?"

"My exempt list?"

"Yeah, that's the list of people you'd have sex with if you knew you could get away with it, no consequences, no regrets, no punishment. It's usually movie stars."

She was so enthusiastic that he had to say something. "Oh, I don't know, Ingrid Bergman – "

"They have to be alive!!"

"Yeah, that would be kind of gross. Let's see. Okay, movie stars: Halle Berry – "

"Every guy says Halle Berry!"

"Halle Berry, Salma Hayek-"

"She's got hair like mine. I like that."

"And that's it. Really. I haven't thought about it." He couldn't tell her that the other three were women he'd noticed – the girl with the nose piercing at the bookstore, his secretary Zoe, and one girl they'd gone to college with together, who still appeared in his memory often.

This omission didn't seem to bother Katherine. "Nicholas Cage, Christian Slater, Harrison Ford circa Indiana Jones, Pierce Brosnan, and Bill Clinton."

"Bill Clinton?"

"Right up to the end of his second term, then he suddenly got old. But I bet he'd be hot. That was what the whole Monica thing was about. If he hadn't been so hot and she was so average-looking, nobody would have cared."

This theory fascinated Jeremy. He sat up, giving her the cue to go on. "Seriously. If a hot person cheats with a hot person – and being powerful made him so attractive – then we all just accept it and move on. When a 10 has an affair with a 5, and his wife's a 9, then something is up and everybody wants to talk about it."

"Hilary Clinton is a 9?"

"The same way Kissinger was." Katherine said it so matter-of-factly that it took a moment for him to realize she was aware of politics. It was so easy to underestimate Katherine; but she was the one who always took the best notes in college. If you told her something, she stored it away in her mind. She didn't always think about it, but it was there, like the Christmas feeling you get when you unpack a box from storage and discover contents you had completely forgotten you had. That was it. Katherine was like a perpetual Christmas.

Jeremy looked into Katherine's vibrant eyes. "So there's nobody we know on this exempt list? That's where I thought you were going."

"No, I was just saying, would it be a turn on for you if I flirted with other guys? Nothing would happen, we'd just go to some bar and flirt, and you can watch like you're not there with me, and I think it would turn you on."

"Sounds like it would turn you on."

"No, I don't care. I just want to keep you interested."

"So tonight, we go somewhere and you flirt?"

"If you want to try it. See how it feels."

That night she'd left the main hotel, as they agreed, and took a seat at the bar in a restaurant nearby where there seemed to be a lot of young, good looking men. Jeremy, as agreed, waited fifteen minutes, and entered to try to find someplace to sit where he could watch her.

There was no place for anyone to sit. He ordered a beer and stood back towards the exit door, watching Katherine sit and wait for someone to offer her a drink.

It wasn't happening. Jeremy looked around. Nobody was even looking at her. How rude was that? Sure, she wasn't twenty-two anymore, but –

Oh God, he thought as he double-checked. Every couple there was comprised of men. They hadn't realized it, but they'd chosen Aruba's one gay bar to try the new experiment in. Jeremy felt himself being checked out as he retrieved Katherine.

"So soon?"

"This isn't our kind of place, hon."

"What do you mean?" Katherine hadn't noticed.

"You see any other girls here?"

Katherine looked around, then laughed out loud, finally garnering some attention. "And here I thought I just had a competitive advantage!"

They laughed about it after making love that night in their room. When they were done, Katherine asked, "didn't that turn you on a little? I mean, before you found out I was in a gay bar?"

Jerome shrugged. Maybe it did.

"Let's think about it, then. Maybe sometime after we get back home."

Six months later, he was watching Katherine command every man's attention in the pool-hall side of a bar on the other side of Milwaukee. She was getting good at it. This was the fifth time and the fifth pub, and whatever shyness she reported on the way to the first attempt, she was clearly beyond it now. Jeremy couldn't make up his mind how he felt about it.

She wasn't going to go to bed with any of them, and strangely, they all seemed to know that. There was a certain aura about her—they knew she was somehow unapproachable, which is why her flirtations were even more outlandish. Katherine told Jeremy it was all a game, and she was learning how to play it.

The game she played the most was "help me, I can't play pool very well." There was never a shortage of volunteers who were willing to lean over her, place her hands in the right position on the long hard pool cue, and when she'd screw up purposefully they'd laugh and reset her hips to a more suitable angle. Usually the guys in the area would stick around long enough to see who could get away with the most, which meant a lot of 'accidental' caresses on the small of her back, touches on her arms as she spread out into position, the requisite comment about her firm backside as she leaned over the table.

As their experiences grew, Jeremy became less worried about her behavior and safety, and more bothered by the guys in the bars. They all did the same thing. How could this possibly work? How could any of these idiots pull the same moves on this beautiful woman that they might pull on a bar skank and expect it to work? He began to wonder if he'd been so obvious, so vulgar, when he was dating.

Tonight, one guy was different. His name was Wayne, and like everybody else, Wayne was eager to put his arms around her as they played pool. She seemed to roll back into his embrace playfully, as though that's where she belonged. He definitely liked it, and as soon as he showed it too much, with one glance down too many, she'd back away, flitting off to talk to another one of the boys (never Jeremy) or to take another poorly planned shot on the pool table.

Even after months of processing this, he couldn't understand what she was doing. Was she trying to tell him something? Was he supposed to say something, to get jealous? Or was he supposed to be secure and enjoy the attention his wife generated from other men? Which response was normal? Which did she want?

Katherine laughed him into alertness. Some guy he'd never seen before was trying to teach her how to play pool. He stood behind her, giving instructions, and waited for her to automatically assume the shooting position, crouching down, sticking her ass out. When she did, it settled right into his crotch for a moment. She jumped away and yelled "oh my god!" and started laughing.

Jeremy felt himself grin a little as Katherine looked over at him, her eyes flashing. His grin went away as he realized she wasn't sharing anything with that look. It wasn't a 'look what this guy did' look, or a 'don't worry, honey, I'm only yours' look. In fact, it was as though he were another part of the wall, like he blended in with the tacky old ceramic signs and neon beer ads behind him.

It only took him a second to realize that wasn't happening. She was definitely trying to keep him interested. Katherine didn't lie about anything.

Jeremy was momentarily distracted in his internal debate when Wayne had to slide past him in the crowd, his hands laden with two drinks that were apparently called "cocaine shooters." Jeremy stood up a little straighter between the pool table and the wall to let him past.

Wayne smiled at him. "Hey, this is going well." He whispered with an aire of complicity.

Without realizing it, Jeremy laughed and said, "give it your best shot, buddy."

"Oh hell, man, she's just playing. I don't know who she's going home with, but it isn't any of us. Her old man probably can't get it up anymore. Never hurts to try, though, right?" He shuffled optimistically towards her.

Jeremy cocked his head, surprised. He should be furious. He should go over and pour the cocaine shooter down over this clown's head, grab him by his wet nasty hair over the pool table, and shove the cue up his ass to teach him from hitting on married women. Especially if he somehow knew she was married.

Except he agreed to this experiment, so he couldn't do any of that. Jeremy watched Katherine laughing and realized, deep down, that a part of him, down at the base of his spine, was tingling. With the jealousy, with the adrenaline of the fight he was imagining, and, he had to admit, with the idea of another man actually having sex with her.

This excited him. Katherine was right.

That night, Katherine seemed slightly distant when they were making love. Not the kind of distance he could perceive when she knew she wasn't in it for an orgasm and was therefore performing a service out of marital affection—but an honest dissatisfaction. Even the slow sway of her breasts as he moved above her seemed to suggest disappointment.

"What's wrong?"

"I don't know."

"Are you drunk? Those shooters were pretty strong – "

"You had one?"

"I wanted to know what he was buying you. I had to water it down."

"Oh. Yeah. I didn't finish mine."

"Was he a jerk or something?"

"Yeah, kind of. Not in a real way, but he reminded me too much of—(she couldn't say Zach or the Butch woman)—I just didn't like the way he looked at me. I haven't liked the way any one of them has looked at me. I'm sorry."

"Why on Earth be sorry?"

"Because I wanted this to be something you'd like, gorgeous." Jeremy loved it when she called him gorgeous, even more than when she called him handsome. He knew he wasn't handsome, but it would take someone in love with him to call him gorgeous.

He smiled. "I kind of liked it tonight. It was tingly, in a this-place-is-gross kind of way."

"I know, we were like the only ones there over thirty-five, except for those old divorced women who were just begging for someone to talk to them."

"You noticed that too?" Jeremy laughed. "I almost went to buy that redheaded one a drink, but I was afraid she'd devour me."

The word redhead quieted Katherine immediately. "Yeah, you'd be taking your life into your own hands there." She paused. "Jeremy?"

"What, my love?"

"Let's not ever be that lonely."

He kissed her and rolled off of her, pulling her so she could fall asleep with her head on his chest and her hair all over his shoulders. She absent-mindedly massaged his left arm. "I don't like doing this."

"Then we won't do it."

"And you'll still love me? You'll still want me? I know my body's changing."

"Don't be silly. I'll always want you."

"You have to tell me what you'd want me to do for your fantasies."

"I told you," Jeremy lied, "there's nothing more I could ask from you."

She sighed heavily, and as he felt her begin to drift away into sleep, he knew that she was still uncertain. There was going to be a next step. That fact disconcerted him a little; but he had to admit, as his eyes closed, that given Katherine's imagination, she'd propose something interesting soon.

"Some old man at home who couldn't get it up." Maybe the whole time Katherine had been asking for more playfulness it was to get a sign of more virility from me, Jeremy thought. But that would be borderline manipulative, and he'd never put Katherine in that category.

He slept fitfully at night, and dreamt he was a smoker who wore leather jackets everywhere.

Tiffany looked at Tim's new BMW 535 and frowned. Tim was surprised.

"I thought you'd like it."

"It's not really you, though."

"Maybe it is me, and I've never had a chance to explore this part of me before."

"You're forty-eight years old."

"So?"

Tiffany paused. She hadn't counted on Steven to just up and disappear, although she wasn't very surprised by it. She thought he'd fight harder for Anthony. When he was around, she had a foil, someone she could blame almost anything on, and Tim's energy would be spent defending her and being her white knight on a horse.

Without Steven to defend her from, Tim was left on his own too often emotionally. He had nothing to worry about, so he spent his energy trying to impress Tiffany instead of working harder for all of them. It started when he spent far too much money decorating her apartment with expensive Chinese furniture, then when he started wearing only highly visible expensive logo clothes, and now this. She was fine with his old convertible Chrysler, even if it was a wreck. It told her that he was more interested in moving forward than in staying in place.

The BMW was too self-satisfied, she thought. He hadn't earned that yet. And someone was going to have to pay for it, because Tim had been forced to disclose massive credit card debt during his divorce, which almost made her want Steven back. Steven didn't spend money he didn't have; and if he did, he certainly did not keep it a secret.

"You realize we can't afford this."

"Oh, we'll make it. I'll get promoted soon anyway."

"So can't we wait to spend the money until the promotion actually happens?"

"This isn't for me, really. I wanted you to have something to drive that didn't smell like grease all the time."

Tiffany looked at Tim as he propped his head up with a fist under his chin, his belly having grown even larger since the Steven event (it was best not to call it by any other name, as any other name would divulge her role in setting him up). Tim could look amazingly stupid sometimes.

That gave her an idea. How stupid was he? How committed was he? How much did he care about who she really was?

"Well," she said with a hint of tenderness, "obviously you can't give as much to Lisa as before. There's no other way we can pay for this."

Tim stood upright, dropped his hand from his chin, and looked away, suddenly deep in thought. Tiffany watched him like a cat waiting for a grasshopper to come back into view.

"You're right. Besides, I overpaid her last year," He paused. "I think."

Tiffany smiled and patted the BWM on the hood. "It's beautiful."

# CHAPTER TEN

## Your child may become easily bored.
## Try to vary his activities.

Those who had dinner at Jeremy and Katherine's house always found them to be more attuned to each other than most. If you were a guest for a meal there, you didn't sit with Jeremy in the living room and talk Derrida while Katherine banged out a meal in the kitchen. Everyone got involved in the food preparation.

For their part, they'd been doing this long enough that they each knew what to ask of the other. Jeremy was a great sous chef, and seemed to know from sheer routine what Katherine would ask for, and when she'd ask for it. In fact, often she didn't have to ask; she'd make a quarter turn in the kitchen and Jeremy would casually offer a bowl of diced onions, and she'd take it and add it to her dish without a thank you. Not because she wasn't grateful – but because this is simply what they did. Thanking him for that gesture would be somehow inappropriate.

So they did live together quite well, for some time after the "flirt with a stranger" experiment. She would help him with maintenance chores around the house, he'd let her, and wordlessly correct her handiwork when she'd gone — she'd show him interesting sites as the Internet became more and more populated. They'd watch the same television shows and have similar views on them — this always made her happy, because she knew Jeremy didn't like television much, and when she brought him a suggestion for a show, it had better be good.

To see if they could stretch their culinary muscles, she'd even bought a pasta maker that she used precisely twice, because good lord, how could anything be worth that much effort. They got a perfect lasagna with home-made spinach-semolina pasta. On only the second try. And that was enough. She'd grown basil on their back porch too, and loved how happy it made Jeremy to have fresh herbs.

But if there was any consistency in her desires, it was this: once she'd accomplished a goal, it was hard to interest her in doing the same thing again. Become a realtor? Great. Sell a house? Fantastic! What, keep start-ing over and do that again and again? No thanks.

So Katherine went from career to career, trying her hand at decorating for as long as it took to take the courses, pass the exam, and do one client's house. Take a cake decorating class, spend five weekends trying to master a chiffon cake, and give away all her piping bags once she'd done it.

It wasn't just about things for herself alone. To spend more time with her husband, one month she proudly announced, interrupting a football game Jeremy was only mildly interested in, she took up chess, which she knew he'd always loved as a kid and she wanted something to do with him. Beginning that moment, during a wrenching Packers loss that Jeremy was trying simultaneously to follow and forget at the same time, they began their chess experiment.

They played game after game after game, almost nightly, for months, until the rainy Sunday afternoon when she finally beat him — he'd made a silly mistake with his knight, the kind she normally would not have noticed, but she'd been taking chess lessons by secretly playing the chess program that came with her new computer; the one that taught her what she'd done to lose the game. She obsessed about it — she even dreamt of chessboards and brilliant moves —

But once she'd beaten him, there seemed to be no motivation at all for her to play again. She'd set out a goal, accomplished it, and it was time to move on.

This is one of the reasons I don't blame her for Steven as much as you might think later on. Ours might have been the last American generation to be encouraged to go out to play, but we might well have been the first generation to view mastery as play. *Sesame Street* taught us nothing if not to get really good at something and then move on to something else to get good at. As much as it encouraged early reading and command of basic mathematics, it did not exactly prepare its audience for repetitive tasks or assembly line work.

In fact, the opposite mindset was ingrained in most of its audience, and it had become so obvious by the time the initial Streeter kids were twelve years old, that when postal workers in several parts of the country began showing up with guns and killing co-workers, one of the easiest ways to explain the phenomenon was that the U.S. Postal Service was a horrible place to work because it required people to ignore their imaginations and do repetitive tasks that even the auto industry was no longer requiring people to do. They had been treated meanly by mean people who only expected them to be machines. When this happens, angry feelings can build up, and without the emotional vocabulary all the Streeters were mastering, these pour older souls had nothing to do but snap.

This was a very common argument advanced via teachers (especially in gifted programs, where Steven, Jeremy, and Tiffany thrived, and who were more than willing to feel superior to postal workers) and in the evening news, which was by the early 1980s written for Katherine's fourteen-year-old level of literacy and understanding – after all, she'd change the channel (or get her parents to) if they didn't encapsulate the story quickly enough in simple enough terms. This argument was to make the parents, who were raising free thinkers for the first time in history, to believe they were doing the right thing. Nobody talked about this; media critics just lamented the fact that the news, especially with the sudden advent of cable, was being dumbed-down for the masses. That's not why it was being dumbed-down. It was being dumbed-down for the Streeters, who were suddenly in their teens, and the parents who were so proud of raising them on Street principles.

But an awful lot of what makes a marriage work is dull repetition. I wanted to point out here that as badly as Steven adjusted to it, when it came to their marriage, Jeremy and Katherine were actually doing pretty well. For years. The sexual experiments had been to improve their intimacy – and had largely worked. They handled the repetitive acts of their marriage with more than the usual joy – or at least so they'd answer when they were finally in counseling – but at this point, in the absence of the repetitive acts of childhood, Katherine felt a growing problem in their relationship.

Jeremy was different enough to continue to worry Katherine from time to time. She knew she was more intuitively correct in most areas (I will use the cliché of Street Smart), but that Jeremy was somehow just plain smarter (much more *Sesame Street* smart). He had a way of doing tiny things that seemed to almost purposely remind her that he could have been a philosopher if he weren't a marketing advisor, and she couldn't seem to hold a job despite being the only one who could throw from the left field line back to home plate, or catch anyone who made an error in a repetitive task. It didn't matter that he never said that, and Katherine was certain that he didn't really mean it. But the result, which was now seeming to manifest itself as a cycle every couple of years, was that Katherine would start to doubt whether it was within her power to make him happy.

She never quite made the connection herself, but that cycle would usually begin again after a friend or relative would have a baby, and everyone she knew around that person would gather and celebrate and welcome the new life into the world with increasing fanfare as Jeremy and Katherine grew older. It was getting to the point where being a mother was now some kind of deified creature (my words, not hers. She'd say something like "why do they treat moms like they're 'all that?'"), when in the past motherhood was something you just did, and if you did it well, your kid turned out okay. Now moms had to be perfect, kids had to be exceptional, and the failure of a woman to create a new partnership with her husband through having a child meant that eventually, he'd be unhappy. And, the thought continued to her in a far distant voice, so might she. Maybe.

One afternoon after showing a house to a pregnant couple, whose every comment about the dwelling seemed based upon what their unborn child should have ("oh, we simply must close this staircase," etc), Katherine drove past a middle school that was just letting out for the day. The entire street was jammed with traffic, as parents took off of work early or stay-at-home parents rushed to make sure they could all pick up their children from school. Some had to have lived only blocks away. The buses in the school's parking lot were nearly empty.

She might have been expected to look for little versions of her and Jeremy in the crowd of children. But she was looking for tall, athletic red-headed girls instead. Once she realized that, she left the school at beyond a safe speed and had to talk her way out of a ticket.

"Do you know how fast you were going, Ma'am?"

"Do I get a prize for knowing?"

It was a risk, but after a moment of consideration, she continued. "It looks like my husband picked up our kids, which means I'm the one late getting dinner ready. I'm sorry."

The policeman gave her license back. "Just be more careful. Hate to see your kids not coming home because another parent was rushing to cook dinner."

"You're right, of course." And that was how you did that.

One the way home she ruminated. She never got a ride to school from her parents in her life. If she missed the bus, she walked. What was every-body afraid of? "Perverts" was the easy answer, but it didn't seem to account for the fact that all the parents seemed happy to be there. This is how they avoided monotony: having children was anything but boring, right? It was the most beautiful thing in the world, the ultimate act of creativity, as she'd heard almost every one of her friends say as their children grew older.

Jeremy would be a great picker-upper from school, she knew that.

How much was he missing by their lack of a child? She began thinking again about how she could keep him entertained enough to stay with her. It gnawed at her, even in the slightest moments when Jeremy would read a new book—one that she wouldn't understand, she was sure—and call one of his old college friends to discuss it. And she knew he really didn't like working for the city, so his job wasn't fulfilling. It had been a while since he had looked so completely fulfilled. And that she had achieved only by doing something that most of her parent friends couldn't do.

It was up to her. She had to do that again.

That night, she got online and started entering search terms she'd nev-er have thought of before. And she found someplace special.

It looked like any other bar from the outside. No unusual signs, no pictures of naked women or men in the single window next to the front door. Except for the understated neon sign – could neon be understated? Jeremy decided at that moment that it could be – there was no indication that it was anything other than an old warehouse, or maybe a machine shop. The brick walls were painted a clean (if not shimmering) white, and it was only when he opened the door for Katherine that the red lights from inside spilled out, and the sound of music in an adjacent room signaled that it was indeed a social club.

"Are you members?" A friendly looking, massive man asked as they walked into a foyer that was lit rather like a photographer's developing room.

"We'd like to be," Katherine spoke up first, a slight quaking in her voice. Jeremy was glad she was nervous, and doubted that her reservations were even in the same universe as his. He had to keep his hands in his pockets to keep them from shaking.

"Fill this out. That'll be sixty dollars for the two of you." He handed over a clipboard with a membership application.

Jeremy reviewed it, and it was remarkably clinical. It looked like a credit card application, except for the fine print wasn't about interest rates, it was about sexuality.

"I agree not to offer payment, accept payment, or conduct any kind of financial transaction in exchange for sexual contact.

"I understand that the dues paid to Amplexus do not guarantee that I will have sexual contact with anyone in the Club, nor does it guarantee I will observe any sexual activity in the club.

"I affirm I am not a member of any law enforcement agency, a government official, a representative of a government agency, or a member of the press.

"I/we promise to use a condom for any sexual contact that is not with my spouse or long-term partner who I know not to have any sexually transmitted diseases."

Everything was pretty straightforward, it seemed. Jeremy wondered what it was they were getting into – and noticed that Katherine seemed pretty nervous herself as she filled out the form. Her handwriting flowed messier than usual across the clipboard, and at one point, she even turned and placed it against Jeremy's chest for stability.

"You up for this?" Jeremy asked, directing the question largely at himself. His job was to attract people to the wonders of downtown Milwaukee. He was pretty sure this wasn't what Uncle Ted had in mind when he got him the job.

"I think so." She giggled and shrugged. All of a sudden she looked like a twelve-year-old girl on her way to a pet shop.

She returned the application, and Jeremy offered his credit card, and thirty seconds later, with a signature on a grey carbon receipt, they were officially swingers.

Inside Amplexus, Jeremy felt an odd electricity in the air, like the entire place was a sexual playground. Actually, he had to correct himself: it looked just like any other non-alcohol-serving club, he imagined, except for the excitement he was bringing to the place with the knowledge that every other person there was more sexually sophisticated than he was.

There were some thirty other couples mingling in the common area, and about the same number of single men and women. The single men looked a bit wolfen, he thought, and had to fight the urge to claim Katherine with an arm on her shoulder or around her waist. Unlike the bars they'd visited before, this was a place where everyone there was not only looking for action, but could reasonably expect to find it. The men who noticed Katherine here were perfectly within their bounds to ask her to have sex.

And this was a place where she could say yes, and Jeremy had given her his blessings as they'd gotten dressed earlier.

"I think we're going to have to know what the boundaries are beforehand." Jeremy had said, staring at his shoes as Katherine applied her lipstick with more than usual attention.

"That's probably a good idea."

"So. What are the boundaries?"

Katherine looked at him in the reflection of her vanity. "I think they should be whatever you're comfortable with, honestly."

"What if you want to go further than I want you to go?"

"I don't."

"Is it that simple?"

Katherine turned around and looked at him with disarming directness. "Yes, it is."

She walked into the closet and started looking at shoes.

"Well, if someone wants to join us, I think that's okay." Jeremy kicked an imaginary ball back and forth between his feet. Sally was off limits still. "But I'm not sure—"

"Not sure what?" Katherine walked out of the closet with red heels.

"I'm not sure I'm ready to be the odd man out."

"Okay. That's fine. What do you think of these?"

"I like them."

"Yeah, I know, but are they sexy?"

Jeremy looked at Katherine, her makeup so expertly applied that he could barely tell she was wearing it – she was wearing a black transparent blouse with a black bra that heightened the rise of her breasts, and a black and white skirt that framed her hips so perfectly that Jeremy was certain that anyone who saw her would feel his hands drawn there.

But red was the wrong color for her shoes. "Try black."

"You're right, you're right." She nearly dove back into the closet.

And now they were approaching the public rooms – and while Jeremy had seen several men scoping her out, nobody had approached them. Maybe nothing would happen.

They arrived at one area with several couples staring through a window. As they neared, Jeremy could see it was a one-way mirror, and the four couples on the three large round beds inside the room couldn't see their observers. This was called the Aquarium Room, according to the sign above the mirror. Jeremy wondered how it was decided who was in and who was out of the aquarium.

Jeremy stood behind Katherine and began absent-mindedly rubbing her shoulders as they moved up to the glass. Each of the four couples was preoccupied with their own actions; this was sex among others, but not group sex in the classical definition.

Jeremy laughed at himself. Was there a classical definition of group sex? Did Plato's definition vary much from Queen Victoria's?

It occurred to him that this was the first time he had ever observed in person other people having full-on sex. One couple was devoted to the missionary position in the nearest bed. Another bed had a woman leaning forward on it, her legs draped down to the floor, while her partner mounted her from behind. The other two couples were on the far bed, with both women astride their partners, rocking back and forth, almost like two race-horses nearing the finish. The blonde with three earrings by a nose.

Jeremy felt Katherine breathing more deeply, and he caressed her sides, from her underarms down along her hips. He looked over to the other observers, and found most of the men were taking far more liberal approaches to caressing their partners. Of the five pairs of hands he could see, four of them were firmly cupping breasts, and the other seemed to be busy working further down.

Katherine's rapid heartbeat was palpable even at her waist. This was what she wanted. And it was okay.

"Do you like this?"

"Yes." She said quickly. "Are you cool?"

"Yeah," Jeremy said, noticing he was better endowed than the man closest to him in the Aquarium Room. That was at least a bit encouraging.

Katherine leaned back against him, and drew his hands up to her breasts. She must have seen the other couples, Jeremy thought as he felt his penis firming up against her skirt.

She squeezed his hands against her and pushed firmly into his crotch, her head leaning back, her eyes closed.

Seeing her, even glimpsing the faint reflection of her in the glass, feeling her coming alive in his hands, Jeremy suddenly felt a surge of power, of generosity, of immense well-being. She wanted to explore and they were exploring, together. This was what she wanted, and so far, he was strong enough to give it to her. He smelled her hair and kissed her on the neck, eliciting a soft moan as she reopened her eyes and watched the bareback couples.

Jeremy smiled. She was so childlike in following her desires, so simple in what she wanted, and so grateful that she was getting it. Jeremy kissed her neck again, and she leaned back even harder against him, moving his erection into her skirt. She was beautiful, young, sexual, and completely his.

The Great Studebaker tour had lasted almost a year now. The routine was the same in every city. Get a job at a local pizza delivery boy. Try to make a few bucks to get ahead. Meet some nice people, sometimes get approached for a management position.

"Ever been in trouble with the law?" The manager would ask, often without looking up.

"Nope. You?" This usually made them laugh, but what gave each interviewer pause was the fact that Steven drove a Studebaker. How do you even get parts for that thing?

"I scrounge 'em up. Kept this one going for longer than the cars your drivers are using."

Et Voila. He had a pizza delivery job. It would usually last about four weeks until the local corporate office did a routine check on his background, then he'd be fired, move to another town that was run by another franchisee, or even once he just put on an old nametag and started working at another branch of the chain. He knew he had a month. He usually got it.

In that vein he saw Albuquerque, Sacramento, Seattle, Coeur d'alene, Lincoln, Des Moines, his Studebaker putting along, his mind slowly and inexorably turning against him. He wasn't going crazy: he just formed a chasm between what he could do in an ideal world (the one he could inhabit before he slammed into Deputy Dawg's golf cart) and the one he was living and breathing now. Occasionally he'd see an ad for a technical school and wonder if he could make a living long enough to get certified in computer repair or network maintenance. But that had always been Tiffany's bag. He was more theoretical: the work he did was big boy work.

And the big boys weren't having him back anytime soon. So he worked with the little boys (literally — as his tour wore on, he found his fellow drivers to be younger and younger. The older ones, one at a time, came up with something to do with their lives.)

He walked into the Pizza Dude near the campus at the University of Wisconsin-Milwaukee. It was this third week, so he wasn't at all surprised when Karen, the store manager, called him into her office.

Pizza manager's offices smell the same everywhere. Here comes the speech.

"Steven, I'd like to talk to you about something that's come up."

Steven sat up and waited to turn in his apron.

She pulled out a flyer. "This is your kind of thing, right?" She said, pointing to the title: *Cat on a Hot Tin Roof*. They're doing a production of it here. Auditions tomorrow. Think you'd be interested?

Steven was taken aback.

"Call me a theatre geek – I graduated with a degree in folklore, now manage a store serving 2800 residents the pizza of their choice on a daily basis. But I know a good actor when I see it. Or," she said, patting a stack of oddly green paper, "when I read about it."

"You can just fire me, there's no need for torture."

"Don't be silly. I'm not going to fire you. Because believe it or not, the great state of Wisconsin has no problems with felons who have broken their probation making the food their children eat. They just don't want them driving nice cars."

"What are you saying?" Steven was rarely speechless, and unaccustomed to the phenomenon.

"I need someone to assistant manage my kitchen. And you need some stability, and frankly, you're a thespian if I ever saw one."

"It's not a very grown up job."

"You're not a very grown up boy. Perfect fit."

Steven left the office in a daze. Auditions? Tiffany and he used to fantasize about them both somehow entering show business, but it was the same crap every couple who thinks too highly of themselves thought. Tiffany had even stopped reading *People Magazine* when she decided that she'd be in it one day and didn't want to read it as a civilian. She'd told him that once in the line at the grocery store and they both cracked up. They were buying two huge boxes of diapers, that when stood in front of either of them, completely obscured their field of vision. The fantasy was a way to see through them.

He left the office wondering what Tony's sizes were now; and if he got the part, should he tell her lawyer or her directly?

Jeremy's head was filled with the sound of his own thoughts, coming furiously at him. How do you stop infidelity? If the entire premise of your relationship has been that you have to be open, free to love each other, then why does it hurt so much that she'd consider loving somebody else?

Jeremy was close to losing his mind, he was sure of that. He sat in the basement rumpus room and talked to himself to try to stay rational.

You asked for this. You told her she should fulfill all of her fantasies, and she took you at face value. Can you possibly go in there now and tell her it's too hard? Can you take your word back? What kind of person does that make you?

It makes you human. It makes you like everybody else, fallible and natural and honest. This is hurting too much. When you told her you could live with an open marriage, you didn't realize how much it would cost you emotionally.

So I have to admit I'm just another middle class bourgeois who clings to his wife because I'm afraid some other man will take her?

What's wrong with that?

I'm supposed to be above that.

That doesn't mean that watching your wife make it with strangers should give you pleasure. There's something to be said for wanting your spouse to desire you only.

Jeremy flipped through the channels on the TV, trying to distract himself. She'd come home soon, he hoped, and they'd go to bed again, and she'd go down on him, stopping every few seconds to tell him some detail about the man she'd had that evening. And her voice would be so tender, with so much trust in it, like they were the only two cool kids at a slumber party, so cool that they had to whisper their secrets so none of the normal kids would hear.

He couldn't keep doing this. His eyes flashed to the wall clock above the TV ten times in one minute. He couldn't stand the waiting, the knowing that somewhere out there, not too far away, his wife was sharing her body with someone he'd never met.

Wasn't that supposed to make you feel like you're generous? You're sharing your bounty with other men.

That sounds like a caveman talking.

Maybe there is something cave mannish about the whole thing. Katherine always said it was a primal urge that was driving her.

But she also gave you so many chances to stop this. She checked with you at every point to see if you were comfortable, and even when it wasn't comfortable, it was exciting enough for you not to mind. And you didn't speak up when you were supposed to, so you can't very well go speaking up now.

The Brewers lost again. No surprise there.

Jeremy gathered himself and considered going to see a movie.

He checked. All the movies playing nearby were about bad marriages or new passions. There wasn't a good shootout movie available – or he could go down to the University and catch a screening of *Jules and Jim*. That didn't seem like a good idea either. Whatever sexuality he'd see on screen he'd magnify in his head.

The sessions at Amplexus had accelerated too quickly. It wasn't just the first time he watched another man kiss her as she caressed Jeremy's erect penis, or the time she rode atop him wile giving fellatio to a man whose name they didn't know. He'd even enjoyed having sex with Katherine in the "mass hysteria" room, comprised of six giant circular beds put together, being one of ten couples having sex in front of each other without shame, without fear – and sharing touches with polite questions: "please, may I?"

None of the people at Amplexus were people anyone would peg as alternative sex practitioners just by looking at them from the street. What struck Jeremy, in fact, was how natural it all seemed. Katherine had even leaned over to him during one of their first visit and said "I thought I'd be seeing a lot of freaks or something. Everyone here is just like me! I mean, us!"

Jeremy looked around and saw a dozen or so couples, dressed in street clothes, eating finger foods from a surprisingly well-appointed buffet. Except for the odd man or woman in lingerie, this could have been a networking reception for real estate agents.

Jeremy watched Katherine taking it all in. "Just like us? Are we this boring?" He meant to laugh just a bit so she'd know he was being self-deprecating, but as he heard himself he realized he'd issued a snobbish type of laughter instead. An audible smirk. Katherine dismissed it with a quick flutter of her eyes in his direction before going back to her people-watching.

"Look at them. I bet he's so strong. She can count on him for anything."

"Really?" The man was a balding insurance salesman type. His wife (or partner) was younger, vivacious, and he seemed to be enjoying watching her have a good time.

"Yeah. It doesn't matter what she wants, he takes care of her, and she takes care of him. I think it's the healthiest couple I've ever seen."

Jeremy felt proud of himself. Katherine's father just wrote checks until he died. Her stepmother always approached her as though she were walking onstage to play "the Aggrieved Stepmother" long enough to get a review, then it was always exit stage left (someone would call, she had an errand in town, always something whose immediacy was directly proportional to how far away Katherine's current obsession was from Mary's sense of propriety).

Maybe she liked this couple because she'd never seen a healthy relationship; so she didn't know what they looked like. Or maybe because she had never been spoon-fed what a healthy relationship was supposed to look like, she could find them where others wouldn't consider to look.

Jeremy was so busy contemplating this that he didn't immediately notice a good looking, black haired blue eyed man approach her. His name was Alex, and almost before Jeremy figured out what was going on, he asked Katherine on a date, and she didn't hesitate to say yes. Jeremy had watched it happen in its entirety, horrified — but when Katherine turned to him with a big, loving smile that seemed to say "aren't you proud of me, honey?" Jeremy found he couldn't object. He was at the helm of the healthiest relationship Katherine ever had.

But that first date night he could feel him touching her, he knew exactly how she would feel in his arms, how she'd look at him before kissing him, the way she'd moan slightly while pinching his lower lip in her teeth . . .

How could he convince her to stop this? With every step she seemed to grow bolder and bolder. Two months ago she never would have gone home with somebody else, even if it was just for sex. Three months ago she was still too shy to go anywhere but Amplexus, because she didn't think guys in regular bars would be as careful.

So what was next? Jeremy couldn't stand not knowing. Something had to change, something had to give, and he was going to make sure it happened.

Listen to yourself, kid. There's no way you're going to stop her. What are you going to do, threaten her? Beat her? That's not you.

But it hurts.

You asked for it.

I can ask her to stop.

Would she stop? He could see her not going out for a few days. She'd stay in, they'd cook dinners together, watch a few movies during the week — and then, by the second weekend, she'd get the urge to go to Amplexus again. And then they'd go, and somebody would watch her dancing, and she'd notice, and start flirting with him, and the slightest flirtation would open this wound completely up again.

And worse, she'd enjoy it, then she'd start making secret dates with some of these men. "I'm in an open marriage, but I'm discreet about it," she'd say, as if any of them cared. None of them did. They just saw how beautiful she was, and so long as Jeremy wasn't a pro football player or a mob boss, it wouldn't change their approach.

Then she'd work late, driving him crazy. He'd wonder if every moment she wasn't with him if she was cultivating another man, another relationship. Milwaukee had so many places to go and meet people, she could have affairs anywhere and he'd never know it. And when Amplexus didn't work for her well enough, she'd go online and find men to chat with. It was driving him slowly insane.

Even with this pain, at least it's a pain you know, Jeremy thought. At least you know exactly where she is and what she's doing, even if you don't like it. You still have that innermost intimacy with her, the one in which she tells you everything, and you're truly sharing this experience.

Just so long as he never had to worry about her keeping secrets from him with other men. That, he was certain, would be too much.

*SportsCenter* was on television. Two minutes had passed; two much information. There was nothing he could do about it. Time was going to go at its own damn rate, and he was just going to have to ride it out.

He wanted to drink. He wanted a big drink. But that always just made him sick. Maybe he should eat something. But he had a pretty big meal already, and Katherine was pretty attuned to his weight. No use in giving her another reason to look elsewhere for physical pleasure.

The TV, the wall clock, the TV, the wall clock. He had to take a walk.

As he went upstairs, he heard a car driving up. Was it in this driveway, or next door? He couldn't tell. Suddenly, he was nervous about where he was – if he was right by the garage door, it would look like he was hanging on her return, and that might make her nervous. No, he had to return to the living room, quickly.

Be in the TV room, watching *Sesame Street*.

No, you should be reading, doing something intellectual that shows you don't have a care in the world. You're casual about this. You're her strong, strong husband who's so in love with her he lets her spread her wings in every possible way. You're her dream partner, you can't be seen obsessing over where she's been for the last two hours.

. The garage door opened. Katherine came in and kissed him on the cheek.

"How'd it go?"

"Get undressed and go to bed, I'll tell you all about it."

"You can't tell me now?"

"I'll tell you one thing: I got the part!!!"

Jeremy got up unsteady. Got what part? He decided it didn't matter. You made it through another night, kid. Congratulations.

Steven didn't quite believe in total sobriety, reality never having favored looking at it directly, anyway. He'd decided some time ago, between the second and third week of 'the tour' as he now called it, that reality was very much like Medusa. You couldn't look straight at it, or it would paralyze you. The only way to examine it closely without turning to stone was to see it reflected, and what better reflecting pool than the calm surface of a glass of Jim Beam, with one ice cube.

Which is why at first he didn't believe the recruiter. A real job doing real engineering right there in Milwaukee: designing tools to work in air conditioning plants, smaller, lighter, computer-driven tools that would allow the plants to double production and reduce their size by half. This was challenging work. This was taking science where it belonged, into the real world. Steven was astounded he even rated an interview, but Paul apparently gave him quite a good recommendation, and everyone seemed to understand that you go through some downtime after a divorce.

He was glad he had gotten into the habit of screening his calls on his road trip. The next day, calling from the parking lot, completely sober, he did wonderfully on his interview, even if he did have to hang up twice to think of the proper answer for tough questions – the beauty of being on a cell phone is that people expect to lose the signal.

After he got the job offer, he turned on PBS on the motel room's television and watched that idiot character Elmo scream "Hello boys and girls!"

about ten times a minute. *Sesame Street* had changed from an inspirational, educational program to an institutional babysitter. He hated it. He was just glad he'd caught it at its best. Everything just might turn out okay if he worked hard and was nice to people.

Two weeks later, he began packing all of his possessions in anticipation of having a real apartment rather than a hotel room. The restraining order, as he found out while trying to mention that he was to play Brick's understudy, meant the threat of jail if he called Tiffany, even if it was to tell Anthony his daddy got a job; so he left a message with Tiffany's lawyer saying he'd be in touch with a new address as soon as he had one. He wondered if they'd assume he got a new job and would pursue him for child support – mutual friends had taken great pleasure in letting Steven know that Tim was far more in debt than he'd let Tiffany believe - but decided that he'd deal with it squarely when the time came. The call was a good-faith measure, and that had to stand for something.

Milwaukee was every bit as green and lush as Austin was, and with a cool breeze coming off of the lake, making August a great deal more tolerable than it was down in Texas. Between line memorizations he looked around several neighborhoods before choosing a small loft just south of downtown, in a converted warehouse. It was great to live in an industrial building, even if it was in a one bedroom apartment, it had fifteen foot ceilings, which meant it was already larger than his any of his hotel rooms were wide, a freight-style elevator, and a view of the old Gas company building with the Art Deco glass flame on the roof. Milwaukee was going to work out: so what if the Mexican food would suck. This was a cool place, and they still made beer there.

Steven unpacked his things, called his uncle and thanked him for co-signing the lease on the apartment, then sat down amidst all three of the boxes of his clothes and contemplated his next step. This is where it would happen. This is where he would rebuild his life and start over again. Already he felt stronger, and The Tour had done him an immense amount of good. It stung not being able to contact Anthony, but that time would come, and before long, with this salary, he'd be able to challenge the court order and start fresh with his family.

It was easy to feel this way. The air smelled fresher than he expected, and he liked how cool it got at night. He was even looking forward to the winters, hearing that the snow could come down almost horizontally during some storms. He was ready to walk out of his apartment, dressed for work in a long overcoat, and drive some new car to an office where his work mattered.

Steven looked out the window. Everything else, he'd figure out eventually. This was the starting over place. He smiled spontaneously, utterly without cynicism, for the first time in as long as he could remember. He remembered the cast was getting together for drinks and decided to join them. Maggie the Cat was an interesting girl.

# CHAPTER ELEVEN

"I told you all along there was a Snuffleupagus,
my best pal, but you never believed me."

–Big Bird

Jeremy sat in the truck outside of Ysidro's and waited. Time wouldn't move at all, and the clock on his radio wasn't helping. He stared at it, amazed that it could remain on 8:14 for so long. It had to be broken, there's no way a minute could take that long to pass.

And she was in there, with this guy. Not an anonymous guy, not somebody she was just going to screw and come home and tell him about. This was somebody she'd already lied to him about, somebody who meant more.

That changed everything. Suddenly he wasn't the strong husband, he was the chump. He was the guy she mentioned in hushed tones, as in "Shhh. Don't let my husband know."

He was officially broken. It had been all bearable, slightly, only so long as he was in her innermost circle, so long as she confided everything in him, shared that journey with him. As long as she did that, everything could somehow be suffered through and endured.

That was all over now that she was pretending to be in a play. Katherine doesn't do irony, and theatre is nothing but irony. He could line up fifty academics to say so (actually, he almost smiled at the thought of lining up fifty academics. It's like herding cats). Instead of this being a phase that would burn itself out, now Jeremy himself was probably the phase. She was actively looking for something different, for someone different, and it was a matter of time before she left him behind. She'd say it was because he didn't grow enough with her, or that she'd developed into something new and he hadn't – and tidily forget that he was the one who encouraged that growth, who suffered through every minute that she indulged herself. She was denying him her perspective on things, her point of view, and sharing them in chat rooms and with Amplexus buddies. Once he realized he had no idea what she was really thinking anymore, he knew that this was the definition of infidelity, a much more painful offence than just sharing her body.

Jeremy got out of the truck and looked in the back of the cab, deciding to leave the baseball bat there. He wasn't crazy, and he wasn't going to do anything crazy. He was just going to put a stop to it, right now.

He walked through the parking lot, feeling dizzy, and wished he were able to drink hard liquor again. That was supposed to take the edge off, wasn't it? Maybe he'd have a drink later, and after going through all this, maybe he'd be able to stomach it this time. Real men were supposed to be able to do that. He felt more like an angry child than he did even when he was an angry child. What would an adult do? What would Uncle Ted do? He didn't have time to call and ask. His marriage was in the act of being violated right inside of this restaurant.

The lot was full, and Jeremy briefly considered waiting until he saw Katherine come out with whoever this guy was, pay attention to which car he got into, and call in Uncle Ted and report him driving drunk. Almost everybody who leaves a bar is technically intoxicated anyway, especially with the .08 blood alcohol standard.

That would mean waiting outside for who knows how long. He checked his watch. 8:16. "This is stupid," he said softly as he hurried back to the truck, turned the key forward one click to activate the stereo, and tried to listen to music. Maybe listening to classic rock would make time go faster.

A few notes from a song on CD would begin, and he'd fast forward it to the next, play it for a matter of seconds, and fast -forward it again, until the CD was finished. The radio was a band of commercials and country music, which only made him think of Katherine's first dance with that stranger, the way she arched her back and straddled his leg, letting her crotch rub against him obscenely, even with that innocent smile on her face. . .

Jeremy almost leapt out of the truck this time, and threw the door shut. He had to put an end to this right now. Either she stops seeing these other men entirely, cuts it completely off, agrees to be his wife and his wife alone, or . . .

She'd leave him first. Jeremy stopped in his tracks. Good god, she'd leave me.

What would that be like? Would it really be that bad? She'd walked all over him, been indifferent to how her actions had made him suffer – she'd even blamed his current depression on his job, and wondered aloud if he wouldn't be happier in another career or even another city.

She was already preparing to divorce him, Jeremy suddenly realized. This was all part of that.

There was no sense in going in there.

Jeremy took a few steps back to the truck before he stopped again. This was driving him crazy. Whether she was going to leave him or not, he had to stand up for himself. Let him be the jealous husband or the cuckold or whatever, but he couldn't spend another night in the basement trying to watch *The Muppet Movie* on Nick at Nite waiting for the sound of a car in the driveway. This was too much. He'd stand up for himself and ride out the consequences, whatever they may be.

She can't leave me, he thought. I just won't let it happen. I'm going back in there to claim my wife.

Beneath the jealousy, behind his fury, Jeremy realized in a weak, passive way that he was now in danger. As he opened the door to the bar, he realized he was walking like everyone else, and was attracting no attention. It was as though he were watching himself as he went to the bar and casually ordered a Guinness, thinking that jealousy and barroom confrontations might be aided by an Irish stout more than by any other drink, especially since gagging on whiskey rarely makes a manly impression.

I've done it, Jeremy thought as he placed down the empty glass. I've gone crazy. This is what it feels like.

It took him a few moments, but he finally saw where Katherine was sitting. She was facing towards Jeremy, and the man she was with was making her laugh. He had short, black hair, and a resonant voice that seemed to cut through the noise of the bar, even though he wasn't speaking loudly. Jeremy could almost make out the conversation from there, but the exact words just wouldn't reach. Something about "Big Daddy" and "Skipper" and "not being able to get it up anymore." Jeremy couldn't help but wonder if his marriage were the subject of a joke.

Whatever he was saying, Katherine was laughing almost constantly — not the flirtatious, seductive laugh they used together in Amplexus, but something more frightening and genuine. She really liked this guy, whoever he was.

Jeremy stepped away from the bar and walked along the far wall, coming no closer to Katherine and the guy, but hoping to move sideways enough to get a glimpse of his face. He reached the corner booth of the bar and sat down, peering over at them.

He wasn't ugly, but he wasn't a looker, either. Kind of pasty-faced, like a guy who hadn't spent a day outside in years. One of those computer geeks or something, but Katherine would never lie to him over a computer geek. That was just beyond comprehension. What in the world was she doing with this guy?

Laughing. Again. And he was grinning, the bastard, kind of a casual, manly grin that made him look like he was in control of the situation and he knew it.

Jeremy couldn't just sit there and watch, he realized. Sooner or later Katherine would sense something was wrong and look around, and she'd spot him, and she'd excuse herself and come over and they'd have some fight, and after that she'd go back to the table and say something like 'my husband is crazy' and he'd believe her and Jeremy would be sitting back outside waiting for her date to be over, watching the clock as it advanced only ten seconds every five minutes or so.

No, he'd have to take the initiative, and put an end to all of this. And it had to happen now.

Jeremy wished he'd had another beer, but the one he'd already drank was making him feel a little queasy. His hands were trembling, and as he noticed them, for a moment, he almost felt normal again, as though he were making far too much out of all of this, and all he had to do was go home, take a sleeping pill, and the next day have a calm and rational discussion with Katherine about how much this all has been hurting him, how he just wasn't strong enough for them to have this kind of marriage, and then they could come to an agreement about moving forward or divorcing, and everyone would act with grace and maturity, and there wouldn't be any kind of public unpleasantness.

Then Jeremy felt himself get up from the booth, and he realized that he wasn't in control of this anymore. His pain itself was walking him slowly, inexorably, towards Katherine's table. The only rational part of him left was the part of him that was observing all of this from an eerie distance, and the phrase "slouching towards Bethlehem" seemed to invade that rational observer to the point where even that lone thread of sanity couldn't reveal to him exactly what kind of rough beast he was about to become.

Steven briefly turned and signaled to the waitress that they'd each have another glass of wine. It was nice to relax with Katherine, and Steven felt more at ease than he had in months.

He shifted back in his seat and looked across the table at her. Nothing had to happen, he realized. He didn't need to sleep with her, didn't even really need to kiss her, though it would be nice if that happened. Just being an engineer again, sitting in a civilized place across from a young, beautiful woman again, was enough for right now. He liked that she was only thirty-four (he was unaware that Katherine had long stopped telling people she was just past forty – it just seemed to freak them out) and still found him interesting, usually he was a boring engineer to most women who didn't know he'd spent the last few years as a delivery guy. And he could read the Milwaukee phone book out loud and she would laugh at it. Maybe she really did like him. If that's the case, there's no rush, and he could ease into it. He didn't have any illusions about how strong he was. Work was going great, and he was enjoying getting to know the city, but there was still too much of him that was broken, torn down, in ashes. Like Uncle Lawrence said, he'd be a real gift to someone right now. He'd probably cling to any woman who showed interest, and especially someone as beautiful as Katherine.

He'd always had a thing for hazel eyes, and hers were unusually large and clear – unless she were laughing, and then they'd close up, almost until they were mere crescent-shaped slivers, almost like a doll or an old fashioned cartoon. And her lips formed an almost unnatural pout when she listened closely, only to explode into a wide smile when she laughed. She wasn't a woman who could laugh with her mouth closed. It just wouldn't work.

But of all her features, even though he'd been attracted by her slim body and the fullness of her breasts, which were still young enough to be firmer than the bra she was wearing – it was her hair that captivated him the most. Long, chestnut brown, flowing down her back or over her neck, trickling down like a mantle on her shoulders. It was her hair he longed for more than anything, to feel it along his face, to smell its freshness, to be tickled by it as it trailed down along his chest if they were to ever make love.

Steven was astonished at how he was letting himself go in this. Tiffany's hair had enchanted him too. He had to work not to think of her in that moment, or to think of Tim. It was hard to ignore the flash of anger that emerged whenever Tiffany wandered into his mind. He wanted those thoughts gone – they were keeping him from concentrating on the task at hand.

What was the task at hand?

"What's that?" Steven spoke suddenly as if coming out of a trance.

"I just think it's cool how you've traveled, that's all."

"I haven't been that many places."

"What's your favorite place?"

Steven thought of Canyon Lake in central Texas, how he and Tiffany used to go skinny-dipping, how she'd come and tease him underwater, how they'd lie in the sun and dry out slowly, where he could close his eyes and smell the coolness of the grass and feel the all the colors of the springtime on his skin.

"I don't know if I have a favorite." He said, cocking his head to one side. "But I've got to say I'm liking this place better and better."

Katherine laughed. "There's a place I like in Madison by the lake. I love swimming there, when the water's not so cold. That's only a few months out of the year, and even then it never gets warm, you know?"

Steven nodded.

Katherine leaned forward, conspiratorially. "I have a question for you."

"What's that?" Steven was again completely there, having taken another five-second mental field trip into Tiffany and Jim's bedroom.

Katherine looked confused, and stopped her fingerplay along the glass. Then she looked up suddenly and her eyes widened, taking on almost giant proportions, which startled Steven.

He turned and looked up to see a man standing over him; not menacingly, but unsteadily, as if he were about to fall. He was large, taller than Steven, and looked pretty strong as well.

Suddenly, nothing felt right about the situation.

"I need you to come with me." The man said softly to Katherine.

"Jeremy, go away. I'll talk to you later." Katherine's voice was firm.

"You know him?" Steven asked.

"I just need you to come with me, Katherine. That's all." Jeremy's voice was shaking. That element didn't bother Steven as much as the fact that he was clearly outsized.

"No, Jeremy, just go – I'll talk to you later, okay?" Katherine's voice had an edge of fear in it, and it made Steven worried. He stood up and positioned himself between her and Jeremy. This guy outweighed him by some twenty pounds, and looked like he knew how to handle himself. This was not going to end well.

"I don't think she wants to talk to you right now, my friend." Steven was calm, trying to appeal to the larger man with the incredibly probative eyes. "Let her call you later, okay? There's nothing going on here."

Jeremy shifted his stare to Steven, who was a little frightened by it. He looked far away, this man. Steven felt himself go into the cold stare you wear when you're challenged, and for the first time in his memory, he actually felt scared: not nervous, but an outright, there's-a-train-heading-for-me scared. Katherine hadn't mentioned any crazy ex-boyfriends, but he clearly had one on his hands.

"This doesn't concern you. This is between me and her." Jeremy's voice was calm enough to be frightening.

"I know you feel that way, but if the lady says she doesn't want to talk to you right now, you need to accept that. Go get some rest."

"I'm not tired." Jeremy said coolly, and Steven began to realize that he hadn't blinked in an unnaturally long time.

"Jeremy, go home. Please. I'll talk to you when I get there." Katherine pleaded, her voice rising further.

Other people in the bar had stopped talking, and suddenly Steven felt dozens of eyes on him. "Listen, buddy, just take it easy and go, okay? She doesn't want to talk to you right now. She says she'll talk to you later. Can't you just do that? Don't worry about anything." Steven lifted a hand to gently guide Jeremy away.

Jeremy's left arm flew up as though to block a punch, startling Steven. Steven felt a rush of adrenaline, as though Jeremy were about to blow, and instinctively threw his right fist towards Jeremy's stomach. It landed heavily, and Jeremy began to double over, when Steven instantly threw his left fist upwards in a hook, squarely catching Jeremy on the chin.

Jeremy fell, limp. The entire sequence had taken less than ten seconds.

As Steven heard the rest of the bar patrons rushing towards them both, holding Steven back and tending to the fallen man, a sentence began to ring out in his head. "I'll talk to you when I get there." He turned and looked at Katherine, who was standing now, looking down at Jeremy.

"Do you live with this guy?" Steven asked, his voice higher than usual.

Katherine looked at him sadly. "He's my husband."

Steven felt his head tilting backwards, and suddenly he was dizzy, looking at the ceiling. "Damn." No wonder this guy was upset. How many times had he wanted to do the same thing, find Tiffany and Jim and confront them both? He'd never had the courage. And now this guy, who probably hadn't even thrown a punch in his adult life, was on the floor and completely still. And nothing had even happened between him and his wife.

Steven turned to Jeremy and tried to offer his hand. "Buddy, I am so sorry. I had no idea—"

Two large men from a nearby table wanted to make sure the fight was really over, and held Steven by the shoulders in case he was trying to sucker punch Jeremy while he was down.

"Let me go, guys, come on."

They didn't.

The bouncer, a bald black man of about 5'7", but seemingly just as wide, slid in front of Steven. "I think you need to go."

The men eased their grip on Steven, and Steven felt himself backing away. "I didn't know he was her husband."

"That's not my thing, man," said the Bouncer. "You just need to go."

"I was trying to keep him from hurting her."

"Door's over there. Come on."

Steven looked back at Katherine as the bouncer guided him away. She was staring at the fallen man, who only rolled a little from side to side, almost crying like a child. He knew the feeling. Is this how it would have ended up if he'd confronted Tiffany? Was he that weakened during that time? Was he any stronger now?

And it suddenly occurred to him Katherine hadn't looked in his direction since the punches. She was just staring at her husband, saying something under her breath, something that was apparently bothering the man even more.

The door opened, and the bouncer escorted Steven outside.

"Look, I'm cool, I was just trying to stand up for the lady."

The bouncer nodded. "It's not my thing, man. Just need you to stay clear of the place for six months, alright?"

"Whatever."

"This wasn't but a thing, so we're not gonna call the police, alright? But you need to be out of the parking lot in five minutes, or we'll have to change our mind about that. Alright?"

"Sure, man."

"You take it easy."

The door closed. Steven looked around at the cars in the lot, and honestly couldn't remember what he drove. This was too much too soon. He really wasn't ready to date yet.

Inside, Katherine had finally bent down next to Jeremy. He couldn't believe what had happened. One minute he was staring at Katherine, the next he was on the floor, feeling like he couldn't open his mouth.

"He's okay, he's okay." He heard her assure the other people in the bar.

"You sure?" A masculine voice, softer than the one the other guy had, came from a few inches above his head. "He looks like his jaw might be broken."

Jeremy realized, his hands covering his face, that he'd been bawling for an indeterminate amount of time, and suddenly felt extreme embarrassment.

"Jeremy, come on, get up."

"No—" Jeremy said, his voice strangely muffled.

"Jeremy, look at me." Katherine's voice cut through his feelings and hit him like a command. He opened his eyes and saw her between his fingers, like he was looking at her from a jail cell. "That man was a friend, that's all."

Jeremy shook his head, and whispered, harshly. "You're lying."

"Come on. Get up, sweetie. Let's go."

"I don't want to." Jeremy felt his legs pulling up into a fetal position.

"Jeremy, don't be silly. You're making too much of this. Come on, honey." She grabbed him by the arm and tried to lift him.

Jeremy let himself go limp, making his body heavier, and flopped back to the floor.

She gathered her purse and stepped over Jeremy. "Jeremy, you're making me angry! I am not your mother!" She began walking away.

"Wait . . . " His voice trailed weakly after her.

She continued to walk. He heard the door open and close, and took his hands away from his face. Everybody was looking at him.

"I think you'd better see a doctor, bud." One man nearby said, his eyes a mixture of pity and disgust. "Your mouth looks pretty bad."

Jeremy nodded. Two men helped to lift him up.

"Can you drive?"

Jeremy nodded again, then tried to walk. His legs were too weak, and he stumbled.

"He needs an ambulance. He might have hit his head or something."

The bartender squinted disapproval, then shrugged it off. "Yeah, probably." He picked up the phone.

Jeremy let himself be eased back into a booth and looked around. Katherine was gone. He'd blown it. He hadn't even had a chance to say what he wanted to say. This was a bad, bad idea — and he couldn't even find within him the logic that made it ever seem like a good idea. It was as though the madness was gone, leaving in its place only a deeply, deeply felt embarrassment. It resided in his stomach, where the hole felt so wide that Jeremy was certain he could never eat again.

Steven emerged from the holding cell to see a man in a wrinkled brown suit straightening his tie. He looked nervous, and with good reason – the tie was never going to be straight, one of those cheap ties you get for five dollars at K-Mart, where the fabric and print themselves are off kilter, so just wearing the tie makes you look undressed.

Steven owned several of those ties, and wore them for engineer's night at the annual Simpkins party, and once for Paul's Christmas party, where he'd gotten insanely drunk and danced with that Polish receptionist until her husband got pissed. He hadn't put one on since. Even his uncle's old tuxedo came with a pre-formed knot in the tie.

"Steve?"

"No, Steven."

"Good. Call me David." Steven shook his hand, which was sweaty. "Sorry about that – pretty humid out, isn't it?"

"Can't say as I'd know." Steven sat down, casually.

"How are you doing? Do you need anything?"

"Not much." Steven didn't want small talk, he wanted to know his options, and decided to sit and wait for David to get around to explaining them. David seemed to grow uncomfortable in the silence, and started talking, his voice unsteady.

"Well, here's what we're facing. The prosecutor is pressing for felony assault one, which would be two years in jail, probably out in eight months with good behavior."

"Uh-huh. And?" Steven's eyelids felt heavy.

"And they might accept misdemeanor assault, but that kind of depends on the victim."

"Who's the victim?"

"His name is Jeremy Schultz. His family is pretty well known around here."

"What's wrong with him?"

"Didn't anyone tell you?"

"Listen, what's your name—David? I went to work yesterday morning, and before I'm done with my first cup of coffee five cops walk in to arrest me. Not one, not two, but five, and they've all got their hands right on their guns. I get dragged off in front of everyone I work for, and I've only just started at this place. All I know is I'm in jail for assault because I tried to stop a guy from killing his wife."

David nodded vigorously. "I kind of see your point. The problem is, as I see it, is that you're the only one that any witnesses are saying actually threw a punch, and with your record—"

"I don't have a record. I have a paper violation of an even dumber paper that never should have been filed."

"Well, it just makes it easy to imply a tendency to violence on your part. It looks pretty open and shut for the prosecution."

"What's wrong with this Jeremy Schultz guy? Is he claiming whiplash or something?"

"Steve, you broke his jaw in four places. It's like you just shattered it."

"That's impossible."

"No, the police tell me it happens pretty often, but you have to catch a guy just like this . . ." David moved towards Steven and slowly demonstrated where the fist would meet the jaw that could cause so much damage.

As David pulled back to resume the interview, Steven was certain that he detected the unmistakable scent of Tiffany's perfume. That was absurd.

Helen Moscowitz's office was tiny. Large enough for a desk, her leather chair, and a small sofa —- a love seat, actually. The idea was that even feuding couples are more apt to communicate if their hips are touching.

She'd been highly recommended by Uncle Ted's secretary, Ms. Adams. In private practice for nearly twenty years, she had even gone across the country giving lectures on the rebuilding of trust after an affair. Ms. Adams did not say how she knew her.

Jeremy could see she had a spare decorating style: only her degrees, a half-open Japanese umbrella, and an architectural drawing of Frank Lloyd Wright's Robie House on the walls. The rest of the office was taken up with bookcases, papers, and a filing system that would be best described as somewhat fluid in nature.

Jeremy and Katherine sat, hips touching, in the love seat and waited for Helen to endow them with wisdom.

"The important thing is to know what each of you wants. If your desires for the relationship are too far apart, I don't think there's much sense in trying to save it. If your goals are compatible, and you're up to it, I'll see what I can do to help. Does that sound fair?"

Katherine said, "Yes." Jeremy nodded, the wires around his jaw making it too painful to talk unless absolutely necessary.

"Who wants to go first?"

Katherine turned to Jeremy. "Maybe he should."

Jeremy didn't have the strength to argue, it would hurt too much. He shrugged.

"Don't be afraid," Helen said, "I know it hurts, but that's why we're here."

"I want," Jeremy had to pause for a moment as the pain shot through his jaw and up behind his eyes. "A normal life."

"So do I, I really do." Katherine immediately and sincerely repeated.

"That's interesting. What do you mean by normal? Could you expand on that?"

Jeremy felt dizzy. He looked over at Katherine, who seemed so eager to have any kind of communication, and decided he'd try again. "Just me." Excruciating pain. "And her." He tilted his head back after speaking and closed his eyes. He needed more codeine.

"I see," said Helen, suddenly aware that Jeremy's discomfort may be physical rather than emotional. "So what you're saying is, you'd like your relationship to be exclusive again?"

Jeremy nodded.

"And you don't want her to continue her affair?"

"But I never had an affair!" Katherine injected painfully, "we were just having a drink! Nothing else happened!"

Jeremy glared at Katherine, then looked over at Helen.

"Okay," she took a deep breath, "Katherine, what do you want?"

"I want everything to be like it was. That's all I want."

"Do you think that's possible?"

"No." Katherine played with her fingernails.

"So what do you want to become of your marriage?"

Katherine chewed on her thumbnail. "I don't know."

Jeremy sagged.

"Jeremy, you seem a little uncomfortable. Why don't you sit in my recovery room for a little while. Katherine and I are going to talk about what she wants, and I'll come get you in a bit. You can stretch out and even nap a little if you can. Does that sound good?"

Jeremy realized that when you can't talk, people treat you like an infant. What's worse, the temptation to respond by acting like an infant was almost irresistible. He nodded and stood up, and began shuffling out of the room behind Helen. Just as he reached the door he turned slightly to see Katherine waving at him with her fingers, smiling optimistically. He nodded and went in the other room.

This room was more opulent, with more things to see. About four Persian style rugs were there, one on the floor, three hanging from the pale yellow walls–they were detailed designs that were there to encourage concentration and recovery. Or at least Helen was saying something like that as she eased him down onto a pea-green leather sofa. "—just let me know, okay?" Was all he could make out when he started paying attention to her again.

He nodded, and leaned back against the leopard-print pillow she'd nudged behind him. He watched the ceiling as he heard her shut the door.

They were determining if he had a marriage anymore, he thought, and I'm stuck here, waiting. How did he ever get reduced to the guy who sits with a broken jaw waiting for a total stranger to decide whether his marriage is going to last?

Boy, was Uncle Ted throwing the book at that other guy. As soon as Katherine'd called him that night, after she found out about the jaw, Ted went into action. He probably would have put him on his own docket if he thought he could do so without appeal. Steven had told Katherine enough about himself that they could track him down, and arrested him at work the next day. Turns out he had a criminal record, which Katherine didn't know, and part of that had been in domestic violence. Katherine'd said that he made her a little nervous, but that she didn't know entirely why.

And she'd never had sex with him, she assured him of that. She'd have told Jeremy if she had, just like always. In fact, this guy was a little odd, he didn't seem to want to have sex with her. He was interested, she thought, but he'd been reserved. She thought it was gentlemanly at first, but considering everything that happened and what they'd found out about him, it was probably because he was a freak, and she was lucky they'd only met in public places.

Like all this was supposed to change the fact that she was dating this guy, Jeremy thought. Just because they hadn't slept together yet doesn't mean they weren't going to, and he knew, he knew something was different about her feelings for this guy. He could read it in her face before, and he saw it in the bar. This guy had potential for her – thank god Uncle Ted was handling it.

That was the odd thing, though. Even today, on the ride in to the therapist, Katherine was very much in favor of pressing charges. It was something Jeremy didn't want to do, but Uncle Ted insisted, and was going to flex his judicial position to make sure that the County pressed charges if Jeremy wouldn't, and since Jeremy didn't want to look bad to Uncle Ted, he went along. Uncle Ted was always careful not to allow anyone else in the family to abuse his position: they all paid their parking tickets, nobody ever got out of that–and everybody knew, if they got yanked for a DUI, Uncle Ted himself might sentence them to an extended jail term. He just didn't tolerate behaving badly; so when he told Jeremy that this guy needed to do time for felonious assault, Jeremy just nodded, and signed the statement that he and Katherine had given the police.

But why Katherine was into it, he couldn't quite figure out. Maybe she was telling Helen everything.

Jeremy's eyes closed, and he felt himself drifting.

Katherine was entirely different. Either she'd decided it was all over, and she'd be polite out of respect for his injury, or . . .

He couldn't think of another reason, and sighed, letting himself fall asleep.

He awakened to feel a hand on his shoulder, gently tugging at him. The motion made his head sway from side to side, pressing the outside wire of his jaw harness against the leopard skin pillow, making him feel like his teeth were being yanked one way, and his jaw the other.

Screaming out, "Jesus!" Was all he could do to react.

Katherine jumped. "My god, you scared me!"

Helen gave Katherine a short, supportive hug to calm her down, then turned to Jeremy, who was just sitting up.

"Well, we've discussed it, and we're going to try to save the marriage."

Jeremy nodded, hoping he still had teeth. He looked up at Katherine, who was staring at him sweetly, with tears welling up in her eyes. "I love you so much, Jeremy."

Helen smiled approvingly and walked back towards her office. "We agreed on all of us being here next week at 11:30. Sound good?" Before Jeremy could nod his answer, she was back in her office, the door closed.

Later, as she got ready to drive them home, Katherine was effusive. "She's wonderful, baby. We had such a good talk about me and how bad I've been to you."

Jeremy looked over at her, questioningly.

"I've been so selfish."

Jeremy cocked his head. Not after just one session. Not after everything they've been through. Katherine was either too calculating or too naïve to have even known what she'd put him through over the last six months. How on Earth could she just turn around and admit it? Did it mean she knew all the time how badly she was hurting him? He'd based a lot of his patience on the fact that her childlike self-obsession kept her from realizing a lot of things in the world. Was he just fooling himself?

What else was he fooling himself about?

"You look so tired, honey. Let's get you home, I'm going to put you to bed and make some soup."

Jeremy nodded and let her help him to stand.

"Vichyssoise."

"What did you say, darling?" Katherine's eyes were sparkling, true, and full of love. Jeremy didn't trust them.

"Vichy. Swaz." The 'swaz' required a pursing of the lips that forced the jaw backwards, and he grimaced.

"I think we need to get your prescription refilled. Then I'll make you a nice soup. Tomato okay? Come on."

Jeremy followed her out of the recovery room, out of the building, into the cool air of a lakeside August day.

Steven's trial was remarkably brief. The bouncer took the stand, the victim took the stand, and Katherine took the stand, all to say that Steven stood up, tried to block Jeremy's path, then punched Jeremy in the jaw when he wouldn't back away.

Katherine wouldn't make eye contact with Steven during her testimony, and claimed during cross-examination that she was a little afraid of Steven before Jeremy even showed up. Jeremy, on the other hand, looked at Steven several times, almost apologetically, and Steven struggled to figure out what that meant.

David claimed before the end of the trial to be able to produce someone who could affirm that Jeremy tried to throw the first punch, but ultimately, nobody stepped forward with that information.

The judge didn't seem to be giving anything away by the look on his face, but Steven was still hopeful that he'd made the right choice by asking the judge to reach a verdict rather than a jury. People seemed to be too bothered by the fact that he'd had a restraining order, a point the prosecution repeatedly hammered at.

Prosecutor: Did you know that Steven was under a restraining order, an order he had violated before?

Katherine: No sir, I did not know that.

Prosecutor: If you did know that, would you have agreed to have a drink with him?

David: Your honor, this is speculation.

Judge: And it is reasonable. Overruled.

Katherine: No, I definitely would not have.

David had sat down harshly and looked over at Steven with a sheepish shrug. Steven sat up suddenly and leaned over to him and whispered harshly, "this isn't like we're watching some football game somewhere. This is my life we're talking about!"

David leaned back, a little surprised, and nodded. "Sorry. Just some things going on at home have me a little distracted. You know how it is."

Midway through his closing argument, David called the judge "Judge Schultz," when his name was actually "Judge Arnhem." The Judge quickly corrected him, and David continued after a brief apology. There was a Judge Schultz in the building, but he rarely presided over such cases; it was not until two weeks after being released from jail that Steven would discover that Judge Theodore Schultz was actually Jeremy's uncle. He would never discover, however, that Judges Arnhem and Schultz were widely considered to be unbeatable partners at pinochle, largely owing to the fact that Arnhem could communicate a wide array of bidding suggestions through a complicated series of eyebrow movements.

The Judge came back from lunch with the same dispassionate face he had when he left; and except for an odd habit of moving his bushy eyebrows up and down before speaking, there didn't seem to be anything that Steven could use to augur what was going to happen.

He was asked to rise, and he did, along with David, soon to be a father of twins.

"In the matter of State vs. Atkins I find you guilty of felonious assault in the second degree. I'm sentencing you to a twelve-month term at the state penitentiary in Green Bay, and I hope you take a lesson from what's happened here. Do you understand your sentence?"

"I do, your honor."

"Very well. Mr. Prosecutor, Mr. Miller, thank you for your time, this court is adjourned. Docket to resume in one hour."

Before the judge could get out from behind his dais, David had his hand out for Steven to take. Steven, automatically, took his hand, and watched with a sense of disbelief how vigorously David shook it.

"It could have been much worse, I think. He reduced the degree, you'll be out in six months, maybe sooner, I don't know how things work in Green Bay."

Steven nodded, and wondered if his Uncle would notice not hearing from him for six months. He just didn't feel like explaining everything.

Just as the bailiff arrived to take Steven away, David asked "is there anything else I can do for you?" Steven, stupefied, answered simply, "file an appeal?"

David appeared to think about it sincerely, then answered: "I think you'd find that an expensive process, and with the Judge's workload it would take three or four months for us to do it right – and you'd be in jail the whole time – unless you have some family who can post bail or get a more commercial lawyer?"

Steven just shook his head. He could never bother Uncle Lawrence with something like this.

"Good luck, Steve."

"Steven."

"What?"

"I prefer Steven. I've told you that, like, ten times." The Bailiff led him away.

In the minivan on the way to Green Bay, Steven asked the guard if he'd be allowed to write home, or to make calls.

"Prisoner access to communications is spelled out in the handbook your lawyer should have given you after the trial."

"I didn't get one of those."

"Then one will be made available to you during your first week of incarceration."

"Can't you just answer my question?"

"Too many inmates do something wrong and then say 'hey, Guard McNary told me I could do it.' So we don't allow that no more. You'll get your handbook of guidelines like everybody else."

Steven sat back and watched out of the chain-screened windows as the late summer sunlight washed green over the fields near Manitowoc. Linden trees, poplar, and rolling fields where corn was still growing. He'd be out before the NFL playoffs began, and the regular season usually wasn't worth watching anyway. It was just six months. He could stand anything for six months.

"Does that mean sending mail?"

McNary ignored him. Wisely, Steven thought.

# CHAPTER TWELVE



"Now leave me alone and get lost!"

-Oscar the Grouch

Tiffany was watching *Law and Order* on cable and waiting for her newborn son Tommy to awaken when Tim barged in the door. It was unusual for him to be home before six. For a moment, she resented the intrusion as though he were trying to catch her with another man. But a look at his face told her this was the farthest thing from his mind.

"I'm toast." Tim threw his briefcase on the floor.

"What do you mean?" Tiffany tried to remain calm. Tim could be dramatic, and it was her job to refuse to enter that realm when he did so. It was part of their partnership.

"I got skipped for the promotion."

"Why?"

"Your fucking ex-husband."

Tiffany sat down to digest this. In truth, she didn't know what it meant. So it was wisest not to say anything until Tim had made himself clearer.

"He sent the emails we wrote to each other to everyone in the office. Everyone, even in corporate. They know I fired my wife to make room for you. They know you invented his abuse to cover up our affair. I'll never get out of logistics. Ever. And it was all I could do to keep that job today."

"How could he have done that?" Tiffany decided building up a rant was the right thing to do, but she was interrupted.

"You're the geek, you tell me." Tim was pacing now, stopping to slap the side of a Chinese wedding cabinet. "You know what? It's my own god-damn fault. He isn't wrong. I did everything he accused me of doing. And I believed you when you said he was crazy. He wasn't crazy. He was just seriously pissed off."

"He is crazy."

"No, babe, he acted in a very rational manner."

Tiffany paused for a moment. "That was a long time ago, even before we were married."

"They just showed up. The whole mailroom was full of these manila envelopes."

"Oh." Tiffany's mind was racing. "Who is getting the new VP slot, then?"

"Pitts. He was right there, ready to pounce."

Tiffany nodded. Steven was living underground. He didn't have the balls to do something like this. But Sam Pitt, he did. So how would he have gotten the emails – hell, how would he even have known about them? He and Tim were close once, but after Tim's ex-wife Lisa got fired, they didn't have much to say to each other. Mostly because Tim fired her himself to ensure she wasn't in the way of his seducing Tiffany. Sam always liked Lisa, Tim said.

Oh shit. Oh no.

"Hey baby, did Sam know, about us?"

Tim looked down at Tiffany suspiciously. "Maybe. I think I told him something way back at the beginning. Wasn't anything detailed."

Except for the fact that Samuel Crockett Pitt was the son of James Bowie Pitt, who served in the legislature exactly one door down from Leonardas Morales the Second.

Tiffany sat down and moaned softly, her hands covering her face. What on Earth had she done. Oh god, please no. Steven had never said a word to Leonardas. Steven had never betrayed her. Until now.

"I can't believe this, Tiff." Tim's voice cracked. "Tiff?" Tim's demand for comfort was becoming unseemly, she thought.

Tiffany knew what this would take. She stood up and walked to Tim slowly, and hugged him from behind, letting her breasts tickle the small of his back. In case he didn't notice, she made sure to ease herself up and down slowly so that he'd feel her and think of something else. Maybe she would too. "He's insane, baby." She said with less conviction than ever.

Tim pulled away abruptly and faced her. "No, it has nothing to do with him. It has everything to do with me. You told me he was dangerous and I didn't listen."

He slammed his drink. Tiffany saw only fear.

"Fuck him." Tiffany said without real passion; she couldn't stop thinking about how Steven looked that last morning.

"That's only natural, darling." Tim smiled. "He's fucked us for the considerable future."

Tiffany felt her back stiffen. "What. Happened."

Tim seemed to be entirely too relaxed about it, as though he were Cary Grant explaining his plight to a lover in a Hitchcock film. "Nothing, darling—he just happened to speak up right when this opportunity arose. Sure, they think he's crazy too. I think he's a son of a bitch. But he made sure I'll never be a vice president. Our emails to each other 'break the ethical code' that the company has to at least pay lip service to."

"Everyone knows that was years ago."

"Yes, but the public lawsuits against this very public company are less than a year old. They can't afford the PR crap they may face if they promote me. But hey, there is good news—"

Tiffany braced herself.

"They're letting me work for shipping. In LA. I'm to run operations in Long Beach and stay out of Austin and stay vewy vewy quiet." He laughed slightly and let himself slump down into his chair. Tommy watched the two of them like he was watching a tennis match.

"Is that Hollywood?" Tiffany held out hope for just a moment that they would be rescued from obscurity. She could get in shape. She could get auditions. She could be in commercials. Fuck Maria and her Ribbon in the Sky.

"Not even close." Tim said, absently watching Tommy. "But, you know, the Goodyear Blimp lives about a block from the office. Apparently you can see them launch it from the windows."

This was not what Tiffany wanted to hear.

Tim had now officially let her down too. Fucking liar. He said there would be no problem with how he divorced his wife, and together they'd ensured that Steven was regarded as a crazy menace by the criminal justice system—and more importantly, by Tim's bosses in family-friendly Texas.

All he had to do was get promoted. What the hell was so hard about that? She watched his legs as he bounced his feet up and down nervously, and felt a disgust grow within her. Another fucking weakling. She sure could pick 'em.

After a moment, Tiffany realized she hadn't heard his last sentence.

"What?"

"I'm asking you to support me. Please, Tiff, this has been harder than I ever expected."

Tiffany stared at him for a moment, then felt a steely sensation in her back. She would not give in to this weakness. It was unduly feminine, it was a boy trying to be a man, it was someone who believed that the world was going to give everything to you, when she knew at her core that the only way to get what you wanted was to take it from the strong gnarly fingers of the universe. Why was her father the only person who knew this?

"I-" Tiffany stopped herself. She was about to cry, which pissed her off immensely. He didn't deserve emotion. He had to be told the way things are.

"What is it?" Tim was supportive and accepting. Fuck him.

"I don't have anything to say to you." Tiffany said, then sucked in a new breath of air and held onto it. It would have to wait a while. As she said it, she felt her chest rise along with her chin: she was taking a stand, and this weak excuse for a man in front of her had better take her example and grow a pair.

Tim nodded. "Yeah, I guess I deserve that."

This was not the response she wanted. They would be broke in four months if he didn't get a promotion. The value of their property was already falling. And staying in this crappy job where the company wouldn't promote him was unacceptable: the only choice was to resign. What did he expect, for HER to work? After five years of his keeping her out of the job market so she could raise his goddamn child, who still was behind the average on all developmental tests? No way. No fucking way.

"You don't understand me. I have nothing more to give you."

This got Tim's attention, and he turned to her in what seemed like disbelief. "What? Tiffany, come on. I've given you-"

"All you've done is taken from me. This is the simplest corporation in the United States, and you still found a way to get them to keep you from running it. I have nothing for you. Don't look to me for support. You fucked this family up. And we both know you can't fix it. You've fucked up too many times already."

"So what do you suggest I do?" Tim looked suddenly defiant. "It's not like you've done anything to make us work."

Tiffany was ready for this. "Why don't you just fuck off. Leave tonight. Tommy won't even miss you after a few months."

Tim nodded nervously. Weak bastard.

"Maybe that's what I should do."

He set down the glass and headed out the door. Tiffany suddenly found herself in a panic.

"You're leaving right now?"

"You told me to." He strode to the door and left, slamming it.

There was only room in any house for one door slammer, she decided. He'd get wasted at some no-tell bar and slink back after midnight, hoping the reek of the cigarette smoke wouldn't awaken her.

The next morning, as Tim remained passed out, she stood naked in front of her bathroom mirror and appraised her body. She was getting to be too old to be a trophy wife. And she never wanted to be one anyway. But how was she going to survive this? She leaned forward and examined her face. Still pretty, but not a knockout. She never wanted to be a knockout, just smart and efficient and ready for anything. It was anything time.

She pulled forward the loose skin that had been filling out under her chin and looked at herself in the mirror again. She was five pounds too thin to be unthreateningly chubby; and five pounds too heavy to be a power woman.

Thing is, she was a power woman. She yanked the same skin backwards, and as it tightened, she realized she could use Los Angeles to her advantage. That kid in high school always wanted to photograph her. She'd lose fifteen pounds, get her pictures done, and see what happened.

That was a stupid idea, she decided. More likely, she'd find a job doing tech support again and spend all the money paying some illegal immigrant to raise her children.

But she still had Leonardas's cash.
She hated everybody in that moment. Absolutely everybody.
So it was time to get head shots done.

Steven's Uncle Lawrence was pushing a wheelbarrow full of gravel from the driveway to the back yard. It was shaping up to be the worst drought in twenty years in Fort Stockton, and he and Loretta were getting too old to maintain a lawn. So as she watched Oprah Winfrey, Lawrence set about to build a drought-proof property.

Loretta found him two hours later, and closed his eyes. She calmly walked back into the house and called the ambulance. When it arrived, she was sitting on their dusty sofa, the television blaring advice on domestic relationships; Loretta remained utterly unresponsive to the EMTs who attempted to revive her. Sometimes they die sitting up, one medic said to the other respectfully. They called for the coroner, and left without realizing that the woman they were bagging at that moment had made the call to report Lawrence's death fifteen minutes before.

Lawrence's body remained in the unfenced back yard, where it was mauled by coyotes for two nights before a neighbor spotted it.

He had no heirs that anyone knew of. He'd adopted his nephew, they all remembered, but didn't he die of rheumatic fever right after college? Nobody had seen him in nearly twenty years, so that became the consensus.

Life in Green Bay hadn't been all that hard. Steven had managed to avoid any major fights, and only had to spend the football season incarcerated. The jail was close enough to Lambeau Field for everyone to hear the crowd during the Packers' home games, but the sounds were muffled by echoes. It became a science to know what a first down sounded like compared to a touchdown, but interceptions were always easiest to identify.

So he read. He read everything he could, mostly magazines: it's a myth that prison libraries have the classics just sitting around waiting for a brilliant inmate. No, they have stuff he should have read by middle school: *The Mouse and the Motorcycle, The Phantom Tollbooth*, an illustrated and truncated version of the Bible (Jesus was conspicuously white, but had been colored in with brown crayon at some point). By far the most interesting book he found was The *Temple of the Golden Pavilion,* about a Japanese monk who burns down a temple, largely because it's beautiful. He read it twice in a row, then tucked it under his pillow, knowing nobody would ever miss it. Even when it was found during a surprise inspection, the guards left it there. Part of being a guard in a Wisconsin prison is not caring what dead Japanese guys thought about anything.

When the letter came from his new employer stating he had concealed his past criminal record and his services were no longer required, Steven laughed. He had been, for at the least the last month, indisposed. The fact that they sent the letter anyway only told him that legal had been contacted by Tiffany and fired him well after HR had. One of Tiffany's lawyers would have clicked on Westlaw to find out he was employed again, and after hearing the news she'd have relayed to his new company the information about his past conviction in the most helpful way possible. It was the only way for her to justify how she destroyed both their marriage and Tim and Lisa's. It couldn't be because she wasn't rising meteorically enough, or because she wasn't provided for enough to give up outside work. No, it had to be because Steven was a monster.

The better letter was from the playhouse. It caught up to him late also:

Thank you for your participation in our production of CAT ON A HOT TIN ROOF. Your contribution has been felt by all of our cast and crew, and we are grateful for your interest in the Community Theatre.

Unfortunately, there are certain political realities we must be aware of and recognize, as we are a community organization, and depend upon the grace of the community for our support. Certain aspects of your past activities may threaten that support, and we cannot risk that in a time where community support for artistic organizations have never been weaker.

Steven, I assure you that I myself have had to make many sacrifices of a similar nature to maintain the political peace in the organizations I serve, and I hope that you will understand that this is in no way a personal judgment, and I encourage you to consider assisting the CT in other, less public ways.

Thank you for understanding our position, and the best of luck to you in your future theatrical endeavors. Hans tells me you are a bright star ready to rise; I wish ours were the sky to host you.

Best regards,


Sylvia Warring
Personnel Director, The Community Theatre


He briefly considered writing back to Sylvia Warring, whom he hadn't even met. But who would that serve?

Drinking in prison was tricky, but it could be done. He'd help other inmates with jailhouse appeals, pretending to have been a legal assistant, when only his advanced literacy skills distinguished him from his clients. His first brief actually was heard and considered by the court, resulting in an inmate leaving jail four months earlier than scheduled, which dramatically increased his reputation among the less literate inmates. In exchange, they'd sneak in cheap whiskey, which he'd pull from under his cot late at night. He could handle this. When he got out, he'd start over again. This might even be the best thing for him: on the Pizza Tour's Omaha stop, he swore the whites of his eyes were becoming yellow. Having only a fifth of whiskey a week would allow his liver to recover.

Steven played basketball, learned when to speak up, and more importantly, when to shut up, which was a skill he admitted he'd sometimes lacked. His general mood even seemed to improve. Contrary to what the cop shows portrayed, most guys in prison knew what they did and why they were there. Some had been screwed by the system, as he felt he had been, but it didn't mean they ignored the fact that their actions led them there. Steven didn't have to punch that Jeremy kid out, even if he weren't the nephew of a judge. Too macho. Too much.

He'd just gotten to that place of relative inner quiet when, as he was watching TV in the day room, a commercial for a nationwide rental furniture store came on: and there was Tiffany, explaining how she couldn't afford to buy nice furniture, but now that she'd gone to this store, her apartment was a hit with all of her friends. At first he thought it was just an actress with an uncommon resemblance to Tiffany, but after the third airing of the commercial in one hour, he closed his eyes as she talked and realized it could be nobody else.

Shaken, he walked back into his cell and sat upon his bed. It made the sound of crushing cellophane, and he leaned up to see a letter from Tiffany's lawyer. Knowing her, it was probably a request to keep him in jail for his full sentence, instead of being released the next month for good behavior. He actually felt optimism as he opened the mail-even bad news doesn't sting so much when you know it's coming, and Tiffany had nothing on his good behavior. It was a Wisconsin standard, enforced because Wisconsin couldn't afford to hold inmates for their entire sentences. He'd have had to have shivved someone to be held past next month.

That wasn't the topic at all. Uncle Lawrence had died of a heart attack. Tiffany's lawyer found out about it and wanted Steven's inheritance in Fort Stockton. It was a worthless little house in a flat little town. It had almost no cash value. But they were laying claim to it, and he had thirty days to respond – which meant four days after his release he had to somehow get back to Texas and mount a defense.

And by the way, he'd owe attorney's fees to Tiffany if he lost, and her husband had gotten a big promotion and they now lived in Los Angeles.

Steven held the letter in his hand until it began to tremble so much that he couldn't read it.

Uncle Lawrence was gone. Steven had done a good enough job laying low that only Tiffany found him. But Uncle Lawrence was gone. Steven closed his eyes and tried to remember his mother for a moment. Anything would do: her voice, her hair, her scent, anything.

Nothing came to mind and the moment passed, and all that was left was the fact that Tiffany could find out about his uncle before he did, and was using a loss, something she knew would cripple him, to terrorize him again. She always looked at attachments as a weakness, and the only thing Steven was attached to was his uncle, although he could go years without talking to him. They'd pick up the phone like they'd spoken the day before. Always. He'd been looking forward to calling him next month.

There was no way he was calling his public defender, who wasn't licensed in Texas anyway, and any Texas attorney would take one look at the value of the property and decide it wasn't worth even their retainer to defend it for Steven. But a part of Steven couldn't let that happen, a growing part, something rising from almost within his stomach.

Steven felt physically ill. He turned and leaned over the stainless steel toilet.

Come on, get it out, come on—he leaned farther over, waiting for his stomach muscles to contract. The toilet smelled of antiseptic. Steven tried to use that to cause his throat to loosen, hoping for a gagging effect.

Nothing happened, but his stomach continued to churn. He had to get this out—but it was no use.

Steven turned and sat down on the floor next to the toilet. It was only now that he realized he'd been crying. He hoped nobody had seen him on the way down the hall, but even the sound of his dry wretches probably drew some attention. He'd have to say he ate something bad.

Suddenly an idea hit him, just as he noticed how cool the rim of the toilet bowl felt against his forehead. He had to stop Tiffany. Completely. Her lawyers won't work without a client, and he could fix that.

He sat back up, feeling instantly sicker. He threw his face into the bowl just in time to watch the contents of his stomach flow into the water. It was only grey bile. One purge, two—and he fell back against the wall.

But still, it wasn't an awful idea. He'd already done the time, hadn't he? Felonious assault without ever assaulting someone, losing how many opportunities because Tiffany decided the best defense was a good offense. He'd already paid for crimes he hadn't committed, over and over again. He'd keep paying. It wasn't going to stop anytime soon, or anytime at all. Every day that Anthony grew would be a day more that Tiffany's lawyers would charge him for—he'd never get on his feet, ever, if they had anything to say about it.

You couldn't kill anybody, you weakling. Steven swore he heard that voice, actually heard it, there in the cell. No, he wasn't going crazy, he thought—but that voice wasn't his. That thought wasn't coming from him.

It was coming from Tiffany. That's exactly what she would say if she saw him right now. She'd laugh, say something about Tim getting a national job and them moving to LA, living in a giant house, raising his now nine-year-old son–and he could just see her telling Tim that she was so happy to have gotten away from such a weak, pitiful man.

And now, he was hearing her taunting him, teasing him, telling him he was too weak to do anything about it.

He wasn't too weak, though. That was what only Steven knew as he heard the rushing water of the flushing toilet. He could still do something. He could stand up for himself and make a statement: that you can't just ruin a man's life with impunity; that you cannot lie about a man without consequences.

Steven began to stand up, and as he did, he realized, for the first time, that he was, in fact, capable of ending another person's life.

He looked at himself in his scratched up aluminum mirror, and decided his last three weeks would reveal him to be a model prisoner.

Tiffany woke up again, almost violently, and found herself sitting upright. She looked down beside her, relieved she had not bothered Tim. He'd ask if she had a bad dream, then pester her about it until she'd have to make up one that was sufficiently Freudian for him to believe.

Because he stopped deserving to know what she thought a while ago, when he made her move to this stupid house in LA (let him commute to Long Beach. She had things to do in town), a house that was being constantly overflown by helicopters, especially at night. He didn't deserve to know who she truly was. So screw him if he asks.

That night she wasn't so sure it was a good idea to be so hostile. The ranks of people who cared about what she thought about anything were undeniably shrinking. Anthony was just getting old enough to care more about his friends than about his mommy; and Tommy, well, she knew she loved him. She just didn't like him very much.

Why couldn't she have just had a girl?

Just take what you're given, she told herself. You rolled the dice, you lost. There are worse things than getting a national commercial spot. People in the grocery store would occasionally recognize her, without knowing why; she got used to those looks, and it made her feel the comfort of being a credenza again. They don't know me, she thought, but they think they do. They won't tell me so. This was high school. Everything was high school to Tiffany.

And it hadn't been a bad dream anyway. She was just awakened with unexpected clarity by the sound of Leonardas's voice. What it said, she couldn't make out, but it was vaguely panicked, as though asking of Tiffany something that she knew Tiffany could not provide. But it wasn't a disappointed voice either: just loving, accepting, and recognizing that Tiffany would never be who he wanted her to be.

Tiffany eased back down onto her pillow and listened to Tim faintly snore. He'd rolled the dice with her too, and all he had to show for it was a wife who was angry all the time for no discernible reason.

She didn't have to be that person, she realized. She could throttle back the anger.

Maybe. A lot had brought her to the anger place. It would take a lot to come back. And life with Tim just seemed to be digging a whole even deeper to dark parts of herself she couldn't identify.

She closed her eyes and tried to remember what Leonardas had said to her in the dream. No discernible words, just something akin to a long hum, like you'd feel if you were in some kind of papoose as a baby and your mother was talking to someone else.

Oh, Tim would love to hear about that dream. He was convinced all of her problems were her dad's fault; how could Tim be responsible for anything that went wrong between them? How could she not love the great Timothy? Being unhappy in his presence had to be a pathology on her part, his attitude suggested. It disgusted her.

She opened her eyes and watched the ceiling as the occasional car drove past. As they'd go by their reflected lights made the light through the windows seem to dance from one side of the room to the other. She wondered how to plot those motions on a graph. Depending on any mid-pass changes in speed, they'd most likely be purely parabolic curves. She ached to do real math again, to live in a world where the right answer was plottable, and nobody cared whether you could bend your back or toss your hair or be a girly girl or a tomboy. Someplace where only the work mattered.

Tim burrowed into his pillow, half awake. He always woke up when she'd have unspoken conversations next to him, as though he could hear every word that she thought. She'd have to get some sleep. She had a call-back tomorrow for a FedEx commercial.

"I dreamt of my father last night," she told him at breakfast.

"Really." This meant, "of course you did."

"Yeah. He was juggling three chainsaws and speaking Arabic. And you know what? I think I understood him."

Tim deflated somewhat, and he turned his attention back to the newspaper. Tiffany laughed slightly. Tony and Tommy, not understanding but not wanting to be left out, laughed with them.

Tim's eyes glistened when he looked at her. There were worse things than that.

# CHAPTER THIRTEEN

## The World is full of possibilities.

Steven took a few steps out of the McDonald's on Business 10 before stopping to take in the view. The sun doesn't go gently into the good night in West Texas, it puts on a show as it dies. Thick bands of yellow, orange, red, and even grey seemed to lounge on the horizon to the west along the Davis Mountains, as the giant cumulonimbus clouds to the east towered in pink and purple. This was a living rainbow of life, he thought, as he bit into his quarter-pounder. This was something more people should stop and see.

His key didn't work right away. It took a few minutes of maneuvering before he could coax it into the old lock that barred his uncle and aunt's front door. There'd been a realtor's key-safe there for some time, but the house hadn't sold since they died, and despite Tiffany's efforts, it wasn't about to. Fort Stockton, Texas, is, frankly, in the middle of nowhere. Farther from any metropolitan area than almost any other town in the continental US – and seeing how the major cities nearest to it are San Antonio and El

Paso, Steven wasn't sure if that counted at all. It was Montana without the romance, and that's saying something.

When the door opened it seemed to call upon every ounce of dust in the room to spring up to its defense, and the particles danced in the last streams of sunlight as Steven walked to the sofa in the front room and pulled it away from the wall. It was a yellow plush monstrosity with light brown carpeted patterns on it; perhaps it was meant to convey royalty or wealth or something. But to Steven it always shrieked of the worst of 1960s design, and when his aunt unilaterally decided to put a clear plastic cover on it following the Dairy Queen debacle of 1974, he found it even more hideous. But he was looking for something else today.

It was just a precaution, Steven thought. Then he actually laughed out loud, his breath disturbing the easy flow of the golden flecks of dust – no, this wasn't a precaution.

But you're not really doing this, are you?

He didn't answer that question to himself. He'd stopped answering it long ago. The sofa yielded and slid away from the wall, and a large oblong box became visible on the floor.

He placed the box on the sofa and paused ahead of the ferocious sneezing fit that was the house's last show of defiance to its intruder. To someone not in Steven's head, it appeared he was dancing from the old rabbit-eared console TV to the sofa and back again, convulsing with a spirit worthy of a Baptist preacher on a sin-hating tear. Steven himself simply went through the sneezes, waiting for them to stop, confident it was just a reaction. It would rain soon.

The box was permanently left unlocked, Uncle Lawrence had explained, because if he locked it, he wasn't sure if it would open again. It had been in their family for almost 100 years – and was brought to Ft. Stockton when the US Army had to repel the invasion of Texas by the Mexican army in the days just before America entered World War One. They'd taken a lot of land very quickly, but it was land nobody lived on, and the Army had to simply assemble with a token force to convince the Mexicans to withdraw.

Aunt Maria always disputed this, largely because the Mexicans had always fought so bravely to keep Texas in the past that she couldn't stomach the idea of them simply running from cannons. But their hearts weren't in that war; they'd marched across an empty border, and anyone who looked at this land knew instantly it might be worth fighting for, but it truly didn't belong to anyone.

The gun itself lay in the box. It wasn't a manstopper. Just a .22 rifle, single shot, meant to deter coyotes and other creatures from harassing the houses on the frontier, and to shoot prickly pear cactus. It was used by the Army, but never considered a serious weapon. It was cheap to make and looked good on the shoulder, which is all that was required during the defense of Texas in 1917. The Mexicans retreated, then officially refused the Zimmerman telegram's request, and the event faded into history without any loss of life. The US entered the war soon after, and most Americans outside of Pecos County never knew that part of their country had been briefly invaded.

Steven wasn't really into firearms. He'd never found handguns attractive, and was bewildered by the people who did. But he knew that as a paroled felon, he'd never be able to buy one. But this was an heirloom, it didn't have papers, there were no registration hassles to be faced. It might not have been powerful enough to kill even a coyote, but it could sure piss one off, which was usually enough to get a pack to retreat from the property.

More importantly: when they did the ballistics report on Tiffany, they wouldn't know what in the world killed her. Or at least, they couldn't trace it back to him, he was sure of that. Thank god for inheritances.

He pulled the lever that allowed the rifle to fold open —the barrel was a little dusty, but still clean and fireable. Uncle Lawrence had always kept it well-oiled, and had even had it restored to its original specs just before he died, so Steven figured it didn't need an overhaul for two shots to the head.

He wondered for a few moments about the age of the bullets in the faded cardboard box. Did bullets go bad? Not in brass casings, he decided, as he loaded the chamber. He'd go outside, take a test shot at a cactus, and leave. That's all he had to do at this point.

The rain began as he slid the sofa back against the wall. Not a slow, soothing tropical rain – most people in Ft. Stockton have no idea that such a rain exists. This was a full downpour, as if God had opened a relief valve. These storms came often in warm weather, and were known for their horrible violence and their brevity. It would soon pass. Or not.

Standing in the front door with the antique rifle in his hand, breathing in the scent of the rain, Steven marveled at how miraculously simple such convection storms were, and hoped this one would last the night, as they sometimes did. Then he could lay on his old bed and let the droning sound of the raindrops slapping the tin roof coax him to sleep, and when he'd awaken, he wouldn't have made the mistakes he'd made, his aunt would be cooking migas for breakfast, and the whole world would be wide open to him again. This wasn't a romantic notion. Texas storms do in fact make you believe that weather can wash all things clean.

He aimed the rifle at a cactus. Nothing was flowering; must be too early in the year. The gunsight was level. But Steven wondered, even in the midst of a storm, if the report of the rifle would be noticed. When he was a kid, he heard them all the time. Somebody was always killing something. That's just how it was. But now, McDonald's had a drive thru and nobody trusted anyone. He found these developments to be correlated, but couldn't explain why. He did, however, realize that he didn't want all nine members of the Ft. Stockton police department congregating on the property. So he lowered the rifle without pulling the trigger and went back into the house.

As he sat on the hideous sofa he reconsidered his plan, as he knew the storm would force him to do. Did Tiffany deserve to die, and did he have the arrogance to make that decision for her?

She ruined your life.

Yeah, maybe. But I helped.

This was an unproductive debate that Steven had long grown tired of. But it had gotten him on a plane and into a rental Prius in Midland (the fact that he could rent a hybrid electric car in Midland, a town that literally reeks of oil, astonished him), and now he was home and arming himself, about to make it a considerably less abstract conundrum. Anyone could kill someone in their imagination, or in an idle conversation. Now he had a gun in his hands.

A bolt of lightning struck, probably a mile away. Steven didn't jump. Nobody in Ft. Stockton jumps at lightning. In fact, most of the population was too old to even hear it, he thought. Was Mrs. Walker still alive next door?

He had to strip away his doubts. He had tried too many times to re-build his life, and he had deserved a better one. Tiffany took it from him, and what was more, she took it for so little. It was one thing to be betrayed if Tiffany was going to become famous or significant in some historical way. That was a situation he could live with, he'd long ago decided. But for her to betray him just to have an average life with another man, bereft of real accomplishments, was something worth being punished for. Balzac had written that every fortune was built upon a great crime. She'd committed the crime, but never reaped the profits from it. He wasn't going to shoot her out of revenge for what she'd done – it was going to be a reckoning for what she never became after doing so.

The world is full of possibilities, Cookie Monster once said. You could be whatever you wanted to be in this world. If you're going to torch someone, it better be on the way to the top. To torch someone to become utterly average was offensive in a deeply existential way, Steven thought.

The rain began to subside. He would not be lulled into sleep.

As he left the house and scurried to his rental car, he realized he hadn't locked the door behind him. It wasn't worth going back through the last gasps of the storm to correct – there was nothing in that house that anyone wanted. It was a strong realization that made him oblivious to the fact that he'd left the car radio's volume up at an alarming level, and the static from the AM band seemed to meld with the last few drops of rain on the top of the car. Maybe he shouldn't have rented a hybrid, he thought as he turned the volume down. People notice hybrids in this part of the country.

But not in LA. And if he set the cruise control at four miles per hour over the speed limit, he'd be there in twenty-three hours. It was a pleasant realization, and he pulled out of the muddy driveway to begin his last road trip, the rifle in plain sight in the back seat. And Steven was completely unaware that his uncle, when he had the gun reconditioned just before his death, had discovered that time and a cartridge casing corroded by dust meant that either the rifle, if fired again, would make so much noise it'd wake up every coyote in ten counties; or, it would simply explode in the firer's face, most likely ripping it off.

"Don't see anyone firin' that weapon," Lawrence said, aware that his old friend Bob the Gunsmith was always short of parts for the Stockton Specials. "Just keep 'er as is."

Katherine pulled up to the house and noticed that Jeremy's car wasn't there. He must have stopped at the store on the way home or something, when she called him at work he was headed out the door.

Good. It gave her just a little more time.

She grabbed the bag from the rear seat and hurried inside, turning on one or two lights as she snaked through the house. It would be dark soon, he had to be back in time for the sunset.

She ran upstairs and threw the curtains wide open. It was her favorite feature about their new house, the view they had of the sunset every evening. It was the highest window, and she was only half joking to Jeremy the other day about putting a small dining table there. Jeremy had laughed and said it would make the master bedroom feel like an efficiency apartment, and they'd had enough of those in college.

She'd felt bad then, remembering how he'd hated living in that old apartment, eating that lasagna and his macaroni and cheese and drinking water from the tap. Not like her life was much better before his Uncle Ted got Jeremy the marketing position. She never had that kind of help – she cut herself off. This was a time to rebuild them both, not to obsess over what went wrong.

Even after six months working with Helen, she still had that tendency just to focus on her own immediate desires or memories without realizing how doing so would impact anyone else, especially Jeremy.

What a trip Helen turned out to be. That first session, the moment she returned from the other room where she'd set Jeremy down, Helen wheeled on Katherine and said "you need to grow the hell up, or you're going to do this to every man you meet, and eventually, honey, one of them's going to hurt you back. Badly."

And Katherine hadn't even told her anything yet.

That following hour was spent just explaining everything, from the lesbian experiment to the fantasies to the "fuck buddies" (Helen didn't even blink at the term), all of it. It took nearly an hour just to explain the facts, and Helen had listened impassively, not reacting, not encouraging, not even writing things down. And when Katherine had finally finished, and looked up to Helen for some indication, some reaction, any reaction, Helen had just leaned forward and said:

"Do you think any of these other men cared about you?"

Katherine didn't have to think about that.

"No."

"Do you think that man in the other room cares about you?"

"Jeremy?"

Helen nodded.

"Well, yes. It was stupid, showing up like that in the bar. I think he was drunk."

"What would it take, what kind of pressure, what kind of pain, would he have to be going through to do something like that?"

And just like that, a light turned on in a hidden cavern in Katherine's mind, and she could suddenly see, in the small remnants of recalled conversations, the looks in Jeremy's eyes over the last months, the way he'd always act so nervous before and after she went out, even the way he seemed to want to run away into the closets when they had sex with other people – suddenly all of this fit into a pattern that she'd never been willing to recognize before.

"I really hurt him, didn't I?"

Helen had actually looked surprised at this. "Yes, dear. And I've been in practice enough to know that you're lucky he's the one with the broken jaw."

"Jeremy wouldn't hurt anybody."

"He's a man, dear. A man can destroy anything or anyone if he sets his mind to it."

"What do I do?"

"What do you want to do?"

"I want to make things how they were."

"Can't do it."

"Then I want to fix things."

"What will that take?" Helen was fidgeting with her hands, as though they longed to be holding a cigarette. She seemed to be checking the wall clock a lot.

"I have to be a better wife."

"Is it that simple?"

Katherine looked into herself, and felt stupid. Maybe Jeremy wasn't perfect, and maybe she'd been a little selfish. She could at least be nicer to him, and stop the running around for a while. She was no longer the virgin bride, and she'd met enough men to know that even if Jeremy didn't excite her like he used to, he was constant, and he didn't lie to her.

"Probably not."

"We'll talk next week, then." She then walked out with Katherine, and Katherine had been genuinely surprised when Helen announced that they were going to try to save the marriage. Yeah, she'd thought, I guess that's what I was saying.

Since then, Katherine had been surprised how easy it was to be good to Jeremy. Even sex with him had gotten better, to the point where she couldn't understand why she'd been so adamant about living out this fantasy life.

What kind of phase had that been? What brought it on, and why did she enjoy it so much? Why couldn't she see how hard it had been on Jeremy? And why, she thought as the laid out a linen tablecloth on a folding card table in the master bedroom, did she have no desire whatsoever to do anything remotely kinky again? Honestly, she thought as she looked over at the bed, missionary position with Jeremy is fine, with the occasional turning over or her taking command on top of him — but that's all she needed sexually anymore, and she couldn't conceive of what made her want more than that to begin with. Maybe just some kind of reaction to having waited so long to have sex, and marrying him as a semi-virgin (the high school thing didn't count, she'd long ago decided). All those years of buildup and fantasy just burst out, she thought, not being at all sure if it were true.

Katherine felt herself sweating a little as she hauled two of their formal dining room chairs up to the master bedroom. It was taking shape. Candles in place, and their best china, the wedding gift from Uncle Ted, who had never bothered to find out where they were registered. The plates didn't go with anything else, but they worked tonight.

She stepped back, examining her handiwork. A romantic corner table in a restaurant, right there in their bedroom, overlooking the sunset.

She heard the timer go off. The meal was almost ready.

Further sessions with Helen had been useful. Sometimes Helen was wrong, sometimes she'd get a little carried away, calling Katherine immature and self-centered that one time, for instance. But generally, she was pretty good, and had helped Katherine see that trust takes a long time to build up, and virtually no time at all to destroy. It would take work to bring her and Jeremy back, but they had good things going for them: Jeremy hadn't gone nuts, as many men would have, and had never threatened her or attempted to hurt her. She really hadn't lied to him much, and throughout their fantasy experiences, she'd been as blunt and direct with him as possible, and that left a strong foundation, Helen said, even if the house got blown away during the storm.

Helen seemed to like framing things in terms of houses and storms. She was from Oklahoma.

This new house was even Jeremy's idea, after he got out of the hospital he announced he was tired of them renting a town home, even if it was large, and with a little help from Uncle Ted, they were in a beautiful, if smaller, three story house in Wauwatosa, right on the crest of a hill, with the most beautiful sunsets she'd ever seen. Sure, the neighbors were ten feet away, but it was a charming old 1920s neighborhood, and people didn't mind building so close to each other then.

Katherine drained the water from the pot, added a stick of butter to the pasta, a little bit of milk, and cut open the packet of cheese powder. She began stirring the mixture.

She and Helen had actually started talking about whether or not to continue the sessions. Helen said she didn't like repeating herself, and since the marriage was fundamentally sound (Helen said things like that, they always confused her. Like she was getting an A in a class or something. She always got As when she knew what was expected of her), Katherine knew what to look out for, and the relationship, if she could keep that in check, would likely flourish.

And she'd been amazed at how much she found herself wanting to give to Jeremy. She did his laundry now, and even sorted it properly, without finding it the least bit of a chore. She liked cooking for him, doing the dishes – she found herself thinking, at the oddest times, 'how can I take care of him best right now?' which was an odd, somewhat disturbing question that made her feel a little embarrassed, as though she had transformed into a 1950s housewife or something.

She could tell by the sudden sticky sounds that the macaroni and cheese was ready. Just for fun she threw in some chopped up hot dog pieces, stirred the mixture a little more for good measure, spooned it into Uncle Ted's fabulously expensive china bowls, and brought the meal upstairs.

It was a little odd that Jeremy wasn't home by now, but she was glad to have the surprise ready for him. It's never quite as good a surprise when you're in the middle of preparing it. Then you have to see people react like it's the thought that counts, and if there was anything Helen had taught her, it's that the thoughts don't mean anything if the actions contradict them.

Katherine surprised herself with that thought. Maybe she didn't need to keep seeing Helen. Maybe Helen was already permanently in her head.

Besides, she didn't want to sleep with anyone else but Jeremy, and couldn't fathom that ever changing.

She sat down and noticed that the sunset had begun. If Jeremy wasn't here in fifteen minutes, he'd miss it. She could still light the candles, though, and maybe put on something sexy. Nah. She'd thrown out most of her negligees and merry widows, and now preferred to wear plaid flannel. It made her feel sexy in a completely different way than she ever had before.

The sunset was marvelous, and Katherine found herself staring blankly at it, not really observing it so much as participating in it – her mind wandering to wherever Jeremy was, and totally avoiding any kind of speculation that the future wouldn't be exactly what she wanted it to be. She never looked that far ahead, anyway, but right now, she was a good wife, and she had a spoonful of macaroni and cheese absentmindedly, wondering what Jeremy would think of her surprise when he came upstairs.

He wasn't going to. Jeremy had just cleared security and was about to board a flight to Dallas. Then another flight from Dallas to Leon, Mexico, and a two-hour bus ride to San Miguel de Allende. He pulled out his MP3 player and tuned to the Spanish language lessons he'd loaded on it the week before. He was up to "how to order in restaurants."

He watched the sunset from Billy Mitchell International Airport and wondered how to describe it in Spanish.

"La puesta del sol es muy bonita."

He was certain that couldn't be right.

He picked up his cell phone and called the only number he could dial with his eyes closed. It answered. "I'm sorry, this is Jeremy Schultz again, I promise I'm not a bill collector, but this is the last contact info I have for my mother, Naomi Schultz...." The line went dead, as it always did. So he went over his Spanish again in his head as the last rosy-fingered tendrils of sunlight slowly crawled up the walls of the terminal.

It occurred to Steven that cruise control made so many other crimes more possible. Or at least, it helped you to blend in just a little more, as to reduce the possibility that you might be caught by adrenaline-soaked acceleration. The Oklahoma City bomber was pulled over for a bad brake light; how many bank robbers were caught just for speeding? Steven suddenly realized he didn't know if any truly had: it just stood to reason.

He already felt so conspicuous that he tried to avoid any eye contact during the brief stops he would make for gas and food. He longed for a credit card that wouldn't be traceable to him – all those wonderful card-powered gas pumps would have kept him from being noticed. But paying cash would make his steps harder to trace. Not impossible, but harder. It would perhaps give him time enough to get into Mexico.

If he made that choice. As he drove through El Paso and read the giant words carved into the mountain across the border: "La Biblia is La Verdad. Leela,' he wondered if this was really the kind of place where he wanted to live. It was one thing to have a belief system, and another to lord it, as it were, over your neighbor from the top of a mountain. He smiled at his pun. What the hell. The Voice of America has been doing the same thing for years.

Steven was driving at precisely the speed limit with the radio on, neither foot near a pedal. He was driving through a part of the country where drug crimes were so rampant that police felt they could search your car for no reason, and Steven's trunk contained his future, which your average motorcycle cop on the shoulder of I-10 in El Paso was not likely to understand.

So when Steven passed by one, sunglasses gleaming, radar gun firing right at him, his pulse throbbed and he didn't know what to do. Make eye contact? Ignore him? Do the two-finger man-wave from the top of the steering wheel? He pledged to buy some cheap sunglasses at the next gas station, and drove by the cop as though he never saw him.

The next quarter mile was the most crucial. Steven watched in the rear view mirror to see if Robocop mounted his bike. He knew he hadn't been speeding, but Driving While Under the Influence of Some Really Bad Intentions had to be visible, even at full speed.

The cop mounted his bike. He seemed to be moving – then –

Steven had to slam on the brakes. The Cadillac in front of him, which had been going entirely too fast and had passed him a minute or so before, now decided that the presence of a policeman on the highway required a regulated speed of ten miles below the speed limit. Everyone's brake lights were lit up, and the Cadillac's custom license plate brought the word "arrived" with alarming speed towards him. Steven managed to slow down without swerving or screeching his tires, while the motorcycle cop drove steadily towards him, his lights on.

Just lay off the brakes and go with the flow. Steven took his shaking left hand and tried to steady it against the steering wheel. He could hear the siren now. He looked around at the other cars and saw them all angling slightly to the shoulder. Steven followed. He wanted to turn up the air conditioning but didn't want it too look as though he were pulling something out of the glove box.

The cop flew past him, then got in front of the Cadillac and waved the driver over. Steven slowed down to allow for their exit from the lane, then let his thumb slowly slide over the 'resume' button on the cruise control.

The hybrid's peppy engine decided it was to resume a speed of fifty-five miles per hour within a few seconds, and Steven's heart leapt as the sudden acceleration seemed to be a vehicular confession of guilt. He looked again behind him; the policeman was talking to the driver of the Cadillac, some gray-haired baby boomer.

The policeman never looked up. Steven exhaled with unexpected force and felt his shoulders relax just a little. They had, he suddenly realized, been trying to force their way into his ears.

You're supposed to be able to get used to anything, he thought. Surely he'd calm down by the time he got to New Mexico.

He entered the Land of Enchantment without realizing he'd just blown his left brake light.

# CHAPTER FOURTEEN

"You're Going to a Pretty Awful Place if Getting There is Half the Fun."
— Miss Piggy

Steven woke up in the Travelodge on Sunset Boulevard. His hands were shaking and his stomach felt like it had been ripped out by some exotic animal. Maybe a tiger. Yeah, this is what it feels like to get a tiger claw in the gut. Is that what Siegfried felt? Or was it Roy?

He rolled up and found the bottle of Stolichnaya on his nightstand, perched in the plastic ice bucket, condensed water everywhere. Water escapes through most barriers. Would it spoil the finish on the nightstand? Steven wiped some of it away with his right hand and decided there were few manmade objects that could destroy the finish on hotel furniture.

The vodka was still cool enough for him not to need to shuffle down the hall to the ice machine. The first sip renewed the silvery feeling on his tongue, but he knew that before having a second, he'd have to endure some dry heaving. His digestive system wouldn't keep bourbon down and clearly didn't want any more vodka. But his soul, his soul needed it. You don't kill somebody sober. As he looked out the window at the gray morning light he thought, *hell, you don't do anything on Sunset Boulevard sober*. But that was just a feeling. The inversion layer of clouds would burn away in a couple of hours and everything would be bright again.

He no longer bothered to run to the bathroom when the heaves began. There was nothing to regurgitate. His stomach convulsed, and he leaned over the ice bucket to spit. It pulled at him again, yanking him downwards. This was all to be expected, nothing unusual. He waited until he felt the blood being forced into his face, like he was wearing a collar that was two inches too tight, and then went to the bathroom sink, where a few tablespoons of acid flopped from his mouth into the basin. This is why he didn't wear ties.

Who am I kidding, he thought. Nobody has asked me to wear a tie for five years.

He looked at himself in the mirror. His tomato face during the dry heaves always made him look like a monster. It blew out a few capillaries around his nose and cheeks, and even his eyes flared a yellowish-red. It would subside in about an hour. Then his eyes would be back to a pale yellow color that nobody seemed to notice. He figured there was a connection between his drinking and his eyes, but refused to see a doctor in case his hunch was correct. Fuckup. Perpetual fuckup.

He shuffled back to the bed and grabbed his Styrofoam cup of Stoli. The third drink came easily, and he felt the alcohol easing into his bloodstream. This was better.

Calculations. Drink until you take a nap; then wake up feeling sober enough to drive down the street. Wait until she brings Anthony from school. One shot if you can. Nobody knows where one shot comes from — they can locate it easier after two or three. Then take Anthony, and it's off to Mexico.

He looked at the Hefty Bag containing his change of clothes — you change right afterwards in the Chevron station's bathroom. You drop your old clothes in the dumpster behind that Thai restaurant on LaBrea before 4pm, when the garbage truck came. If you miss that deadline, all the dumpsters in Larchmont Village are emptied about an hour later. The things you learn by following garbage trucks.

He took another drink. He wished he could feel drunk again. It had been so long. Now all he ever felt was a little light headed, and he knew not to drive or go out in public when that happened. It was best to go to sleep; but if he could ever get a restful sleep instead of just passing out, he thought, he'd probably not be in this state of mind.

Another idea came to him. He sat down and added it to his notes. It was a funny thought, but seeing how badly his hand was still shaking as he wrote, he realized it looked like the scribbling of a madman.

And it was. He was certain he had gone insane. She had done this to him. She set this all in motion.

This really wasn't revenge. He wasn't particularly angry anymore, and could hardly remember what it was like to feel hurt or betrayed by Tiffany. He was restoring balance. He was an agent of karma. She had every right to lie about him to cover her ass; but that was far from the middle path. The world corrects when you stray from the middle path. And Steven was part of the world.

He felt the heaving again, and this time he sensed that he had something to lose. He rushed to the toilet and emptied a surprising amount of pale red liquid into it.

It took two more drinks before he felt normal again. He lay down and stared at the ceiling, a bare concrete pad with cracks all around it. Too tight a mix for earthquake-prone areas. This is what happens when a hotel chain orders the same pour for buildings all around the country. No situational awareness; bad engineering.

He ran his hands through his hair and was suddenly grateful he'd had it cut so short. Less chance he'd lose some at Tiffany's house that could be used as DNA evidence against him.

He always looked so much more frightening when his hair got dry and wild during a drunk. Now, with his hair so short, he could actually walk outside without showering if he wanted to, and it wouldn't be obvious.

His hair felt crinkly and dry like an SOS pad. When he was last sober for a few weeks, he remembered, his hair was so soft. It would be nice to have soft hair again.

Jeremy came home from his first Friday of school, satisfied. Four classes, no more than twelve in each. His student bodies also included redheads in their late twenties, which he found somewhat encouraging, and was looking forward to the private teacher-student conferences that the syllabus called for in the third week.

And there was a full bottle of tequila in his apartment. Jeremy sat down in his courtyard, felt the sun gently warming him, the air in San Miguel reaching a balmy sixty-eight degrees that afternoon, and realized that if it was his destiny to be an American alcoholic in Mexico, he had noble precedents enough. He didn't mind living under the volcano.

He was fooling himself, he knew. Liquor didn't make him sick like it had in Milwaukee, but he still couldn't drink much. It made him feel like someone else, and he'd always thought it was the highest goal to feel like whoever he was. His body internalized that somehow and still resisted all efforts to infect himself with anything deleterious.

The school had been his saving grace, he was sure of that. Arrive at eight in the morning, hang out with the other expatriate teachers, talk about sports, start teaching at ten, basic conversational skills, repeating what he'd read in the *Herald Tribune* that morning, or go over the current events the other teachers had mentioned.

Basically, he was getting paid for just being himself in front of four separate groups of people. At the end of the day, he could go home to his journals, or grab a book from the library, which had a surprisingly deep collection.

He'd started dating another teacher. Her name was Elizabeth, she was forty-one, the kind who clearly used to be thin and wiry but had since relaxed herself and her brassy hair into Mexico; far more suited to him than most of the women he'd met there. She'd been an attorney in Boston, made partner, and then gave it all up, including her marriage to another member of her firm. Being divorced told Jeremy that she'd once believed in forever and gotten educated to the contrary, which was something he felt was necessary in whoever he got involved with in the future.

Jeremy examined his tequila ration. Should he hold off, make sure he's good and sober for his date, or should he embrace the warmth that was waiting to envelop his soul? He heard a knock at his door.

Was Elizabeth early? They weren't supposed to meet for another two hours, and even that was supposed to be at the café across from the church. He hadn't told Elizabeth or anyone else exactly where he lived; he couldn't bring himself to get that close to anyone. Not for a while yet.

It must be someone from the school, though, or maybe the landlord. Jeremy took a quick shot of reposado, spit it out involuntarily, then gathered himself and opened the door.

"Jeremy." Katherine stood, her eyes swollen, her arms shaking as she held her hands up to her face. She threw herself into him.

Jeremy's legs felt suddenly weak, and he realized that Katherine was holding him up as much as he was standing on his own. "Katherine – what?"

She pulled back, smiling through tears. "Baby, I'm sorry it took so long to find you."

Jeremy had no idea what to do, and found that his instincts were taking over. "Can I offer you something to drink?"

Katherine laughed. "I'm pretty whacked, sure. Water'd be fine. Oh wait, we can't drink water here, can we?" She moved forward, inspecting the courtyard as she headed for Jeremy's chair.

Jeremy headed into the kitchen and poured a glass of Evian for Katherine, then a similar glass of tequila for himself. He held both up, and thanks to the blue tint of Mexican glasswork, he was reasonably sure his drink looked mysterious. Let Katherine wonder.

This meant the evening with Elizabeth is probably off, he thought, almost amused with himself.

Katherine had taken a seat in Jeremy's hammock chair and was looking out at the mountains. "It's beautiful here."

Jeremy handed her a glass and sat down on the ground in front of her. She took a large gulp and gagged. "Oh my god!" she called out as she coughed uncontrollably for a few seconds.

Jeremy sniffed his glass, then shrugged and exchanged his for Katherine's, while she continued to cough out the last of the tequila she'd inadvertently slammed.

"My god, you don't drink liquor, honey!"

Jeremy smiled. "And I do it very well."

Katherine's face became suddenly very serious. "What are you doing here?"

Jeremy looked down at his feet. A small weed was sprouting between them, and he briefly considered pulling it – then decided it was fine where it was. "I was going to ask you the same thing." He couldn't look up at her. He took a tiny sip of his tequila and welcomed the vibrations it brought.

"I came to get you."

Jeremy nodded. He looked down at his rolled-up long sleeves. Linen suited how he felt here.

"Jeremy, what happened? I thought we were getting so healthy together." He looked up and saw she'd started crying, but not in an overly dramatic way. Not an "I lost my puppy" cry, but rather a "this movie is making me sad" cry. In fact, had he not looked up, he might not have noticed.

"I didn't feel healthy in Milwaukee. Too much happened there."

"You mean with me, the thing with the other men?"

Now's your chance, sport. This woman loves you. She came all the way from the Midwest to tell you that, to bring you back, and you can go back to the house, go back to work, and make it all happen the way you promised her when you married her.

The way you promised her when you married her, he thought again. This wasn't the woman he married. He had no idea who that woman was, but she wasn't here.

"Never mind, Katherine. I live here now."

"That's silly, Jeremy." She turned and looked back at the sunset, angry.

He was grateful to her. By invalidating his choices, Katherine was making it easier for Jeremy to keep some emotional distance, despite the fact that he could still smell the freshness of her hair. It aroused him despite his resolve.

"It's not silly, Katherine. It's what I want."

"Do you want a divorce?" Katherine had obviously rehearsed this conversation, and seemed braced for any answer.

"I don't know."

"Well, if you don't know, then we won't do it right now. Do you want me to leave?"

He looked up at her. Why did she have to be so beautiful? Why did she have to be so naïve? He suddenly thought of the Eric Rohmer film that he'd watched a few weeks before in his quest to catch up with the life of ideas that had marched merrily on despite his sabbatical marriage. It was called "Claire's Knee," and articulated better than anything he'd ever seen the effect of the stupid, mute eroticism of young women, who could excite and repel at the same time, and how angry that made Rohmer and just about everybody else who'd experienced it.

And he was doing it again. This had nothing to do with ideas or French films or existentialism. This was Katherine in front of him, her eyes moist with tears, her cheeks clear and white, her hair draped down in front of her shoulders, nearly reaching her breasts. He'd forgotten about the effect it had on him.

"No. You don't have to leave."

"Can I stay here?"

Jeremy didn't know how to answer that, so he kissed her. She fell into him as though that were the only thing she'd been waiting for, and in a moment, she was on top of him, kissing him furiously. Jeremy loved her when she was like this; he always had, and for a moment, everything seemed absolutely right in the world. He could still smell the freshness of the mountain air, he felt her tears as they flowed from her own eyes down his cheeks, and as she sat up and removed her blouse, Jeremy looked up at her breasts and was overwhelmed with a sense of well-being.

The next morning, Jeremy stirred as sounds rose out across the courtyard from the kitchen. His head was throbbing, but he was getting used to that, and it seemed like something he'd have to accept about living in Mexico. He checked his clock. 7am. He had an hour to get to the teacher's lounge.

He stood up, realized he was naked, and that he didn't care, and walked across the courtyard to the kitchen. Katherine was wearing his U of W – Milwaukee tee shirt and pouring coffee.

"Good morning, sunshine. I used bottled for the coffee."

Jeremy nodded and took the hot drink. As he sat down at the dining table he watched Katherine making herself at home, and realized that a part of him really had no idea who she was, what she was thinking, or what she was capable of. She continued to surprise him, with her fantasy life, with her devotion, and now, with her persistence.

And he couldn't have that. He wanted someone who couldn't surprise him. Was that wrong?

"You working today?"

Jeremy nodded.

"Can you speak today?"

Jeremy nodded again, smiling, realizing he had yet to say a word since waking up; Katherine sat down across the table from him. It was time to tell her to leave.

"What's wrong?"

Jeremy looked into her eyes and felt totally beguiled. She turned her head slightly, as though anticipating a blow, and Jeremy realized it was unrealistic of him to believe that he could ever be anything but in love with her. Her eyes were the very picture of innocence, and he knew she would never understand what he was feeling, no matter how long he took to explain it to her.

He also knew that it didn't matter. He knew that if he closed his eyes and imagined it, he could see himself growing old next to her, feeling her love him through the adoption of some children, through various houses in the Milwaukee area, through the grandchildren they'd have. He could sit next to her on a stoop in forty years, talking about their family and how wonderful it was to have raised it so well.

My god, she was beautiful.

Jeremy took another sip of coffee, then listened to himself talk as though he were an Eric Rohmer character. "I never want to see you again. In my entire life. Ever. If I'm on my death bed, if you have cancer, if Uncle Ted dies. Ever."

"Jeremy, what are you saying?"

Jeremy laughed out loud. This was Katherine. This is who she was and who she always would be.

"Katherine, you don't exist to me anymore. Nothing in Milwaukee does. I don't want you to talk to me, to call me, to email me, or to pop in on me wherever the world I'm living."

"What if you need help?" Katherine was crying again, quietly.

"Nobody gets help, Katherine. That's the thing. We were sold a lie. We get hurt when we're kids and we never get better. Everything else is about buying cars or houses or influence. But most of us never grow up. I know I won't. And I can't not grow up with you."

Katherine was confused enough to furrow her brow, which Jeremy always found irresistible. He turned his gaze to the sky, then continued without eye contact.

"Leave. Today. If you need to get out from under the house payment, tell Uncle Ted and he'll make it happen."

He turned and looked at her as directly as he had in years. "You are the one person I know who has a chance of being happy. And you'll never get there with me."

"What if I'd rather be with you than be happy?"

"Then I would jump off of a bridge."

He stared at her, and was surprised at the maturity Katherine's eyes returned to his gaze.

"I'll do this, because I love you."

"Thank you-"

"Under one condition."

Jeremy was surprised. "What condition?"

"You never, ever, even in a moment of weakness, reach out to me again either. I couldn't handle it. One day we might be able to talk without it meaning the apocalypse of both of our lives, but I don't see it happening. I'll file for divorce, you won't owe anything. But I never want to see your voice or hear your face again."

Jeremy had been surprised that she'd used the word apocalypse; it was easy to underestimate Katherine's mind. But the "see your voice or hear your face" reminded him how difficult it was for her to say what she obviously needed to say. She'd known this was going to be his reaction, and had practiced her response so much that she got it wrong.

"Okay. I have to get to work. Take all the time you need, but I'm back at four today. I would appreciate it if you weren't here."

They both stood up and stared at each other. This is the time in movies where they kiss, or make abrupt turns away from each other, he thought. They did neither. She cleared away the coffee cups, and as Jeremy packed his book bag, she leaned into his bedroom.

"Kitchen's clean."

"Thanks." The top of Jeremy's mouth felt scalded, like he'd bitten into an apple cobber right out of the oven.

Jeremy was dreading the goodbye. He stepped back into the courtyard and looked around. She must be packing her bag, although he couldn't quite remember that she brought one.

He heard her rental car start. It would take only a second for him to be there to say goodbye, to make it something memorable, to bring true closure to the experience.

The car pulled away before he had a chance to decide what to do. He wiped away a tear and left his courtyard apartment through the back door to take the mountain trail down to the school, so he wouldn't have to walk the roads.

Katherine will probably be smiling by the time she got to Leon, he thought. She had the clearest instructions he'd ever given her on how to make Jeremy happy, and would follow them to the letter.

Two years later, after selling the house in Milwaukee and taking a job with a non-profit in St. Louis, Katherine began an affair with the female Executive Director of the organization, Regan. She'd still tell herself she was a heterosexual because her thoughts would regularly turn to Jeremy and how he was doing in Mexico, and it was a point of pride that she didn't contact him; unlike Regan, who couldn't seem to stop calling some guy in Hawaii who curled her toes for a few days, several years ago. That brief affair had made Regan, who was recently married, so miserable she took up beekeeping in her spare time. Katherine remembered her own therapy and knew that volunteering to be stung on a daily basis was a way of expressing misery. If nothing else, wearing beekeeping gear was the strongest symbol she could think of to tell the world to stay the hell away from her heart.

But Katherine was content. She knew what the rules were, and she was following them. She was working hard, she was nice to people, and she knew that her silence would make Jeremy happy. That's all that mattered. That would make Jeremy happy. It would have made Amy happy.

When Regan asked her if they would consider having a baby in vitro, Katherine wanted more than anything to call Jeremy to ask him to donate as the father. Raising his child would make up for a lot. But contacting him would be akin to refusing to grow up and accept him for who he was. It would be childishly self-centered, and she wasn't a child anymore.

"You'd have to get a divorce, unless you want Alan to think it's his child."

"You'd have to admit you're a lesbian. Are you ready for that?"

Katherine chewed on her lip, looked at Regan, and smiled.

The Travelodge had no stationery, which wasn't a surprise. So Steven had half-stumbled up to the Roosevelt on Hollywood and Orange and asked for some. While he was waiting he flirted with an architect named Rachel, who had recently fled back home from a bad marriage in Alabama. She was a thin woman with strong features, and shoulders that Steven could tell were just learning to bear her own burden, as though she'd been carrying the great weight of another's man's baggage, and was now free of it and her muscles didn't know what to do.

So Steven said a few nice things (it turned out that being an agnostic was a huge turn-on; he'd never gotten laid just because of his spiritual doubt), and they figured out together what to do with her muscles in her room at the Roosevelt. She made love with a vengeance. Literally. Steven knew what that felt like and just let the ride happen. It clearly wasn't about him at all. When it was over, he knew she had no intention of ever seeing him again, so he went downstairs, paid for her room and room service on his last credit card – screw 'em if this is how they track me – and went back to the Travelodge.

She smelled like a fresh field with patchouli growing on the far side of it, unable to be seen, only to be detected by the most careful of observers. He liked that, in part because it made him think that perhaps he hadn't completely ruined his olfactory system with vodka.

Back in the cheap hotel room, which smelled vaguely of vomit diluted by antiseptic, he wrote his final words on a tiny laminated desk. The fancy Roosevelt stationery would be a nice touch, he'd decided.

Steven sat outside of Tiffany's house, buzzed, comfortably numb. He had just ended his efforts to find a radio station that would play for him the perfect soundtrack for killing his ex-wife. There are few FM playlists that can pump someone up for murder. That would require a custom made mix, and Steven hadn't gone all OCD on the process.

He didn't expect the house to be so nice. A beautiful Spanish-style house in the middle of Hollywood. Tim must be making money, or maybe the commercials were better paying than he thought. He didn't know how he felt about that, and wasn't interested in exploring the sensation at the moment.

The .22 rifle was lying on the back seat. In the event he was killed running away, he hoped that the oddly assorted pages beneath the gun would explain to anyone why he felt cornered into such a course of action. It wasn't for general consumption: just for the eyes of the detectives investigating the case, and perhaps Tiffany's family. In fact, that's who he figured he had written his explanation for: the dead asshole who turned Tiffany into a monster. He wished Leonardas could have lived to read it and know how complicit he was in the pain he was feeling as he identified the body; his wife would have to do.

Not that he expected to be caught. The plan was working. Tiffany entered her home as expected. It was just her and the baby. Tony would be home from school at any time. Nobody had seen Steven so far as he knew, just a couple of old Russian ladies who seemed to spend their time letting cigarettes burn themselves to the nub on their lips as they watched the neighborhood expressionlessly. One woman had bright orange lipstick and neon red hair, as though she somehow thought it would keep anyone from noticing she was solidly in her 70s. Welcome to Hollywood.

He listened to music. He waited.

The kid wasn't to blame. He hadn't done anything wrong.

To rob a baby of his mother is a crime beyond the pale.

But this child did not choose to be born, he did not choose to have such a bitch as a mother. He doesn't have individual agency yet. So Steven wasn't robbing the child of a mother, he was saving him from one. Tim wasn't a bad guy, he'd raise the boy with hired help—anything better than to be exposed to the constant manipulations that were inevitable in a life with Tiffany.

But still, Steven couldn't open the door of the car. Another song came on, a dance tune that made the idea of killing someone feel remarkably stupid.

Steven grabbed his pint of vodka from the glove compartment and took a long swig. Vodka had long since stopped helping him take leave of his senses; if anything, vodka made his senses possible now.

Why didn't you just move to Mexico and teach English, the vodka asked. Steven didn't have an answer, so he drank again in the hopes that he could drown the thought.

He looked over at Tiffany's front window. In an almost cinematic framing, he saw Tiffany lifting her younger child up and kissing him. She held him in her arms, patting him on the back. The kid had Tim's fat cheeks.

And yet, Steven's car door didn't open.

He stared at the street signs. Street cleaning was Tuesday morning from 9 to 11 am. Cars would be towed. How he found such a sweet parking space on a Wednesday was surprising.

And the car door didn't open.

Could he take a life? Could he deliberately end someone else's existence? Steven knew that he didn't believe in God, and even if he did, he'd have a real bone to pick with him. Or her. Whatever. But to do his or her work? Who made him an agent of the Universe?

We are all agents of the Universe.

Does that come with dental?

I saw Steven struggling with this. And the only contribution I can honestly say I made to this story was to stare at him through the window as he drove past me as I kept watch over the entrance to the old A&M studios on LaBrea where I worked. Steven saw me, recognized me, and slowed down, nearly to a stop.

Someone honked behind him. He just stared at me, barely moving forward.

Something in him changed. I didn't say a word, but my eyes implored him to come up with another solution. You don't have to be religious to know that murder is never right. It doesn't matter how many of your expectations have been dashed, you've been taught the right thing to do. So do it.

Kermit wouldn't kill anyone. It's true, I wouldn't. You know better than that. Every voice you've heard since you were a toddler has told you that you can be whatever you want to be. Now go be that person. It's not too late; it's never too late. Rise above this pettiness and be the man everyone around you has believed you could become.

*She took this from me.*

She slowed you down. She only ends it if you let her. Ending her will end you. Not just if you get caught. You know you'll never sleep through a night again if you commit this crime against everything you hold dear.

*Don't talk me out of this.*

I'm not saying anything.

*I don't want to be talked out of this.*

Steven, you idiot, that's all you do want.

Steven looked at his eyes in the rear view mirror: puffy from dehydration, red and yellow from sleep deprivation and jaundice, darting and unfocused, courtesy of the good people at Stolichnaya.

*I can't do this.*

There's no shame in that. In fact, it might be the first decision you've made that can help you rebuild yourself.

*I'm not into self-help bullshit.*

You don't have to be. Just put the fucking car in gear and leave her alone.

Tiffany was still visible in the window. She was watching TV while her toddler ran all over the place. Thirty seconds from now, it could all be over. All scores would be settled.

But you won't do that. You already know it.

*How can I come this far and not do it?*

Nobody knows about it but me. Go home. Start over.

*I can't keep starting over. I'm forty fucking years old.*

You can always start over.

Steven noticed he was crying, just a slight mist around his eyes. He wiped them.

Don't give her the satisfaction of becoming such a train wreck. You're better than that.

This thought seemed to reach Steven. He sat up suddenly, with a newly-cleared mind. He was awash in a rush of thoughts, none of them clear. He couldn't articulate what he was feeling, so he went back to his old standby.

"This is stupid," he said aloud, and noticed that his voice cracked.

The door opened.

Steven's pulse raced as the lights came on behind him. He had allowed himself, like most drivers in Los Angeles, to creep up in speed on I-10 until he was cruising well above the speed limit. So a cop was signaling for him to pull over just before the Pomona exit, and Steven's rifle was in the back seat, the manuscript beneath it, explaining his rationale for a crime he hadn't committed.

He had no idea his taillight was out.

Steven took a few seconds to analyze his options. Pull over, explain why someone with a restraining order is in possession of a weapon; why he's got a manuscript that contemplates murdering someone just a few miles away; why it should be looked at as something fanciful and cathartic, not a real threat.

*They'll never believe you.*

They'll never believe you. Steven forced down the accelerator on the Prius, which responded with unexpected spirit. Within a few seconds he was going faster than eighty miles per hour. The police car, some domestic horsepower-hog, was keeping an even pace behind him, lights flashing, siren blaring.

"Pull over immediately!" The voice from behind was distorted by the bullhorn, but it clearly had the tenor of a young man. Maybe the policeman had never been on a high-speed chase before. Steven found himself wishing he was in more experienced hands.

They wanted him on the side of the road, but the problem was, the instant they saw the gun they'd make him crawl out of the car on his knees and assume the position on his stomach. Drivers would slow down to watch. They'd arrest him, bring him into some ridiculous holding cell with a bunch of idiot drunks and call Tiffany, and ask if she'd felt threatened lately. She'd lie and say yes, just on the off chance she could put him in jail again. And he wouldn't have a leg to stand on.

Steven didn't know what to do. He called out to me. "What do I do now?"

I didn't answer. This was a teaching moment.

"I'm fucking serious, Kermit! What the hell am I supposed to do?"

I kept quiet. I was always an entertainer; I was never supposed to be a role model. It's not my fault that Jim wanted to be in show business, and the Muppets were the only gig he could get. We paid well, but whenever he tried to make his real dreams happen, he was shouted down; to the point where he confused a life-threatening lung infection with a stress sandwich.

Steven coughed as his eyes darted from the rear view mirror to the traffic ahead. It would be a matter of minutes before he heard the blades of a helicopter overhead: LA news channels love nothing more than watching a high-speed chase. The best form of free entertainment.

The policemen behind him were following the book: don't drive aggressively, don't force the suspect off of the road, just pursue and wait for guidance.

"WHAT THE FUCK AM I SUPPOSED TO DO?"

I kept quiet. This was his problem to solve.

There would be a nail-strip within twenty miles or so. It would flatten his tires and render the car inoperative. He'd try to drive for a little while as sparks flew from his wheels, but ultimately he'd have to crawl out of the car and be handcuffed.

But I didn't even try to kill her, he thought. Add that to the stack of shit that nobody would care about once Tiffany cleared her throat in court. No, all that would matter is the arrest record he had, and the rifle and scrawled ramblings on Roosevelt Hotel stationery in the back seat. And Tiffany would seize on that to lock him up again.

He wasn't returning to jail. Under no circumstances. None.

He yelled out for me a final time.

I kept quiet. If he hadn't learned anything by now, there was no teaching him. Work hard, be nice to people. That ultimately works. He just never got the message. It's not my fault that he confused entertainment with education. At one point we have to grow up and accept who we are without any excuses. That wasn't my lesson to teach: it was a lesson we all assumed kids would learn on their own. Maybe we should have been clearer on that: but our demographic was always too young for that lesson. That wasn't our fault.

Steven obviated that discussion by realizing as he neared a railroad overpass that there was a more elegant solution than any that he had entertained before. And at the end of the day, an elegant solution is what he wanted. There was nothing elegant about a mug shot.

The concrete pylon was thick and old, probably poured during the Eisenhower administration. It would have been designed to withstand a direct side impact from a loaded missile truck with a fully loaded train passing over it. It could endure a direct strike from a Toyota hybrid.

The sirens doubled. Another police cruiser was in the chase. The cars all around him parted the highway. He was becoming an event. This was not what he wanted, not what he wanted at all.

He pointed the nose of the car at the pylon and watched as the concrete structure grew larger and larger. It seemed to be asking a question of him somehow, a question he would easily have dismissed if it had come from anything but an inanimate object.

He realized what he was asking, and what the answer was. It didn't matter what you felt, what made you happy or what made you sad. The real question was: what could you survive?

The self-preservation instinct in him held his foot just over the brake pedal, waiting for the command that would avoid the pylon. It did not come. He found himself overwhelmed to forgive Tiffany, who was not in the least interested in receiving his largesse. He knew that, but felt a strong urge to bestow it regardless.

Steven watched the pylon growing ominously closer to him and realized he would never survive her. That was nobody's fault. It's just what happens.

This breakthrough is the thought; this is my thesis; this is what I had always hoped he could achieve with the gifts that were given him: that nobody but him was to blame for his failures, or to praise for his accomplishments. We are happy when we decide to be happy. If we don't, we have to examine what it is in ourselves that has failed us: blaming others isn't right or wrong, it's simply unproductive. If I gave any lesson in the world, that's it. Watch the footage. I never promised anything more or less than that.

Steven decided his fate, and I couldn't alter it. So I sat post of top of those gates at work, unblinking. Don't you dare blame me for your failures. I couldn't say that on TV, but if you didn't get the point, that's a 'you' problem All I was created for was to was make you laugh: don't think I was supposed to raise you.

Steven heard a crushing noise of his car impacting concrete, and stopped thinking forever.

Tiffany thought the knock on the door was the FedEx guy. The damn shoes were a day late and she'd called to raise hell. It didn't hurt that most of the delivery guys recognized her from the Super Bowl spot, so they usually credited her the shipping cost when that happened. The gig should have come with free shipping for a year. Cheap assholes.

She was surprised to see a young police officer in front of him. "Ms. Tiffany Morales?"

Tiffany considered before answering, and not just because he was using her old name, which she was just getting used to. Tim had been gone for two months, living in some efficiency apartment, calling his ex-wife Lisa three times a day and begging her to come back to him. She knew all that.

But this delivery boy looked like a baby. Twenty-three? Twenty-five? His last name was Morales as well, and he had a light caramel skin tone that she would get if she ever let herself go out in the sun. All young men were starting to look like children to her, and it bothered her on an intuitive level. She didn't like young sentient people who could mathematically be her children.

"Yes."

"You were married to a Steven Atkins?"

None of his business whether they married or not. "What's he done now?"

The police officer shifted his weight. "Um, ma'am, Mr. Atkins died last night."

Tiffany's breath tightened. She stared at the officer's brown eyes for a second while she gathered herself.

She had no idea what she thought, other than a sudden wave of anger. Of course he would do this to her.

"Yes?"

"Well, he had a note with him."

Of course he did. Another one of his rants blaming her for everything. "Yes?"

The officer seemed to cock his head slightly, and ease somewhat. This was hard for him, she thought. Had he not done this before?

"Well, ma'am, when was the last time you were in contact with him?"

"Why do you ask?"

"He had a weapon with him. And one of his notes indicates that he might have intended to harm you."

Tiffany looked down at her feet. Steven wasn't going to harm her, she knew that. What a mess he'd become. How much could she have made of her life if he hadn't been such a loser and stolen those years from her? Now she would have to clean up another one of his messes.

She suddenly realized the police officer was expecting a response. "Harm me?"

"Maybe," Morales said. "Have you seen him recently? You apparently have had a restraining order against him for ten years now."

"I can show it to you if you want."

"But you haven't seen him recently?"

Tiffany looked at the young man. She could tell him anything and he'd believe her.

Steven is dead. Let it go.

Officer Morales was waiting.

"I don't want to talk about it," Tiffany said, and began to shut the door.

"Ma'am, wait – "

As if on cue, Tommy cried out.

She paused. "I've got a toddler and a hot stove. Excuse me."

Morales looked nervous. "We might call you if we need a statement."

Tiffany almost laughed at his incompetence. Her father would have fired any officer who couldn't collect even the slightest amount of information–from a potential victim, even. Nobody knew what they were doing anymore. What was the world coming to.

She nodded solemnly and said, "Thank you, officer." She shut the door gently in his face.

She waited until she heard his footsteps leave the front patio, and leaned against the door, her forehead seeming to support all of her weight on the old Spanish hardwood.

She felt her breath quickening instantly, a sudden series of shallow gasps for air, but it took her a moment to realize she was crying. This annoyed her almost enough to stop, and her breathing leveled. Crying was ridiculous. She didn't love him. She never loved him.

She never loved anyone, she thought again to herself. She slid down the door until she was seated, unable to stop convulsing. This was stupid. Why does it hurt so much. She thought for a moment that Tommy was starting to whine as though he were hurt, and was shocked to discover the wailing was coming from her. She rolled over on one side and felt the Saltillo tile cool her face as her shoulders heaved.

Control yourself. Control yourself.

As though a fan had blown upon her, the tears dried in her eyes almost immediately. She sat up, used an old rickety credenza to pull herself to her feet, and dusted herself off compulsively.

Tommy was sitting on the kitchen floor with a wooden spoon in his mouth. Tiffany removed it and clicked on the remote for the drop-down television hanging from the cupboards. *Sesame Street* came on. Tiffany watched absent-mindedly as Elmo talked about loving everybody.

She caught herself chewing her thumbnail. "Where the hell is FedEx?" she asked out loud, to nobody in particular.

# Epilogue

## Everything Happens Here

His new kitten, Pablo the Magnificent, scurried after an insect while Jeremy rocked back in his hammock chair, slightly buzzed, watching as the last remnants of sunlight slipped away over the mountains outside of San Miguel. It was getting colder at night.

If he closed his eyes, he could feel the sunset, he was becoming convinced of that. It was now an evening ritual: come home, read the *Herald Tribune* or a local Mexican newspaper, drink some tequila (liquor was no longer just possible to consume now, it was pleasantly necessary) and feel the sun go down. It was something he could look forward to, and he enjoyed promising himself that time alone when his classes became too boring.

He could hear her in the kitchen, fixing dinner. Elizabeth was a good cook, better than Katherine was, and it was an unbelievable luxury. He'd never fully appreciated that before Elizabeth. She was undeniably a strong, lithesome woman, and there hadn't been a pair of jeans yet that did her body justice – she could look storkish in the wrong light - but her shoulders sometimes sank as though she couldn't get rid of a great weight. It wasn't Jeremy's job to fix that for her. When she wants to talk, she'll talk. Katherine taught him that.

"Almost ready—" she called. Jeremy nodded, then realized she couldn't hear him doing so, and answered her properly. "On my way, gorgeous."

He stood up and stretched, realizing the sun was down and his daily ritual was complete. There were worse things than living this way.

He yawned, and felt a sudden twinge in his jaw, as happened from time to time. He rubbed it and found himself thinking again, and decided he needed another tequila to head the thoughts off at the pass.

As he walked into the kitchen, however, the routine had begun. Where was that guy who hit him? What happened to him? He had to be out of jail by now. He felt like his sore jaw always asked these questions rather than his conscious self, so he was never in a hurry to answer them. Your body betrays you in so many ways: never be a slave to it. But the questions lingered in a somewhat annoying way.

He'd probably gotten on with his life, and that was a good thing, and Elizabeth was fixing fettuccine carbonara, because she knew he liked it.

Elizabeth was standing over the range, stirring the pasta and egg mixture, her slender long-jumper's body moving in time with the wooden spoon, as though dancing to unheard music. Jeremy came up behind her, brushed aside her softening curls, and kissed the freckles on the neck.

"Hey." She said, softly.

"Smells good."

"Don't jinx me. It might suck."

He kissed her neck again, making sure his teeth nibbled at her slightly.

"Hey – what's that for?" She smiled at him. Even with his hands on her hip, he could feel her body responding.

"Nothing. I'm hungry."

"Well, we'll take care of that," she said, a large smile coming over her face.

Jeremy kissed her on the cheek and sat down. He rubbed his jaw again and looked out the courtyard. It was cool and dark outside, and the soft light from the kitchen stretched out into the night like a blanket that could never feel too warm.

"I got another phone call from Boston. My old firm wants to double my partnership share. Name on the masthead and everything."

Jeremy nodded, utterly unthreatened. She could leave tomorrow and he'd never stop being grateful for the gifts she gave him. He would miss the cooking and that special swirl she knew that he couldn't tell anyone about, but that was a disruption in routine only. And the secret to happiness, he'd decided, was to value the gifts you have, in the moment you have them. We run into trouble when we ask anyone for permanence.

"What do you think?"

"I think there's this woman in my class: Alisa, I told you about her, the one from Atlanta. Her husband went to Iraq and had a whole slew of affairs. He might have even raped someone, he's being court-martialed. She's running away here in Mexico. If she doesn't learn how to adapt to this culture, she'll die going back to the U.S. She's finally realized that Georgia is toxic in her eyes, and I agree. Helping her sort that out is more important to me right now than anything someone like Stodgewood Shippen the Second could offer me."

"Sounds good."

"And I'm pretty deeply in like with you."

"I'm pretty deeply in like with you too."

Jeremy smiled and returned to the hammock with a bowl full of carbonara. He would have added more basil, but he didn't tell her that.

As he slowly rocked, he squinted his eyes so that the lights from the town were unclear and vague in their origin, and he couldn't identify any celestial object but the moon.

He took a deep breath and felt his shoulders relax; because when he let himself de-focus, when he let himself see things without an agenda, when he freed himself from all of his pain and ambition and expectations, he couldn't tell whether it was sunrise or sunset.

How could he give that gift to others, he wondered, then realized he was missing the point. Nothing matters but the sight of the moon and the fact that you worked hard. If you work hard and are nice to people, you can't avoid being happy no matter how hard you try.

Why on Earth didn't everyone else know this?

And why on Earth didn't anyone ever tell him?